OTHER SECRETS

OTHER SECRETS

Farida Karodia

PENGUIN BOOKS

PENGUIN BOOKS

Published by the Penguin Group
27 Wrights Lane, London W8 5TZ, England
Penguin Putnam Inc, 375 Hudson Street, New York, New York 10014, USA
Penguin Books Australia Ltd, Ringwood, Victoria, Australia
Penguin Books Canada Ltd, 10 Alcorn Avenue, Toronto, Ontario, Canada M4V 3B2
Penguin Books (NZ) Ltd, Cnr Rosedale and Airborne Roads, Albany, Auckland, New Zealand
Penguin Books India (P) Ltd, 11 Community Centre, Panchsheel Park, New Delhi – 110 017, India
Penguin Books (South Africa) (Pty) Ltd, 5 Watkins Street, Denver Ext 4, Johannesburg 2094, South Africa

Penguin Books (South Africa) (Pty) Ltd, Registered Offices:
Second Floor, 90 Rivonia Road, Sandton 2196, South Africa

First published by Penguin Books (South Africa) (Pty) Ltd 2000

Copyright © Farida Karodia 2000
All rights reserved
The moral right of the author has been asserted

ISBN 0140 29565 8

This novel is a work of fiction. Any resemblance of any character to any person alive or dead is entirely coincidental.

Typeset by PJT Design in 10.5 on 12.5 point Sabon
Cover design by Claire Heckrath
Cover picture: The Image Bank
Printed and bound by The Rustica Press, Ndabeni, Western Cape

Except in the United States of America, this book is sold subject to the condition that it shall not, by way of trade or otherwise, be lent, resold, hired out or otherwise circulated without the publisher's prior consent in any form of binding or cover other than that in which it is published and without a similar condition including this condition be imposed on the subsequent purchaser.

To Anesia and John for their 'Time Capsule'

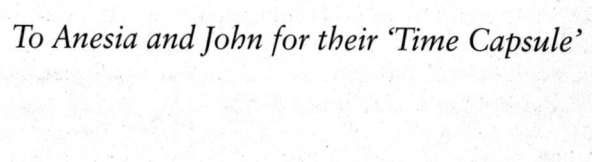

Acknowledgements

I wish to thank Pat Baker, Chris van Wyk and Sandi van Niekerk in South Africa for their valuable comments on this work, Liv Beck and Jan Atkinson-Grosjean in Canada, and Zaheda and Cassim Behra for their input on the Islamic rituals. My thanks too to Alison Lowry and Pam Thornley of Penguin South Africa.

DAUGHTERS

1

WE LIVED in Soetstroom, in the Eastern Cape. A pimple on the face of the earth was the way my older sister Yasmin disparagingly described the small town. The population of 2 795 excluded the Africans and the handful of Coloureds who lived in the African Location, because they were considered non-persons.

We were the only Asians in town and for us, too, there were no census figures. Had there been, the count would have been six: Ma, Papa, our maternal grandmother Nana, an orphaned relative, Baboo, and Yasmin and me.

It was relatively common in the days before mass relocation to find solitary Asian traders living and conducting business in the heart of white rural communities. Isolated because of their racial and cultural differences, they built walls around themselves – surviving like bits of flotsam in a hostile sea, practising their religion and conducting their daily routine as inconspicuously as possible.

Somehow, in this small town we were insulated against the wider implications of apartheid. We survived the effects of the racist laws by being unobtrusive, almost invisible.

On Sundays, in deference to the white congregation who might find an open door audacious, we kept our front door firmly shut. Concealed by the screen of net curtains at my parents' bedroom window, and led by a commentary from Nana, we observed the stalwart citizens assembling for their church service.

Not even Mrs Hattingh's horribly disfigured face elicited sympathy. According to Nana, she was the architect of her own misfortune. The story was that Mrs Hattingh, a manic depressive, had gone to Johannesburg to visit her daughter and one night while her daughter was out she had stuck her head in the oven and turned on the gas. Instead of her anticipated peaceful demise, her hair caught alight. By the time they found her she had suffered severe burns to her face and neck. Now, years later, the keloid tracks had thickened, scoring her face like a map.

Then there was Lynette Cronje in a bold, wide-brimmed black hat. She was despised in this conservative community because of her alleged affairs with some of the more prominent men – including the *dominee* – and was shunned by the other women.

Our presence in town was grudgingly accepted. While there was enough business to go around we were tolerated, but at the first sign of a weakening in the local economy the whites banded together. In retaliation farmers drove their labourers into the town on trailers and deliberately deposited them at the white stores with instructions to stay away from the *coolie* shop – coolie was the commonly used derogatory term for Indians.

My father remained scornful of such tactics. 'Don't worry,' he said. 'They'll be back. At least here at Mohammed's they're treated like human beings.'

Mohammed's Trading Store was a general dealership selling everything from peanuts to bicycle wheels. Like a shy companion, the shop sat next to our house in a side street.

Our house, however, was directly across the street from that bastion of Afrikanerdom, the Dutch Reformed Church. The enormous clock, pinned like a badge to the church tower, boomed every hour.

My father said it sounded like Big Ben.

'Rubbish,' Nana retorted. 'It doesn't sound at all like Big Ben.'

'I know what Big Ben sounds like on the BBC news,' Papa argued.

'I've heard Big Ben on the radio too,' Nana said, 'and it's not like that.'

My grandmother could argue the mundane with as much passion as she argued the imperative.

I always sided with my father, who was like a man who had

wandered into a room through the wrong door and couldn't find his way out again.

Despite the occasional lapses he and Nana got along well. Perhaps they understood each other because they were of the same generation.

When my grandfather died Nana came to live with Ma and Papa in Soetstroom. Although Nana and Yasmin shared a love-hate relationship – probably because they were so much alike – Nana and I were close, closer even than Ma and I.

Papa was thirty years older than my mother, who was his second wife.

My father was seventeen when he arrived in South Africa with his first wife. It was at the height of the Mahatma Gandhi-inspired resistance campaigns. A few months after landing in Durban, he was arrested at a protest and sentenced to three months' hard labour.

Along with his fellow inmates, Papa was sent to work in a quarry. On the second day he crushed his left index finger which eventually became arthritic and inflexible. He claimed also that the dust in the quarry was partly responsible for the cataracts which affected his vision. To protect his light-sensitive eyes he always wore dark glasses outdoors.

After his release Papa moved to the Transvaal, but he found life there much too restrictive and soon headed for the Eastern Cape where he bought a plot of land in one of the small communities. On this land he built a small shack and cultivated vegetable gardens, selling his produce at local markets.

Young and energetic then, and fired with enthusiasm, he had been willing to conquer all kinds of hardships to succeed in his adopted country. Gujaratis, he said proudly, were hard-working, astute businessmen. Had they not pioneered the most remote and inaccessible corners of Africa, or the world for that matter?

My father often spoke about India with great longing, hoping that some day he would return to visit – but, of course, only when Yasmin was old enough to accompany him.

'There'll never be enough money for such a trip,' my mother said, genuinely regretful about not being able to help my father realise his dream.

Much as he wanted her to, I knew that Yasmin would never set foot in India. I, however, would have gone gladly, but never once was my name mentioned in the same breath as India.

It was always Yasmin. Four years older than I, tall and slender, with long brown hair, she was the pretty and adorable daughter, the one who always garnered all the attention.

Ma and Nana still spoke about the beautiful baby who had been so admired by the nurses in the hospital. No one ever raved about me. I must have been quite ordinary.

I was very young when I first heard about my incongruous entry into the world – right there in the shop, behind the counter, when my mother went into labour while serving a customer. Nana said there was no time to drive my mother to the hospital, fifty miles away. My father was away at the time and so Nana, with the assistance of one of the neighbours, delivered me. The word *delivered* was misleading. It was a word my young mind associated with parcels or letters and so I assumed I had arrived through the mail.

I was probably the only child in the entire town who hadn't a clue where babies came from. It was only when I started school at the Soetstroom Apostolic Primary School for Coloureds – SAPS – that I received a crash course in sex education. My teacher was none other than Dora Oliphant, fourteen years old and still in primary school.

SAPS was a two-roomed, whitewashed, concrete building on the town side of the gully – a mere stone's throw from the narrow pedestrian swing-bridge that crossed into the African Location. The two rooms were separated by a dilapidated red velvet curtain so full of holes and rips that it was a miracle it still had enough thread to keep it together. Dora sat near the back of the class and tormented the senior boys through the curtain.

It was common knowledge that Dora had provided practical

sex education for every boy at school. She was a big girl, over-developed physically and sexually. Breasts like melons. Most astounding of all was her knowledge of sex, about where men put things in and where babies came out of.

Winters were cold in Soetstroom. On occasion there was even a light dusting of snow. One year, during a particularly severe winter, fifteen sheep survived after being buried in a snow drift for almost a week.

The high altitude somehow made the summers bearable, except when the Berg Wind, a hot, suffocating current of air, gusted across the mountains on its way to the ocean. It sapped us. Stole our breath and whipped up the gritty dust, blasting the backs of our legs until they felt as rough as the moulted skin of a snake.

There were two outside rooms in our yard. One of these was occupied by Nana and the other by Baboo. There were only two bedrooms in the house. Ma and Papa shared one and Yasmin and I the other.

Nana preferred the outside room because it gave her privacy and a semblance of independence.

'I don't ever want to be underfoot,' was her catchphrase.

It was enough that she ate from her daughter and son-in-law's table, she didn't want to be beholden in other ways too. But Papa had a very generous nature and would never have begrudged her anything.

I adored my father. Despite his age he was still a good-looking man. In his suit, fedora, dark glasses and dust-coat, he looked like an older version of Omar Sharif.

The discrepancy in the ages of my parents was obvious and people often referred to Papa as my grandfather. I remember men coming to the shop and asking for my 'grandfather' and then, when he appeared, going through a secret ritual of flipping a coin – the male code for condoms. It was only when I was much older that I finally figured out what it meant. It was another adult secret. It seemed to me that with all the secrets and complexities of the grown-up world, we children would never fathom the way adult society functioned. Much later in life I realised that even my mother, that quiet, reserved rampart of family life, had secrets of her own.

Whenever I saw my mother staring into the distance, her eyes glazed over as if looking back into her past, I wondered what it was that held her there. Yasmin said that Ma had probably made a great sacrifice, giving up the love of her life, to marry Papa.

'Women are always required to make sacrifices, you know,' she said with such authority that I believed her.

Her comment fuelled my fantasies. But it frightened me that my mother's other life was such a mystery. I told Nana what Yasmin had said.

'You know what rubbish Yasmin comes up with. I would have thought you'd know your sister by now,' she said, her tone reproachful.

Although I never mentioned the matter again, I did start looking at my mother with new eyes. I was curious about the fact that she never spoke about her life before Papa or before us. That part of her past remained a secret place in which she alone dwelled. It was a part of her life which excluded the rest of us.

When Nana spoke about the past she revealed only the ordinary, the mundane. There were no clues to complete the puzzle. It was as though the two women had conspired to bury certain chunks of my mother's life.

She spoke openly about Ma and Papa and their relationship. There was no secret about this and she told us in detail how my parents had met during the last years of the second world war and how difficult life had been for all of them.

'Your Papa was very good to us,' she said. 'He always brought us fruit and vegetables from the market. Had it not been for him, we might never have survived.'

I so wanted my parents to be happy together and tried to put out of my mind all the niggling doubts that occasionally surfaced.

In the romance novel *Forever My Love*, Julie had also sacrificed a great love to marry Austin, a wealthy, older man, in order to save her parents' farm. She, too, had been content with her life until the return of her long-lost love.

While Ma and Nana took care of the shop, Papa purchased produce from the city markets and redistributed it to smaller rural markets for a marginal profit. My father loved travelling to the small towns where he was well known and liked and where he always insisted on supervising the work. The best manure for a man's land was his own footsteps, he used to say.

The marketing business and the profits from the shop provided us with a fairly comfortable living. Occasionally Papa was resourceful enough to sell one of the old cars he had acquired through one of his deals. Ma tried to discourage this money-losing enterprise because each time Papa sold a car, it was returned a month or two later, driven into the ground. Sometimes we had two or three crocks lying in the backyard, chrome winking in the sun, tyres deflated like sagging breasts.

'These are used cars. They don't come with guarantees,' Ma scolded, furious about my father's lack of resolve when the cars were returned.

She was a lot tougher than he. Customers who owed us money avoided her or sent someone else into the shop to call my father out. When my mother was around, she'd confront them and demand that they pay their debts. They always swore on a stack of Bibles that next time they'd pay her before they paid anyone else.

And in the mean time our books grew heavy with unpaid debts.

'You can't knock blood out of a stone,' Papa sighed, when Ma challenged him.

'*We're* bleeding, Abdul,' Ma told him. 'And no one cares about us. When are you going to stand up to these people?'

'Gandhi said . . .'

'Bugger Gandhi!' Ma snapped.

Sometimes Papa was too tired to argue and just walked away.

Yasmin and I were typical young girls growing up in the early nineteen sixties. Our interests, more so Yasmin's than mine, were boys, sleeping in late, and clothes.

Always contrary, Yasmin leapt out of bed on Sundays, but on weekdays it was impossible to rouse her. She would lie under the blankets clutching them around her as Ma and I tried to pull them off. Finally she would emerge, blinking and squinting into the daylight like some night creature blinded by the light.

One Sunday we were all up early. We'd been awakened around midnight by the sound of shattering glass, but waited till daybreak before investigating what had happened. My father was first on the scene in the storeroom where one of the windows had been smashed by a stone. We knew who the culprit was.

'You'd better speak to the principal about Cobus Steyn,' Papa told Ma when she joined us.

'Why don't *you* speak to him, Abdul?' she asked.

'You're better at these things than I am,' Papa said.

'We can't leave the window like that,' Ma said.

'There's a piece of glass in the garage. I'll get Daniel to fix it. He's good at fixing things.'

Daniel, who did odd jobs for us, beamed as Papa extolled his virtues.

'That's not the point,' Nana interrupted. 'Why should *we* have to fix it? That boy's father should be spoken to.'

My father stormed out of the storeroom cursing under his breath.

Yasmin looked on in dismay. She had wanted to confront Ma that morning about the possibility of going to boarding school, but now a broken window had diverted everyone's attention.

'I was scared silly when I heard the window breaking,' I said. 'Weren't you, Yas?'

Yasmin tossed her head. 'I knew it was that idiot Cobus Steyn.'

The rattling of the gate interrupted further discussion. Vukile, wearing an enormous jacket, was waiting outside. Several months earlier Vukile's father Absolom had been arrested at a political rally in Molteno and had later died in jail under mysterious circumstances. His widowed mother Anna was now struggling to feed her family. Ma, who felt sorry for her, had set aside some groceries which the ten-year-old Vukile had come to collect.

'How's it, Vukile?' I called.

He grinned. He had with him the toy car he had built out of wire. About the size of a shoebox, it was manipulated by a thin rod embedded in the front wheels.

The store was closed on Sundays because trading on that day was prohibited by the Lord's Day Act.

We occasionally circumvented the law and did a back-door trade with our African customers, trusting them to conceal their purchases. We needed the extra business and took enormous risks, especially when one considered that on Sundays half the town was gathered at the church across the street.

On a few occasions when my father was caught trading after hours, he pleaded guilty and paid the fine. Ma was afraid that if this happened too often we would lose our licence.

Because of this we ensured that all purchases were well hidden before letting customers out of our sight. The youngsters who were sent to the shop after hours knew the drill and wore loose clothing. By the time they left the shop, they looked like the Goodyear Blimp. I was certain no one was fooled.

Vukile gazed at me, index finger gingerly rubbing the side of his nose, one foot hooked behind his leg, eyes large and watchful.

I fetched the groceries Ma had left on the counter. Yasmin joined me as I stuffed the packages into Vukile's pockets.

'You'd better hide this stuff properly, Vukile, or the police will catch you and put you in jail.'

Vukile grinned disarmingly.

'It's Sunday – the shop's closed,' Yasmin said sternly.

Vukile, weighted down but still grinning, hurried away. Despite our warning and as soon as he was out of view, he removed some of the packages from his pockets and zig-zagged down the street, the illicit cargo prominently displayed on his toy car. It wasn't long before he was spotted by one of the young constables.

Yasmin, who was about to lock the side door to the shop,

turned quickly when she heard the back gate opening.

Constable de Bruin, a young Afrikaner policeman, stood at the gate, scowling. In one hand he had Vukile by the scruff of the neck – and cradled in his other arm were the incriminating packages.

Yasmin glowered at De Bruin.

Nana, who was in the kitchen with Gladys, heard the commotion and shouted for my mother. 'Delia! You'd better go see what's happening in the yard.'

Ma came to the kitchen door, pulled off her apron and hurried outside.

'What's the problem, Constable de Bruin?' she asked as she summed up the situation.

'I caught this *kwedini* . . .' De Bruin started.

'Let him go, you idiot! You're hurting him!' Yasmin cried.

My mother gave Yasmin a quick disapproving look while Vukile tried to wriggle free of De Bruin's grasp.

With all his squirming, a packet of mealie meal fell out of his pocket and smashed to the ground, its contents splattering on the concrete pathway.

'Now look what you've done!' Ma exclaimed.

'It is Sunday. The Lord's Day,' De Bruin said, scowling. 'You know you're not supposed to sell this kind of stuff.'

'I didn't sell anything,' Ma said sharply, losing patience. 'It was a gift for his mother. Ask him.'

'And you think he's going to tell the truth?' De Bruin asked.

While Ma and De Bruin were locked in hostility, Vukile managed to free himself and scampered off.

'Why aren't you out there chasing real criminals?' Yasmin called scornfully.

At the gate De Bruin paused and turned. 'One day I'll get you people . . . you'll see.'

Eyes like daggers followed De Bruin as Ma shut the gate and dropped the latch back into the slot.

Papa knew nothing of this confrontation with the constable. He was in the backyard arranging bags of potatoes to be sent to one of the markets the following day.

For the rest of the day, still angry at his reluctance to deal with the matter of the broken window, Ma barely spoke two words to my father. It was clear she was not going to let Daniel fix the window. She wanted the Steyns to take responsibility, and she wanted Papa to ensure that they did so.

We all knew Cobus Steyn, knew what he was capable of. He was rotten to the core. He was not only responsible for Lucinda's untimely demise, but had for years made our lives miserable.

2

LUCINDA WAS a celluloid doll with violet-coloured eyes, rosebud lips and pink cheeks. She was a present from my parents on my fifth birthday. I named her Lucinda after a comic-book character.

On the morning of my birthday, I awakened anticipating the surprise I knew my parents had been preparing for me. My eyes snapped open and alighted on the doll which was propped up on the dresser. I hitched up my drooping pyjamas and crawled over the bed to where the doll sat with outstretched arms, waiting to embrace me.

I carefully lifted it and wrapped my arms about it. Yasmin was still asleep. I examined the doll, removed its clothes and discovered that its arms and legs were attached to an inside mechanism with rubber bands. I pulled the doll's head out as far as it would extend and peered into the body cavity. The limbs moved with surprising ease, a feature which compensated for the absence of hair which in Lucinda's case was merely an imprint on her celluloid head.

'It's like Lena's doll,' I pointed out to Yasmin when she woke up later.

'That's because Ma bought it off Mrs van Staden.'

'How do you know?' I asked, with a twinge of disappointment that the doll had belonged to someone else first.

'Ma told me,' she said. 'Come on, Meena, let's go find Baboo.'

'No. He might break Lucinda.'

Yasmin steered me past Nana's room to where Baboo was

practising his cricket strokes in the backyard.

Baboo had come to live with us when I was about two years old. His parents had died in an accident when he was twelve, and he had been shunted from one relative to another before ending up with us.

I had no memory of his arrival. Nana told me that he was only supposed to stay for a few months until his uncle in Johannesburg could take him, but three years later he was still with us. He had spent two years in standard six and because he was big for his age, Papa decided it would be best to take him out of school.

Baboo was fifteen and his two closest friends were Moses Dlamini, who lived with his mother in the Location where he attended the African school, and Willem Arendse who lived about ten miles out of Soetstroom on Oubaas Nel's farm.

Willem was the youngest of the three boys and still attended the Soetstroom Apostolic Primary School for Coloureds. Although no longer a student, Baboo used to organise a ragtag team of cricketers. Cricket games were played in the veld where stray dogs and children all participated. Sometimes they got Daniel to join in as well, but eventually he was kicked off the team because Baboo said he had jelly hands.

Cricket was Baboo's all-consuming passion. He knew every major cricketer by name. And even though he had never been able to master his multiplication tables and still had no idea what 7 x 7 was, or even 5 x 5, he could reel off, effortlessly, statistics about famous West Indian, Australian and Indian cricketers. Nana said it was because he spent half the night listening to the radio when overseas games were being broadcast.

When Baboo saw us coming towards him with the doll, he backed away, thrusting his hands into his trouser pockets.

Since Baboo had decided to ignore me, I went to sit on the kerb, hoping that someone would come by so I could show Lucinda off.

I was so engrossed with Lucinda and her inner workings that

I didn't see Cobus Steyn creeping up behind me. Suddenly a hand reached over my shoulder and plucked the doll from my grasp.

Startled, I leapt up and lunged for Lucinda.

Cobus held her just out of my reach.

'Cobus, please!' I cried.

Yasmin heard my cry and came rushing out of the yard to join in the struggle for possession of the doll. Cobus laughed at our futile attempts to rescue Lucinda.

In the ensuing struggle, I managed to grab one of Lucinda's arms. Cobus pushed me and I dropped like a rock on to my backside, my eyes smarting with tears.

Yasmin was still struggling with Cobus. 'You stupid bastard! Don't break my sister's doll,' she screamed.

'Say *Baas* Cobus,' he said, grinning diabolically.

'Never. You're just a piece of shit!' Yasmin yelled, sounding just like Dora Oliphant.

'I'm your *baas* and I can have anything I want.'

'I'm your *baas*,' she mimicked. 'Kiss my arse!' Yasmin continued to struggle and finally got hold of one of the doll's arms. Cobus jerked the doll away and the arm snapped off in her hands.

'Now see what you've done!' Yasmin cried, dismayed, as she gazed at the severed arm clutched in her fist, rubber bands dangling limply.

'That'll teach you!' Cobus said.

Yasmin's cry brought Baboo running from the backyard. He rounded the corner and spun the Afrikaner youth around. The impetus threw Cobus off balance. The next moment the two boys were rolling on the ground.

'You filthy bastard,' Baboo grunted through gritted teeth, pummelling the white youth in the stomach.

'You son of a bitch! I'll break your neck!' Cobus hissed, flailing at Baboo's face. Although Cobus was younger than Baboo, he was a little bigger and heavier. But Baboo's fury lent him added strength.

My anguished eyes sought my sister's. I noticed in a vague, distracted way that her hair, loosened from the restraints of the ponytail, had tumbled to her shoulders. Her dress was streaked with dirt. I tried to gather the pieces of my doll. I found one of the arms and a leg. The head had rolled into the gutter where the two boys were battering each other.

Yasmin joined in the fight, trying to kick sand into Cobus's face. Unfortunately, Baboo became the casualty. He spluttered, eyes shut, as Yasmin continued to kick sand at them.

'Stop it!' Baboo yelled. 'You're getting sand into my eyes!'

'Hit him, Baboo! Hit him!' Yasmin cried, eyes glittering savagely.

Finally Baboo pinned Cobus down and smashed his fist into the other boy's face.

I stepped back, shrinking from the sight of blood. But even more devastating was the sight of my doll's mutilated torso, the celluloid dented and fractured.

Baboo got off Cobus's limp body.

Cobus tasted the blood and blotted his lip with the back of his hand. He stood up and glared at Baboo. At his feet lay the pretty face with its rosebud mouth. Cobus glanced down.

'No! No!' I screamed as Cobus lifted his foot.

Grinning sardonically, he brought his boot down viciously, smashing Lucinda's head to smithereens, her remains spread like confetti in the gutter.

Once across the street and out of Baboo's range, Cobus recovered some of his bravado. 'I'll get you for this, coolie!'

A few weeks later Baboo came home bloodied. Cobus and three friends had ambushed him.

Each day after that brought with it another incident and a new problem with Baboo and Cobus. My parents knew that unless they sent Baboo away, something terrible would happen because of his temper.

Papa hastily dispatched a letter to Baboo's uncle in Johannesburg. He replied immediately, saying that he had just opened a new business and would be delighted to have Baboo come and live with him.

The matter was settled. Arrangements were made for Baboo

to take the train to Johannesburg.

'It's for his own good,' Papa assured us. 'If he stays, he may get into serious trouble.'

Baboo was reluctant to leave the relative security of his home in Soetstroom. Eventually, though, he agreed when he was assured that he could play cricket to his heart's content in Johannesburg.

A few weeks later the whole family gathered at the station in a solemn little group. Baboo's two friends, Moses Dlamini and Willem Arendse, had also come to see him off. They stood awkwardly, studying the scuffed toes of their shoes while they waited their opportunity to exchange a few words with him.

When the train pulled into the station Ma and Papa were both moist-eyed. We had barely managed to say goodbye when the conductor's whistle shrilled and Baboo clambered aboard and disappeared inside.

'You look after yourself and be careful,' Ma called. 'Jo'burg is full of *tsotsis*. Be sure to hide your money, and hang on to your suitcase.'

Baboo leaned out of the window. Yasmin and I walked alongside the carriage until the platform fell away. Willem and Moses trotted alongside the train as it gathered speed.

Overcome by a sense of desolation, as if something precious had been ripped from us, we remained on the platform, waving until the lights dwindled to pinpoints and the train was finally swallowed up by the cavernous darkness.

3

MENTION OF Cobus Steyn had brought all those early childhood memories flooding back. Apart from the occasional incident of mischief on his part, I hadn't given him much thought since. I was twelve years old and the doll incident had melted away like snow in summer.

Yasmin was sitting outside braiding her hair. I accepted without rancour that my sister was the beauty in the family. Even my eyelashes were insignificant compared with hers.

'Don't worry, Meena. Some day you'll emerge from your chrysalis,' she once said when she found me primping in front of the mirror.

Her reassurance, even though facetious, supported me through the days when I became disheartened about my plain face and unremarkable body.

'I've *got* to talk to Ma today,' Yasmin muttered vehemently as she threw herself on to the bench in the arbour. 'She just *has* to send me to boarding school. I'm not staying here one more day!'

I didn't say anything.

'I'll be in standard nine next year, and then what?' Yasmin continued. She was desperate to get away from the constraints of the small community and the family.

She had read *Secret Society*, a story set in the USA and filled with the mystery, glamour and heartache of teenage students belonging to a fraternity. That was what she imagined boarding school would be like.

She didn't want to attend school in the nearest town fifty

miles away, as she would have to commute each day. She clearly wanted to put distance between herself and us.

Ma and Papa had argued about the issue of her education. It was difficult to avoid hearing the arguments because our room was right across the passage from theirs.

'What is the use of sending her away to high school?' Papa demanded. 'One of these days she'll be married.'

'My daughters are not going to end up as slaves in some man's kitchen,' Ma retorted. 'They're both clever and I think they deserve a chance to be educated.'

Papa didn't agree. Nana said when he was determined about something he was like a dog with a bone.

I hated it when my parents argued. There were times when the atmosphere was so fogged with tension that I couldn't sleep. I would lie awake all night listening anxiously to their harsh, angry voices.

Yasmin said it was a feature of grown-up relationships. She told me once that Ma was frustrated with her dead-end life. She had nothing to look forward to, except what she had there with us.

But Nana had always told me that we didn't have too bad a life. We had everything we needed. What more did we want?

I glanced up from my musings to see Papa pulling away from the kerb. He was going to Molteno. Daniel was with him.

Like Gladys, Daniel – a general factotum – had been with our family for ages. Despite all the changes and the clamp-downs on African influx control, he was remarkably invisible.

Although Daniel had been with us for a long time, we knew very little about him. Nana said he had shown up at the gate one day, a piece of rope belted around his waist to keep up his threadbare trousers.

In spite of his appearance, she said that he had had a strange air of dignity about him that had touched them all. Because he couldn't speak a word of Xhosa or Afrikaans, they assumed that he had come from some distant place. Perhaps from one of the Rhodesias because he had mentioned the 'Smoke that Thunders'.

We explained his strange behaviour away by tapping our heads and rolling our eyes. But to my father, Daniel was a crony. A confidant. An accomplice in a house dominated by women.

As an alien without papers he was not permitted to live in the Location, and since Africans were not allowed to live in town, he moved into the backyard with a minimum of fuss, assuming a crab-like existence beneath the rusted skeleton of the Hudson. Fortunately his presence went undetected by the local authorities. Much as Ma wished to see the yard cleaned up, it was going to be virtually impossible to dislodge Daniel.

He was an indispensable cog in the machinery that kept my father going. He was my father's eyes. Although he was almost blind, Papa would not give up driving. Losing that last bit of independence would have sent him to an early grave. Ironically, he felt as trapped in Soetstroom as Yasmin. Daniel had never learned to drive. But it was not for lack of trying. Papa had made several attempts to teach him. But at the last attempt, he had nearly got both of them killed.

Daniel was erratic. His periods of sanity were too infrequent to trust him behind the wheel and in the end my father, with Daniel's assistance, devised a way to ensure that he remained independent.

While Papa sat behind the wheel, Daniel guided him, alerting him to obstacles or oncoming vehicles. It was a system they had honed to a fine skill. When a car approached my father steered over to the left or the right as required. Daniel would let him know if it was far enough or if he needed to move over further. My mother tried to discourage this practice, but my father slipped away at every opportunity. Fortunately the farm roads were usually deserted and when Papa had to go further afield, Ma insisted on driving him.

With a grimace of relief at being able to get on with the cooking, my mother tied an apron about her waist. Nana was already in the process of baking a cake.

These occasions, when we were all together as a family, were my favourite times. There was a sense of camaraderie amongst us and even though Yasmin hated cooking, she would find an excuse to be with us. Amidst the clatter of pots and dishes, there would always be gossip and laughter, especially with Yasmin around because she was so good at mimicking people.

Gladys had built a huge fire in the stove. Each time the oven door opened we were assaulted by a blast of air hot enough to singe the hair off our legs.

Nana's cake was done and she left the kitchen as Yasmin joined us. I guessed that Yasmin was still waiting for the right moment to broach the subject of her schooling.

When everything was going really well and we were all laughing and chatting, Yasmin suddenly said: 'Ma, I want to go away.'

Hip pressed against the sink, she waited for Ma's response.

Ma looked up and studied Yasmin for a moment. A drop of perspiration eased its way down the side of her face. She lifted the corner of her apron and carefully dabbed at it.

It was a long moment. A moment almost suspended in time. Everything seemed to be moving in slow motion.

Gladys entered, slamming the door behind her. Startled, we glanced up. The moment of suspended time collapsed like a burst bubble.

Gladys must have seen our bewildered faces. She grinned sheepishly and, carrying the freshly shaken mats, quickly trotted to the front rooms. Her bulky German-print skirt hung heavily from her thick waist and fleshy hips, buffeting her ankles and bare feet.

'*Yini, Nkosikazi*, almost finished now,' she said when she returned to the kitchen. She straightened her head-dress and waited for Ma's response.

Yasmin, too, waited for a response.

Ma was still imprisoned in her thoughts, her attention steadfastly fixed on the roti dough, which she was rolling savagely.

I felt a familiar tug at my insides. I had long ago made the startling discovery that Ma, like Yasmin, had a soft underbelly of vulnerability. Rarely exposed, I could see it now. I watched their two faces anxiously.

Ma was shorter than Yasmin, full-busted with a slight waist that curved out to rounded hips. Nana had once said that Ma was as voluptuous as one of the maidens in Hindu mythology. Papa, being a Muslim, did not appreciate the analogy.

I mouthed the word 'voluptuous'. The way my lips curled around it made it sound full and fleshy. I tried to conjure up an image of a Hindu maiden, but the only one that came to mind was the picture of the goddess Lakshmi which hung in Mrs Gopal's bedroom.

I'd only seen it a few times and I wouldn't go anywhere near it after Yasmin told me that the container on the altar beneath the picture held Mr Gopal's ashes. Nana dismissed Yasmin's claim. She said that Yasmin made up all sorts of stories when she had no ready explanation.

Ma's face was not as round as Mrs Gopal's goddess. Her face was angular, with a generous mouth and prominent cheekbones framing a captivating pair of eyes. Ma's thick brown hair shimmered and swayed as she moved about.

Setting down her rolling-pin, she turned to Yasmin and said: 'Exactly what are you trying to say?'

My glance darted from my mother to my sister. Yasmin glared at me and I promptly feigned disinterest. Lowering my head I carefully scraped the residue from the pestle and continued pounding. I was anxious not to miss a word and so the pounding was out of sync and I spattered crushed chilli all over the floor. My eyes and nose were running.

'I've had enough of this stupid school,' Yasmin said as I left the kitchen to fetch a tissue.

I returned quickly and tried to ascertain how much I had missed.

Nana had often said that the Soetstroom school was a dead end where the girls invariably ended up being sucked into the morass of Location life – either sinking into oblivion or growing fat and prematurely old with childbearing. My mother shared this view.

Now, however, when Yasmin expressed her sentiments about the school, Ma's brows gathered in dismay. 'I suppose you'd like to add your penny's worth too?' she asked, unexpectedly turning on me.

'Don't pick on me, Ma,' I protested. 'I'm not the one who wants to leave. I'm quite happy here.'

Ma's glance swept to Yasmin and then back to me.

I maintained a prudent silence.

'Yasmin, in just another year you'll be in standard nine. Things may change for us. Who knows? Maybe we'll be able to send you to a decent school. Just be patient . . .' Ma's voice trailed away as Nana entered the kitchen.

'What's going on?' Nana asked, hastening to the stove to peer into the pots.

Ma shook her head.

'What's going on here?' Nana said again. 'Can't you smell something burning?'

Cursing under her breath Ma dragged the pots to the side of the stove, away from the heat.

As she became aware of the tension in the kitchen Nana fixed her piercing brown eyes on my mother and then on Yasmin. The small hump on the bridge of her nose marked the spot where her reading-glasses rested. There were times when Nana's expression bore an unmistakable resemblance to Ma's. Ma and Nana both belonged to that nebulous group generally referred to as 'Coloured'.

Brows arched questioningly, Nana looked at my mother.

'Yasmin wants to leave school.'

'Well, what did you say?' Nana asked, still gazing at Ma.

'I said . . . this school. . . here in Soetstroom . . .' Yasmin began.

'I wasn't talking to you, Yasmin,' Nana snapped.

Yasmin glared.

'What do you really want to do, Yasmin?' Nana asked in a gentler tone as she rearranged the pots on the stove.

'I don't know,' Yasmin muttered.

'You're almost grown up now,' Nana remarked. 'Surely you should know. If you want to go out into the world, you'd better realise it's not an easy place, and you can't run back here each time you're in trouble.'

'Mum, we're not chucking her out of the house,' Ma said. 'All we're doing is considering another school. Perhaps the change will do her good.'

'What do you have in mind?' Nana asked, irritated at the way Ma had once again leapt to Yasmin's defence.

'I'll discuss it with Abdul,' Ma said.

'I suppose she's already thought of something.' The corners of Nana's mouth drooped disapprovingly as she glanced at Yasmin.

Ma banged the spoon down on the table and glared at her. 'Do you always have to be so irrational? I can't discuss anything with you!'

'You don't want to know the truth about your daughters, do you?' Nana said, her voice trembling.

'Let's drop it, Mum,' Ma snapped.

'You've got to stop giving in to her like this, Delia. One of these days you're going to be sorry.'

'Drop it, Mum.'

'OK, but don't come crying to me,' Nana muttered, getting in the last word. She glanced around the kitchen. 'Where on earth is Gladys?' she asked.

'She's finishing off the bedrooms. I told her she could leave early.' Ma's reply was curt and defensive.

'All this pampering,' Nana snorted. 'I'm the only one who ever does any real work around here. But no one shows me any appreciation. No one shows anything . . .' She gave Yasmin a frosty look. 'I'll pick up the *Sunday Times*,' she said, clearly eager to escape.

The train from Johannesburg had come in earlier and the papers would be available at the station café.

'I'll come with you, Nana,' I said.

Nana waited while I finished what I was doing. As I left I paused in the doorway, my glance travelling from my sister, who was sullenly staring at her shoes, to my mother, who was furiously ladling ghee into a pan.

4

THE STATION was at the southern end of town. The gravel road to the left veered north-west to Molteno, and the one to the right snaked around the town for seven miles before it linked up with the main road to Johannesburg.

Three blocks south of our house on Church Street was a small park. The white-owned stores, the two banks, post office and hotel were all located in this vicinity.

Nana and I walked in silence, our curious glances flitting from one side of the street to the other as the congregation in their Sunday best returned from church services.

Mrs du Plessis was at her gate.

'Hello Nana,' she called.

'Hello Mrs du Plessis,' Nana said distantly, obviously resenting the familiarity of the other woman's greeting. 'Familiarity breeds contempt' was one of Nana's assortment of proverbs which she trotted out regularly.

Mrs du Plessis was one of the Afrikaners who owed us money. Although she didn't come near our store now that her debt was unmanageable, we were the ones who had helped her through all the rough times when she was denied credit at the white stores.

Nana said that the moment their circumstances improved, people like Mrs du Plessis and the rest of the poor white community all trooped back to support their own kind.

'*Hoe gaan dit vandag?*' Mrs du Plessis enquired.

'Fine, thank you,' Nana said frostily.

The smiling Mrs du Plessis leaned on the gate, making herself comfortable.

I drew in my breath, expecting a long litany of complaints, but Nana was brief. She was still angry after her exchange with Ma. Mrs du Plessis, realising that it was not going to be easy to engage Nana's attention, lost interest. She cast her eyes around for some other distraction. It came in the form of fat Mrs Prinsloo who waddled up to the gate, leaning on the arm of Tickey, the slight African girl who usually escorted her to church.

Mrs du Plessis smiled at the panting woman and we seized the opportunity to escape.

'Hello Mrs Prinsloo,' Mrs du Plessis gushed as we moved away. I tried for the sake of propriety to keep my eyes averted from the elephantine rolls of fat which engulfed Mrs Prinsloo. The two women hardly noticed our departure.

'I wonder how Piet Prinsloo puts up with her,' Nana muttered.

I turned to stare thoughtfully after Tickey who was allowed to accompany Mrs Prinsloo to the church gate, but could not enter the church grounds. At the gate she had to wait until a member of the congregation was on hand to assist Mrs Prinsloo into the all-white domain.

'What if I end up like Tickey, working for some stupid white woman?' Yasmin had asked one afternoon after Tickey had been in to do Mrs Prinsloo's shopping. The mere thought of such a possibility had sent a shudder of revulsion through my sister. For the first time I got an inkling of what went on in Yasmin's mind, and the extent of her dread of being trapped in Soetstroom.

The vacant lot beside the station was densely treed. A brown carpet of pine needles crunched underfoot as we hurried along the winding path. The heady scent of pine blended with the aromatic eucalyptus in the clump of trees at the far end.

A train whistle shrilled, sending a flock of startled finches into the sky. The crash of jolting carriages and the hiss of steam heralded the departure of a train as Nana and I hastened into the small café where we picked up the paper.

Later that afternoon, when the cooking was done, Papa returned.

'It's about time,' Ma said, peering through the window when we heard the old DeSoto grinding to a halt outside.

My father looked exhausted.

'Go see if your Papa needs anything,' Ma quietly instructed me.

But before I could get out of my chair Yasmin had leapt up and rushed after him. I followed and stood in the bedroom doorway.

Yasmin fussed like a mother hen while Papa pulled off his khaki dust-jacket and threw it over the back of the padded blue chair. Then he rolled back his sleeves and slipped out of his braces. Without saying a word, Yasmin lifted the porcelain jug and poured water over Papa's cupped hands. He splashed his face. As if knowing instinctively what he wanted, Yasmin slowly poured more water into his hands. When Papa was done, he emptied the porcelain basin with its pattern of blue forget-me-nots, one of my mother's treasured possessions, and carefully replaced it on the washstand.

I noticed the strange expression on Yasmin's face. It was as though she were seeing for the first time that Papa had aged. In my eyes too he had suddenly become an old man, balding and stooped, his brown arms covered with matted grey hair. My heart skipped a beat.

'Are you all right, Papa?' Yasmin asked. She was tall like him, with Ma's eyes and his long, lustrous lashes. But that's where the similarity ended.

'We can eat whenever you're ready!' Ma called from the kitchen.

Papa patted Yasmin's cheek and she gave him an affectionate smile. I felt a twinge of resentment as I watched the two of them together.

'Let's go eat,' he said, slipping his arms through the braces, which snapped back into place over his shoulders.

I led the way, Yasmin and Papa following. Papa drew the old wicker chair up to the table and waited for his meal to be served.

Yasmin sat down next to him. 'I'll keep you company, Papa,' she offered.

I scowled as I went into the kitchen to help Ma carry the food to the table.

Papa smiled contentedly, peering at Yasmin from beneath his bushy brows. 'What's the matter?' he asked. Although he had an excellent command of both English and Afrikaans, he spoke with an accent which identified his Indian origins.

'She wants to leave school,' I said, pre-empting Yasmin.

'It this true?' Papa asked, his surprised glance resting on her.

Yasmin narrowed her eyes at me. 'Yes, Papa,' she said sweetly.

'Why?' he asked. 'There's nothing wrong with this school. That woman is no longer here. Miss . . . Miss . . . What was her name? That teacher?' He looked around for someone to supply the name.

I obliged again. 'Miss Durant.'

The mention of Miss Durant elicited varying reactions from us. We all recalled too vividly the incident with the readers.

It was my first day at school and I was thrilled to be there. Yasmin, who was in standard two already, regarded school as a bore. She sat on the steps of the one-roomed schoolhouse, knees supporting her elbows, face propped on her hands in an attitude of total dejection.

My eager eyes swept the playground for the comfort of familiar faces. I was delighted when Willem Arendse arrived, sweat dripping from his brow. Summer and winter, dry and rainy seasons, Willem ran the ten miles to school. He had the easy lope of a long distance runner and Yasmin said that he had hopes of becoming an Olympic athlete. She was probably the only one who believed that he had the ability.

Most of the Coloured students were from the Location; others, like Willem, came from the surrounding farms. During the lambing and shearing seasons the attendance dropped dramatically, returning to normal levels only when the work was done.

I had joined the beginners, who were bunched together, voices pitched with shrill excitement as we waited for the morning bell.

It rang five minutes later and we bumped and jostled one another before organising ourselves into four uneven lines.

Inside, the junior classes were separated from the seniors by a red velvet curtain. Since the only exit was through the front of the building, the senior boys who wished to leave the room, in order to attend to the call of nature or nicotine, had to traipse through Miss Durant's classroom.

Yasmin sat right in front of the class in the first desk to Miss Durant's right, sandwiched between Sarah Schoeman, Anna Klassen and the hefty Dora Oliphant, who had been moved to the front.

While we settled in, Miss Durant carefully cleaned her reading-glasses. Before directing her comments at the older students, she swept a disdainful glance over the newcomers. Satisfied that the young ones were suitably intimidated, Miss Durant perched her glasses on her nose and opened a small notebook.

She ordered us to our feet and, before reciting the Lord's Prayer, we sang out 'Good morning, Miss Durant'. While she checked the register, we were left to our own devices. Although the class was perfectly silent and attentive, she intermittently rapped her desk with her ruler.

Miss Durant first addressed herself to the right where the older children were seated. She crossed her legs and rested her elbows on her desk. Then, supporting her chin on her clasped hands, she surveyed the group as a whole.

'I see many of our old friends are back with us. Some of them have advanced a year, others unfortunately . . .' and here her tone became condescending, 'are still in the same old class.'

Her mood quickly recovered, embracing those students who had moved ahead. 'For those of you who have passed into higher classes, remember I shall be expecting great things from you this year.' At this point she turned her attention to the newcomers. 'I wish to welcome all the new children to SAPS.' She paused. 'I suppose you all know what the letters SAPS stand for?'

A few hands shot up.

She singled out one of the boys who was flapping both his arms in the air.

'Soetstroom Apostolic Primary School,' he yelled.

I was spellbound, but Yasmin merely rolled her eyes. And while Miss Durant's voice droned on I watched Yasmin become heavy-lidded.

'Now, little ones, if I can have your attention for a moment.' Miss Durant rapped her desk again. 'We have finally received our supply of readers,' she announced, pointing to a pile of *Dick and Jane* readers stacked in the corner of the room.

We all craned our necks to get a glimpse of the precious books. Without them the teachers had been forced to improvise with flashcards and other simple reading materials.

'We're very fortunate to get these readers,' she continued. '*Meneer* Bezuidenhout, the superintendent, brought them here for our very own use. And we promised to take extra good care of them.'

On the inside covers the books were marked with the oval stamp of the Soetstroom Primary School for Whites. It was obvious from the style of dress in the pictures that the books were outdated. Some of the pages were so badly defaced that they left great gaps in the story about the pretty white girl named Jane who had two adoring parents and a dog named Rover.

We eagerly studied pictures of Jane and Rover, Jane and her mother in the kitchen, Jane standing by the picket fence waving at her father, who, briefcase in hand, ambled up the pathway to the house. There were the usual giggles which followed obscene comments about Jane's activities, but Miss Durant quickly brought this silliness under control with several sharp raps on her desk.

I did not participate in this frivolity. Yasmin and I had both learned to read at an early age and now, turning the pages, I concentrated on the captions beneath the pictures.

I was oblivious to everything around me as I flipped back the pages to the flyleaf. Beneath the oval stamp on the inside cover were the carefully printed words of a jingle: *Coolie, coolie, ring the bell; coolie, coolie, go to hell.*

Without thinking, I ripped out the offensive page and watched as it slowly drifted to the floor. Suddenly aware of the silence, I looked up. All eyes were on me. Miss Durant was glaring at me in total disbelief.

'How dare you!' she croaked. 'How dare you!' She almost choked on her words as she pushed herself up out of her chair and slowly crossed the room to my desk.

My foot edged towards the page in an attempt to cover it, but it was too late.

'I'm going to give you the thrashing of your life,' Miss Durant declared as she seized her cane and pulled me out of my desk to the front of the class.

'It's only a blank page, Miss Durant,' Yasmin said.

My petrified glance was fixed on the cane, which swished back and forth, catching in the folds of Miss Durant's skirt as it swooped downwards in a tight arc.

'Hold out your hand,' she commanded.

I was incapable of moving.

'You can't cane her!' Yasmin finally found her voice.

'What was that?' Miss Durant's incredulous glance swept to the source of the reckless remark.

'She's only a baby . . .' Yasmin mumbled into her shirt collar, her eyes downcast.

'Well, if that's the case, you can come forward and take her punishment.'

A dark flush spread over Yasmin's face. She licked her dry lips, considering her options. Then she looked up, her eyes lingering on a stain on the wall before sliding sideways to the teacher's face.

Miss Durant fixed her mouth into a hard line. 'Give me your hand,' she said to Yasmin.

Yasmin hesitated. She had obviously not counted on this.

'Now, girl! Give me your hand!'

Yasmin held out her hand. But she withdrew it the moment the cane swept downwards.

'If you do that again,' Miss Durant said through clenched teeth, 'you'll be in a lot more trouble.'

My eyes followed the upward arc of the cane and I anticipated the searing pain. Yasmin squeezed her eyes shut. When the cane landed, it was like an explosion. I could almost feel it biting through her flesh to the very bone. I felt the pain speeding up my own arm, just as it must have gone up hers.

Before she could recover from the first lash, the second scorched along the same path. I bit into my lower lip to prevent the cry which had gathered in my throat.

Incensed by Yasmin's defiance, Miss Durant gave her two more lashes, for good measure.

Yasmin returned to her seat. She had not uttered a single cry or shed a tear. The only audible sound was that of my sobbing.

Miss Durant was transferred soon after this – thanks to Ma.

The mention of Miss Durant brought that particular incident back to both of us. Yasmin's eyes clouded over. I was sure that the memory had its own special pain for her. A moment later, however, she tossed her head, throwing off the unpleasant recollection.

She reached for the salt. 'Who cares about Miss Durant? I've forgotten all about her. All I know is that Soetstroom is a dull, boring pimple on the earth's surface. I bet no one outside this place has ever heard of it.'

'It's more like a valley where all the old elephants come to die.' Papa felt obliged to restore to Soetstroom the dignity that Yasmin had stripped from it by her remark.

Ma dragged her chair to the table. We waited for my father's muttered blessing, *Bismillah*, before we started eating.

'It's a good little school.' Papa was anxious to keep the family intact. 'Miss Durant was no good and we were glad to get rid of her, but you have good teachers now.'

'Papa, you're being old-fashioned,' Yasmin said. 'Those two teachers are numbskulls.'

'Where did you learn to speak of your teachers with such

disrespect?' Ma was aghast.

But Yasmin didn't care. 'Well, it's true.'

I watched the shadows creeping up behind Yasmin's eyes.

'What are we going to do about the broken window, Papa?' she asked, changing the subject.

'I'll get Daniel to fix it.'

'No, you won't,' Ma said.

Papa was silent for a long moment. 'Maybe we'll drive out to their farm next Sunday and talk to Steyn,' he said.

'It won't do you any good,' Nana said as she reached for another roti.

'Why not?' he asked.

'I've already written notes to both the principal and his father,' Ma added. A wisp of hair had come undone, falling over her ear. Her right hand carried the food to her mouth while the left hand reached over to sweep the strands back under the knot. 'The last time was when he threw stones on the roof.'

There was a moment of silence as we all recalled the terrifying sound of stones clattering on corrugated iron.

'Steyn is a big shot,' Nana reminded us. He's an MP.'

'Big shot or not, he'll have to do something about his son,' Papa declared.

Ma and Nana exchanged amused glances.

'There's something wrong with that boy,' Nana said tapping her head. 'Wouldn't he be about the same age as Baboo?'

No one answered.

'Did you speak to Swanepoel today?' Ma asked my father.

Papa nodded.

'What did he have to say about the car?' Ma wanted to know as she got up to refill the dish with dahl.

'Well,' Papa hesitated. 'He thinks it needs more work.'

'Expensive work?' Ma asked.

'Jannie will do the work.'

'Swanepoel won't pay. You're wasting time and money with all the tinkering.' Ma's tone was edged with impatience. 'It's Swanepoel's problem.'

'I'll speak to him,' Papa said.

'That's what you always say,' Ma muttered.

For a moment my father was silent. I watched him and wondered how satisfied he was with his life. There were times when I caught him gazing off into the distance too.

'We haven't done too badly in spite of the fact that everyone thinks this is a dying town,' Papa observed. 'Have we not always had food on our table and a roof over our heads?'

'By the grace of God,' Nana agreed.

'Things will improve.' Papa spoke as though he needed to convince himself. 'We'll live quite comfortably. I can sell that old Dodge in the garage.' His voice was wistful and my heart went out to him.

'Stop dreaming,' Ma said.

'Do we always have to talk about these things at table?' Yasmin groaned.

'One car sale is equivalent to a year's produce sales,' Papa continued as though he hadn't heard a word anyone had said.

'The last time you sold a car the profit was swallowed up in HP costs, legal fees and those two retread tyres we had to throw in as part of the deal.'

'Someone up there is taking care of us. I can't see how else we've managed.' Nana sighed, rolling her eyes heavenwards.

Papa had had about all he could take of this conversation.

'Things are bound to get better,' he said. 'The boom will come and when it does, I'll be right here to take advantage of it.' He pushed his chair back and went into the kitchen to wash his hands.

After supper Yasmin and I helped with the dishes. When everything had been cleared away, Yasmin sat at the stove, absently raking the coals. Mesmerised, she watched as the bright embers plopped into the pan of grey ash under the grate.

Nana gathered her knitting and shuffled off to her room in the backyard.

5

THE FOLLOWING Sunday Ma and Papa drove out to Hermanus Steyn's farm, *Twee Jonge Gezellen*. I went with them. Nana and Yasmin stayed home, both claiming that they wanted to rest.

The farm lay fifteen miles north of Soetstroom on the leeward side of Doringhoek Mountain. My father was silent throughout the drive. It was so quiet and peaceful that Ma stopped the car for a moment. The only sound we could hear was the creak of a windmill, fanned by a gentle breeze.

At the foot of the windmill the rippled surface of a large dam gleamed in the midday sun. Beyond this the landscape was dotted with clusters of what appeared to be cream-coloured rocks but which, on closer inspection, turned out to be sheep.

At the entrance to the farm we bumped off the tar road on to a gravel track and stopped beneath a board on which was emblazoned the name *Twee Jonge Gezellen*.

I got out to open the gate and Ma drove through. Two miles and six gates later we topped the last hill. Below us, tucked into the valley, was a gabled house, as blindingly white as a patch of freshly fallen snow against the green and ecru of the landscape. We passed through the gate and Ma slowed down as three big mongrels with bared teeth chased after the car, snapping at the tyres.

Fortunately, one of the labourers witnessed our plight and came over to assist. With a series of short whistles he brought the dogs under control.

Papa waited until the dogs had slunk back to their pens before he ventured out of the car. 'Steyn, where is he?' he asked, speaking to the tall Xhosa in his own dialect.

The man gestured towards the house. I climbed out and went after Papa. Ma chose to stay in the car. Papa and I had just started in the direction of the house when Hermanus Steyn emerged.

He was fiftyish. Tall and sinewy, his chest was daringly revealed by the three shirt buttons left undone.

Papa stood to one side waiting for Steyn to invite us on to the stoep. Several chairs were grouped on either side of the door beneath two long, shuttered windows.

Steyn's hat was tilted slightly forward over his eyes. He idly scratched the side of his neck and waited with a small contemptuous smile. Finally he growled in Afrikaans: 'Mohammed! What do you want?'

'It's your boy,' Papa responded in English.

'What about him?'

It became clear that he was not going to speak English and Papa was determined not to speak Afrikaans. They continued the conversation in both languages.

Steyn stepped forward, blocking the doorway and thoughtfully tapping a thin leather sjambok against the side of his leg.

'Well, speak up, man. What has my son done to bring you all the way out here?'

'He broke one of my windows.'

For a moment Steyn looked incredulous. Then he laughed, a great insolent roar that seemed to echo across the valley. Clearly perplexed, Papa looked at me. I could tell that he thought Steyn was quite mad.

'You came all this way to tell me about a piece of broken glass!' Steyn gasped as he finally managed to catch his breath.

Papa was embarrassed. Even I felt a little awkward about coming out to the farm to report something as trivial as a broken pane in a window. Fortunately Papa remembered that the glass was not the issue. It was the disdain Cobus had shown for our property.

Papa was standing at ground level. Steyn was on the stoep, four steps above him, almost dwarfing him.

'Come up here,' Steyn said, beckoning to Papa.

'Do you understand . . .' Papa began.

'No,' Steyn silenced him. 'I do not understand why anyone would waste their time like this.'

Papa shook his head. 'It is not the piece of glass, but all the trouble your boy has caused us.'

Steyn studied him. Then abruptly his mood became conciliatory.

'Look, I know that in the past the boy was wild. I was not able to do much with him after his mother died, but they did straighten him out at boarding school.' He fingered his chin. 'Seems to me some time ago I had a note from one of you that he had thrown stones on your roof.'

'My wife wrote that letter.'

'If it is a new window you want, I will pay for it.'

Papa realised that he was wasting his time. He turned to leave. 'If I ever catch him interfering with my family . . .' he said threateningly.

Steyn slowly drew himself erect. 'If you harm my boy, Mohammed, I will pin your hide to my wall.'

Papa winced, drawing his shoulders forward to shield himself from the Afrikaner's insulting manner.

'You remember your place or one of these days you'll be sorry,' Steyn's voice was low, his blue eyes cold and arrogant.

A small vein throbbed at the side of Papa's head. He looked away, embarrassed that I had witnessed his humiliation.

Ma got out of the car and came over to see what was happening. Sensing the tension, she paused on the first step. Papa had his back to her.

Papa said: 'You may be a big man amongst your people, Steyn, but you're not big enough to scare me.'

I witnessed the slow transformation on Hermanus Steyn's face. He had obviously not heard a word Papa had said because his attention was fixed on my mother.

Papa turned and saw Ma. 'I'm ready to leave,' he said.

Steyn's frank and admiring gaze drew a dark flush which crept upwards from Ma's neck. For a brief moment her eyes locked with his, her lips compressing into a thin, scornful line.

Then she looked away, dismissing him.

'*Mevrou*,' Steyn said, addressing her directly. 'I will have your window replaced, and I regret my son's bad behaviour.' His English was heavily accented.

Papa was astonished at the change in Steyn.

Ma nodded and turned away. Grasping my shoulder, she propelled me towards the car. I glanced back. Hermanus Steyn was still staring after us.

Nana was in the shop when Hermanus Steyn arrived on the Tuesday afternoon, accompanied by his carpenter.

My father wasn't home. It was clear that Nana didn't like Hermanus Steyn. Neither did I. I liked him even less when he smiled and casually enquired after Ma who was in the backyard pruning the honeysuckle bush.

Nana had that tight-lipped look which made me suspect that something was up. I remembered the way Hermanus Steyn had stared after us as we left *Twee Jonge Gezellen*.

I watched as he strolled into the backyard in search of Ma. Nana moved to the window which looked into the yard. Eager to see what was going on, I joined her.

Ma looked up when she heard him.

'Good day, *Mevrou*,' he said.

'Good day, Mr Steyn.'

They were standing just beyond the window and Nana and I had a clear view of them. I felt an uneasy jolt as I watched Ma's hand creeping to her hair, smoothing it back self-consciously.

Hermanus Steyn also noticed the fluttering hand, suspended and trembling like the wings of a butterfly.

He smiled boldly. 'I could not rest until I saw you again.'

'I don't think coming here was such a good idea,' Ma said.

Hermanus Steyn looked up and saw us at the window and

the smile left his face. 'Why not?' he asked.

Ma followed his glance and immediately became flustered, as if not quite sure whether to walk away or to stay and talk to him.

The carpenter stood to one side waiting.

Nana grunted, her eyes narrow slits.

'My husband isn't home,' Ma said.

'I am not here to see him. I am here to fix your window.'

Ma had nothing to say and an awkward silence fell between them.

The carpenter was still waiting. He coughed discreetly.

'Where is the window?' Hermanus Steyn asked brusquely.

'In the back.' Ma gestured towards the storeroom.

'*Gaan aan met jou werk*.' Hermanus Steyn instructed the man to get on with his work and returned his attention to Ma.

Ma distanced herself by moving off to watch the carpenter remove the shards of glass from the damaged pane.

'If you'll excuse me, I have a great deal to do,' Ma said.

I wished he would go. I didn't like him and my heart was pounding with anxiety – for my father and for us. The faint scent of Ma's perfume, *Evening in Paris*, lingered in the shop. What were they saying? He was standing so close to her that with the slightest movement he might easily have touched her.

Ma lifted her head and, with as much dignity as she could muster, said, 'Good day, Mr Steyn.'

By the time she entered the store her nostrils were flared and her chin quivering.

'*En toe*? What's the matter with you?' Nana asked.

'That was an unforgivable thing to do,' Ma said, pouncing on Nana.

'What?' Nana asked, all round-eyed innocence.

'You know very well what I'm talking about.'

Nana shrugged.

'You were spying on me!'

'You're out of your mind,' Nana said scornfully.

'Oh, I know you well enough.'

'Isn't that just like you? Why didn't you tell him to leave? Instead you were like a simpering schoolgirl. Don't you care what your husband might think? Don't you know the kind of reputation a man like that has with women? And it doesn't matter what colour they are either,' Nana added.

'Don't be ridiculous!' Then, throwing her hands up in exasperation, Ma exclaimed, 'There's no point arguing with you!'

Nana sniffed, turned her back on Ma and stalked out of the shop just as Yasmin entered. She sensed the tension and raised a questioning eyebrow. I hurried out after Nana.

Papa was surprised to hear that Hermanus Steyn had kept his word and had actually fixed the window.

'Good thing you went to see him, Papa,' Yasmin said as they inspected the repairs. 'It looks like he's done a good job.' She ran her fingers over the smooth surface of the putty.

'I could do a good job like that too, if I had his tools,' Daniel said, looking a bit aggrieved that someone else should receive the accolades.

Yasmin smiled. Sometimes she revealed the softer, gentler side of her nature. These were rare occasions, and when they happened it was like a feathery touch to the soul, making one's heart lurch with happiness. Daniel smiled back at her, his disappointment forgotten.

6

THE PROBLEM of Yasmin's schooling surfaced again a few months later. We watched with a sense of helpless resignation as she became increasingly morose, often bursting into tears at the slightest provocation.

Yasmin had the ability to cry at will – a technique, she said, that actors often employed. 'All you have to do is concentrate on something terribly sad, like the death of someone close to you.'

'I thought you said actors used onion juice,' I said.

'There are all sorts of techniques,' Yasmin said, dismissively.

I sighed. Unlike Yasmin, I knew so little about life. Nana had once remarked that Yasmin inhabited a world quite apart from ours. I suspected that it was her way of escaping an environment she found so completely inhibiting.

Our parents' lack of concern about finding her an alternative school incensed Yasmin. 'All they ever do is talk, talk, talk,' she complained. 'One of these days they'll end up with varicose veins on their tongues.'

At supper one night while she was listlessly picking at the food on her plate, Papa asked: 'What's wrong, Yasmin?'

Yasmin lowered her lashes, squeezing out the tears. I watched in fascination as two large drops trailed down her cheeks.

'I wish I were dead!' With that she leapt up and ran to the bedroom, slamming the door behind her.

There was a moment's silence. Ma sighed. 'I've made enquiries about the Elizabeth Grey Private School for Girls near the city. Perhaps we should make an appointment with the headmistress.'

Papa thought about this suggestion. He was reluctant to send Yasmin so far from the protection of our home. There were too many pitfalls awaiting a young girl like her. There was the equally important consideration too of whether such a school would provide halal food.

'She'll be much better off here at home,' he said.

'What happens about matric?' Ma asked.

'Why would she want to do matric? One of these days she'll be married.'

'What if she isn't?'

'She will be.' Papa spoke with great conviction.

'What are you up to, Abdul?' Ma demanded.

'Nothing.'

'Who've you been talking to?' she asked.

But Papa would say no more.

Nana listened to the debate without comment. She returned to the kitchen to dust the china dinner service that had belonged to my great-great-grandmother who had purportedly arrived from Ireland with her husband bearing this treasure. Ma and Nana both valued the china, which had been passed down from one generation to the next. Nana said that the dishes would one day be passed on to us.

Yasmin had already said that she didn't want the china or the gold jewellery Papa had given Ma when they married. The necklace and earrings were typically Indian, heavy and clumsy in appearance.

With the issue of Yasmin's schooling still unresolved the atmosphere at home was tense. Yasmin was impossible to live with and I took to spending more time alone.

One Sunday Nana and I took a walk to the station for the newspaper. It was a warm autumn afternoon. The setting sun hovered above the horizon, shading the clouds in various hues of crimson which gave the illusion of protracted twilight.

'It's the ash from the volcanic eruption in Hawaii,' Nana explained.

'I'd like to be in a spaceship to see all of this from up there.'

Nana shrugged. 'I just wish they'd stop tampering with things that should best be left alone.'

A goods train pulled out of the station, slowly chugging north along the tracks which skirted town. We walked in silence, Nana glancing reflectively around her. 'Getting ahead here,' she observed, 'is like King Sisyphus and the rock. I don't suppose you've heard of him?'

I shook my head. I'd heard of King Solomon, but not this other king.

'He was condemned to roll a rock up a hill . . . What the blazes . . . ?' Nana exclaimed as we reached the station. 'Isn't that Yasmin? Why is she dallying here?'

Not too far from Yasmin sat Cobus Steyn.

Nana hurried towards Yasmin who was visibly shaken when she saw her.

'What are you doing here?' Nana demanded.

'Buying a magazine at the café,' Yasmin said, quickly recovering her composure. She had obviously not expected to see either of us there. Cobus's gaze was mocking. Nana glared first at him and then at Yasmin. She had seen the way Yasmin was fluttering her eyelashes.

'You're cheapening yourself,' she hissed.

'I wasn't doing anything!' Yasmin cried.

Nana's eyes flashed a warning and Yasmin pursed her lips into a delicate little bud and lowered her lashes.

'You'd better watch out, my girl, or you'll be spending the rest of your life behind bars. Are you forgetting that he's white?' Nana asked in a low voice, glancing at Cobus, who sat with his arms stretched along the back of the bench. 'You'd better get home now, young lady.'

Yasmin sauntered ahead of us and then, with an over-the-shoulder glance at Cobus, waited for me.

'Nana's afraid that there's too much of Ma coming out in

me,' she muttered under her breath.

'What do you mean?' I asked.

Yasmin shrugged.

'What do you mean, Yasmin?' I persisted. But it was no use. She had nothing more to say.

'Don't pay any attention to her,' Nana snapped.

'What were you doing with Cobus?' I asked.

'Mind your own business.'

Nana studied Yasmin, who had walked off ahead of us. There was a determined look on her face. Nana told me that it would be in everyone's best interests to get Yasmin out of Soetstroom, for the longer she stayed the more likely she was to get into serious trouble. After what she had witnessed at the station she was sure that it would be wisest to send Yasmin away.

'You see,' Yasmin said to me later with an insouciant smile, 'there are many ways to skin a cat.'

7

MOHAMMED'S General Store specialised in dry goods and catered to the African trade. The interior was filled with stacks of blankets which reached all the way to the ceiling; billy-cans hung from the doorway in tight bunches and the three-legged cast-iron pots popular with Africans for outdoor cooking were propped up against the door; beads and colourful bangles festooned shelves stacked with rows of plastic shoes.

Most of the other general stores in Soetstroom were similar, shelves filled with inexpensive, heavy, blue cotton prints which the African women sewed into voluminous skirts. In those days the white-owned stores had separate entrances and cubicles for African customers.

We were talking about this state of affairs one night when Nana said that it was no better than the time when Africans were required to do their buying through a hole in the wall without the benefit of viewing the merchandise.

'Remember, Delia? At Kruger's Butcher Shop the Africans had to ask for two shillings' meat and then got a small parcel containing all sorts of rubbish, like sheep's hooves or . . . snouts.'

Nana didn't want to say pigs' snouts in front of Papa because the mere word pig was offensive to a Muslim.

'This country's gone to pot under the Afrikaners,' Nana complained.

'It is a legacy of the British,' Papa insisted. 'They did the same thing in India.'

'India, India! You're always comparing this country to India.

The British had their faults, I'd be the last to deny that, but don't forget what your own people did to each other. The Hindus murdering their Muslim brothers and vice versa. Who can forget the atrocities committed by Indian upon Indian?'

Papa fell silent. After this he was a little more careful about making comparisons. But Ma agreed that the British, as a colonial power, had been responsible for a lot of misery.

Despite the segregation and humiliation, shopping was still a major social event for the farm labourers. At Mohammed's General Store the African customers milled around the doorway or sat on the sidewalk, knobkerrie in one hand, the other clasped around the bowl of a long-stemmed pipe, their conversation punctuated by jets of crimson spittle aimed into the sand. The women usually did the buying, unselfconsciously peeling out their breasts when they paused to nurse their infants.

The white farmers were again boycotting us and dropped their black workers off at the white stores, where they were forced to shop. We lost a substantial amount of business. Even Papa now complained about unfair competition.

It was because of these unfair business practices that the rumour about a recruiting office for black mine workers, purported to be opening in Soetstroom, caused so much excitement.

'It means more people will be passing through the town,' Papa declared happily.

'Pretty soon they'll be closing the railway line,' Nana reminded him.

'Never!' Papa declared. 'This town is the junction for all the smaller towns around here. They would never do anything so stupid.'

Nana was not convinced. She ticked off all the stupid things that the government had done. But Papa was convinced better things were coming our way.

There had been talk about mining exploration on Boesman's Hoek. Papa said he had long suspected that the mountain would one day yield its riches. Whenever he drove through the mountain pass, he always mentioned that there was probably untold wealth lying beneath it. Then, too, there was a government proposal to build an irrigation dam not too far from us. It was never done.

'Things are going to get better,' he said contentedly. 'This town is going to grow and we're going to grow right along with it.'

Nana sighed. There was no use arguing when Papa was fired up like this. 'Your father has all these high hopes. He's floating somewhere up there,' she pointed to the sky. 'You know what they say. The higher you go, the harder you fall.'

'We're in the right place at the right time,' Papa announced. He was so exhilarated that he could speak of nothing else but the expected improvement in the local economy.

Ma watched all these goings-on with a strange remoteness.

Lately, she had become increasingly frustrated. 'Our lives,' she said to Nana one day, 'are so small and so limited. Each day is exactly like the next.'

Nana listened in silence, a frown on her face.

The winter that year was bitterly cold. Frost remained on the ground all day in areas protected from the sun's rays. Water pipes froze and burst. Each night before going to bed, Ma built a large fire in the kitchen stove, but the house was designed to permit draughts, not to exclude them, and by morning it was so cold that we dreaded leaving the warm comfort of our beds.

It was during this spell of cold weather that the response arrived from Miss Jones, the headmistress of the privately run Elizabeth Grey School for Girls.

'Where will we get the money?' Ma wondered after a sleepless night of worry.

'We'll find it somewhere. Tell Miss Jones we'll see her,' Papa said, having resigned himself to the fact that Yasmin could no longer be kept at home against her will.

'The money, Abdul. Where will we get the money?'

Papa sighed. 'I don't know, but if something should happen

to me, at least one of the girls will have had an education. It'll probably be the only legacy I can leave.'

'I thought you had plans for her,' Ma remarked.

'*Inshallah*, she's the eldest. I should make sure she's settled. I've talked to some families who have sons of her age. Pity she's difficult. And such a sharp tongue too. Perhaps an education will help to make the package more attractive.'

Ma just shook her head wearily.

'Your mother is right,' Papa said. 'Look what happened to Baboo. No education – and now he's working like a slave for his uncle in Johannesburg, dreaming of some day becoming a famous cricketer.' He paused reflectively. '*Inshallah*, if all goes well, perhaps we'll be able to educate both the girls.'

'This is the first sensible thing he's done in a long time,' Nana observed when Ma told her about Papa's decision. 'This is no place for a young girl. It's too easy to get into trouble. The devil will find work for idle hands.' Nana had not forgotten Yasmin at the station with Cobus Steyn.

'I'll inform Miss Jones that we'll see her next week.'

Yasmin was thrilled. She persuaded Ma to make her a new dress for the occasion. She selected a delicately printed blue crêpe from the fabrics in the store.

'That's too grown-up for you,' Nana protested. 'Besides, it's too cold for such a flimsy dress.'

Yasmin insisted. Eventually both Ma and Nana gave in.

The drive of one hundred and eighty-five miles to the city was a miserable one. We left early that morning. It was still dark and in the cold our breath soon iced up the windows. Shivering, we huddled under the comforter while Ma strained to see in the weak light from our headlamps.

'Are you all right?' Papa asked her.

She nodded. 'Are you girls sleeping?'

'No,' Yasmin and I replied in unison.

'I expect Miss Jones will be asking quite a few questions,' she said, speaking over her shoulder to Yasmin. 'It would be best if your Papa and I provided the answers.'

'Yes, of course.' At this point Yasmin would have agreed to anything.

We reached Stutterheim at about seven o'clock, just as the sun was coming up. This was a convenient place to fill up with petrol before continuing the journey to the city. Ma stopped at a garage and we took turns freshening up in the lavatory where the shivering Yasmin changed into her new dress.

I was awed by Miss Jones, who met us in the lobby. Papa removed his hat and tried to generate an air of confidence, but he was nervously squashing the crown of his fedora, then pounding it back into shape again.

'The education of the girls is not entirely academic,' the prim Englishwoman explained as she led the way to her office. 'There are several courses for their physical development too, as you can see from our playing fields and stables.' She opened the door and swept in, the rest of us trooping close behind her.

She waited for us to be seated in front of her desk before settling comfortably into her black leather armchair. 'I regard education as the promotion of a delicate balance between the mind and the body. *Mens sana in corpore sano*. A healthy mind in a healthy body. Don't you agree?' She looked directly at Papa, who had his attention fixed on his hands.

There was a moment of silence. Papa nodded his head and stored the statement for later consideration. She pushed her small frame to the very edge of her padded chair, giving all her attention to Yasmin.

Apart from the initial glance, Miss Jones ignored me completely. Papa struggled to concentrate on what she was saying, nodding whenever she paused. Ma, too, was unusually quiet, and so all the talking was left to Miss Jones.

'Since we are catering not only to the Coloured community but also to the Indians, which of course includes those of the Muslim faith, we provide halal for them and vegetarian for the Hindu students.'

Papa waited for her to continue.

'We purchase all our meat from a *bona fide* Muslim butcher in the city. So you see there really is nothing to worry about.' Although Miss Jones concentrated her attention on Papa, she recognised that Ma should not be underestimated.

It was apparent that Yasmin had impressed her. Yasmin looked radiant in her flimsy dress. It was as if the attention from Miss Jones had made her immune to the cold. A paraffin heater burned in a corner of the office, warming the room.

Miss Jones clasped her hands under her chin. 'Yasmin is a very beautiful young girl. And I am sure she is a talented one too. She needs a stimulating environment, one that will encourage her to blossom. I don't think your little town can do that. Am I right?'

'Yes.' Ma spoke up.

Miss Jones smiled knowingly. 'It is imperative that young girls have ambition in life.' She looked steadily at Yasmin as she spoke. 'It is this which provides the motivation and drive to get through school. A career is most important.'

Papa's expression tightened. I didn't think he wanted some Englishwoman telling him how to raise his daughters.

Before we left home, Nana had wondered aloud what a 'Miss' would know about raising children. No doubt these were Papa's exact thoughts as we sat in Miss Jones's office.

Yasmin, needless to say, was quite taken up and was hanging on to every word, her eyes darting frantically between Ma and Papa, fearing that Papa might say something to embarrass us all.

'Nursing is a very desirable career,' Miss Jones continued.

'No daughter of mine is going to be a nurse.'

'Well, what about teaching?' she enquired.

Papa shook his head emphatically. We knew that Papa was being contrary purely because the suggestions had come from Miss Jones.

She fell silent. She had listed the possibilities available for non-white girls and now discreetly dropped the subject.

'How much is this going to cost?' Papa asked.

'The fees do run high,' Miss Jones said. 'And there are extras that have to be paid for.'

'How much?' he persisted.

She told him and he regarded her in disbelief.

'The school is a private one. Believe me, it's a much-needed institution for Coloured and Indian girls who have found themselves in the same predicament as your Yasmin.' She glanced at Papa again. 'We even have girls from as far afield as Mafeking and Louis Trichardt. Of course, we do have bursaries . . .'

I could tell from Papa's expression that this information was of little interest to him. Having already retrieved his hat from the side of the chair, he was ready to turn down the whole idea.

'We're quite willing to make sacrifices in order to give Yasmin a satisfactory education and get her out of the Soetstroom environment.' Ma feared that the opportunity for Yasmin's education would be lost if she had to depend on Papa for a decision. 'I'd like to think about it,' she said.

'I hope you won't take too long,' Miss Jones cautioned. 'We have only a limited number of places left.'

'You'll hear from us as soon as we've made a decision,' Papa said firmly.

'What time is it?' he asked Ma as we rose to leave Miss Jones's study.

'Almost twelve o'clock,' she said.

'Too late for the market,' he muttered irritably. 'We might as well go home. There's no point in going into the city now.'

'What about a visit with Cassimbhai? You haven't seen him in ages,' Ma urged.

But he declined with a sharp 'No'.

'We'll be in touch with you soon,' Ma said to Miss Jones.

On the way home Yasmin and I listened to our parents speaking in incomplete sentences.

'I don't think so,' Papa mumbled, massaging his head.

'It will be a good thing,' Ma countered.

'I don't like her.'

'That's nonsense. She struck me as a very competent person.'

'Too expensive. For that kind of money they should be eating biryani every day.'

Ma chuckled. 'It's not that expensive. You said we'd find the money.'

'How was I supposed to know that it would cost so much?' he asked. 'All that rubbish talk about extra courses. Where in Soetstroom or anywhere else in this country will she use any of them, eh?' As far as he was concerned, an education involved reading, writing and arithmetic, not any of this other nonsense.

The conversation continued in that vein, the unsaid hanging delicately balanced in the air. Ma was very persuasive and wore Papa down until he raised his shoulders in resignation.

Yasmin clasped her hands in glee.

8

YASMIN'S LETTER of acceptance arrived. She was required to register in January, at the beginning of the school year.

Thrilled with the news, she indiscriminately bestowed smiles, hugs and kisses on all, including Nana.

Her high spirits were infectious and Ma surprised us at breakfast one morning when she announced: 'I'm going to have the house renovated, the outside painted and that damn backyard cleared.'

Our mouths dropped open. I looked anxiously from one parent to the other. Lately, the anger between them had sputtered like an electric current, dragging the rest of the family into its eddies.

'Where will we get the money?' Papa protested. 'Already there is the expense of sending Yasmin away.'

'We don't need much.'

'We don't have anything to spare!' Papa cried.

'I have a bit saved,' Ma said.

There was an angry pause from Papa who took his time spooning oatmeal porridge into his mouth.

'With all the talk about the government moving Indian traders out of the small towns, it would be best not to draw attention to ourselves, especially when we're right across the street from their church. You know yourself what's been going on,' Ma continued, undaunted.

Nana studied Ma from under lowered lids. 'Don't you think fixing the house will draw attention?' she asked.

'That's right,' Papa said. 'There's nothing wrong with this house. It's been good enough for us all these years.'

'*Ja*, I know. But let's face it, Abdul,' Ma said cajolingly, 'it needs work. Look at the mess in the backyard. Look around you. See how the smoke from the stove has blackened the ceilings. They're more likely to evict us because of the condition this house is in, especially right in full view . . . on the main street.'

Papa sipped his coffee and the silence intensified. Then he spoke. 'I suppose . . .' He was beginning to falter.

'Don't worry,' Ma said quickly. 'I told you I have something put aside.'

'If you ask me . . .' Nana started.

Ma flashed her a warning glance. 'But no one's asking you, Mum,' she said.

'. . . if they want to move us, they will,' Nana continued, undeterred by Ma's angry eyes. 'Spending money on this house is not going to make a difference. You'll only be throwing good money after bad.'

'What do you know about any of this?' Ma demanded.

'You need material and labour. It's not that easy,' Nana said hotly.

'Stay out of this, Mum,' Ma snapped.

Yasmin blurted out something unintelligible which was meant to ease the tension. She, too, was praying that Nana would keep quiet. Nana was determined to have the last word, though.

'It's a stupid idea,' she said.

'I can get whatever we need quite cheaply from the auction sales in town. Perhaps, with everyone helping . . .' Ma's glance swept the table and came to rest on Papa.

But this was too much to expect.

Nana shook her head.

'What's the point? Look what we have next door,' she said, gesturing towards the neighbouring house.

'I'll speak to Mrs Ollie.' Ma's tone had lost its edge.

Our neighbour, Mrs Ollie, kept three jersey cows in her backyard.

Although this was in violation of the town's health regulations, no one did anything about the flies or the stench. Mrs Ollie astutely supplied us and several of the town officials with milk.

We had learned long ago that the round-faced, cheerful woman had many aspects to her character. She was an Afrikaner with a strong sense of justice who dovetailed right into our lives.

Although Ma said she would talk to Mrs Ollie about the condition of her backyard, she never got around to it. She was too busy planning and organising help for her own projects.

Two weeks later the shacks in the backyard came down, leaving only the outside rooms intact.

I helped Papa to search through the rubble for salvageable material, but Ma stubbornly insisted that everything be carted to the dump.

'I want that old post,' he warned her.

'It's rotten,' Ma protested.

It was true. I had spent countless hours watching the termites march off with the core, leaving only the husk behind. In Papa's present mood, however, I wasn't about to argue.

'You leave it alone. It's a good solid piece of wood. We'll find a use for it. When times are bad everything has its use, even a dead snake,' he declared. He was still dismayed about Ma's extravagance, but Ma had closed her mind to all arguments.

Next, Daniel's home, the rusted Hudson skeleton, was unceremoniously tossed on to the donkey cart and hauled away.

'I hope you're satisfied now you've left Daniel without a roof over his head,' Papa said, bristling.

'He can sleep in the garage. There's enough room at the back for a mattress.'

'There's not enough room, Madam,' Daniel said, vexed that he was being treated with so little consideration.

'You should kick him out. Let him stay in the Location like the rest of us,' Gladys told Ma later, quite irritated at the fuss Papa was making about Daniel.

'He can't stay in the Location. He has no papers,' she reminded

Gladys.

'Then let him go back to where he came from,' she sniffed.

'Please, Ma, can we have an indoor flush toilet?' Yasmin pleaded. 'It's such a stupid idea to have a shower right next to that stinking hole you call a lavatory.'

'It's been good enough all these years, my girl. It'll be good enough now.' Nana was quick to squash any grandiose ideas Yasmin might have.

Yasmin ignored Nana and continued to badger Ma.

'Not now, Yasmin. I have a terrible headache,' Ma complained.

But Yasmin persisted.

'OK. OK.' Ma threw up her hands in surrender. 'But first I have to see how we make out with Daniel's help.'

'If we were living in the city like civilised people, we'd have no trouble finding workmen,' Yasmin remarked. 'It's different in this God-forsaken hole.'

'You watch your tongue.' Nana glowered.

'It's all right, Mum. I've been thinking of installing an indoor toilet anyway.' At that point Ma probably would have promised anything to restore peace.

'I don't know what's happening to this family,' Nana said in disgust. She glared at Yasmin as she tucked her knitting bag under her arm and marched outside to the arbour. In the shade of the grapevine she lamented loudly about the state of the world, and the curse of having children.

The day before Yasmin went off to school the indoor toilet was ready.

To mark the occasion, the whole family, including Mrs Ollie, assembled while the first bowl of water was ceremoniously flushed away.

'This is a historic event. The first of its kind in the town.' Ma laughed as she depressed the handle, all of us watching as the water gurgled out of the bowl.

'Wait until the council cuts the water this summer, then I'd like to see how they're going to flush that contraption,' Mrs

Ollie said to Nana as the two of them strolled towards the shop.

'*Ja*, but do you suppose they'll listen to me?' Nana said, shaking her head. 'Best thing for them is to learn their lessons the hard way.'

Most of the young people were leaving Soetstroom.

Moses Dlamini was one of only two non-whites to gain admission to the Witwatersrand University Medical School. Willem Arendse, his dreams of Olympic fame unrealised, got married and moved to another town. Cobus Steyn, we heard, was at the University of Stellenbosch. And Yasmin had left to begin her first year at the private school.

Yasmin, of course, went not in search of academic excellence, but in search of freedom. In order to pay for Yasmin's education, Ma had sold everything of value that she owned, including the jewellery my father had given her. Whatever little was left, she used for the renovations to the house.

All the structural changes had been completed, including the glass-enclosed sun-porch where Nana and I spent evenings listening to the radio. Sometimes, when sports commentators discussed cricket scores, we thought of Baboo and knew that he would be up until the wee hours listening to Test matches being played in Britain, the West Indies and Australia – countries that he would only ever visit in his imagination.

There was talk about television coming to South Africa, that eventually we'd have a window on the world. But my grandmother had her own ideas about this. She said that television would not come for a long time yet. It was her contention that the only way the government could keep its grip on the population was by keeping them ignorant and that was why censorship was so strictly enforced.

'It looks fabulous!' Yasmin squealed when she arrived home for the short Easter break.

'Fabulous' was a new expression she had picked up at school. For two weeks she gave everyone a good dose of it, laughing when Nana grumbled 'I never want to hear that word again.'

We celebrated my thirteenth birthday while Yasmin was home, and Papa surprised us with two bicycles which he had bought from Mr Naude who had no use for them because his daughters had married and moved to Cradock. One had a lamp operated by a battery, the other a noisy horn attached to the handlebars.

'They look like leftovers from the Second World War,' Nana remarked as she examined the rusty frames.

'They're Raleigh bicycles,' Papa informed her. 'A good, solid English make.'

'Good? Solid?' Nana sniffed scornfully. 'This is post-war rubbish. The same kind of rubbish they compensated the African veterans with when they returned from North Africa. In those days the African men got bicycles instead of pensions. That was the thanks they got for risking their lives so the whites in this country could be safe from Hitler.'

I didn't care whether they came from Timbuktu. A bicycle was a bicycle. I eagerly leapt on to the one with the noisy horn and wobbled around unsteadily for a bit before getting the hang of it.

'You're still such a child,' Yasmin said scornfully.

Of course, she would have preferred to sit astride a horse in jodhpurs and riding habit.

Papa couldn't understand her lack of enthusiasm.

She gritted her teeth each time I went careering by, shouting 'Papa, Papa, look!' But Papa had eyes only for one person, and it wasn't me.

Yasmin knew that Papa was disappointed by her lack of interest. 'How am I going to explain to him that I hate the damn bicycle?' she asked me.

I shrugged. 'You'd better pretend to like it or his feelings might be hurt.' In fact, I hoped that Papa would be very upset with her.

She was in the kitchen making a cup of tea later that afternoon when Papa asked: 'Don't you like the bicycle, Yasmin?'

Yasmin's lowered lashes created great shadows under her eyes. 'Oh, Papa. Of course I like it. It's just that I'm so tired.'

'Are you ill?'

'No. It's just been so hard at school, Papa. I thought I could rest while I was home.'

Nana happened to enter the kitchen in time to hear this. 'That's all you've been doing since you got home,' she snapped. 'We've all been running in circles around you.'

'If she's tired, she'd better rest,' Papa said. 'The bicycles will always be there.'

'It's all right,' Yasmin said, ignoring Nana and turning her sweet smile on Papa. 'But you shouldn't have got us such expensive presents, Papa.'

'Nonsense,' he said. 'What kind of a father would I be if I couldn't spoil my daughters once in a while?'

Nana snorted loudly and left the room. 'I can't stand any more of this doting. For people who don't have much money, you're certainly throwing it around. First the house, now the bicycles.'

While Yasmin was at home rumours began to circulate about the new arrivals, a count and countess who had moved into the area. The local people spent much of their time idly speculating about the VIPs.

Some hoped that with relatives in the neighbourhood the royal family might some day stop in for a visit. The townsfolk focused their energies on dreaming up suggestions to beautify the town in the case of such an eventuality. One of the priorities would, of course, be the tarring of the main street.

Ma expressed her relief that the house, exposed as it was on the main street, was presentable, even though the gleaming exterior was only whitewash.

Apparently the count and countess had formerly owned a sheep farm in Australia and were planning to start a similar operation in the district.

There was much excitement and discussion about how one behaved in their presence. Yasmin, the fount of knowledge, briefed everyone on the correct protocol.

'I'm not bowing and scraping to anyone,' Papa declared.

'Nor am I.' For once he and Nana were in agreement.

'Royalty is special,' Ma informed them.

'They're only distant relatives,' Papa argued.

'The fact remains they're titled.'

Under Yasmin's expert instruction I practised my curtsy.

'Everything has to be perfect,' Yasmin said when we were advised that the count and countess were expected to call on the stores.

Since we were the only ones handling fresh produce, there was little doubt that we would be honoured in this way.

The entire day before the anticipated visit was spent dusting, sweeping, polishing and shining. Yasmin, who had no interest in labouring for the cause, showed no reticence about giving unsolicited advice.

At first Nana was reluctant to put herself out, but when she realised that I was going to be left to do all the work, she took charge.

'*Yini, Nkosikazi*, who are these people that we are killing ourselves for?' Gladys complained.

'They are the Queen's family.'

'But they are not your family or my family . . .'

'Madam, she doesn't understand. She's never been out of Soetstroom,' Daniel said, scornful of Gladys's ignorance.

'What do you know?' Gladys demanded.

'Never mind, Gladys. Let's just get on with the work,' Ma said, trying to keep the peace.

By ten o'clock that night there wasn't a speck of dust anywhere. Nana finally straightened up and pressed her hands to the small of her back. Her braid, long since unwound, swung loosely below her waist. She checked the shine on the counter surface. Satisfied that the job was done, she packed away the cleaning materials.

We were up early the next day. It was a cool autumn morning and Yasmin persuaded Papa to wear his good clothes. Despite his earlier reluctance to participate in what he considered frivolous activity, he entered the store dressed in his dark suit, the one which he generally wore to weddings and funerals. The stiffly starched collar pinched. He pulled and tugged, stretching his neck to relieve the discomfort.

'Your Papa looks like a trussed turkey,' Nana laughed as she watched him fidget with his collar.

Yasmin was wearing a pale yellow dress and new black shoes with small heels and open toes which provided a tantalising view of her long, slender feet. She walked with the lithe gait of an accomplished ballerina rather than the novice that she actually was.

I wore a white dress patterned in green with little sprigs of red flowers – a trifle short and tight around the bodice, where I had filled out. Perhaps I was finally beginning to emerge from my chrysalis, I thought, as I studied myself in the mirror. Ma entered, looking radiant in her good dress, a powder blue crêpe which hung in soft pleats from the shoulders.

Nana, however, was determined to look her worst in an old pink smock which was slightly soiled where she had deliberately wiped her hands to achieve the desired effect.

By midday the count and countess had not yet made an appearance and Papa was becoming more uncomfortable and disgruntled by the minute.

'It serves you right for pandering to Yasmin's whims,' Nana remarked when he made the mistake of complaining to her.

Yasmin was the first to see them. She was standing behind the counter when they arrived, accompanied by the member of parliament, Hermanus Steyn, and his son Cobus who was on holiday from university.

I recognised Cobus immediately, even though his appearance had changed from the miserable, pock-faced youth we used to know to a tall, angular, younger version of his father, with the same brilliant blue eyes.

The count and countess were both in khaki work clothes. They were indistinguishable from the locals.

The countess smiled, grey eyes sparkling. 'My goodness me,' she gasped. 'I wasn't expecting a welcoming committee.'

Yasmin had no qualms about approaching the newcomers;

she curtsied, then politely introduced herself. Cobus watched intently.

Yasmin paid no attention to him. It was easy for her to dismiss the incident with the doll, which in her opinion had happened a long time ago, but I was not so forgiving.

Ma was outside in the backyard and Hermanus Steyn cast his eyes around the store, looking for her.

Papa entered from the storeroom, bowing stiffly. The countess extended her hand to Papa. 'My name's Jill,' she said, introducing herself. The count also stepped forward.

'Oh, please,' the countess laughed, 'treat us like any of your customers, Mr Mohammed. We're farmers now.'

The Steyns remained in the background, the rest of us trying to ignore them.

'Wasn't she just fabulous?' Yasmin said after the visitors had gone. 'I'd love to be like her some day.'

'Not in this country,' Nana said quietly.

'I know. Still, I can't help thinking. Some day I'd like to be rich, and do whatever I want.'

Nana smiled wryly.

'Perhaps I'll leave the country,' Yasmin said dreamily. 'Go to Australia . . . Did you notice her beautiful tan? I bet that's where she got it. I liked her husband. Wasn't he just ravishing?'

'Oh, yes,' I sighed.

'I must admit that they did seem like nice people,' Nana observed. 'But I suppose eventually they'll also change, and they'll become Baas Edward and Miesies Jill.'

Before returning to school Yasmin confided that she had kissed a boy. She described in detail how his lips had lingered on hers, gently forcing her mouth open so that their tongues met.

'It's a French kiss,' she explained.

I listened attentively. I had never yet been kissed by a boy, but from what Yasmin said it sounded dreadful, something I wouldn't be caught dead doing. I could not imagine having someone else's tongue roaming around my mouth.

'You'll understand it all one of these days,' Yasmin said, giving me the benefit of her experience.

Even though Yasmin knew a great deal more than I about such things, I doubted whether I would ever be interested. She spoke with passion, her face glowing with a radiance that seemed to illuminate her eyes, softening them with a sensuality that I had not observed before. I wondered who the boy was. He had obviously made a big impression on her.

Yasmin was hardly back at school when Ramadan was upon us. During this month of fasting, like millions of other Muslims throughout the world, we were up before sunrise to prepare and eat the last meal of the day. After this meal nothing could be consumed until sunset – not a crumb of food nor a drop of water could pass our lips.

In summer fasting was exhausting. I was constantly dehydrated and counted the days to the end of this gruelling period of deprivation. Papa's conviction that fasting was not only a religious necessity but also taught self-discipline was of little interest to me. My only interest at that time was to get a fraction of the attention monopolised by Yasmin.

To take my mind off my growling stomach I watched the progress on the taffeta skirt Ma was sewing for me. This was for Eid, the day of celebration following the sighting of the new moon.

Ma was doubtful about whether she should use the same fabric for Yasmin's skirt, but in the end she took Nana's advice and made us identical skirts of the same taffeta. She also decided to make us crinolines to wear under the skirts.

Nana suggested that cotton netting might do for the crinolines. I helped her cut small pieces from the roll and watched as she experimented until she found that soaking the netting in a sugar and water solution made it stiff enough to flounce out the taffeta skirts.

I wondered what my sister would have to say about the home-made garments. The last time Ma had sewn for us Yasmin had never stopped complaining.

'Why do I always have to wear stuff like this when other girls get to buy their dresses from a store? Why do I always have to look like a frump? I hate home-made clothes!'

I was glad when Ma had finally thrown her sewing down and, placing her hands on her hips, had looked sternly at Yasmin.

'Now look here, young lady, you seem to forget that your Papa had to make great sacrifices for you to attend that school. In fact we've all made sacrifices, so I'd like to see a little more appreciation from you.'

That had put a stop to Yasmin's complaints for a while.

I loved the dark blue taffeta, which seemed to shimmer in the light, constantly changing colour just like the sunset.

Outfitted in a pair of black pumps with a strap over the instep and wrapped in the swirling luxury of my skirt, I almost drove my parents and grandmother out of their minds as I pirouetted from one end of the house to the other.

'At least she's enjoying it,' Nana remarked.

I could hardly wait for Eid. I could already see myself in my ballgown, like Rochelle in *Island Child*, a Cinderella story of a little island girl married to a wealthy plantation owner in Mississippi. I imagined floating down the staircase in my gown, the eyes of all the men in the room riveted on me. I raised my head, pointed my feet out like a ballerina, took a few steps and tripped over the carpet, hitting my head on the corner of the table. I lay quite dazed for a moment, and then without a sound I got up and composed myself. I could already feel the huge bump rising on my brow, topped by a dark blue bruise. No doubt I was destined to end up looking like a unicorn on Eid's day.

9

'WE'LL ONLY be gone for a few days, Daniel,' Ma said. 'There's no room in the car. You can see for yourself.'

Daniel turned his woeful gaze on Ma, his eyes large and aggrieved like an abandoned puppy.

'Oh, *please*,' Ma said stiffly as Papa was about to intercede on Daniel's behalf. 'He'd only have to sit on your lap.'

That put an abrupt end to any further argument. We were in a hurry to get away. We still had to pick Yasmin up. Her school was allowing the Muslim girls to spend the festive occasion with their families. The same concession was made for Hindu girls at Diwali.

We were looking forward to getting out of Soetstroom for a while. Papa hadn't seen Cassimbhai in ages. Cassimbhai was an older second cousin from Papa's village in India. They had come to South Africa at about the same time. Papa enjoyed spending time with him and his other Gujarati friends. Whenever they were together Papa and Cassimbhai went to see Indian films. But Papa's real passion was the big sprawling market-place.

Yasmin visited her girlfriends to gossip and engage in girl talk, or else they spent their time doing each other's hair and making up their faces.

I was drawn to the beach, to the warm water pools amidst the rocks which were full of the swish and scurry of crustacean life.

We arrived at Cassimbhai and Aishaben's home at around six o'clock on the evening before Eid.

They heard our car pulling into the yard and were both at the door to greet us. The sky was overcast, but the new moon had been sighted in Johannesburg.

I knew it would be. I had seen the full moon two weeks before, hanging from the sky, bright and bulbous like a pregnant woman's belly.

Yasmin and I were jubilant. The prospect of another day of fasting was totally unbearable. Ma, Nana and Aishaben had lots of news to catch up on and immediately disappeared into the kitchen. Yasmin and I started to carry our luggage into the house, but she immediately found some other distraction and I was left to finish the job.

At supper Papa enquired about Farouk.

Cassimbhai was reluctant to talk about his son. He seemed angry and disappointed about the fact that he wasn't coming home for Eid.

There was an exchange of comments in Gujarati between the two men.

'He has exams. Universities don't close for Eid,' Aishaben explained.

'What about Yasmin?' Cassimbhai asked. 'How is she doing at school?'

'She's doing well.' Papa didn't elaborate. He was too embarrassed to talk about the horse riding and frivolous things that Yasmin was doing so well at. He would have preferred to say that she had got an A in maths, or an A in some other academic subject. But that, of course, had not happened.

'How's business?' Cassimbhai asked.

'Slow, very slow,' Papa complained.

Cassimbhai considered this response for a moment, then said: 'You should have come to the city when I did. It won't be too long before all the Indians will be moved out of the *dorps*. The white-owned stores can't take the competition.'

Papa nodded. 'It is happening already.'

'We are the Jews of Southern Africa, hated and envied,' Cassimbhai continued. 'Scapegoats, that's what we've become.'

Papa nodded. He had always told us that he and Cassimbhai had come with nothing in their pockets. All they had were brains and determination. And they had worked tirelessly, scraping and scrimping.

'I was thinking just the other day,' Cassimbhai said, 'about that time we pushed the cart all the way from Jamestown to Aliwal to sell the produce before it rotted in the heat. Remember, the donkey died and we had to push it ourselves?'

Papa laughed as he recalled the incident.

He often spoke about those difficult times. But Cassimbhai had gone to the city while Papa had chosen to remain in the small towns.

In the end Cassimbhai had succeeded in accumulating a fortune, while Papa continued to struggle, eking out a living wherever he could.

'Those damn Dutchmen. Sitting in their ivory towers, arms folded, trying to steal our hard-earned money. They want what we worked so hard for, Abdul. You and I.' He paused for a long time. Papa, sensing that something was wrong, had his attention concentrated on Cassimbhai. 'The Group Areas will strike here too,' he said. 'It's just a matter of time.'

'Where will you go?' Papa asked.

Cassimbhai shrugged. 'Who knows.'

Papa shook his head. 'Is no one safe?' he asked.

'Don't make yourself too comfortable in Soetstroom. I've heard that there is already a plan to move all the Indians out of the small towns.'

'Where will they move us to? Surely they won't create a whole area just for us.' Papa was hoping for reassurance.

'Don't be a fool,' Cassimbhai said.

Papa was visibly upset. This was news he didn't want to hear.

Cassimbhai studied Papa for a moment. 'If they want to move you, they will,' he said. 'They're doing it here and in other cities. There's nothing to stop them from clearing the small *dorps* too.'

There was a long silence between the two men. Then with a sigh Cassimbhai got up from the table and declared vehemently:

'I will not move from my house. I'm telling you now, my friend. They'll have to carry me out of here. This is my home and I will not give it up.'

We were so settled in our small town that it never occurred to us that things might change.

Nana said that the word 'removal' had gained a sinister new meaning. She told us how, some nine years before, the people of Sophiatown in Johannesburg had been 'removed' to desolate areas under the government's policy of separate development. She said she had been visiting friends in Johannesburg and they had seen with their own eyes how people had been evicted from their homes, their belongings thrown into the streets, their houses bulldozed.

It seemed that everyone was on the move. Coloureds and Indians were being moved out of the towns to peripheral areas around the cities. Nana said it was the great trek all over again, only this time people were being force-marched not in search of better lives, but to be dumped in the veld, miles out of town, each homeland created within specific racial and tribal boundaries.

The Group Areas Board was a government body that had been formed to deal with the classification of racial groups and their removal to particular areas set aside for the different groups. New townships sprouted along the outskirts of towns and cities to accommodate the dispossessed.

Nana said that the rumours about a 'plan' to remove Indian traders from small towns to an area specifically created for them would have been laughable, if it hadn't been so frightening.

On Eid morning the menfolk trooped to the mosque for prayers while the women stayed home to prepare snacks for the well-wishers who were expected to stop by after the service.

I waited impatiently as my mother carefully unwrapped Yasmin's taffeta skirt, then held it up to the light for my sister to admire.

Yasmin blanched as Ma said: 'You and Meena have look-alike skirts.'

'No one at my school would dream of wearing something like that,' Yasmin said.

Ma flicked the skirt to show how the material caught the light.

'Oh God, Ma-a-a,' Yasmin groaned.

I held my skirt up to my waist and swirled around in an attempt to encourage Yasmin. But Yasmin's lower lip swept the ground. My mother was terribly disappointed.

An unpleasantness built up. Yasmin sat in the yard looking miserable and angry. Ma ignored her, as did Nana.

Eventually Yasmin came around. She went into the room and unpacked her skirt. Ma followed her.

'Here, look at this,' Ma said, holding up the crinoline.

'We soaked it in sugar,' I said as I joined my mother and Yasmin.

'Oh, God!' Yasmin wailed, tossing the crinoline on to the bed. 'How could you? What'll happen when the ants get hold of me?'

Aishaben came to see what the fuss was all about. She started laughing when Ma told her why Yasmin was upset. It did sound terribly funny and soon we were all laughing, including Yasmin.

Yasmin had no alternative but to wear the skirt. She had nothing else to wear.

'So, after all the ructions she's actually wearing the skirt,' Nana remarked.

'She's really not a bad child, Mum . . .'

'I know,' Nana muttered. 'But it's hard to see the gold under all that tarnish.'

We returned home. Yasmin was back at school and the weeks dragged by. I was bored at school. Like Yasmin, I was beginning to yearn for something more. A change. But I had no idea what to look for or how to bring about change in my life. It was a strange restlessness – like an undefined itch, like a yawn that couldn't be stifled.

I felt as though I wanted to run away. To escape. To melt into the darkness and disappear into a huge hole. I felt as though I was losing my mind. I knew now what Yasmin had been talking about all those years.

I had read every book in the house, including the dozen or so fly-encrusted romances that were strung up in the front window of the shop and had been there ever since I could remember.

One morning Ma was sorting the post as usual. And as usual most of it was bills. She was looking for cheques from the markets. At the bottom of the pile was a manila envelope with the government crest and a departmental stamp. She carefully scrutinised the envelope as though the information on it might provide some clue to the contents.

She opened the envelope, read through the letter and gazed at us, her expression stunned.

'What's that?' Papa asked.

'A letter from the Group Areas Board.'

There was a long silence.

Then Ma looked up as Papa asked: 'What do they want?'

'They've assessed our property,' she said, her hand trembling slightly as she scanned the typewritten page again, as though it needed another reading to digest the contents.

'And . . .?' Papa asked anxiously.

'They've settled on a value for our property. The house and the shop.'

Startled, my father sat down. He ran a hand over his head as he waited for Ma to continue.

'They've offered us twelve hundred rands,' she said.

Papa's jaw dropped, his mouth working like a fish gulping for air. He looked incredulously at Ma and the letter in her hand. 'For the house *and* the shop?' he asked.

'Yes, Abdul. How many times do I have to repeat myself?'

'But they must be mad,' Papa said. 'Twelve hundred for this property. Right here on the main street? It's valued much higher for property taxes. You know how much we pay in property taxes?'

'Of course I know,' Ma snapped impatiently. 'Why are you

telling *me* this? Save the story for them.' She flapped the letter in front of my father's nose.

He got up and slowly, with shoulders hunched, walked away. 'I'll tell them,' he muttered. 'I'll tell them.'

Ma was too agitated to respond.

At the door Papa turned to ask: 'When did they assess this place?'

Ma shrugged. 'They don't say. But I think it was the time that Afrikaner came by to inspect the property about four or five months ago.'

'Why don't I know about it?' he asked.

'You were the one who spoke to him,' she reminded him. 'Remember, you thought he was here to assess for property taxes?'

Papa had forgotten all about the incident. He nodded as it came back to him now, his eyes narrowing. He had asked the man what he wanted, but had got no answer. At the time he had thought nothing of the episode. Now, however, it took on a new significance.

In the days that followed, I listened as my parents rehashed the incident, reading all sorts of relevance into how the man had walked, looked around and refused to answer questions.

'They're going to take over our home and our shop,' Ma said, aghast. She could not accept the inevitable. She glanced from Nana to Papa as though she hoped they would refute it.

'Not while I have a breath left in my body!' Papa stubbornly declared. Then he laughed. 'This is just another bureaucratic bungle. It's a mistake. Don't worry about it.'

'What if it isn't?' Ma asked.

He sat down and considered her question.

'What are we going to do?' she repeated, thinking that he hadn't heard her.

'I don't know. But I won't let them walk in and take what we've worked for all these years! This is our house. We've built all of this from nothing,' he said, spreading his arms. 'We'll put up a fight. You just wait and see.' Papa's eyes darkened and a vein stood out on his temple like a knotted rope. His clenched hand jerked open and involuntarily twitched as it rested on the surface of the old rolltop desk.

'Fight with what?' Nana asked. 'They'll come with bulldozers and flatten it, regardless of whether you're in it or not. I've seen how they operate. They're not interested in owning these buildings. What they want is to get us out of here. They don't care about your life or what you've put into this place. They don't care about anything except getting you out.'

'I don't think they'll break this down,' Papa said hopefully. 'It's a solid structure. I think someone wants it – probably old Faurie or Van Wyk.'

'We should have seen it coming, especially after what they've done in the other small towns,' Ma said. 'Still, I think Abdul's right. We should put up a fight. We can't just go like lambs to the slaughter.'

Papa leaned forward in his chair, a tormented expression on his face, and drew a hand over his head. 'What else did they say in that letter?'

Ma looked weary. 'Nothing. I've read this letter to you more than a dozen times already, Abdul.'

Papa came upright so quickly that the old spring in the swivel chair twanged. 'Then read it to me again. I'm almost blind. If I could see I wouldn't be asking you!'

'I told you not to spend all that money fixing the place,' Nana said, giving my father more ammunition.

Papa's eyes glinted.

Ma stormed out, glaring at my father and my grandmother.

'They've given us six months to find another place, or the alternative they've presented here, which is to move to McBain,' Papa said as the door slammed behind Ma.

'I know,' Nana said. 'I saw the letter. I don't know what on earth we're expected to do at McBain.'

'It's in the bush. A pile of bricks in the veld beside the road.'

'I know,' Nana repeated. 'We've passed by it hundreds of times and never given it a second glance.'

They talked about nothing else but what was happening or

what was going to happen. It was on everyone's mind.

'Dear Lord,' Ma sighed tiredly as she and Nana discussed the issue yet again. 'My home . . . both children were born here. I love this place.'

Something really frightening had happened to our family. Filled with dread, I stood to one side watching my parents. A spectre loomed over us. The future looked dark and hopeless.

'We'll see a lawyer,' Ma said early one morning. 'Abdul's right. We'll fight them. Why should we give up our home? Our livelihood is tied up here.'

They were at the lawyer's office when it opened that morning.

The lawyer told them that there was nothing they could do. It was the law, an act of parliament, that each racial group be confined to its own area. He said that we had no alternative but to abide by any decision made by the Group Areas Board.

They came home angry and disappointed.

'That man is a *mompara*,' Papa said as they stepped in the door.

Nana and I knew instantly that things had not gone well.

'They leave one with nothing,' Nana said, 'not even one's dignity.'

'What's happening?' I asked.

Ma shook her head wearily, too preoccupied to explain it all to me.

'What's going to happen?' I persisted.

'Everything will be taken care of,' Papa answered.

My parents and grandmother latched on to the phrase, taking refuge behind it whenever they became impatient with my questions. I wished that Yasmin was there. I missed her. I had no one to talk to.

One afternoon following her return from Johannesburg, Mrs Dlamini, Moses' mother, stopped by to see us. Nana made tea. We were anxious to hear about her trip because she had taken a parcel and letter for Baboo.

'Where did you stay in Johannesburg?' Ma enquired.

'In Alexandra Township with Moses,' Mrs Dlamini said. 'Here in the Location I have a home, a brick house built for us by my husband before . . .' She swallowed quickly. 'Now my son lives in a tiny shanty, worse than anything I have seen here in the Location. I hated leaving him. It would have been better for our boys to stay home. Johannesburg is a terrible place.'

Ma quietly absorbed this information. She had long suspected that Baboo was having a hard time with his new family.

'It would have been a waste for Moses to stay here,' Ma said eventually. 'And by now Baboo would probably have been in jail because of that Cobus Steyn.'

'I saw Baboo,' Mrs Dlamini said.

Ma's anxious glance sought hers.

'Moses went with me. The two boys were overjoyed to see each other. But we hardly had time to talk to him. That man he works for is a slave-driver. Wouldn't let Baboo talk to us for more than five minutes. The boy works hard, seven days a week. He has no time for cricket or anything else. Moses said he would go to see him again. You know how fond they were of each other. But they are both so busy now.'

'Did you see his place – where he lives?' Ma asked.

'No. We did not go back to see him. That man he works for is a bad person.'

'It's his uncle.'

Mrs Dlamini pulled a face. 'He is still a bad man.'

'How does Baboo look?'

'He has grown tall since you last saw him. He is a man now, but I can see he is not very happy.'

'If it weren't for that damn Steyn boy . . .' Ma paused, remembering that any day now we might also be without a home.

Mrs Dlamini removed her glasses, wiped them with a handkerchief, then pulled a blurred picture out of her pocket. It was a photograph of Moses with two of his friends. She passed it around. The friends looked like thugs, but of course we didn't say so to Mrs Dlamini.

She continued in a sombre tone. 'He will have to find a place closer to the university. Not only is he a long way from the medical school but few buses run that route, so he either has to walk, and run the risk of being attacked by *tsotsis*, or else he has to get up at four o'clock to catch the bus into town. This country is hard on its black people. It's even worse if you're a black woman. To think how I struggled to raise that boy. When they came to take his father . . .' she swallowed the lump in her throat. 'That is why I feel for Anna. Now she has no one – only Vukile. I went through the same thing. I prayed for strength and the Lord helped me. I pray that he helps Anna too. It's been two years and she still sits in the door of her hut, waiting for the husband who won't return . . . it's hard.'

Mr Dlamini had also been taken by the police. He had disappeared about three years before they took Vukile's father. They came for him one night and charged him with sedition. He was never seen or heard from again. He was the second man to be arrested in Soetstroom. It was surprising that in this small town two people had already been ferreted out as anti-government activists. This small town where, according to Yasmin, nothing ever happened, had suddenly become a hot-bed of 'terrorism'.

Nana said that the two men were guilty of nothing more than objecting to the way the government treated the blacks who were constantly being arrested for pass-law infringements.

'It's amazing what our people have to go through for an education,' Ma said. 'It's a miracle that anyone ever succeeds.'

'It will make my heart very sad if Moses gives up medicine. He likes what he is doing even though there are so many frustrations. He says when they are to dissect a white cadaver he has to leave the room, and then of course he misses the work and has to get the notes from one of the white students. If they are bad whites . . . *kaloku*, he gets nothing.'

We reflected on this in silence.

Mrs Dlamini sighed and clicked her tongue.

We had not told anyone about our impending eviction. It wasn't something one talked about, but Ma succumbed to the urge to unburden herself to Mrs Dlamini.

'We might not be here much longer,' she told her.

'Why? What is happening?'

'The Group Areas Board . . .'

'*Yini, Thixo,*' Mrs Dlamini responded, shocked.

'We had a letter from them.'

'*Kaloku,* this is madness. Where will you go?'

'I don't know. Abdul says we're going to stay and fight.'

Mrs Dlamini stayed on to talk for a while longer, the three women discussing the possibilities open to us. Listening to them, I began to realise how limited our options were.

10

WEEKS LATER a registered letter arrived from the Group Areas Board with a cheque for twelve hundred rands and a covering letter advising us that we'd be able to rent the house from the Board for an interim period of two months while we made the necessary plans to relocate.

Again, McBain was suggested.

'What are we going to do?' Ma cried.

'We're not moving,' Papa said firmly.

'You'd better look for another place,' Nana urged. 'Or they'll be on your doorstep one of these days. Cash that cheque. That's all you're going to get out of them.'

The cheque sat on the desk for weeks, because Papa refused to accept what they had offered him.

Nothing further was heard from the Board. My father relaxed. He said we had nothing to worry about. They'd probably forgotten about the whole issue. They'd come to their senses.

I felt that we were living on the edge of a precipice. At any moment now we would tumble into the abyss. Be swept into oblivion.

But time passed with no further communication from the Group Areas Board.

Business picked up over the Christmas season.

Yasmin came home and once again the whole issue of our move became topical. Nana warned that we had to be vigilant.

Papa had still not cashed the cheque, and in his convoluted reasoning this meant that the government had no claim on our property. The cheque sat on his desk, winking at him, reminding him of our jeopardy.

Fortunately we were busy and didn't have much time to dwell on our misfortunes. During the last two weeks before Christmas there was barely time to eat. We were busy right up to Christmas Eve, and then we spent a quiet Christmas Day recuperating.

'This has been the best season we've had for many years.' Papa was almost his old self again.

'It's also probably our last season,' Nana reminded him.

'Perhaps things are turning around for us,' Ma said hopefully.

'Miss Harper says that you should always be on your guard when things go well.' Yasmin was tired. She could barely raise a hand to help with the Christmas dinner.

'Sounds like that teacher is filling your head with nonsense,' Nana remarked.

Yasmin shrugged; that was all she could bring herself to do. She was much too exhausted to argue.

Papa tolerated the Christmas festivities because of Ma and Nana's Christian background. The usual Christmas gifts to the town dignitaries were delivered by Yasmin and me. The mayor, the police sergeant and the town clerk received the more substantial boxes of chocolates. The lower-echelon officials were given bottles of orange squash.

Each day Papa glanced at the cheque and then put it back on his desk. The lawyer had advised him to cash it. He warned that if it became stale and lapsed, the Board could very well come back with a lower offer.

Finally, and with great reluctance, my father decided to deposit the cheque into the business account and within a matter of minutes it was all gone, gobbled up by his many debts. He had nothing to show for all his work. Nothing. The money wasn't even in the account long enough to make a difference to our lives.

Papa was in a panic now. He could see that his world was about to crumble. So distracted was he by this new threat that one afternoon he got into his car with the intention of driving out to one of the farms. Two blocks down the road he smashed into a road works barrier. The car wasn't badly damaged, but Papa's licence was withdrawn.

This did not deter him. For months afterwards he continued to sneak around, driving himself because there wasn't always anyone else around to do so. But as his eyesight deteriorated, even he began to recognise that he presented a danger to other motorists.

Throughout this time Nana kept on reminding us that we were in a precarious situation and that we couldn't afford to relax our vigilance.

She'd been through all of this before when they moved her out of her comfortable old home on the banks of the Orange River in Aliwal North to a flat, arid, treeless tract of land outside the town.

No one paid attention to Nana's warning.

One Sunday afternoon Ma left the house early. Nana and I were in the backyard.

'I wonder where your mother's off to,' Nana said as she drove away.

I shrugged. Ma hadn't said anything to me.

She was gone for several hours, during which time Nana speculated about where she had gone. Papa had come out of the house once or twice to enquire after her. Nana told him that she'd gone for a drive, which was not what I'd heard her mumbling earlier. The name Steyn was quite clearly mentioned under her breath on more than one occasion.

When Ma got home Nana was waiting in the backyard. I heard the car and went to the back door. Neither of them seemed to notice me. They were too busy arguing. Ma was trying to push past Nana who was barring her way.

'So I was right,' Nana hissed under her breath.

'What on earth are you talking about, Mum?' Ma asked.

'Is it Hermanus Steyn? Have you no pride?'

'Are you mad?' Ma asked. 'What are you talking about?'

Nana peered at her through angry slitted eyes.

'Sometimes I don't know what goes on in your head,' Ma said. 'When are you going to learn to trust me?'

'I'm not blind. I saw the way he was looking at you.'

'What do you want me to do about it?' Ma asked angrily.

Nana was incensed. 'Dear God! I see you in Yasmin all the time. I fear for that child's future. Please God, save her from the same fate!'

Ma hurried away, leaving Nana to glare after her. I hadn't seen my grandmother so angry in a long time. I wished I knew what was going on.

My senses tingled. There was something heavy and musty in the air, like the smell of an old suitcase being opened for the first time in years – a suitcase full of dark secrets. But I knew as I watched Ma storming off and Nana gazing after her, that the lid had been snapped shut again.

Yasmin's exams were over and schools were closing for the June holidays. I accompanied my parents when they picked her up on their way to the city.

We arrived at the school on the Friday shortly before midday. There was a message that Miss Jones wished to see us, but Papa was impatient to get to the city in time for noon prayers.

'Tell her we can't wait,' he instructed the secretary, who disappeared through one of the doors and promptly returned to say that Miss Jones would see us right away. Yasmin joined us and we were shown into Miss Jones's office.

We listened impatiently to her preamble about the forthcoming vacation. 'It's a well-deserved rest before the difficult haul to the departmental examinations in November, which will conclude her education at this school,' she commented, giving Yasmin a wry smile.

'We are aware of this,' Papa said testily. 'Is this the matter you wished to discuss with us?'

Miss Jones raised her hand. 'Yasmin is expected to attend a coming-out ball,' she said. 'It will be held when the school closes in December.'

Papa looked puzzled. 'What is a coming-out ball?' he asked.

'It is a tradition at this school,' Miss Jones replied. 'All the girls in their final year will be débutantes.'

'I don't know what this is all about.' He wiped his brow and shook his head.

'They will be graduating as young ladies, you know.' Miss Jones's glance fluttered between Ma and Papa while Yasmin and I listened attentively.

'The occasion, of course, will also serve to present the eligible girls to the society in which they'll be making their contributions. Many important families from your community are expected to attend the ball. I'm sure you'll be interested in meeting them. You know, in England this would be quite a social event. Débutantes are often presented to the Queen.'

Papa stared at her in disbelief. 'I have no intention of allowing my daughter to parade herself. In fact, plans are already under way for her future.'

'What plans?' Ma demanded.

Yasmin fidgeted anxiously.

Miss Jones continued. 'She has profited from an education that has transformed her from a country bumpkin into a sophisticated young lady.' She paused, looking condescendingly at Papa. 'She has reaped the benefits of ballet, elocution and deportment. We even indulged her with extra riding lessons because she felt she was not as good as the other girls. We went to a great deal of trouble to procure a special instructor for her while our own Miss Fitzsimmons was away.'

'Yasmin didn't mention this,' Ma said, turning towards Yasmin.

'I wanted to surprise you, Ma.'

'Well, you certainly have.'

'There's nothing wrong with her wanting to develop other skills,' Miss Jones said. 'Many of the girls here are accomplished riders.'

'Why are you teaching her to ride a horse?' Papa asked. 'What kind of school is this?'

But before Yasmin or Miss Jones could answer, Ma interrupted.

'You mentioned a special riding instructor . . .' she said.

'He's the son of one of our neighbouring farmers. As I said, Miss Fitzsimmons, our regular riding instructress, was away and this young man, Andrew Jordaan, very kindly volunteered some of his time. Occasionally he earns a bit of pocket-money from us when he's on holiday from Rhodes University.'

Fortunately, I was the only one to notice that Yasmin had turned two shades darker at the mention of Andrew Jordaan. I wondered if this was the French kisser.

'I had no idea . . .' Ma sat forward in her chair.

'Don't take it to heart, Mrs Mohammed. Yasmin has some very fine qualities, and of course the school has nurtured her like a delicate flower. A flower, you know, will not grow in a desert. It requires a certain milieu.' Miss Jones paused, then laughed. 'When you think of it, our job is much like that of a horticulturalist.'

Papa wasn't amused. 'What is involved in this coming-out ball?' he demanded.

'Only the cost of a long white formal gown,' she assured him.

Papa hesitated while Yasmin wrung her hands.

'Please, Papa,' she pleaded.

'Yes.' Ma spoke up. 'Yasmin will attend.'

Yasmin had informed Ma and Papa that she wasn't coming home for the September break because she hoped to spend it at a friend's home in the city.

'I can hardly wait for the holidays,' she had confided.

'I'm going to miss you.'

'I'll see you in December, silly. What about my dress, Ma?'

'There's a lot of time for that, young lady. Right now we have other problems on our minds, like the prospect of moving.'

'Why don't we just move to the city?'

'Oh, and do what there?' Ma enquired.

'We can open a store.'

'Where do you suppose we'll get the money?'

'Well, they paid you for this place.'

'The money went to pay the merchants. There's nothing left.'

'Oh,' Yasmin pursed her lips thoughtfully. 'As soon as I find a job I'll be able to help,' she said.

'What kind of work are you thinking of, Yasmin?'

'I'd like to be a fashion model.'

'My poor child. You're such a dreamer, just like your father.'

Yasmin's eyes narrowed. 'I'll be rich some day, you'll see . . . even if it means leaving this country and going elsewhere.'

Ma sighed, and then hugged her. She held her tight, as though afraid of losing her.

Yasmin was a little sad about returning to school. It seemed that the family crisis had drawn us all closer. There had been some wonderfully warm moments shared in the kitchen as a family. Remember this . . . Remember that . . . It was all about the past. The future did not exist.

It was like waiting at a station for the train to depart with a loved one on board. I remembered the wrenching feeling I had had when Baboo left, and the feeling I got whenever I thought of losing Ma and Papa. Waiting to say goodbye to our home brought with it the same ache.

The days were short and cold, but when Yasmin left for school I often went to sit on the green park benches, ignoring the 'Whites Only' signs. I watched the squirrels darting in and out of the trees. Now and then they'd come to an abrupt halt a few feet away, black eyes blinking curiously while they sat on their haunches to observe me.

I just had to get out of the house. And in that peaceful environment I had time to dwell on Nana's theory that troubles came in threes.

What else lay in store for us? There were so many questions and so few answers. Time was running out for me at the Soetstroom Apostolic Primary School for Coloureds, but with so much else happening I didn't dare think about my education.

It was a cold, blustery day in July and we were in the kitchen baking a cake. There was an atmosphere of gloom in the house and Ma gave more than her share of weary sighs.

'We don't want the batter beaten to death, just mixed,' Nana said drily.

Ma looked startled. Then she laughed.

'I was just thinking that it won't be long now before Meena will have to start her matric too,' Nana remarked.

I glanced up from the hateful chore of pitting raisins as hard as pebbles.

'I don't know what we're going to do, Mum,' Ma said.

'Why can't we send her to the city? I'm sure she could stay with Aishaben and Cassimbhai,' Nana said.

'I don't know, Mum,' Ma said. 'I really don't know. I don't think I want to ask Aishaben. I hate to take advantage of our friendship with them.'

'What about Jo'burg? I could stay with Baboo,' I suggested hopefully.

'Don't be ridiculous. You can't stay with Baboo,' Ma snapped impatiently.

'Why not?'

'Because Baboo's a boy,' Nana said. 'Besides, he only has a tiny room which he rents. It can't be much, and who knows what mischief he's into. Jo'burg is a big city.'

'It would be best to have Meena reclassified Coloured,' Ma said. 'At least then we'll have a few more options.'

'Are you mad?' Nana demanded. 'Do you really want to put yourself through that kind of humiliation?' Nana paused thoughtfully. 'Remember Albert Makalima? He married a Coloured woman, Ellen Monroe. They used to live around the corner from us.'

Ma didn't say anything.

'How can you not remember them when you used to practically live on their doorstep?' Nana asked.

Ma smiled at the recollection.

'His daughter had to be reclassified to go to a Coloured school, remember? They went to Pretoria to the reclassification offices and you know what they had to go through?'

Ma shrugged, but I waited expectantly for Nana to continue.

'With her father African and her mother Coloured, Felicity's hair was thick and coarse. So they did the comb test on her. Right there in the office, in front of her parents and everyone else, they drew a fine-toothed comb through her hair. Poor girl. Imagine the humiliation when the comb got stuck in her hair. The idiots refused to reclassify her and they chased her and her parents out of the office like dogs.'

'But it'll be different with Meena . . .'

'It'll be no different, they probably won't do a comb test, but she's Indian. She looks Indian. They're likely to insist on all sorts of stupid things – probably make you speak Afrikaans or stand on one leg, or something.'

Ma didn't say anything. Her head lowered, she was thinking about what Nana had said.

'Look, it's up to you, but don't come crying to me if they humiliate you,' Nana said.

'What am I going to do then?'

'Something will come up. It always does. I'm on my knees every night.'

Ma listened in silence. She was desperate, but the thought of being humiliated by some white lackey made her angry.

'Don't worry about these things, Delia,' Nana said. 'Right now we've got too much else on our plate.'

'The children must be educated, Mum,' Ma insisted.

'Look, I'll pay for her education out of my pension. I don't mind. I don't need much. All I'm saying to you is wait a few months. Meena is still young. It's Yasmin we have to worry about.'

'Your pension is too small,' Ma said, dismissing Nana's offer. 'There's hardly enough for you . . .'

'That's enough!' Nana said sharply.

'I regret that Baboo didn't get much of an education,' Ma added.

'You did your best for him,' Nana said. 'Besides, it's all water under the bridge now. He'll survive. He may not have an education, but he does have a lot of common sense.'

'Can't I go to Jo'burg, Ma?' I pleaded.

'Didn't you hear what your Nana and I just said?' Ma asked.

'But I don't want to be reclassified. I don't want them to humiliate us. I want to be Indian. I *am* Indian. Why must I be something else?'

'Don't worry, child. We'll get you sorted out soon,' Nana said, breaking the eggs and separating the yolks.

'When?' I asked.

Nana took a deep breath. She dusted flour from her hands then reached behind to tie the bow that had come undone on her blue gingham apron. I helped her. Nana turned to me. She gave me a long, hard look. 'I think you've got spunk,' she said.

Ma watched us, smiling gently. 'What you are is a South African, and since you can't be that in your own country the next best thing is to be something that will at least give you an advantage,' she said. 'We're not trying to deny your birthright. The government has already done that. What we're trying to do now is make the best of a bad situation.'

Nana winked at me. 'Here, grease these,' she said, sliding the cake pans towards me. For a moment it took our attention off the issue of reclassification.

'I don't know why we're even discussing this. Abdul will never agree.'

Reclassification was still clearly an issue for Ma.

'I don't always agree with Abdul, but I think this time he's right,' Nana said, wiping her hands on her apron.

I wasn't listening any more. I couldn't believe that my mother was seriously considering having me reclassified.

'Don't you worry about what anyone says,' Nana told me. 'You're a South African. That's the only thing that matters. The government's dirty tricks to keep us divided won't make any difference when the day of reckoning comes. What'll count then is who we are as human beings. Colour and race won't be important.'

'I suppose it's a matter of self-respect,' Ma said, 'of pride, especially as far as her father is concerned.'

'Things will change. It might take time and it might not happen in my lifetime, but change will come.'

'I doubt it,' Ma said, shaking her head.

'There are people out there, men like Walter Sisulu, Oliver Tambo and that Mandela fellow. Men of Rivonia. Things will change some day. I'm just sorry I won't be around to see it.'

'Not much they can do sitting in jail on Robben Island, is there?' Ma said.

'We'll see,' Nana said. 'But Meena, you hang on to your pride and self-respect. Even though they've tried, it's the only thing they can't take from us.'

11

OUR EVICTION was like a bullet in the head.

The men from the Group Areas Board arrived at our door on Papa's birthday. Nana had baked a cake for the occasion and we were just about to sit down to tea and cake when we were interrupted by a loud commotion at the front door.

On our doorstep were two men. Strangers in khaki shirts and trousers. One of them had a beard.

Parked in front of the house was a police car and the local police van. A third man in a blazer was peering over the wall.

All of this registered instantly, almost like a photograph in which small details were captured.

Sergeant Klein stood to one side, shifting uncomfortably, eyes averted. Ma's first thought was that something had happened to Yasmin.

'What is it?' she cried anxiously.

When she saw the guns, her face turned ashen.

Constable de Bruin and one of the black policemen got out of the car. De Bruin, wearing a small, almost triumphant smile, watched us.

'What do they want, Ma?' I asked.

My mother shook her head, waiting for an explanation.

'These men are from the Group Areas Board,' Sergeant Klein said finally, gesturing towards the three strangers. 'They are here to evict you . . . I'm sorry.'

Ma's face was stark. She was too shocked to say anything.

Papa appeared in the passageway behind us wanting to know what was going on.

'What is it, Meena?' Nana asked, joining us in the doorway.

'I don't know, Nana.'

Nana's questioning glance flew to the khaki-suited strangers and then to the local constables, finally coming to rest on Sergeant Klein, who was our only salvation. He, however, was studying the tips of his boots.

'We're locking up the property,' said the man in the blazer.

'Now?' Ma asked, aghast.

'But you can't do that,' Papa said. 'It's all a mistake.'

The bearded man laughed harshly.

'You can't just march in here,' Ma said. 'You're supposed to give us notice. Why are you doing this to us now?'

'According to these men, you received an eviction order some time ago,' Sergeant Klein said. He still stood apart from the others as though disassociating himself from them.

'No, we didn't,' Ma said.

'We have a copy of the letter,' one of the men said.

'But we didn't receive it,' I cried.

'The letter was registered,' the man in the blazer said drily. 'You got it all right.'

I looked at Papa and it all became quite clear. I realised that he had received the notice and had destroyed it. It explained his recent strange behaviour.

'You've had enough time. Now move out of the way,' one of the other men said.

Constable de Bruin brought one of the dogs out of the van. Sergeant Klein gestured angrily to him. De Bruin hesitated, preferring to take instructions from the khaki-suited men. But none of them said anything and so he returned the dog to the van.

The drumming of voices and the clattering in my head made it almost impossible to hear clearly what was being said. Despite all that I had heard, I couldn't believe that this was happening to us. We had spent our lives amongst these people. Some of them were our friends. We had helped many of them – we had given them credit when no one else would. There was no need for this. Who of them could possibly have hated us so much?

'We need time,' Papa said.

'Go phone our lawyer,' Ma said to him, her voice ragged.

But Papa was too dazed to respond.

My mother's bun had come undone; her large eyes were filled with anguish. Her hands dropped to her sides in a gesture of helpless resignation.

This was the image of my mother I took with me as I hurried inside to phone the lawyer.

When I returned two of the younger constables had pushed their way into the house. One of them was dragging the blue padded chair from my parents' bedroom.

'What are you doing?' Ma asked, as he tossed it on to the sidewalk.

My father pressed his hand to his chest. I helped him outside, righted the chair on the sidewalk and sat him in it.

'What did Attorney Joubert say?' Ma asked.

'He said there was no point in him coming over,' I said. 'There is nothing he can do.'

Mrs Ollie appeared and led Nana over to her house, while Papa remained in the blue armchair on the sidewalk looking totally disorientated.

'Are you all right, Abdul?' Ma asked.

Papa nodded. 'I'll be all right. Just get my pills,' he said to me.

I rushed back into the house to find my father's nitroglycerine pills. The two policemen were carrying out another chair.

'*Yini, yini!* Come quickly!' Gladys cried. There was a crash from the kitchen and Ma rushed into the house.

'No! No! Please!' I heard my mother's horrified cry.

I found her kneeling amidst the chaos in the kitchen. She was clutching a shard of china. A thin trickle of blood oozed from the palm of her hand. Her eyes, bright with tears, were fixed on the young constable.

Sergeant Klein appeared in the doorway.

'What's going on here?' he demanded.

'I dropped the plates,' the constable said sheepishly.

Blood was still dripping from my mother's hand as I helped her to her feet.

'It belonged to my great-grandmother,' Ma said as I drew up a chair for her. 'She brought it from Ireland.' She turned a pleading gaze on the sergeant. 'Please, I'll pack the dishes myself.'

The sergeant looked distraught. Ma lowered her head, tears falling into her lap. Sergeant Klein glared at the constable. 'Go wait outside,' he said.

'Why are you doing this to us, Sergeant Klein?' Ma cried. 'Why?'

'I'm sorry, Mrs Mohammed. Very sorry. I wish . . .' his voice broke and he walked away.

'What are you doing to these people?' Mrs Ollie asked, blocking his way. 'I know them. You know them. They're not criminals. Why are you treating them like this? In God's name, man, what are you doing?'

'Look,' Ma cried, gesturing to the broken crockery. 'My dinner service, look at it!' There was a loud crash from the bedroom. When Sergeant Klein and I got there we saw the fragments of Ma's precious porcelain basin and jug on the floor.

My mother blocked the doorway. Constable de Bruin placed a hand on her shoulder intending to guide her out of the room, but she jerked away angrily.

'I'll take her out,' Mrs Ollie said anxiously.

Sergeant Klein nodded.

Ma leaned against the dresser. 'All of it destroyed,' she whispered. 'We took such good care of it all these years – three generations of us and now . . . look at it. A few minutes with them – and look what they've done to it.'

'Come Delia,' Mrs Ollie said. 'Let's go to my place. Your mother is there. I want to take a look at that hand.'

Ma held out her hand which was still wrapped around the piece of porcelain. Mrs Ollie pried her fingers open and threw the bloodied fragment of porcelain into the gutter. 'That's a deep cut. It needs attention. Come.'

Ma offered no further resistance. She paused to ask my father how he was. Papa had his head buried in his hands in an attitude of utter despair. It was as though his life was over. There was nothing left. Nowhere to go. Nothing seemed to register with him as he watched our belongings being carried out of the house.

Ma hesitated when she saw how defeated my father was. But Mrs Ollie was firm. '*Kom nou*, Delia. *Kom*,' she urged, glaring at the policemen.

Ma stared vacantly at our scattered possessions.

Many of the townspeople had gathered. Some of them helped, others stood around, uneasy witnesses, shuffling from one foot to the other.

I tried to salvage what I could. Some of the bystanders picked up our clothing and helped me to pack what was left of our lives. One of the women offered to pack the china. She found newspaper and carefully wrapped what remained of the dinner service.

Mrs Ollie stuck her head out of her front door and called me. '*Kom Meena, vat vir jou Papa 'n lekker koppie tee.*'

I dropped what I was doing and went to fetch the cup of tea for my father.

'Thank you,' Papa said. He took the tea from me, but made no attempt to drink it. When I returned the cup Mrs Ollie and Ma were sipping their tea in silence, Ma with her head bowed, the cup and saucer in her lap. Mrs Ollie had poured the tea in her best china.

'Under the circumstances you might find this hard to believe,' Mrs Ollie said in Afrikaans, 'but we're not all like that.' She gestured to the police. 'I've been your friend for a long time. I know what you're going through. Hardship and pain are the same, no matter what colour you are.'

'You've been a good friend to me all these years, Sinnah.' Ma smiled sadly. 'Sinnah Olivier . . . I'd almost forgotten your last name. All these years you've been Mrs Ollie because the children couldn't say Olivier.'

As I was leaving Ma said: 'Keep an eye on your Papa please, Meena.'

Sounds from outside carried indoors and her eyes welled up again. They were emptying the store in the same manner as they had emptied the house.

'I'd better go,' she said to Mrs Ollie.

'You can store your stuff in my shed. The cows will be all right outside,' she said, accompanying Ma to the stoep.

'Thank you,' Ma said. 'Thank you so much. I'll leave the big items here . . . for a short while anyway.'

'What are you going to do now, Delia?' Mrs Ollie asked.

'I suppose we'll have to move to McBain. There's nowhere else for us to go.'

'That's ridiculous. The place is nothing but ruins.'

Ma shrugged.

Mrs Ollie sighed. She didn't have to say anything. It was all there in her eyes.

Ma turned to go. 'Thanks for the tea . . . and everything,' she said, offering her hand, but the Afrikaner woman ignored her outstretched hand and embraced her, right there in the middle of the street with half the town looking on.

'Good luck,' she said.

Gladys said that she would join us later when things were more settled. I didn't know whether to believe her or not. Daniel didn't want to come either. He didn't want to leave the house unattended.

'It's not ours any more,' Ma tried to explain, but Daniel refused to listen. He was determined to stay, and that was that.

We loaded the car with as much as we could. Mrs Ollie had an old *bakkie* which she offered to lend us as soon as we were settled.

With the help of some of the men from the Location, we transferred as much of the shop's goods to the shed as we could. After all the fuss we'd made about the jersey cows, we'd now put them out of their abode to store our goods. Nana was right. Life had a strange way of backhanding you when you least expected it.

It took several more hours to sort things out. The constables and the men from the Group Areas Board had left. Sergeant Klein stayed, waiting to padlock the shop door. He stood in the backyard with Ma for a moment. Ma absently stroked her bandaged hand.

He gazed at her with an expression so profound that I felt moved. I knew that he wasn't responsible, but in the end it all came down to the fact that he was one of 'them'.

His expression remained with me for years afterwards. It was only later, much later in life, that I understood what it meant.

Ma took one last sad and regretful look at her garden, her eyes filling with tears, and then she walked away.

Gladys stood on the sidewalk until the car turned the corner at the end of the street.

We were leaving behind not only our home but also a big chunk of our lives. Tears slid down Ma's cheeks as she watched Gladys's forlorn figure in the rear-view mirror. She glanced at my father's face and saw the anguish. Wordlessly, she squeezed his hand.

I turned around for a last look. Both Gladys and Daniel had been such an integral part of our lives, one of the many threads woven into the fabric of our existence.

'There's no use dwelling on the past,' Ma said, brushing the dampness from her cheeks. 'We have to go on.'

'Some day they'll pay for this,' I muttered.

'Not them. We're the ones who pay,' Nana said.

'What will happen to Daniel?' I asked.

'I don't know. I suppose he'll come to McBain . . .'

'Is that where we're going now, Ma?' I asked.

'I don't know, Meena. I don't know anything any more,' Ma said as we turned the corner and turned our backs on our past.

12

BEWILDERED, LIKE a man whose whole world had collapsed, my father stood in the veld taking in the desolation at McBain.

He couldn't bring himself to look at my mother.

The only structure still partially intact was a building which had a roof and four walls standing. It was late afternoon and like lost sheep we searched for a spot to nestle into.

'We'll have to sleep in the car tonight,' Ma said. 'It's too late to go anywhere else.'

'We have friends in town . . .' Nana started.

'This is our home now, Mum, and the sooner we get used to it, the better,' Ma said harshly. Then seeing Nana's pain, her tone softened. 'There's no use procrastinating, Mum. We've got to get a roof over our heads and we've got to do it soon.'

My father still stood aside, beaten down by the speed of events.

'Why didn't you tell us, Abdul?' Ma asked.

My father turned his dazed expression on my mother.

'Why didn't you tell us about the eviction order?' she asked. 'At least we'd have been prepared.'

Papa sighed, drawing his hand across his head. 'I didn't want to worry you. I didn't believe that they would actually carry out their threat. No one could be so stupid or inhuman.'

'Well, here we are. Kicked out into the veld,' she said with a touch of bitterness as she gazed vacantly into the distance.

'I told you,' Nana said.

But it was too late. None of us wanted to be reminded of the fact that we'd been wrong. We didn't want to hear what Nana had to say now.

Ma realised that Papa was hurting. 'We'll get through this somehow,' she said, taking his hands. It was the first time in ages that I had seen my parents demonstrating affection for each other.

'When will it end, Delia?' Papa asked. 'When? All my life I've been kicked around. I'm tired now. Very tired.'

The desolation and the rubble of the ruined buildings which confronted us at McBain merely added to his misery.

He sat down on a crumbling wall and massaged his head, repeating over and over in Gujarati that it was too late for him to start over.

'How can I do it, Delia?' he moaned while my mother listened in silence. 'How can I? Look at me. I am an old man already.'

Ma, many years younger than he, looked on helplessly.

Nana and I, mute with anguish, were too stunned ourselves by what had happened to offer words of comfort or consolation.

The government had stolen my father's life. He had nothing to show for all the years of toil and sacrifice.

Conditions at McBain were much worse than any of us had expected. There was nothing salvageable amidst the rubble.

Everything, including my schooling, was forgotten in the wake of this new catastrophe. The only important and relevant issues were those related to our survival.

Ma didn't waste much time on self-pity. With the help of two labourers from the neighbouring village, she cordoned off an area in the ruined building which we used as living space. The beds and heavy pieces of furniture had been brought to McBain on the back of a lorry.

Our living area was large enough to hold three cots and a table. My parents and Nana each had a cot. I made a bed for myself on the top of two packing cases. The further off the ground I was, the better I felt about not being attacked by crawling creatures.

'To think that we used to have a flush toilet,' Nana said wryly.

'And now we're reduced to performing our business like animals in the open veld.'

Some distance beyond the trading post, on the other side of the railway line, was the McBain siding with its water tower, painted army green, and two storage sheds.

Our daily routine began with the drawing of the day's supply of water, which was hauled from the railway siding. After this the meals were started on the primus stove. Once breakfast was over everything had to be stowed because animals strayed on to the property and foraged amongst our possessions.

We had become the first victims of the government's grandiose scheme to move all Indians out of small towns into one central area, a task so impossible to implement that it eventually had to be abandoned.

But for us it was too late. We had already been 'expropriated' and had lost everything.

Not only had the government evicted us from our home, but they had torn our lives apart. They had stolen what we had spent our lives working for and had shunted us into the veld, twenty-eight miles from the nearest town.

McBain was an area so remote and so desolate that it was like being catapulted into another world. On one side of the railway siding were three cottages occupied by white railway workers. Across the tracks, the ruins of what had once been a farmhouse were now our new home.

While Ma and Nana worked with a desperation born of uncertainty and fear to put a roof over our heads, Papa sat outside despondently contemplating our inhospitable environment.

In the weeks following our eviction he had grown old beyond his years: fingers gnarled, the dark leathery skin on the back of his hand speckled with white patches. A vacuous glaze had settled over his eyes and the cataracts had rendered him almost completely sightless.

Yasmin was still at school. She had been spared the horror of being dragged out of our home.

It took two months for us to establish ourselves in this wasteland. At times not another living soul would be seen for hours on end. Voices from a distant village occasionally carried on the still air. In the oppressive silence even the drone of a bluebottle was exaggerated to irritating proportions.

One morning I caught sight of a familiar figure trudging along the dusty road.

'Isn't that Daniel?' I asked.

'Yes,' my mother said, shielding her eyes as she stared into the distance.

When Daniel reached us, Papa asked, 'How did you get here?'

'I walked, *Oubaas*.'

'Why didn't you take the train?'

'No money.'

'I'm so glad you decided to join us, Daniel,' Ma said.

'I will only be staying for two weeks, Madam.'

'But why? There's nothing in Soetstroom any more.'

'It's a voice, Madam, which tells me not to leave the house.'

'The house doesn't belong to us any more.'

'That's not what they have told me,' he said.

'Who told you?' Ma asked.

'The voices, Madam.' His tone was reproachful.

Nana tapped her head and exchanged glances with Ma.

'Where are you staying in Soetstroom?' Ma asked.

'In my room.'

'Which room?' Nana asked.

'My room in the garage.'

'Don't tell me you're still on the property, Daniel.'

'Yes, Madam.'

'They probably don't even know that he's there,' Nana said.

'What's happened to Gladys?'

'She'll be coming here to work for you soon, Madam.'

'Good,' Nana said.

Daniel shrugged disconsolately.

We worked hard to bring some kind of order to the property. Daniel was of great help and so were three men from the village, who exchanged their labour for provisions of tobacco and mealie meal.

Papa was happy to have Daniel's company. The spring in his step returned. Ma was relieved; she had worried about him sitting on the stoep day after day, gloomily massaging his head as though he had lost the will to carry on. But with Daniel back it didn't take long for them to pick up where they had left off in Soetstroom.

'Madam, this is very bad,' Daniel said one day, putting his hands behind his back and inspecting the property like a general inspecting his troops. 'I shall write a letter to the CIA,' he added, taking a yellowed piece of paper from his pocket.

'What's that?' I asked curiously.

'It's a letter of identification from the CIA.'

'Let me see it.' Ma held out her hand. Daniel gave it to her. She read it and then, raising her eyebrows, she passed it on to me.

The yellowed piece of paper was an old receipt issued by a Mr Bernstein to a Mr Jantzen for some item that was indecipherable. Daniel had obviously picked this scrap of paper off a rubbish heap somewhere. It was so old that it had been scotch-taped along the folds where it had come apart from constant handling. I solemnly folded it and gave it back to Daniel.

Most of the perishable goods from the store in Soetstroom had long since expired and had been discarded. The rest of the merchandise was unpacked and dusted as we prepared to open for business. Nana and Gladys arranged the shelves.

The open veld was encapsulated in a cocoon of hot air. In the distance heat waves shimmered off the tracks. The only sign of life was a herd of goats resting under a scraggy thornbush.

'Good Lord, it's hot,' Nana complained, dabbing at her damp brow with the front of her smock. 'Do you know the Bible story about the plagues, Gladys?'

Gladys gave her a wide-eyed stare.

'You've read the Bible, haven't you?'

Gladys looked shamefaced.

'Never mind,' Nana sighed. 'There's always something sent to torment you, whether you're a good Christian or not. Here in this country it's the white man, the heat and the snakes.'

'And the flies,' Gladys added.

'*Ja*. That's right.'

Gladys had learned that in this heat it was essential to conserve energy. Later, when it cooled down, she would pick Nana's conversation apart, chuckling quietly to herself.

Not long after Gladys's arrival Daniel, seized by one of his strange moods, had once again packed up and taken off. We weren't unduly worried, suspecting that he had returned to Soetstroom.

But it didn't take Gladys long to settle in and she soon made friends with the villagers.

'I'll be darned,' Nana observed. 'I think she actually likes it out here. Have you noticed? She's quite a different person.'

Gladys spent hours gossiping with villagers who stopped by. But it was Nana who was the first to notice that the old chief from the local village had taken a fancy to Gladys, often calling to talk to her. It was quite a sight, the chief leaning on his knobkerrie for hours on end, like some English squire, while Gladys giggled and twittered like a young girl.

Within a matter of weeks, Gladys informed us that she would shortly become the chief's wife. A few weeks later she moved to the village. She continued to work at McBain, walking the two miles to and from work each day. By keeping her job at McBain she was able to feed the chief's children who were half-starved because of the recent crop failures.

'Seems she's quite happy with her situation,' Ma commented.

'I hope it lasts,' Nana responded. 'I think the only reason the old bugger's taken her as a wife is because she feeds his family.'

The chief had seventeen children from three wives; Gladys was his fourth wife. Ma thought that perhaps the chief's children filled the void in Gladys's life. She had never had children, and her husband had left her because of this.

The younger children from the village came often to McBain. While she fed them and cared for them, not so much as a peeling was discarded from the kitchen; every morsel of food was saved for them. The rest of the time, however, she jealously guarded her position from the other villagers, often scolding them when they made a nuisance of themselves.

Finally, the cottage was habitable and we moved in. The front door faced north, overlooking the store. The bathroom was a concrete pad with a little duct that drained the water outside, water which was still carried from the siding each day. A bucket was suspended above the pad to serve as a crude shower. The lavatory was still only a hole in the ground covered by a shack hammered together from planks taken off the packing cases.

We often thought of Soetstroom and of how well off we had been there. Ma hoped eventually to have running water, but Papa said that it would cost too much to sink a borehole on the property.

None of the Afrikaner railway workers set foot in the store. They did their shopping in the nearest town, twenty-eight miles away, a town large enough to provide all the amenities found in a city. We depended on the almost non-existent passing traffic and the small trade brought by the surrounding villages, some of them almost five miles away.

Business was extremely poor for us at McBain but Papa, whose spirits had lifted a little, clung to the view that the main road would eventually pass right by our front door and business would boom. We had our doubts that this would ever happen.

It took a while to get used to the sound of jolting carriages, hissing steam and the occasional boisterousness of the railway workers, especially at night when everything was so quiet.

The passenger trains sped by, but during the course of the day several goods trains hauling freight halted for water and coal.

There was no need for us to buy fuel for the stove as we had done in Soetstroom. The gummy thorn trees made excellent firewood. Occasionally, too, we picked up pieces of coal along the railway tracks, even though this practice was outlawed.

Towards the end of November the letter came from Yasmin's school informing us that she would be home at the end of the week.

'We'll meet her in town on Friday night,' Ma said.

'You know what's going to happen when she gets here,' Nana groaned. 'We'll all be expected to wait on her and none of the work will get done.'

'She's not that bad, Nana,' I replied.

'We'll see, my girl, we'll see,' Nana said.

On the Friday afternoon we closed the store at five o'clock, and although I had volunteered to stay home, Ma wouldn't hear of it.

Instead, she asked Gladys to keep an eye on the place.

13

THE FIRST to spot her, I ran alongside the train until it stopped, impatiently beckoning the rest of the family.

Like Samantha in *Manhattan Green*, Yasmin stood in the entrance to the carriage, placed a cautious foot on the step and gazed down at us. There was a brief hesitation, her wide, round eyes filled with trepidation. Then her eyelids came down like shutters and she took a delicate step down into Ma's excited embrace.

She'd cut her hair. She looked gorgeous. The wispy fringe emphasised those wonderful eyes.

Ma held her at arm's length and gazed at her.

'Such beautiful hair and you've cut it all off!' Nana exclaimed.

Papa waited impatiently. Yasmin broke free of Ma's embrace and hugged him.

'You're as thin as a rake,' Nana commented drily. She didn't deceive me for one moment. She was as happy as the rest of us to have Yasmin home.

We lifted Yasmin's luggage into the boot and she squeezed into the front seat between Ma and Papa.

'Are you all right, Papa?' Yasmin asked.

Papa sighed and shook his head. '*Inshallah*,' he said. 'Things can't get any worse. I'm just grateful the family's together again.'

'I should've been here to help,' Yasmin muttered.

Nana and I exchanged amused glances.

'It doesn't matter. You're home now,' Papa said.

I caught a glimpse of Ma and Yasmin's reflections in the rear-view mirror and was astounded by the resemblance. The two had never looked more alike than they did that day.

Ma spoke about the move to McBain and everyone had something to add. Before long we were all talking at once.

Yasmin's disappointment about our new home was evident the moment we arrived. It wasn't much by any means, and in the stillness of the veld it looked even more desolate than ever.

Ma and Papa had both climbed out and were waiting for her. She slid along the seat, keeping her eyes lowered, as though afraid of what would be revealed when she lifted them.

I gazed at her. She turned her head, but not before I saw again that flash of fear in her eyes.

'It's so nice to have you back,' Papa said.

'I'm glad to be home, Papa,' Yasmin lied.

None of us said anything as we waited for her comments.

'God, it's so . . . so . . . what can I say?'

'What did you expect?' Nana demanded. 'The Taj Mahal?'

'Nothing's changed,' Yasmin muttered as Nana walked away.

She was right. Nothing had changed. Somehow we had managed to pick up the threads again and our life continued as before.

Ma, who had spent most of the previous day in the kitchen preparing a superb feast for Yasmin's return, hastened towards the house, inviting Yasmin in for her favourite – a glass of *felooda*, a special drink prepared from poppy seeds, agar-agar and rosewater. Ma had gone to a great deal of trouble to satisfy every possible whim of Yasmin's.

But Yasmin had no appetite. 'No thank you, Ma,' she demurred.

'It's been a long trip. You must be exhausted,' Papa pressed.

'It's the heat.'

Ma marched ahead to the house while Yasmin lagged behind.

She was in no hurry and sauntered, taking in her surroundings.

Papa's fond gaze followed her as she linked her arm through mine.

'And you, little sister?' Yasmin asked. 'What have you been

105

up to?'

I considered the question. 'Nothing much. It's only been three months since I last saw you,' I reminded her. 'What about you?'

'I can't remember the last time I did anything exciting,' Yasmin said, her voice smooth and languid.

I stood with bowed head, drawing geometric designs in the sand with the toe of my sandal.

'You've changed.' Yasmin pounced on me as she had done when we were youngsters. 'You're different.'

'It's nothing,' I said, averting my eyes.

'I know you,' she persisted.

'It's nothing . . . really. You're imagining things. What could possibly happen here in the veld?' I was impatient with her for wanting to drag something out of me that wasn't there.

'Did you meet a boy?' she continued.

'Are you crazy?' I asked.

Yasmin turned her beautiful smile on me, holding me at arm's length, exactly the way Ma had held her at the station. 'It's time, of course, that you met a boy.' She inclined her head to one side. 'You've grown up now. You're beautiful.'

'Oh, for God's sake, Yasmin. Nothing about me has changed. You make it sound as though we haven't seen each other in years. But things *have* changed for the family. Look at us,' I said, spreading my arms. 'This is real, Yasmin. Not your fantasy about me being beautiful.'

She looked at me in amazement.

'I'm only trying to help you. You're growing up, Meena.' She took my arm. 'You're not a baby any more. It's time you learned about boys and what happens between boys and girls.' She smiled her sweet smile. This was Yasmin the *ingénue* at her best.

'I know what goes on. What do you think I am . . . an idiot?' I slapped her hands off my arm. 'Let's go into the house. I guess Ma and Papa are waiting for you.'

She stared at me in amusement.

'Why are you looking at me like that?' I demanded.

'So you're still a virgin.'

Irritated with the line of conversation, I stormed off.

'OK, OK.' She ran after me. 'I give up!' She caught up with me and, grabbing my arm, spun me around.

'Do you have to spoil everything?' I demanded angrily.

She laughed, a quiet, husky sound developed since her last trip home. 'OK, but I don't know why Papa doesn't find a husband for you instead of worrying about me. If you're not careful you'll end up being an old maid. Life's a journey, darling, and I want to enjoy the ride. I don't want to be like you. Saving it all so I can sit on it.'

I'd heard enough. I walked off in the direction of the cottage. Yasmin followed, stumbling over the stones in her high heels.

'At least I don't throw it around the way you do!' I cried.

'I won't die wondering what it was like. *I know*,' she called out after me.

'Are you girls quarrelling?' Ma demanded as she came out to see what the fuss was about.

Yasmin shook her head while I pushed past Ma.

'Your Papa wants to talk to you, Yasmin.'

Yasmin came inside then, cautiously stepping across the threshold as Ma affectionately took her arm.

'I'll show you the rest of the place later. It's not much, but I have so many plans. You can help me now that you're home again.'

Later, Ma showed Yasmin around the living quarters, taking great pride in what we had accomplished in such a short time. She followed Ma into the bathroom.

'One of these days we'll sink a well and lead water to the house,' Ma said.

I was in the next room and I could hear Yasmin's high-heeled shoes tapping on the concrete floor as she continued her inspection.

'What about a lavatory?' Yasmin asked.

'There's one outside.'

'Oh God, Ma!'

'I know it's a little primitive.'

'A *little* primitive?'

'We have lots to do still. Right now it's merely a boxed-in pit. We'll build a flush toilet in the house like we had in Soetstroom. But we can't do any of that without water.'

In the silence that followed I heard Ma's slippered feet padding across the floor to the front room.

'I'm so glad you're home,' Ma said quietly.

'So am I,' Yasmin said, trying to sound enthusiastic, but failing abysmally.

'Trapped!' Yasmin muttered. 'It's even worse than Soetstroom.' She banged the teapot on the kitchen table.

I didn't say anything.

'I sensed it the moment I stepped off that train,' she continued. 'Christ, life in Soetstroom was bad enough, but it's like being buried alive here.'

'You'll never change, Yasmin,' I said watching as she swirled boiling water around the teapot.

She paused and then gave me one of her sweet smiles. 'Forget all my bitching. Old habits die hard.'

I suspected that something was going on that she wasn't telling me about. I questioned her, but each time I seemed to get close to answers, she changed the subject.

Something in her attitude convinced me that she wasn't going to be with us much longer. She obviously had plans. I studied her, looking for clues whenever she wasn't watching. Whatever it was, she'd have to tell us sooner or later and I dreaded that it might end in another confrontation.

We talked a lot the first little while, often lying in the dark, our door shut so that our parents couldn't hear us. I had missed her so, and I knew that she'd missed me too. Sometimes we got up in the middle of the night to sing and talk into her tape recorder. We made up elaborate and affected conversations that had nothing to do with our real lives. They were fantasies in which we assumed the role of celebrities, Yasmin an actress visiting

McBain and I the interviewer.

After the first week we were all played out and her boredom returned. Ma and Nana built a facade of normality which stifled her. She was right, of course; there really wasn't much to do at McBain. We were isolated – no one to see or talk to outside the family. The arrival of a car sent us scurrying outside, eager to catch a glimpse of another face.

Yasmin seemed to mark the passage of each day like a stroke on a cell wall. Nana sensed her restlessness and was quietly reproachful. There was very little one could hide from Nana. She had that uncanny knack of getting at the truth, working at it until she had sucked the marrow out of the bone.

When we were young Yasmin and I always tried to outwit her, but never quite succeeded. She knew everything. And when you least expected it, she would pounce on you. Ma once said that Yasmin and Nana were more alike than either of them would admit.

Even Nana was bored. Lately she seemed to be more cantankerous than usual. At least in Soetstroom she had kept herself occupied picking people like Mrs du Plessis and Mrs Prinsloo apart. Now there was only her family.

'How long does it take you to get dressed?' she asked Yasmin from the doorway.

'I'm putting on my make-up.'

'Make-up! Why would you want to wear make-up out here? Who's going to see you?'

And so it went on. What did it matter how long Yasmin took? There was nothing to do anyway. If she took two hours to dress in the morning, it shortened the day by that much.

To keep us from going completely insane Papa brought home a box of books bought at an auction in town. Most of them were old romances, as irrelevant to our present-day life as the *Dick and Jane* readers had been, but I devoured them, I even read some of them twice. Yasmin said she wasn't interested in the rubbish I read. She would have liked a good mystery.

I tossed aside the book I was reading. I'd read all of them

anyway. At that point, like Yasmin, I was all 'read out'.

'I'm so bored,' Yasmin complained, joining me at the back of the house where I was sitting in the shade.

Nana, standing by the kitchen window, overheard this remark.

'You won't be bored if you do some work around the place,' she called out.

'I've done my share,' Yasmin protested. 'There's nothing more to do.'

'You can always find work if you want to.'

'Nana, I've helped to put up fences and I've moulded and fired bricks, I've raised walls and helped to put up the roof,' Yasmin said irritably. 'I've had enough. They should have moved us to the city instead of this hellhole!'

'Not much we can do about that, is there?' Nana said tartly.

'This is the bloody end,' Yasmin muttered, storming away. I watched her go and grinned as Nana pulled a wry face.

We fixed the driveway, carrying rocks from the top of the hill to fill in the ruts. While Yasmin cautiously lifted individual rocks, cradling them in the palm of her hands to protect her nails, I carried armfuls. After each trip from rock pile to rut, she inspected her nails for damage.

Yasmin had sulked throughout the exercise, complaining that life at McBain was worse than hard labour on Robben Island.

Needless to say the job was never finished.

Ma and Nana talked about Soetstroom endlessly. It awakened memories of the SAPS crowd. I told Yasmin that Willem was in town, Moses was still at university in Johannesburg, Dora was dead. She had tried to abort her baby, using a knitting needle, and had haemorrhaged to death. Sarah, one of her other classmates from Soetstroom, now worked for a white farmer, and the rest of them had sunk into oblivion. Yasmin shuddered, obviously thinking that this might well have been her fate also.

Yasmin was thrilled when she discovered that Gladys's husband, the chief, owned a chestnut mare. I knew about the secret arrangements with Gladys to let her ride occasionally, and I discovered too that she paid Gladys with extra rations at the end of the week.

'If you let her ride that horse,' Nana said, 'we'll never get any work out of her.'

'She takes good care of it; she's good girl,' Gladys said emphatically. It was no secret that Yasmin was Gladys's favourite.

Yasmin beamed triumphantly. Nana always said that there was a little bit of the scoundrel in each of us. Perhaps, like everything else, Yasmin had received more than her share.

We were going through an extremely hot spell. It was months since we'd had rain.

'It's hotter than hell,' Yasmin complained, retiring to a shady spot beside the house. Nothing stirred between the hours of noon and three o'clock. Nana was lying down and eventually I dragged a folding chair over to join Yasmin.

From this elevated position we could see the road and the occasional car passing by.

Few cars wandered off the main road on to the dirt road which passed by our property. Papa still hoped that a new road would be constructed to by-pass a dangerous railway crossing not far from us. There had been several fatal accidents there. Papa said that if they brought the main road past our property, business would pick up.

Daniel showed up a few weeks later. He had finally been kicked off the Soetstroom property. Ill, hungry and with no place to go, he had returned to us, this time with all his belongings in an old orange sack. His shoes, laces tied together, were hanging around his neck. There was nothing left of them. The soles were completely worn away. The only parts of the shoes that remained were the uppers.

'Seems like he's here to stay this time,' Ma remarked as Daniel stacked his belongings in the corner of the stoep.

We could never be sure what Daniel would do.

Nana was right; he was madder than a hatter. And we were the closest thing he had to family.

Ma and Yasmin were the only licensed drivers. Yasmin, now nineteen, had recently passed her driving test, but I was only fifteen and still too young to learn.

Perhaps it was out of desperation, rather than any act of charity, that prompted Yasmin to teach Daniel to drive. Papa had become increasingly dependent on Yasmin to drive him around.

Nana warned against it. She said it was absurd to teach Daniel to drive.

But Yasmin ignored all our concerns and insisted that it would be a good idea. All he had to do was stick to the back roads and make sure Papa was seated next to him, so he didn't go off the rails while behind the wheel.

Despite Yasmin's assurances, Nana and Ma still had their doubts about sending Daniel out with Papa – the two of them alone in the car and subject to Daniel's erratic moods.

But in the end Yasmin prevailed. From the safety of the stoep, we watched with mounting trepidation as Yasmin and Daniel bounced over ant hills and ruts in the veld, amazed at the patience she displayed with him.

On the day of his last lesson Daniel drove home.

Negotiating the turn into the gate, he drove up the driveway and, grinning from ear to ear, pulled up in front of the steps.

Yasmin had accomplished what we all thought would be impossible.

But although Daniel could now drive, he would never be in a position to apply for a licence. Apart from the fact that we didn't think he would ever pass the test, he possessed none of the required documentation. He had nothing, not even the pass book – the *dompas* as it was known – which recorded every facet of the lives of black people.

Ma thought that since Yasmin had been so successful with Daniel, she could also teach me to drive. She suggested this to

Yasmin who was very reluctant.

'Fine,' I said. 'If you don't want to, I'll teach myself. How hard can it be?'

At fifteen, I was too young to drive legally but I thought that, like Daniel, I could drive the back roads. At least it would be of some help.

Yasmin eventually agreed. She took me out on the same route she had chosen for Daniel. But from the moment we stepped into the car there was friction.

Nana had warned that husbands ought never to teach wives to drive. The same applied to mothers and daughters, but she did not warn about sisters.

Yasmin was grudging and unwilling. It was obvious she wanted to be the only one on whom Papa focused his attention. She wanted to be indispensable.

She was impatient with me. She yelled, insulted and swore at me when I made a mistake.

Once we almost got into a fist fight.

'Can't you read, stupid? R is for reverse. See, R...R...R...' She jabbed at the transmission indicator on the dashboard when the car lurched forwards instead of backwards.

She slumped back in her seat, clutching her head. 'I have a headache,' she said. 'Let's go back.'

'I suppose this is how you yelled at Daniel too,' I said sarcastically.

'I didn't have to. He might not have all his marbles, but he's not as stupid as you.'

After a week of this abuse from my sister, I gave up the driving lessons.

Business had increased marginally, but it was a far cry from our better days in Soetstroom.

'It's all penny and tickey lines: beads, bangles and mirrors,' Papa complained.

One morning at breakfast, Papa said: 'I hear that Prinsloo bought our store from the Group Areas Board.'

'Where did you hear that?' Nana asked.

'Daniel.'

'I hate to think of someone else living in my house,' Ma muttered.

A comment such as this always led to a session of reminiscing. Yasmin hated it. A look of irritation crept over her face, but Ma's eyes clouded with nostalgia as she reached back into the past. Yasmin fidgeted through breakfast and as soon as we could get away, we hastened to the village to borrow Blitzen.

I marvelled at the way the horse's condition had improved since Yasmin had started taking care of her. The mare's coat was lustrous. Yasmin said that the brushing did it. I thought this was probably why Yasmin's hair was so beautiful too; without fail, each night she brushed it at least a hundred strokes.

The horse recognised Yasmin and nuzzled at the pocket where she usually kept a small reward for her.

I climbed up behind Yasmin, wrapping my arms about her waist, face pressed against her shoulder. I enjoyed these moments with my sister. She loved riding, claiming that it gave her a sense of freedom and power.

A track turned at right-angles off the main road and wandered across the veld, following the line of an earlier footpath. It led to the dry river bed which snaked around the village into the hills. Yasmin urged the horse through the *donga* along an easterly track.

The countryside was undulating veld, broken here and there by koppies which appeared as distant specks from McBain. We rode through more *dongas* and gullies, all of them dry now. Spiral whirlwinds lifted the sand from one heap to another. The mare slithered down the wind-eroded embankments, whinnying and snorting while I held on for dear life.

The gum trees were covered with finches. I had never seen so many birds in all my life. Disturbed, they swooped into the air, blotting out the sun. Massing and turning, wave after wave of them returned to find new perches.

Black crows cawed and bobbed on the skeletal trees, picking

incessantly at the twigs and branches while they waited for carrion along the road where man and machine left a bloody trail of dead rabbits, squirrels and field mice.

The short brown grass was matted, but ahead of us it shimmered and danced in silver mirages. There were a few clouds in the sky and the oppressive heat was a portent of a break in the long dry spell.

That night the humidity in the house made it difficult to get to sleep. Awakened by a clap of thunder, I saw Yasmin getting out of bed. She crossed the room and stood by the window, staring out as the rain came down in steady sheets.

Then she tiptoed out of the room to the front door. I went to the window and watched the rain cascading down the walls, forming little lakes on the stoep before flowing to the parched ground.

Stark naked, Yasmin stood on the stoep, illuminated for a moment by a flash of lightning. Water glistened on her body.

Amazed, I rushed outside where she was splashing and plopping through the puddles, going through her old ballet routine.

'Are you mad?' I called. 'Someone'll see you.'

She laughed. 'Come on. It's beautiful.'

'You'll catch your death of cold.'

'Nonsense. The rain is warm. It's beautiful,' she said, sensuously stroking her body. 'Come on, take off your nightie.'

I shook my head, waiting for her madness to end, but she continued her cavorting while the rain pelted down. 'Come on, Meena!' she urged.

I hesitated and then, realising that I couldn't stop her, I thought I might as well join her. I pulled my nightie over my head and stood shivering for a moment.

After the first shock of the cold water I was surprised at how pleasant it was, especially after the unbearable humidity.

'Isn't it wonderful?' Yasmin grabbed my hand and dragged me off the stoep into the open.

I nodded, throwing my head back and allowing the rain to wash over my face. 'Yes.'

'You see. I wouldn't lie to you. You must learn to loosen up. You can't always take life so seriously.'

I laughed, shaking the water from my hair. We frolicked like two nymphs, oblivious to everything except the sheer joy of our freedom, uncaring about whether anyone was watching.

Exhilarated, we crept back into the house and dried ourselves.

Yasmin fell asleep instantly. I remained awake, listening to the clatter of the rain on the roof. Towards sunrise it subsided and although the new day broke with invigorating freshness, it brought with it the sad news of Baboo's death.

The letter from his uncle arrived in the post that morning. He wrote that Baboo had died two weeks before. The only information he supplied was that Baboo had been gunned down in front of the Majestic Cinema in Fordsburg.

It was shocking news. We had no idea why this had happened – whether his death had been an accident or whether he had been murdered. Ma was angry that the uncle had taken so long to contact us. She wanted to phone him and give him a piece of her mind, but Papa said there was no point.

'What difference is it going to make?' he asked.

We were all terribly distraught by the news. My mother blamed herself. She said she should never have sent him to live with his uncle. Nana said that none of us was to blame. We could not change what had happened. It was meant to be.

We spoke about the way things might have been, had he stayed with us in Soetstroom.

'He might have been killed there too,' Nana reminded us. 'Remember why you sent him away in the first place, Delia.'

'That damn Cobus Steyn,' Ma muttered. 'If it hadn't been for him . . .'

14

CURIOUS ABOUT what was happening to our old property, we drove out to Soetstroom one Sunday afternoon. The shop door was still padlocked. There was obviously no one living on the property and the place looked derelict.

Mrs Ollie was delighted to see us and promptly took her good teapot and cups off the shelf. Ma questioned her about the house. She'd also heard that Prinsloo wanted to buy it, but she didn't think he had the money.

'We're all struggling,' Mrs Ollie said. 'The town is dying. I don't know how much longer the trains are going to be running through here.'

Ma was hungry for news and she and Mrs Ollie caught up with what had happened after we left. She told us that Cobus Steyn was home from university and was expecting to be drafted into the army soon. Afterwards Ma went to take a look at the house. She stood at the gate for a long time, looking at the overgrown garden. All her beautiful rose bushes had died.

Later we called on some of our old customers who still owed us money. It was a disappointing exercise because only five of the twenty people we had hoped to see were home and they promised to pay as soon as they could. It was the same old story.

The day of Yasmin's coming-out ball arrived. We had all been called on to help with the outfit. If this was only a débutantes' ball, what on earth would Yasmin's wedding be like, I wondered.

The dress, a cloud of white voile, was ready and packed. Yasmin and Ma went by themselves as Papa was not in the least bit interested in going.

While they were gone, though, he paced the front room, complaining about how quiet it was without them. They were gone for two days because Ma wanted to spend a day in the city with Aishaben.

Nana and I were in the kitchen when they got home, waiting excitedly to hear all the details. Yasmin said it had been boring. Her escort had been some clumsy creature who had stepped all over her toes.

'I didn't think he did that badly,' Ma said.

'You weren't dancing with him,' Yasmin said. 'This is how you dance the waltz, not the way he was traipsing around the floor. May I, Nana?' she asked, taking Nana's hand.

They were both in a silly mood and Yasmin slowly whirled Nana around the kitchen in a parody of a stately waltz.

None of us had noticed Papa at the door. All our attention was focused on Nana and Yasmin. Ma, who was usually alert, was too busy vicariously reliving the experiences of her own youth.

'The hall was a sea of white dresses and the boys all wore black suits,' Ma said. 'All the girls were escorted . . .'

'What escorts?' Papa demanded.

We swung round. Yasmin, in mid-motion, unceremoniously dropped Nana into the nearest chair.

'What escorts?' Papa asked again.

Ma had inadvertently surrendered an item of information that both she and Yasmin had agreed to keep from Papa, knowing what his reaction would be.

'The boys merely partnered the girls in a waltz, Abdul,' she explained.

'How dare you parade her around a room full of people and in the company of another man?' he demanded. He slammed his fist on the table. 'You know that I am thinking of a match for her.'

'No, I don't,' Ma replied.

'With whom?' Yasmin demanded.

'Cassimbhai and I have been talking about you and Farouk.'

'Never!' Yasmin cried.

'Abdul, they did nothing but walk around the room once and dance a waltz together,' Ma pleaded.

'Dance!' Papa spat out the word. 'Since when does a Muslim girl dance a waltz? What are you trying to do to her?'

'I want you to know, Papa, that I am not marrying Farouk.' But Yasmin's protest again went unheard.

From time to time both Ma and Papa glared at me, sucking me into the current of their anger.

Ma left the kitchen. The rest of us quickly took our cue from her and dispersed to attend to various chores that suddenly required our immediate attention.

School was part of Yasmin's past now and she made no further reference to it. Matric was over and done with. She had passed. Ma didn't know what was going to happen about furthering her education.

Papa was adamant that his daughters were going to stay home. The waltz-dancing episode was the last straw. He wouldn't listen to any of my mother's arguments. He was deaf to anything she said about Yasmin. He was more determined than ever that she be married to Farouk. To his way of thinking, this was the perfect match. Cassimbhai was an old and trusted friend, he was more like a brother, and in Papa's view a match between Farouk and Yasmin was an ideal way to cement the relationship between the two families.

One Sunday afternoon while Yasmin and I were sitting on the front stoep I tentatively broached the subject of our futures. She looked at me in a strange way.

'Do you think I've changed?' she asked.

I did not answer.

'Come now, Meena,' she persisted. 'Tell me.'

'What's the matter with you, Yasmin?' I asked.

'I'm in love,' she sighed.

I should have guessed, I thought as I studied her. 'With whom?' I asked.

'It's a secret.'

'Tell me,' I urged.

'Nope. If I tell you, everyone in the whole world will know.'

'I promise . . .'

She laughed coyly.

'Nana's right, you are incorrigible,' I said.

Ma and Nana joined us, and Yasmin tackled Ma right away.

'Why are you people trying to palm me off on Farouk?' she demanded.

'It's not a matter of palming you off, Yasmin. Your father and Cassimbhai would love to see you and Farouk married. You've known each other since you were children. Why not accept your father's decision?'

'Never. And you can't make me.'

'Yasmin, please . . .'

'It's only because I'm a girl. It's not fair! I'm telling you now – I won't marry Farouk and I don't care what Papa says.'

'Your Papa has only your best interests at heart,' Ma said quietly. 'He wants to see you secure and happy.'

'I'll marry when and whom I like.'

'You could do worse than Farouk,' Nana said.

'Then let me!'

'It's easy to talk, but when you make a mess of your life, we'll be the ones who'll have to clean it up,' Nana said.

'If I were a boy things would be different . . .'

'Yes, and while we're on the subject of boys, your Papa wants to know why you were taking riding lessons with that special instructor.'

'Papa wants to know?' she asked sarcastically, glaring at Ma.

'What's his name?' Nana asked.

'Andrew Jordaan.'

I waited with bated breath.

'And how old is this Jordaan fellow?'

'A few years older than me, I think.'

'He must've been the young man I saw you talking to on the night of the ball.'

'Yes.' Her tone was matter of fact, intended to dismiss the subject.

But Ma was like a dog with a bone. I could tell this was building up. Something was about to explode.

'So he was giving up his free time to teach you to ride.' Ma studied her for a moment. 'He was giving you free lessons, wasn't he?'

It was all beginning to close in on Yasmin.

'Of course. Isn't that what Miss Jones told you?' she said.

'I'm asking you.'

Yasmin clapped her hands over her ears. 'All these questions!' she cried shrilly.

'I'm waiting for an answer.' Ma's eyes were like tacks, pinning her to the wall. 'What did you do in return for the lessons, Yasmin?'

'Nothing . . . I told you!' Yasmin cried.

'Tell me again.'

'What do you want from me?'

'The truth.' Ma's gaze was piercing.

'I don't want to talk about this any more.'

'I want to know what's going on!' Ma grabbed her by the shoulders.

'Leave me alone!' Yasmin cried.

Ma's hands dropped to her sides. She tried to compose herself.

'A white man – what were you thinking, Yasmin?'

Trapped, Yasmin searched for a way out.

'He is white, isn't he?' Ma asked, even though she knew the answer.

Yasmin nodded slowly.

'The two of you went out by yourselves?' Nana asked, aghast.

'Yes! Yes! Yes! Are you satisfied now?'

Yasmin fled then, almost knocking Gladys and Daniel over in her anxiety to get away.

15

'I WANT to see the world,' Yasmin declared as we sat outside on the stoep one hot summer's evening. 'I want to do things I've never done before.'

'Hmmm,' Nana muttered with her usual disdain.

'What sort of things?' Ma asked curiously.

'This can't be all there is to life,' Yasmin said, gesturing at the empty landscape.

'We have a roof over our heads and three meals a day,' Ma said. 'What more do you want?'

'I can't believe we were put on this earth just to eat and sleep.'

'A lot of people would settle for just that,' Nana said.

'What about you, Meena?' Yasmin asked. 'What would you like?'

I knew what I wanted, but I kept my mouth shut and gave an indifferent shrug. I didn't dare tell them that I wanted to be a revolutionary like Catarina Estrada in *Havana*. I had imagined myself drawn into the passion and intrigue of that mysterious island – dancing the flamenco with my lover's steamy eyes on me.

'Come on,' Yasmin insisted. 'Tell us.'

'You don't want to hear about it,' I hedged.

'Of course we want to hear about it,' Ma said.

I wondered how I could possibly put such images into words. My family would be shocked if they knew what went on in my head.

'I'd like to go to Cuba,' I said.

'Cuba!' There was a moment's silence and then gales of

laughter.

'Cuba!' Yasmin repeated.

'Yes, Cuba,' I said.

Amused, Ma shook her head.

'Old Fidel Castro, that cigar-smoking rascal,' Nana laughed. 'What on earth do you know about him? And what would you want to do in Cuba?'

'I know all about him!' I said, a little peeved at their reaction.

'If anyone hears you mention the word Cuba or Castro,' Ma said, 'you'll be thrown into jail.'

'If you're so keen on intrigue, you can get it right here,' Yasmin teased. 'We'll come and visit you in jail. You don't have to go all the way to Cuba to be a revolutionary.'

'Don't joke about something so serious,' Nana said.

Nana's comment injected a sombre tone into the conversation. I realised that although we were not actively involved in the political protest, politics always lurked just below the surface. Even my comment about wanting to go to Cuba was immediately interpreted as a political stance. I didn't bother to correct them. In fact their assumption merely planted another romantic notion in my mind.

'The resistance can't continue without leadership. It's like a snake without a head,' Ma said.

'The snake will grow a new head,' Nana said. 'When they imprison one leader, another springs up.'

'*Ja* and all we ever do is sit around talking,' I said drily.

'What good would it do if we were all in jail?' Ma asked.

'I agree with Meena,' Nana interjected. 'We do talk a lot. Maybe it's time we did something too – even if it means jail.'

'Do you always have to be so contrary, Mum?' Ma chided.

Nana clamped her mouth shut.

'You people must be crazy to think that being beaten or thrown from windows is something to relish,' Yasmin added, stretching lazily.

'You've always said you won't be pushed around,' I reminded her.

'Hah,' she laughed scornfully. 'Look, kiddo, nobody pushes me around. I've learned to take care of myself. But I don't need a gun to do so. God,' she laughed, dismissing the seriousness of the issue, 'look at us, here we are talking about guns and jails when what we need is a bit of fun.'

'All you ever think about is fun,' Nana said.

'There's nothing wrong with having fun. I'm sure even revolutionaries have fun,' Yasmin retorted. She paused thoughtfully. 'What I want, though, is power.'

Nana chortled.

'Don't be so quick to laugh, Nana,' Yasmin said sharply. 'You watch me. I'm going to be rich some day. It's only the rich who have power and who get respect.'

'Well, my dear child, you can forget about that dream,' Nana said. 'You'll just have to be content with what you have. And believe me, happiness doesn't come with money. In fact money can bring a lot of unhappiness.'

'I'll take my chances with money,' Yasmin said. 'You people can sit around here and be happy.'

'Typical, isn't it?' Nana said. 'All you ever think of is yourself.'

Yasmin, who'd heard this before, did not react.

'Mind you, my girl, you're not going to get any of what you want lying around the house like this,' Nana added, irritably.

'I don't intend to spend the rest of my life lying around here,' Yasmin said.

Startled, Ma glanced at her. 'What do you mean?' she asked, peering at her in the half light of the stoep.

'I'd like to go to Cape Town. I've heard that it's not too hard to find a modelling job there.'

'Modelling!' Ma exclaimed.

'Yes. I'm not going to be a nurse or a teacher. I want to be my own boss.'

'Who's been filling your head with this rubbish?' Ma asked.

'It's not rubbish, Ma. I can't hang around here for ever. I want to make money. I told you, I want to travel.'

But there was more. I could see it in her eyes and I wondered if it had anything to do with Andrew Jordaan. Was this the reason she wanted to go to Cape Town?

Nana raised an eyebrow at Ma.

'What about Meena,' Yasmin said, 'is she also going to rot here?'

'Yasmin!' Ma was appalled.

Once again the tone of the conversation had changed. Suddenly it was charged with undercurrents of tension.

Nana sighed. 'You young people of today are all so restless. So impatient. Everything has to fall into your laps right now.'

'I don't intend to wait around, Nana. You and Ma have spent all your lives waiting. And for what?'

'On top of it, we lost what we had . . . it was taken away from us,' I added before Ma could respond.

'Things here won't ever change for us,' Yasmin added.

Ma said: 'The elections are coming up soon . . . maybe we'll see a change.'

Nana shook her head. 'Those buggers are all alike. The good Lord just gave them different faces so we could tell them apart.'

'I'm not going to wait around here for the elections in the hope that something may change,' Yasmin told Ma.

Ma was hurt and disappointed. 'We'll discuss this later,' she said grimly.

Nana said: 'If it's work you want, why not look for a job in the city? At least you have friends there.'

'I don't want to be locked in some silly office filing papers all day long,' Yasmin snapped.

'*Ag*, Yasmin. Can't you for once be like a normal person?' Nana asked. 'Why do you always have to be different?'

'And don't worry, we haven't forgotten about Meena,' Ma said, touching my arm. 'There's a good school in town. You can travel in by bus.'

'Jobs are not that easy to come by,' Nana continued. 'There are long lists of people waiting, willing to take what they can get.'

'I'm exhausted,' Ma said, getting up off the step and shaking the dust off her skirt. She seemed relieved to have us all gathered under the same roof again and couldn't deal with the idea that any of us might be wanting to leave.

'If I go back to school, it'll have to be in Jo'burg,' I said, reminding Ma of her promise, but I could already feel Jo'burg slipping away.

'It might not be Jo'burg, Meena,' Nana said, 'but you will get an education. That I promise you. Without an education there's not much you can do.'

'There's not much you can do with one either,' Yasmin chipped in.

'Well, I'm going to get ready for bed now.' Ma yawned. 'Coming, Mum?'

'Yes. I suppose I'd better go to bed too, although at my age it's no longer a pleasure,' she complained. Yasmin and I each took an arm to help her out of her chair.

In bed that night I replayed our conversation. The thoughts, Nana's aphorisms, the clichés – our very existence so narrow that it seemed to be turning in an ever tightening gyre.

One evening after a ride on Blitzen, Yasmin and I were out on the stoep, content to sit in silence and watch the sunset.

The orange orb suspended above the distant horizon had turned the bleached grass into a field of fire. As it dipped below the mountains it splattered the sky with pinks, softening the colours on the ground until the low thorn scrub spread out tentacles of lilac shadow. Then, as it dipped even lower, the lilac shadows ran together in dusky hues.

With a start Yasmin glanced at her watch.

'It's getting late. I'd better return Blitzen. Coming?'

'No,' I said stretching languidly. When I saw her look of disappointment, I changed my mind. 'OK, I'll walk with you to the main road.'

She walked beside me, leading Blitzen. When we reached the road, I stopped. 'This is as far as I'm going,' I said.

She put her foot into the stirrup and gracefully swung her leg over. The horse trotted along the shoulder of the road, Yasmin sitting perfectly erect. She was a good rider. She told me that Miss Fitzsimmons had often complimented her on her excellent posture.

I could see why, I thought, as I watched her. I was really proud of her, but I was a little concerned about the situations she got herself into. First it was Cobus, now it was Andrew Jordaan, the French kisser.

I stood watching her until she got to the turn-off. She looked back once and waved. I was deep in thought and oblivious to the traffic, although I had noticed a small red sports car, which sped by, then stopped, backed up and turned around at the lay-by on the hill. There was something vaguely familiar about it, but Yasmin had already turned off at the track and I didn't give the car a second thought.

By the time I reached the house the sun had edged beyond the horizon and I watched the last rays of sunlight dissolve into darkness.

At nine o'clock Yasmin had still not returned. I made regular trips to the window to peer out, but there was no sign of her. Ma said that she was probably talking to Gladys. She didn't appear to be too concerned, expecting that Gladys would walk her home. Ma, Papa and Nana went to bed, but I stayed up to wait for my sister.

I had a nagging feeling that something was wrong. The image of the red sports car haunted me. But I still couldn't remember where I'd seen it before.

When the others were asleep, I quietly slipped out of the house. The DeSoto was parked in front of the shop. I freed the gear and ran it to the gate. It took ten minutes for me to reach the village because I had to turn off on to a dirt track gutted with pot-holes. There was no sign of Yasmin.

Gladys told me that Yasmin had spent only a short time unsaddling the horse. She had stayed to listen to the drummer for a few minutes and had then left. She said she had told Yasmin not to walk home by herself, but Yasmin had insisted she'd be all right.

The fires in the village had changed from brilliant tongues of light to fists of coal. The young boy was still sitting outside beating his drum, creating a primitive rhythm which in the fading light from the braziers kindled a yearning in me. I wanted to stay longer, but I was worried about Yasmin.

An evening star flickered like a large jewel set in a glittering bed of smaller gems. I could understand why Yasmin had wanted to walk home alone, but I would have felt a lot better had she allowed Gladys to accompany her.

'Maybe she wanted to think,' Gladys said.

I shrugged. 'Maybe she's home by now,' I said hopefully, but I decided to drive across the veld, following the second track to a grove of trees near the road. She often rode in that direction.

Although there was a full moon and it was fairly bright out, I was still unnerved by the immense silence. I drove slowly, bumping over the tracks.

I was thinking about the knack Yasmin had for upsetting me when I picked her up in the car's headlights. She was lying by the grove of eucalyptus trees. My heart almost stopped when I saw her. I leapt out of the car.

'Yasmin!' I cried, running to her. She was lying very still. I shook her, a little more violently then I had intended to. She stirred and opened her eyes.

'Yasmin, what happened?'

'Cobus . . .' she said, struggling to sit up. I helped her to her feet.

It was obvious that something terrible had happened to her. I remembered the red sports car. It all fell into place.

'Oh God, Yasmin,' I muttered as I helped her into the car and turned on the interior lights.

She was a mess, her face dirt-streaked and swollen on one side. She had been crying; there were tracks down the sides of her cheeks. Very gently I touched the bruise on the side of her face.

She winced. 'He hit me,' she said.

I quickly withdrew my hand.

'Please, Meena. Please, I want you to promise that you'll never tell anyone. Ma or Papa or Nana . . . Please . . .' she pleaded, fingering her swollen lips. 'You must promise.'

I hesitated. It was too much to ask of me.

'Please, Meena, not a word . . .'

'But . . .'

'No buts. They'll only blame me. Everyone will blame me.'

'No, they won't. They'll know what to do,' I urged. If only I had gone with her, this might never have happened.

'He was waiting for me. God, it was terrible.'

'Yasmin, we must tell Ma and Papa. They'll know what to do.'

'No!'

'Why not?'

She sobbed quietly. I held her shoulders. 'It's all right,' I soothed. 'It's all right.'

'It was so awful. I tried to get away, but he pinned me down. I fought so hard, Meena. He hit me,' she said touching her cheek.

'Yasmin, we can't keep this to ourselves. We must tell them.' Already I could feel the burden of this terrible secret weighing me down.

'No! He said if I told them, he'd kill them. He'd kill us all.' She paused, fumbling for a tissue. 'We can't tell them, Meena.' She blew her nose on the hem of her blouse. 'I tried to get away.' She tugged again at the ragged hem of her blouse and dabbed her eyes and nose.

I watched her, wondering how we were going to explain her appearance to our parents. In any case, Gladys would know something had happened. We'd have to persuade her to keep quiet.

'He dragged me into the trees. I struggled. I begged him to stop. He said he'd kill me. He was crazy, Meena. I was so scared.'

'Let's not talk about this any more,' I said quickly, putting my arms around her. We sat like that for a while, my mind racing, trying to find an explanation for my parents.

'Promise you won't tell anyone.'

I couldn't say the words.

When we arrived home, Yasmin went straight into the bathroom. She was there for ages and when I went in to see if she was all right, she was scrubbing herself with a brush. In the corner lay her blood-stained panties. Blood and water dripped down the inside of her thighs. I wrapped a towel around her and led her to bed.

16

'MY GOD, Yasmin! What happened to you?' Ma exclaimed in horror the next morning when she saw Yasmin's face.

'Blitzen threw me,' Yasmin said unsteadily.

'I told you!' Papa cried. 'I told you not to get on that damn animal!'

'I'm all right, Papa,' she said, close to tears.

'Why didn't you wake us?' Ma asked sharply.

'I knew you'd fuss. It's nothing really. It was my own fault. We were crossing a track, a branch hit me in the face and I was knocked off the horse.'

'You'll have to see a doctor,' Papa said. 'Something might be broken.'

'Nothing's broken, Papa,' Yasmin said. 'I'll be all right, really I will.' She tried desperately to reassure them.

I sat mutely watching Yasmin, wondering how much longer she could keep the truth from Ma. Already Nana was studying her in the peculiar way she had when she suspected something was not quite right.

'Are you sure that's what happened, Yasmin?' Ma asked, also not quite satisfied with the explanation. 'Are you telling us the truth?'

I wished Yasmin *would* tell them the truth. They'd know what to do. Instead she excused herself and went to lie down.

She bathed constantly. I tried to talk to her again, but each time I mentioned the incident, she compressed her lips into a tight, angry line. Although I felt angry enough to kill Cobus, I was in fact protecting him with my silence.

At night I tried to calm Yasmin as she thrashed around in a frenzy, calling out from the depths of her nightmare.

Would anything ever be the same? Would she ever be able to put her life together again?

'I don't know what's going on with Yasmin,' I heard Ma saying to Nana. 'I don't like it. Something's happened and she's not telling us.'

Ma questioned me. Yasmin, I insisted, had told me nothing. Ma had a way of looking at me, a look which seemed to penetrate to the very core of my being. But loyalty to Yasmin and the fear of Cobus's threat to kill us forced me, against my better judgement, to remain silent.

'Meena, tell us what's going on,' Nana pleaded.

'I told you,' I said. 'I don't know anything.'

But I knew that Nana didn't believe me.

The atmosphere at home crackled with tension. I tried to bury myself in romance novels, transporting myself away from McBain to distant places. The uncomplicated lives of fictional characters was preferable to reality.

Yasmin was morose and uncommunicative. She sat staring into space all day long. It was no wonder Ma and Nana were suspicious.

One Sunday about three months after Yasmin's incident, I accompanied my parents to Oubaas Nel's farm where Papa had arranged to slaughter a sheep.

'Meena, I don't want you around to watch,' he said. 'You always have nightmares. Best you stay home.'

'I'll sit in the car,' I said, desperate to get away from the tension at McBain.

'In that case, you can both come along,' Ma said, directing this comment at Yasmin. 'It might do you good to get out, Yasmin. We've all been cooped up and getting on one another's nerves.' She was clearly hoping the drive would cure whatever was ailing Yasmin.

Yasmin declined. Sensing my anxiety, she cautioned me not to say anything.

We left late that morning. Daniel came with us to help Papa.

Our route took us through Soetstroom. The sight of our old house, as always, stirred memories, and for one exquisite moment I imagined that the old days had returned.

Ma slowed down when we neared the house. It was still vacant. The board identifying Mohammed's General Store was still tacked up and the windows were shuttered. Papa smiled, getting some satisfaction from seeing the property unoccupied. I imagined it would have been a small triumph for him if it stayed that way.

The bare veld was baked to a crust, the ground criss-crossed with cracks. Perched on the naked branches of the trees were the inevitable crows, their cawing an eerie sound in the vast stillness.

The expected bumper crop lay in ruins. The crops planted earlier had shrivelled and died. Ma turned off on to a narrow stretch of tarred road about five miles from Oubaas Nel's farm. Here the wind had eroded the edge of the road leaving large pot-holes which Ma tried to avoid.

She turned into Oubaas Nel's farm.

We stopped at the last gate and Daniel leapt out to open it.

A thorn tree, limbs grotesquely reaching for the sky, provided scant shelter for a herd of goats. Daniel, with a vigilant eye on the crows, waited impatiently for Ma to drive through. He slammed the gate shut the moment we were through and ran for the safety of the car.

'If they're hungry they eat your eyes,' he said in response to my quizzical look.

'That's ridiculous, Daniel,' I said.

'I don't know where you get all these stories from, Daniel,' Ma said, gazing at him in the rear-view mirror.

Oubaas Nel's home came into view.

Aaron Arendse, Willem's father, who still worked there,

directed us to the kraal where Papa, with Daniel's help, selected a young ewe.

After some preliminary exchanges Papa found a level spot, scratched a depression into the ground, removed a clean handkerchief from his pocket and covered his head before starting his prayer.

The animal was brought to Papa. It sensed the danger and resisted. Aaron and Daniel pulled the animal off its legs on to its side, pinning its fore and hind legs.

Papa whet the edge of the knife on a stone, praying as he searched for the jugular vein.

The trapped animal bleated shrilly, its eyes terrified while it awaited the inevitable. Papa parted the wool around its neck, then sliced into the flesh.

'*La, illa ha Illaha* . . .' He started another prayer as the blood pulsed from the severed vein. The sheep's legs jerked and twitched. It shuddered once more and then was still. An opaque film crept over the eyes, freezing its terrified expression. It was all over.

Daniel, with Aaron's help, skinned the sheep and rubbed salt into the hide in order to preserve it for the tannery in town. The offal was gathered for Gladys and the eviscerated carcass was rinsed with the water we had brought with us. While Daniel trussed the carcass into the cardboard box, the crows hovered, lured by the scent of death.

When we got home the carcass was hung in the bathroom, the coolest spot in the house. After two days, just as we were beginning to smell it, Ma instructed Daniel to cut it up into smaller pieces.

On the Wednesday night Ma prepared the sheep's brain for Papa. This and the kidneys were the only organs we saved. The rest were given to Gladys.

Nana looked disgusted when Papa cleaned off his plate with a piece of bread. 'How can you eat that stuff?' she groaned.

Suddenly looking stricken, Yasmin excused herself.

'What's wrong?' Ma asked sharply.

'Nothing,' Yasmin said, as she hurried from the table.

Ma watched her go. She got up from the table and, exchanging a significant look with Nana, she followed Yasmin to our room.

Yasmin was sitting on the edge of the bed. I could see the apprehension in my mother's eyes. It was a look of unspeakable dread, as if she had been preparing for this moment all her life.

She took a deep breath. 'Do you have your period?'

Yasmin shook her head.

'When was your last one?'

Yasmin hesitated.

I sent out a silent prayer for her to tell Ma.

'I asked you a question.' There was something in my mother's tone which sent a shiver down my spine.

'Tell her,' I whispered.

'Tell me what?' Ma demanded.

'No,' Yasmin answered. 'No.'

'You tell me or I'll damn well beat it out of both of you!' Ma said angrily.

Yasmin turned her face to the wall.

'You must tell them,' I said again.

'What's wrong with you, Yasmin?' Ma asked, suspecting that something quite cataclysmic had happened to Yasmin.

Without warning, the story poured from Yasmin's lips.

The transformation in Ma was frightening. She grasped Yasmin's shoulders, shaking her.

'He forced me!'

Dazed, Ma got up off the bed, her anguished eyes finding Nana. She turned from Yasmin and with a wail like that of a wounded animal, she pounded her fists against the wall. 'Why? Why? Dear God, why this?'

Nana, ashen-faced, watched in silence.

Sapped of strength, Ma buried her face in her hands. We waited, stunned, Nana holding Yasmin's hand, shaking her head as if all of this was too much even for her.

I stood aside, watchful and quiet.

Ma turned from the wall and fixed an accusing glance on me. 'You knew about it, didn't you?'

'I made her promise not to tell,' Yasmin said.

'Dear God, Yasmin, why didn't you come to me?'

'I was scared,' she whispered. 'So scared . . .' She burst into tears.

Ma sat on the edge of the bed.

'I was so scared, Ma,' she sobbed.

Ma reached for her, wrapped her arms around her and cradled her head against her breast.

'You should have come to us, Yasmin,' she said, rocking her in her arms. 'No one should have to go through something like this alone. We love you. Oh Yasmin, child, what is it with you?'

Ma knew that Yasmin was pregnant. There was no doubt, though, that the worst was still to come.

'What can we do, Mum?' Ma asked.

'It's too late,' Nana said. 'There's nothing we can do. She should have told us sooner. It's been three months already. What proof do we have now? It'll only be her word against his if we go to the police. You know the law is always on their side.'

We sat on the edge of the bed, our world slowly crumbling. In those few minutes my mother seemed to have aged a lifetime. Nana and I looked on silently. There wasn't much either of us could do.

'This will kill Abdul,' Ma whispered as she caressed Yasmin's hair, holding her tight, afraid of letting her go. 'I wish you'd come to us when this happened. Now it's too late . . .'

'He said he was going to kill all of us if she told anyone,' I said, wanting my mother to understand why Yasmin hadn't gone to them immediately.

'I'm sorry, Ma,' Yasmin whimpered.

Ma tried to comfort her, but it was too much for both of them.

'I don't want this baby,' Yasmin said vehemently, as though wanting to cast her pregnancy off like an item of clothing.

Already she hated the child she was carrying. How would she feel when it was born?

'I don't want it. Get rid of it,' she wailed, over and over again.

Ma drew her into the circle of her arms, stroked her hair and tried to calm her.

'I want an abortion!' Yasmin wailed, teetering on the brink of hysteria.

'We don't know if it's possible, Yasmin. We can't have it done in some filthy little shack where you'll end up with blood poisoning.'

'I don't care if I die! I just want it out of me.'

Ma took Yasmin's face in her hands. She gazed at her for a long time. I noticed then how dull my mother's eyes were, dull and ringed from sleeplessness. 'My child, you've been through so much,' she said. 'If only Meena had gone with you that night . . .'

'Don't blame Meena,' Nana snapped. 'She's suffered enough already. Let's concentrate on what we've got to do.'

It was as though the heart had been ripped out of our family.

Devastated, Papa shrank into the shadows, leaving the women to deal with the situation. He seemed to be miles away, and we often had to repeat ourselves two or three times before he heard or understood.

Once the decision had been made for an abortion, Nana telephoned a friend in Aliwal. It was best to go where Yasmin was not known. An appointment was first made with a doctor to confirm the pregnancy. Nana was impatient. 'We know that she's three and a half months. We don't need a doctor to tell us the obvious.'

Nana's friend Queenie agreed to make arrangements with a local midwife. She had, however, expressed reservations about the abortion, fearing that Yasmin might be too far advanced in her pregnancy. But Nana would not give up.

The Friday evening before the appointment I went into the room where Yasmin was stretched out on her bed, arms folded across her chest, eyes open and unblinkingly fixed on the ceiling.

For a moment I thought she was dead. 'Yasmin!' I cried, grasping her by the shoulders.

'What is it?'

I laughed with relief. 'You gave me a fright.'

'Why?'

'Oh, never mind. How do you feel?'

'Just two more days,' she said, laughing mirthlessly, 'and this thing will be ripped from me.'

'It's not a thing,' I protested. 'It's a baby.'

'You don't understand, do you?'

'All right, all right,' I soothed.

She pushed me aside, leapt off the bed and fled out of the house.

I hurried after her.

The moon was full, just as it had been the night she was raped. I followed as she fled across the veld, stumbling over rocks and lurching into thorn bushes.

'Yasmin, come back!' I called, but she kept on running.

Out of the shadows loomed the dark hump of a koppie. The veld was bathed in an eerie silence. I slowed down. 'Yasmin!' I screamed. There were so many dangers ahead, large crevasses and *dongas*; worse still were the things that could not be seen in the dark. 'You'll get us both killed,' I called desperately.

'Go back!' she cried.

'No!' My voice was shrill with fear. 'You'll hurt yourself.'

I suspected she was heading for the koppie.

She was getting away from me. I ran after her, my terror giving me the added impetus.

I caught up with her and I threw myself at her, knocking her off balance. We fell together, limbs intertwined.

She came to her senses then. 'It's all right, Meena,' she said, out of breath but a lot calmer. 'I'm all right now. I won't try anything stupid again,' she promised.

Supporting each other, we carefully picked our way through the thorn bushes and over the rocks back to McBain.

17

THE DOCTOR confirmed what we already knew: the foetus was fourteen weeks old. He was sympathetic, but because of our fear of a system of justice which punished the victim and rewarded the offender, we told him nothing.

Afterwards we went to the midwife. When we told her that Yasmin was fourteen weeks pregnant, she would have nothing to do with the abortion. Although we had half expected her response, we were disappointed.

We spent the night with Queenie and left for home early the next morning. Yasmin was stretched out on the back seat, looking deathly pale. I was perched on the edge of the seat next to my sister. Watching the movement of her eyes beneath the closed lids, I knew that she was awake.

The drive home seemed interminable.

In the grey light of dawn I was touched by a strange longing, a vague nostalgia that tugged at my heart. Nana sighed and seemed to settle deeper into her seat.

In *Desperate Moments*, Jennifer had said a tearful goodbye to Martin at the lake. It was sunrise then too. Sunrise. The dawning of a new day, a new life.

We passed farmhouses where animals grazed in open kraals, then again we returned to miles of veld, scorched and baked by the sun.

The DeSoto laboured up the hills, wisps of mist hovered and then trailed away behind us. Down below us a valley opened in a patchwork of green and ecru and the mist thinned and dissolved.

The haze from the cooking fires and braziers covered the valley.

Ma coasted down the hill past the turn-off to *Twee Jonge Gezellen*. Afraid of upsetting Yasmin, we said nothing; instead, Ma pushed the car into gear before it could grind to a halt and the engine jerked into life.

When we approached the turn-off to Soetstroom she slowed down from force of habit, then remembered that we no longer lived there and increased speed.

'What are we going to do now?' Nana asked.

'I don't know, Mum.'

'If only she had spoken up earlier,' Nana said tiredly.

We were all suffering from the same weariness. A weariness which seemed to weigh down one's soul, drowning it in misery.

'What is it with our girls, Mum? There's Dora Oliphant and her tragedy too. I thought getting Yasmin away from Soetstroom . . .' They spoke in low tones, not wanting us to hear the details of Dora's death. These, however, were common knowledge to any student who had ever attended SAPS.

Ma shot an anxious glance over her shoulder. Yasmin's eyes were still closed.

'Well, Delia,' Nana said. 'I never had much call for the way you and Abdul spoilt her. In my book, pretty isn't everything. Neither of you gave her a chance to grow. You were always there to pick her up and carry her over the bumps. She's not a bad girl. Beneath all that vanity and self-centredness, there's a spark of something really special . . . If only you'd listened to me . . .'

'Please don't start, Mum,' my mother said irritably.

'Poor child. Always hankering for something just beyond her reach. I feared for her from the day she was born. I always hoped she would accomplish something special with her life. That's why the private school seemed a good idea. It seems we were wrong.'

Ma brushed away her tears.

We reached the turn-off to McBain. Aware of the change in road surface, Yasmin's eyes flickered open.

'Are you all right?' I asked.

Yasmin smiled bravely, grimacing as the car bumped over a pot-hole.

Dust filled my nostrils and hung in little puffs in the car. Ma tried to avoid the ruts in the driveway. But we were home and her shoulders relaxed.

It was still early and the place was deathly still. For the first time in my life I felt completely overwhelmed, like a small speck of dust in a gigantic universe.

In the weeks that followed Yasmin lost interest in everything. Ma had to persuade her to get out of bed long enough to bathe. Her beautiful hair was plastered to her scalp in limp strands. I waited anxiously for the old Yasmin to reappear; Ma and Nana exchanged worried glances as they waited too.

To escape the tension, I started walking along the railway tracks, skipping stones off the rails. Home was not a place I wanted to be any more.

Whenever I passed the railway cottages, I noticed a young girl of about my age standing in the yard of the middle cottage. She was always watching me, eyes wide with curiosity.

Sometimes I followed the tracks to the crossing, skipped over the lines and hurried towards the koppie, wanting to sit at the top of the world so that I could regain perspective.

From the summit I had a good view of McBain and the siding. Alone in this vast open space, the problems lifted away. It was winter and a cold wind whipped at my hair as I huddled into my jacket. In the distance the railway tracks snaked out of sight.

I climbed even higher, hoisting myself up on to a flat boulder. Down below me the thorn bushes were clustered in small clumps. Aloe bushes dotted the landscape; tall cacti with lance-like leaves crowned by racemes of bright orange flowers, they stood aloof and majestic against the barren landscape.

Yasmin had always dominated our lives. Somehow we had always recovered, rolling with the punches, but this time I doubted that our lives would ever be the same again. This tragedy had virtually crippled us. I tried to understand what it was about

Yasmin that could make one love her passionately one moment and hate her the next. I felt a twinge of guilt about the direction my thoughts had taken and tried to banish the anger and disappointment.

Nana said that Yasmin attracted trouble like a magnet.

But she had also said that this was a period of darkness. Yasmin could not be blamed for what had happened to her.

There was yet another life to worry about. A child. Her child. Disowned. Despised. I imagined a little face, tiny hands, groping. I sat for a long time trying to sort out my jumbled thoughts. By the time I made my way down the hill, the sun had already edged towards the horizon. A few weak rays clung to the mountain, penetrating the clouds, bathing them in an incandescent light. These were soon dragged down, leaving large shadows in their wake.

Ma decided that it was essential for Yasmin to have regular check-ups and made an appointment to see Dr Hoffman in town.

I waited with Ma in the office while Dr Hoffman completed his examination of Yasmin.

He followed Yasmin out of the cubicle into his office, shutting the door behind him.

'You have neglected your health,' he scolded. 'Look at all this' – pointing to the reports on his desk – 'one thing after another. Are you a little bit crazy?'

Ma leaned over to catch a glimpse of the reports while Yasmin's eyes blazed defiantly.

'All right, never mind,' he said. 'I don't care about your craziness. But I care about your baby.'

Behind the doctor hung a painting of a scene entitled *Platteland*. The subject was a derelict farmhouse in the midst of wheat fields in the Orange Free State.

'Your pelvis is too small and your baby is not in a good position,' Dr Hoffman explained.

Yasmin's eyes shifted indifferently to the *Platteland* painting.

'You have gained too much weight. There is no excuse for

such neglect,' he said reproachfully.

Yasmin remained detached. She had hoped right from the beginning that the baby would die. She had even thought of going the route of Dora Oliphant, but I told her that it would be a horrible way to end her life.

Dr Hoffman's lips moved, but Yasmin was not listening.

Suddenly she gasped and placed a hand on her stomach.

Dr Hoffman smiled. 'Was that the first time you have felt it move?' he asked.

She nodded.

He exchanged glances with Ma. '*Ja*. It is a bit early, but not unusual,' he said, studying her, his thick brows coming together. 'I want to see you again next week.'

Yasmin nodded, a little more alert now.

'All right then. See you next week Monday.' He held the door open for us.

My father's shoulders had become permanently stooped, as if the invisible burden he carried had become too much for him. His whole posture was that of a man grown weary of life.

'I hope his heart doesn't act up again,' Ma said, watching him.

Yasmin grew bigger and more awkward, caring nothing about her health. She ate to excess against the doctor's instructions. She had gained twenty-five pounds and was enormous. Once she had accepted that nothing could be done to terminate the pregnancy, she bore it with grim stoicism.

'I think she's going to have a girl,' Nana predicted. But Yasmin shut her ears and her mind. She had withdrawn from all of us, sitting by the stove like a statue through that cold winter, while the rest of us worried about her.

Life went on in its rhythmic, endless cycle: in spring the rains came, succouring the thirsty grass roots, washing away the dust which for months had crept over everything. The farmers were overjoyed as the rains filled the rivers and gullies, the parched earth lapping up the moisture, healing the cracks and restoring the vitality to the land.

'Come on. Let's go for a walk,' I suggested one Sunday morning after the sky had cleared. 'The doctor says you need lots of exercise.' The sun was out again and it was a beautiful fresh day. A new day. A new beginning.

Yasmin looked at me listlessly. She had no interest in doing anything at all.

After the rain the veld was a festival of insect industry, life having returned to the slaked earth: butterflies, ants, termites, centipedes and slugs all scrambled for food.

I took huge gulps of the fresh air. Thousands of white butterflies hovered above the pale green stubble. The air was alive with the flutter of wings.

'Yasmin,' I said timidly. 'I'm so sorry about everything. Talk to me, please.'

She stopped in her tracks and stared at me for a minute. Then she walked on, increasing her pace so that I had to hurry to keep up with her.

'Yasmin, this isn't your fault. You have nothing to be ashamed of,' I called after her as I stumbled over the stones. She ignored me. 'Yasmin!' I called again.

She paused, turning to wait for me. I caught up with her and when our eyes met for a brief moment, I thought I saw a flicker of the old spirited Yasmin. Then it was gone and she turned away from me, shutting the door again. 'I don't want to talk about it,' she said.

'It's only a baby. The poor thing knows nothing about you, or its father, or the way in which it came to life.'

'I told you, I don't want to talk about it,' Yasmin snapped.

'It's innocent.'

'No, it's not! It breathes. It moves. It knows everything. How could it be innocent?'

My sister was clearly not going to listen to reason.

'I'm going back home,' Yasmin said abruptly. 'You can go on if you like. I'm not in the mood for any of this.'

18

ONE EVENING while we were sitting outside on the stoep my mother told us that my father had gone to see Hermanus Steyn. She said he had done the right thing, but had ended up being humiliated. My mother was trying to keep her emotions under control for Yasmin's sake but, irritated by the direction the conversation was taking, Yasmin got up and went indoors.

She returned later with a cup of tea and stood in the doorway for a moment. Suddenly she drew in her breath sharply, her expression amazed, almost incredulous, as a thin stream of liquid ran down the inside of her leg.

Her waters had broken. Ma was the only calm one amongst us. She helped Yasmin to a chair and then hurried off to telephone the hospital and Dr Hoffman. Nana grabbed a few items of Yasmin's clothing while I helped her to the car. We were not prepared because she wasn't due for another three weeks.

Papa insisted on accompanying us and sat in the front seat with Ma, staring into the darkness, occasionally muttering and massaging his head as he did whenever he was troubled.

Nana and I sat in the back seat, comforting Yasmin whenever she cried out. Papa never turned his head, but he seemed to cringe, sinking deeper into his seat, each time she had a contraction.

Dr Hoffman was angry because we had not come sooner and swore softly in German. Ma tried to explain that we had left the moment Yasmin's contractions started.

Yasmin was wheeled off to the labour room. There was a strange, ethereal quality to the scene.

We followed Yasmin, but one of the nurses instructed us to remain in the waiting-room. Dr Hoffman's voice reached us through the door, shouting for Yasmin to bear down. As soon as the nurses were out of sight, Ma and I peeped through the small window in the door. Yasmin's legs were in a stirrup and one of the nurses was preparing a syringe.

I recognised the sickly sweet odour of ether. Soon it would be surging through her veins, freezing her blood, I thought.

Terrified, Yasmin cried out for Ma. Ma squeezed my hand anxiously. Yasmin was facing away from us and we could see only the top of her head and her stirruped legs.

A nurse gestured for us to get away from the door, but we kept creeping back.

A young nurse leaned over Yasmin encouraging her as she writhed and struggled, pushing until her body, arched and rigid, lifted off the bed.

'You'll be all right,' the nurse reassured her. By this time Yasmin was beyond caring, drifting on a cloud of narcosis.

Dr Hoffman was squatting out of sight between her raised legs. Only his voice could be heard as he called out gruffly: 'Bear down now, Yasmin! Bear down!'

There was no response from Yasmin.

'Come on! Dammit!' Dr Hoffman's angry voice sent a chill through me. 'Do you want to kill the baby? The cord is wrapped around its neck!'

'Yes! Yes! I want to kill it!' she screamed.

'Get the tray!' he shouted at the nurse. 'The baby is in the passage!'

We heard the clatter of stainless steel on stainless steel.

'What are you doing to me?' Yasmin cried.

'Come on, push!' Dr Hoffman shouted.

'Leave me alone!' Yasmin screamed.

'Here, let me help.' Dr Hoffman had appeared from below somewhere. It had to be from hell, because at that moment he was like a demon. The nurses moved aside while he placed Yasmin's right foot against his shoulder.

'You hate me!' he shouted. 'You have your chance to fight me now. Come on!'

In a surge of helpless rage she kicked against him and pushed.

'Good! Good!' he cried.

They placed a mask over her face. Dr Hoffman disappeared again and when he straightened up we saw the baby covered in blood and birth fluid, eyes tightly shut, writhing in the doctor's hands.

I heard the first cry; it was weak but persistent. I stared at the tiny scrap of humanity, tears coursing down my cheeks. It had come into the world hated and rejected, but there was something in its cry, a tenacity perhaps, that clearly indicated a determination to survive.

This was a baby that was not going to be pushed aside. It already had a personality of its own, I thought as I watched it – mouth wide open, screaming at the top of its lungs.

The baby was a beautiful little girl with pale blue eyes and although her hair was dark, there were indications that it would become lighter. She was the most beautiful infant I had ever seen. My heart went out to her. None of us could tear ourselves away from the nursery where the baby remained in an incubator.

'Yasmin, you can't take your anger out on the child. It's not her fault,' Ma pleaded when Yasmin refused to visit her baby.

But Yasmin merely turned her face towards the wall.

'What are we going to do, Abdul?' Ma asked.

'We're going to take our grandchild home when she's well, whether Yasmin wants it or not,' Papa said.

'Yasmin, you'll have to name the baby.'

'Do what you want,' she said listlessly.

'Why don't you call her Fatima?' Papa suggested. 'It was my mother's name.'

I suggested Soraya, after the Empress of Iran. I had seen pictures of her and thought her the most beautiful woman in the world.

Ma seemed a bit hesitant to stray into that exotic domain,

but eventually compromised. The baby was named Soraya Fatima Mohammed.

'Fine,' Yasmin said, shrugging.

She was discharged a week later and two weeks after that the baby was strong enough to come home. Yasmin remained detached from both the baby and the family, displaying very little interest in either. The rest of us doted on Soraya, tending to her every whim.

'You've got to pull yourself together, Yasmin,' Ma scolded. 'Your baby needs you.' But Yasmin was in such a deep depression that none of us could reach her, not even Dr Hoffman who tried his best to get through to her.

Eventually Ma was obliged to tell him about Yasmin's rape. He was appalled that none of us had reported the incident.

'If you had taken her to a doctor right away, things might have been different,' he said. 'Now you can prove nothing.'

'It would have been a waste of time,' Ma said bitterly. 'The man's white, the son of a prominent member of the Afrikaner community.'

For two months we struggled to get through to Yasmin. Then quite unexpectedly she seemed to recover and became her old jaunty self again, spending hours before the mirror, curling her hair and applying her make-up. Ma watched, filled with misgivings. Nana, too, gazed penetratingly at her.

'What are you doing?' Nana demanded.

'I'm making myself presentable,' Yasmin responded. 'Isn't that what you want?'

'It's what *you* want that counts,' Ma interjected.

'Oh no. Up to now it's been what you want.' Yasmin got up from the dresser, her eyes blazing with defiance. 'I had that baby because you wanted it.'

'What are you talking about, child? You know that it was too late. There was nothing we could do.'

'I hate it! I never want to see it!' she said, storming out of the room.

'Yasmin!' Ma was horrified. She looked helplessly at Nana.

There were new undertones to Yasmin's emotional state. Nana sensed it and was afraid.

'Don't bottle your feelings,' I urged. 'Talk about it. You'll feel a lot better.' She was in the kitchen, reluctantly helping to prepare Soraya's formula. 'Life isn't all that bad. You have your baby now and . . .'

'Life! What do you know about life?' Yasmin cried, clamping her hand on my arm.

I stared at her in astonishment.

'What do you know about life?' she demanded again, her voice hoarse with emotion.

'What do you mean?'

'I mean like living and hurting. Not hiding in this damn place.'

I knew a little, I thought. I'd also been hurting for a long time. 'I know,' I said eventually, trying to free myself from her hold. But she wouldn't let go.

'What do you know?' she demanded, her face contorted. 'Do you know about being raped . . . and . . . and wanting to die?'

I shrank from her.

'How can you know about anything?' she cried. 'All your life you've been protected by two fussing women. In their eyes you're a saint. You can't do a thing wrong, can you? I'm the devil. Maybe I am. I've been through it all.' She paused for breath. 'I wanted to tear that baby out bit by bit. How can I be expected to love it after all the loathing and hate I feel for its father?'

'Then hate the father, but not the child!'

'I've had nine months of hate growing inside me!' she spat, each word like the thrust of a knife.

'What makes you think you're an authority on pain and suffering?' I retaliated. 'What about the suffering of others? What about that baby?'

Yasmin covered her ears.

'Yes, *your baby*!' I cried. 'How can you blame a helpless little baby? And what about us? We have to stand by and see you tearing yourself apart, watching while you turn from that child which is a part of you. Don't you think we suffer too?'

Yasmin hunched her shoulders, pressing her hands against her ears.

'Instead of pulling yourself together . . . pulling your life together, you're wallowing in self-pity. You still think you're so damn special! Sometimes I think you deserve to be miserable.'

Yasmin dropped her hands. 'I don't think I'm so special.' Her voice had lost its brittleness.

I screwed the top on the feeder. Suddenly I felt worn out.

'Forget everything I said.' Her voice had changed again. It flowed like warm syrup.

19

UNABLE TO sleep that night, I crept out of the bedroom and went to lie in the front room. I stretched out on the sofa and squeezed my eyes shut until bright points of light shimmered and danced before my aching eyeballs. I tried to force myself out of that miserable environment into the tranquil world of my childhood, but it seemed impossible to make the transition.

The little space in which I had taken refuge as a child no longer existed. Instead, I felt myself being sucked into a vortex of colliding images. Terrified, I tried to stop myself from plummeting into this maelstrom. My hands were clammy, my heart pounding anxiously. A fine film of moisture had formed on my body and I could feel myself shivering with fear.

Suddenly a voice called. I heard the voice as if from a great distance – the urgency of its tone dragging me back. My eyes were tightly shut, part of me not wanting to relinquish the dream.

'Meena! Meena!'

It was Yasmin.

Reluctantly, I opened my eyes. My vision slowly adjusted to the darkness until I was able to discern the faint outline of my sister's body, nightgown wrapped tightly about her.

'I know you're here,' she whispered. 'I can hear you breathing.'

'I'm on the sofa.'

Yasmin groped her way in the darkness. Her hand brushed against my legs and I quickly withdrew from her touch.

'Move up, Meena,' she hissed impatiently.

I could see her clearly now.

'I want to talk to you.'

'What about?'

'About the baby.'

I waited, but she was silent.

Finally she said: 'Meena, I'm going away.'

'Why? Where? Are you mad?' Questions tumbled from my lips.

'I can't bear the thought of causing any further unhappiness.'

'You're going to leave your baby and you want my approval?' I asked, laughing mirthlessly.

'Stop it,' she said. 'I've tried . . . I can't.' Her voice was ragged. 'I'm sorry.'

'Don't say sorry to me! Have you told Ma and Papa?'

She did not answer.

I sat up. 'You've always known how to hurt people, haven't you, Yasmin? You're an expert – especially at hurting those who love you. And after you've done, you flutter your eyelashes and say you're sorry. Well, sorry isn't good enough. When are you going to grow up? When are you going to face your responsibilities? Face the fact that Soraya is your daughter, and nothing you do is going to change that!' The anger flew off me like sparks off a flint.

'None of this was my fault,' Yasmin protested.

'It's never your fault,' I mocked. 'It's always the next person. Look what you've done to this family!'

There was no response.

'No, you'll never know,' I said, her silence reaching me. 'You don't care about anything or anyone.'

'I'm sorry,' Yasmin whispered.

'Sorry doesn't bring the broken pieces together, Yasmin!'

She remained silent. I flicked the light on. Her eyes were tightly shut against the pain of my words. She sensed the light on her face and her eyes flew open.

I stared at her, brought my face up close to hers and in the voice of a stranger I hissed: 'I should never have pulled you back off that koppie.'

Yasmin looked away.

'Maybe we would all have been better off with you dead,' I said harshly.

The colour drained from her face. I immediately regretted my outburst and went to her. I put my arms around her and held her close, sharing her anguish as only a sister could.

Yasmin was subdued. I didn't know whether or not to tell Ma about her plans to leave. There appeared to be a new level of hostility between them. They weren't speaking, avoiding each other for days on end. It was all building up. I could only hope that Yasmin would come to her senses.

The storm broke one Thursday night when Yasmin, in a state of depression, neglected to feed Soraya.

'Starving your own child!' Ma shouted angrily. 'You're a monster!' Without a word, Yasmin turned and walked away.

'Come back here and take care of your baby!'

Yasmin ignored her.

'You get back here!' Ma, blinded by rage, caught hold of her and swung her around. Then she struck her with such force that Yasmin was thrown off balance.

It was the first time in Yasmin's life that either of our parents had ever raised a hand to her. She was stunned, but the look she gave Ma was filled with such unspeakable contempt that Ma, startled, took a step back.

That night the house was very quiet. Something deep and disturbing had taken place and we all felt it.

When we got up on the Friday morning, Yasmin was gone. Ma sat staring at the fire, Soraya in her arms. Papa went to her, but she remained motionless. He put his arm around her; still she did not move. Finally, she got up, handed Soraya to me and went to the phone. She spoke to the police in town. Then she phoned Aishaben. She asked them to let us know if they or any of their friends heard from Yasmin.

'Where does one begin to look?' Ma asked.

She drove around like a crazed woman, conducting a senseless search. Then she ranted about Yasmin's selfishness. 'What about her child? Does she not care?'

Nana shook her head.

'She's always thought only of herself, never considered the next person,' Ma cried.

'It's too late for recriminations now,' Nana said.

Ma broke down then, her body heaving with uncontrollable sobs.

Nothing we said or did could comfort her. All her pent-up frustrations, disappointments and anger were released in torrents of tears.

'It's a period of darkness,' Nana explained. 'It comes into everyone's life. Yasmin chose her own course a long time ago.'

Ma tried to compose herself. She wanted to generate an aura of calm strength, but Nana was the one we leaned on in those difficult days.

The house seemed desolate.

'Yasmin is strong-willed,' Nana said. 'She's a survivor.'

Ma desperately needed reassurance and Nana gave it gladly.

'Yasmin's more capable of surviving out there than anyone else I know,' Nana said. 'The baby will be better off with us and she knows it.'

I tried to blot my sister out of my mind but, as always, she dominated our lives, even in her absence.

'There was nothing here for Yasmin,' Nana remarked. 'This place is like a desert.'

'This is our home, Mum. A place of refuge.'

Nana disagreed. 'Not here, not in this country. It won't be long before they'll be back again with their dogs and their guns.'

The issue of Yasmin and what to do now was like a huge boulder heaved into the tiny pool of our lives; the ripples from that boulder were like a tidal wave that threatened to engulf us.

MOTHERS

20

SORAYA WAS a baby, barely two months old, when Yasmin left.

'She'll be back,' Nana said.

But I was not as sure as my grandmother that Yasmin would return. Too much had happened.

We all blamed ourselves. I couldn't forget my final confrontation with her. The ugliness of the things that were said . . . but then one never knew where one stood with Yasmin. Nothing about her was predictable.

Meanwhile, life continued. Yasmin would never know what she'd put us through. And there was no word from her. For all we knew she could have been dead. It was a thought that had crossed all our minds, but none of us dared voice it.

In the weeks that followed Yasmin's departure, I watched as my parents' anger and disappointment quietly consumed them. Like a cancer it devoured their love, poisoning them against each other.

Their silence only increased my own feelings of isolation. Whenever I mentioned Yasmin's name in my mother's presence, her eyes would become distant and she'd retreat to some safe place in her mind, cutting herself off from the rest of us.

Nothing we said or did relieved my mother's anguish at losing Yasmin. I tried to comfort her, but it was as if she had turned to stone. Confused and hurt by her indifference, I turned to my grandmother for comfort.

It took a long time for Ma to come to terms with her pain.

Resentful and bitter, she blamed me for the way Yasmin had left.

I hated Yasmin for what she had done to us, hated her for the way she had torn us apart, and in particular for the way I had been set emotionally adrift by my mother.

Nana was still there for me, pouring out affection and attention. She was the one who insisted that I keep up with my studies while I waited for my parents to find a suitable school for me. Yasmin's actions had left us all dangling in a state of suspended animation. All I could do was wait for the decisions about my future and these seemed to take for ever.

Finally, after months of debate, my parents agreed that I could attend school in town, twenty-eight miles away, commuting back and forth daily. I started the following February after having missed more than eighteen months of schooling.

Private school, of course, had never been an option for me. The cost of keeping Yasmin at a private school for two years had practically wiped out our resources. Even if we had been able to afford the fees, my father would never have consented. I accepted this decision. Without rancour or complaint, I travelled the twenty-eight miles to school and back each day.

In the mornings the rickety bus owned by Venter & Son stopped across the road from McBain belching smoke. There was no fixed schedule and I often had to wait alongside the road for ages. In winter, shivering with cold, I used to try to keep warm by stamping my feet on the frost-covered ground.

The passengers, a mixture of workers and students, sat with eyes closed, heads lolling, numbed by sleep.

Sandile, a young African student who attended the Bantu School in town, was a tall skinny boy, two years older than me. Our friendship developed on the bus to school.

Sandile lived in a hut on the Bosman Farm about eight miles from McBain where his father worked as a labourer. His older brother worked in Johannesburg and when Sandile outgrew the small flat-roofed, one-roomed farm school, which only went up to standard three, his father, determined to give him an education, sent him to the town school.

We felt comfortable with each other. His large, sombre eyes seemed to look into all the little nooks and crannies where my secret thoughts lurked. I told him things that I would never have dreamed of telling anyone else. He, too, told me things that he had never spoken about before.

One day as we bounced home in a nearly empty bus, he told me that he was going to be a doctor. He said this with such conviction that I never doubted him for a moment.

Sandile showed me a scar on his leg which ran almost the entire length of his calf. He told me that when he was about seven years old he was attacked by a crocodile when he and his friends were swimming in a river. He was lucky to have escaped with just the scar. He could have lost his leg or, worse still, his life.

I could only imagine the horror of being dragged into the murky depths of a river, a crocodile's jaws clamped around my leg.

'My mother believes it was a miracle that I was not killed. She thinks my life was spared for a special purpose – to become a doctor.' He paused. 'I never missed one day of school. I was lucky that this happened in the holidays and the nurse at the clinic near my village stitched it all together.' Sandile smiled proudly, wearing his scar like a badge of honour.

I thought about Sandile, his mother and the crocodile and once again struggled to understand the vagaries of life.

In the mornings the loud and noisy banter between passengers made communication between us difficult. The two of us, squashed between sweaty bodies, stood swaying in the aisle, Sandile straddling his big suitcase.

Tied to their backs, women carried screaming infants, or parcels of goods they hoped to sell at the market. Live chickens wrapped in blankets or tied in cloth bundles, agitatedly pecked at their restraints.

In winter the windows fogged up, making it impossible to see out. At each stop the driver, using his balaclava, took a desultory swipe at the inside of the windscreen. As soon as the doors closed, the windows fogged up again.

The odours of food, wood smoke, sweat, unwashed bodies,

tobacco, mother's milk and urine remained trapped in my clothes and hair. My mother, still heart-broken over Yasmin, noticed none of my discomfort.

Months after Yasmin left the house was still littered with reminders of her. Her brush on the dresser still held strands of her hair and her sandals remained neatly placed under the bed. The top dresser drawer held her jumble of hairclips, half-used tubes of dried-out lipstick and cracked cakes of jet-black mascara, which Ma couldn't bring herself to dispose of.

But these constant reminders of Yasmin only served to increase my loneliness – a loneliness which seemed to creep over me, paralysing me. I continued to escape the tension at home by walking along the deserted rail track, one foot carefully placed ahead of the other, arms extended like a tight-rope walker balanced hundreds of feet above the ground.

Nana was the only one who noticed my restlessness. 'Yasmin escaped, but at what price?' she warned.

Despite the heartache, our lives were not completely hopeless. Occasional incidents provided lighter moments, like the marriage of Tandi, one of Gladys's stepdaughters. She was a few years older than me and quite lovely and Gladys was very fond of her.

There was much discussion and anxiety about this marriage. One would have sworn Nana was giving away the last of her daughters. We attended the reception in the village for a couple of hours. A cow was slaughtered and the celebrations continued for three days – with Gladys all the while hovering around Tandi like a broody hen. Soraya was a bit jealous of the attention lavished on Tandi.

But although she cared for all her husband's children from his others wives, especially Tandi, Soraya always had a special place in Gladys's heart.

We were very protective of Soraya. Later, whenever she needed someone to wipe her tears or hear her stories, one of us was always willing to listen. No one was more willing than Papa.

Right from the time she was a baby, Papa had always made

sure he was within petting distance of her. When he and Daniel sat on the stoep weighing mealie meal, Soraya would be close by in her baby carriage. Daniel, too, doted on her, especially now that his status had been elevated from labourer to friend and companion to my father.

Daniel, however, still had his way of tuning out to things around him. Although he smiled and nodded, most of what Papa said seemed to slide right past him.

He had stories of his own, a fantasy world pieced together from the FBI and John Wayne movies he used to watch through a broken window at the Soetstroom hall.

'I am FBI,' he would say.

Occasionally, when the mood took him, he'd whip out the faded, water-stained letter salvaged from a rubbish heap to prove his claim. But we were accustomed to his eccentricities and paid no attention.

Often Daniel marched around the yard, a broom held up against his shoulder like a rifle while he strutted like one of Hitler's goose-stepping soldiers and gave the Nazi salute.

Daniel loved war films. One of the ways his madness seemed to manifest itself was in his impersonation of Hitler. He had once even tried to grow a moustache like Hitler's and Nana swore he was trying to coax his hair over his forehead – an almost impossible feat when one considered the texture of his hair.

'Imagine having another Hitler. And a black one *nogal*,' Nana laughed. 'What greater madness than that!'

The idea was so preposterous that we could only watch helplessly and despairingly as he sank into and then emerged from his bouts of madness. There was nothing we could do for him because Daniel had none of the documentation required to get him the help he needed.

While Papa and Daniel swapped stories, Soraya kept Ma and Nana busy.

Meanwhile I continued my walks along the tracks as I struggled to come to terms with the complexities of the adult world.

I became familiar with the feel of the steel rails beneath my bare feet. Eventually I was able to detect the approach of a train by the slightest tremor along the rails.

Like *songololos*, the long, flat freight trains slowly crept through the veld each day. There were two passenger trains, one from Johannesburg in the morning and the other in the opposite direction in the evening. The three short blasts at the crossing, and then a sustained whistle as it entered the siding and sped by, were a familiar feature of life at McBain.

On my walks I skimmed pebbles off the rails, enjoying the 'ping' of stone ricocheting off steel.

Solitude became a way of life. The sluggishness of our environment encouraged it.

The whites at the siding kept their distance, preferring to shop at the OK Bazaar in town. The villagers, with their small purchases of staple foods, were the only ones who regularly patronised our little trading store at McBain.

'Patience,' Papa said, as he stared at the desolate landscape from the back stoep. 'Patience. Things will come right. One of these days they'll build the main road past our place and business will boom.'

Nana's scornful gaze settled on Papa. 'Patience! Look where we are!' she cried indignantly, making an expansive gesture towards the veld.

'All you ever do is talk, talk, talk!' Ma complained, having heard the same debate many times before.

I missed my sister terribly. I was not as clever with words as Yasmin, who had the ability to shock the adults with her irreverence. That was the Yasmin I had known and loved. The laughing, teasing, impossible Yasmin. Not the sullen, hollow-eyed, troubled girl she later became.

About four months after Yasmin left, I became friendly with Elsa Botha, the daughter of one of the Afrikaner railway workers at the siding.

The Bothas' cottage was the smallest of the three. It sat, squat and awkward, between the two other cottages. Anna Botha, Elsa's mother, face eclipsed in the shadowy interior, watched from behind the screen door as I passed the cottage on my excursions into the veld. She never left the house. Ma and Nana were critical about the way she neglected her children.

None of us knew then that in the dim interior of their cottage Elsa's mother was drinking her life away.

The cottages all faced the track, the hub of the railway workers' lives. Our house, about three hundred yards away, had its back to the tracks and faced the road.

Elsa's father started coming to the shop. Unlike the siding master with his cascading belly, Mr Botha was tall and thin. He addressed my parents politely as Mr and Mrs Mohammed. Nana he addressed as *Mevrou*. Whites usually called Papa 'Abraham' – a generic term used to address Indian males. It didn't matter what their names were, to the local whites all Indian men were Abraham. It never dawned on them that the name was identified more frequently with the Jewish culture. Women did not even warrant acknowledgement. Whites spoke over their heads as if they were invisible. But Mr Botha was different. He seemed humble and respectful, almost diffident.

Whenever he came over he and Papa conversed about issues of common concern, usually about the railways and the impending closures. Mr Botha was afraid that the government was about to shut down most of the lines in the surrounding towns. Over time a dissatisfied tone crept into his voice, as though he felt betrayed by his government. How was he going to support his family, he wanted to know. Already they were struggling to survive on his paltry salary.

Papa didn't have to be told about struggle. Out of habit his eyes turned veldwards. 'They can't close this line,' he said quietly, almost hopefully. 'It's the main line, an important line to the coast.'

Mr Botha, one foot on the top step, the other two steps down, leaned into his bent knee, scraped the dottle from his pipe and then filled it from the pouch of Horseshoe tobacco he carried in his pocket. His gaze followed Papa's into the veld as he placed the pipe stem in his mouth. Thoughtfully chewing on it, he asked: 'You really think so?'

Papa nodded, convinced that some day the main road too would pass right by McBain.

The two men fell silent, bound by a common dream.

With my nodding acquaintance of Mr Botha, I began to forge my friendship with his daughter Elsa. Sometimes from the kitchen window I saw her standing in their backyard – tall and slender, leaning forward like a young sapling bowed by the wind. The cotton dress with its pattern of yellow daisies hung as shapelessly as a sack from her bony shoulders. She appeared and disappeared like an apparition: one moment standing perfectly still, the next she was gone.

Elsa was typical of the poor-white Afrikaner communities. She had very little experience and almost no education. She was a year and a bit older than me and although she had been there all the time, across the tracks at the siding, I hadn't paid her the slightest attention while Yasmin was around. Now loneliness compelled me to pursue her friendship even though I had heard her disparagingly refer to me as a coolie *meid*. After we became friends I talked her out of using the 'C' word.

Education for whites was compulsory, but somehow the Botha family had slipped through the bureaucratic cracks. No one seemed to know or care that Elsa was not at school. Her father, having minimal education himself, did not consider education a priority for girls.

Elsa loafed around the house all day long, ostensibly taking care of her mother and her brother. It was only during her mother's few hours of sobriety that Elsa pretended to care. In the afternoons she slipped away immediately she saw me arriving home from school, waiting for a detailed account of my day's activities. Almost seventeen years old, she could barely write her own name.

Despite her scornful attitude, I taught her to read and write. She was surprisingly clever and it didn't take her long to learn. I taught her to read from an old English reader: the same *Dick and Jane* reader which first Yasmin and then I had used when we had started school.

Faded and yellowed with age, the offensive lines *Coolie, coolie ring the bell; coolie, coolie go to hell* were still visible on the flyleaf which had been pasted back into the book.

After months of tutoring, Elsa was able to read and write. Like a locust, she devoured every book in sight, especially the comics and picture stories, most of which were love stories.

Educating Elsa was not entirely one-sided. I learned a great deal from her, too. What she taught me, though, was often unrepeatable. My acquaintance with profanity came directly from Elsa's lips, either shouted at the top of her voice as we walked the rails, or whispered into my ear when Nana was around. Once when Nana heard her swearing, she threatened to scrub her mouth with soap.

Throughout those years of friendship with Elsa, her mother, Anna Botha, remained a mystery. It didn't matter what time of day I went by, she was always either at the back screen door or at the front door, staring out.

'Does your mother ever leave the house?' I whispered as Elsa and I tried to slip back into the yard without being seen – an impossible feat because it seemed that Anna's eyes were everywhere.

The figure behind the screen door melted into the shadows and Elsa, alarmed, hurried away. 'I will come to your house later!' she called after me.

When Elsa and I were together, we spoke Afrikaans, but there was a sense that the two of us were like the railway tracks, travelling side by side, but destined never to meet.

Elsa had been in our home countless times but I had never once been invited into hers. I had to wait in the yard. Mannetjie, Elsa's four-year-old brother, would be playing bare-bottomed in the sand, nose crusted with dried mucus, his little willie curled like a worm.

Elsa occasionally left McBain without saying a word. Because her father worked for the railways, the family could travel at minimal cost and went to Pretoria regularly to visit Elsa's aunt.

Those were lonely times. I had friends at school, but we never saw each other outside school hours. Besides, I thought Elsa and I had a special bond. I thought we were best friends.

The first time she left, Ma, Nana and I speculated as to her whereabouts.

'Perhaps they've sent her away to school somewhere,' Ma said.

'I don't think so.' It didn't seem at all likely to me that Elsa's parents would have sent her to school.

'I don't know what their mother does all day . . . That poor boy,' Nana said, when she spotted Mannetjie in his usual neglected condition.

Weeks later Elsa returned. I waved frantically from the back stoep, but she ignored me. This was a facet of Elsa I had not seen before – arrogant and distant.

With a dismissive gesture, she told me that walking the rails was childish. As we spoke, I sensed her mother's eyes boring into us.

'Get back in here,' she called from behind the screen door.

'Fuck,' Elsa muttered. 'It's best you don't come here any more.'

'Why?' I asked.

She lifted a bony shoulder and shrugged. 'My mother doesn't want you to come here.'

'Why not?' I asked, surprised that after all this time Elsa's mother would object to our friendship.

'You can see for yourself,' she said, making a wry face.

My glance leapt to the kitchen door where her mother's shadowy figure skulked. She rattled the door impatiently. With a look of panic, Elsa hurried inside. At the door she paused for a moment to look back over her shoulder. In that split second when our eyes met, I saw her trapped, anxious look, eyes like dark, murky pools. There was no opportunity to speak to her the following day because it was Sunday and the Bothas went into town on Sundays.

Sundays at McBain were quiet, uneventful times spent lounging about or reading the paper. In the evenings we turned out the lights and sat on the stoep in the dark. In winter we gathered around the stove in the kitchen and played whist. More often than not, Ma and Papa spent the day worrying about how they were going to pay the merchants.

We had already sold everything of value. Soon after Yasmin left Ma sold the remaining pieces of the precious dinner service, the heirloom which either Yasmin or I was meant to inherit some day. But Ma said there was no point trying to store memories and keepsakes. There was no use growing attached to things because they would only be taken from you.

Nana said one always had to be vigilant.

Had we not been vigilant before? What had we got for all our vigilance? Ma wanted to know.

Nana had no words of reassurance. We had lost our home despite our vigilance. Ma said it was no use having dreams in a country that crushed the aspirations of its people.

Bit by bit Ma had sold every piece of jewellery she owned – all the pieces Papa had bought for her in the good years. Much of it had already been sold to pay for Yasmin's education.

'It's all water under the bridge,' Nana commented, weary of the struggle. 'It's all water under the bridge.'

I thought about the water and the bridge and knew that it was hopeless to wish things back to the way they had been.

I could only stand by and watch helplessly as everything I cherished began to crumble. I also thought of Yasmin and her selfishness.

Nana told me that people with gentle, forgiving natures usually ended up being martyrs. Yasmin was obviously not one of those.

I vowed that I would never end up like my mother, sacrificing myself for others. I didn't want to be a struggling wife and mother, weighed down, breasts sucked dry.

Elsa and I continued to see each other for another year or so.

But whenever I went to her house to look for her, Elsa behaved furtively. It was only when we were away from the house and well on our way into the veld, that she shed her inhibitions.

'One day,' she told me, as we sneaked off to walk the tracks, 'I'll go where no one will ever fucking find me.'

'Why?'

'Just because,' Elsa said, viciously flinging a stone into the distance and narrowly missing a hawk which had swooped down to catch a field mouse. 'Fuck! Fuck! Fuck!' she screamed at the startled hawk.

And then Elsa left for Pretoria once more. I went to the house and her mother spoke to me through the screen door.

'She has gone away for a while,' she said.

'Again?'

'Yes,' she replied.

'For how long?'

'A couple of months, maybe more, maybe less.'

Those few sentences, exchanged through the screen door, constituted the first and only conversation I ever had with Anna Botha.

There was no sign of Elsa's little brother, Mannetjie. Mabel, the Bothas' maid, told us that Mannetjie had been removed to a foster home. Mr Botha didn't come anywhere near the shop for weeks. Nana said he was probably embarrassed that his wife, staggering drunk, had been put on the train to her sister in Pretoria.

21

AS THE months passed Nana began to slow down. At night, unable to sleep, her body racked with pain, she wandered around the house like a ghost. In the mornings she struggled out of bed, complaining about being as stiff as an old plank.

She became increasingly cantankerous, looking for umbrage where none was intended. Gladys, the only one who never questioned her judgement or contradicted her wisdom, sat with her on the stoep, sipping tea from a chipped enamel mug. Gladys understood Nana, she knew what it was like to be a woman, to grow old and have no one to understand the fears and anxieties that kept her awake at night.

I was becoming tired of school and the interminable journey there and back each day. I'd had two years of it now. I couldn't bear the thought of the same routine for another two years. So I made up my mind, worked up enough courage, and told my mother that I had no intention of finishing matric. I wanted to attend Junior Teacher Training College and for this I needed only a standard eight certificate. Apart from nursing, teaching was the only other option available to me.

My father rejected my plans. He had too many misgivings about a boarding establishment; the memory of what had happened to Yasmin still lay heavy on his heart. As a last-ditch effort, Ma pointed out that my salary as a teacher would be of great help because there was barely enough business to keep our heads above water. I waited on tenterhooks while they discussed and argued my fate. My mother finally wore my father down and he agreed. I was to start college the following January.

And so began the next chapter in my life.

The women's college was strictly supervised. The only time I came into contact with the opposite sex was when I went on teaching practice. But none of the boys I met interested me.

I occasionally thought of Sandile, sometimes with such passion that it felt as though something had been ripped out of me, leaving a vague longing.

I listened as the other girls talked about their boyfriends, crudely describing the type of intimacy that I had not experienced yet.

Even if I'd wanted to go as far as some of them had, the knowledge of what had happened to Yasmin was always present. It was only in my fantasies that my lovers were given free rein.

I sometimes imagined myself with Sandile, the two of us as characters in a novel, always by a windswept shore. I have never understood why I had this obsession for windswept shores, or my affinity for water, especially since I had never learned to swim.

I did well at college. I brought my reports home and proudly showed them off. My mother read the comments aloud. Mrs Brodie, my 'methods' instructor, once wrote that I was a 'born teacher'. She had taken me under her wing, compensating for my absent family. I still missed home terribly, though, and visited at every opportunity.

During my last term at college, Papa bought an old model Austin from a deceased farmer's estate. It needed some minor repairs and adjustments which Mr Botha was quite happy to help with and when I started teaching at the primary school in town, I was able to drive to school each day, the nightmarish bus trips finally relegated to the past.

The Austin was like a bug crawling along the road at a top speed of thirty miles per hour. Occasionally some impatient driver whizzed by, hand flung out of the window in a rude gesture. I didn't care that the car was slow. It was my carriage and I was a princess, waving regally to the adoring masses – usually groups of kids walking along the road to one of the farm schools. There were to be many times in my life when the edges of fantasy and reality became blurred.

Soraya loved the old car too and used to wait for me at the gate in the afternoons so she could ride the short distance back to the house with me. She was four years old now and the problem of her isolation remained of concern to us all. Nana worried that she had no friends her own age.

Occasionally Gladys brought over one of her grandchildren to play with her, but she bullied and ordered the other children around so dreadfully that they refused to return. Florence was the only one able to stand up to her.

She was turning into a precocious little girl who preferred to hang around the adults: interrupting, demanding attention, standing on her toes in agitation and tugging and fussing whenever she was ignored. It was clearly time for her to go to school, but Ma said she was too young to commute.

The problem of Soraya's schooling was eventually solved when Ma bought an old blackboard, chalk, slates, books, a table and a couple of chairs. She converted the storeroom into a classroom for Soraya and Florence. While my mother taught the two children, my father insisted on supervising every aspect of Soraya's education, nearly driving us all crazy.

Nothing had changed much in our six years at McBain. Our lives continued along a predictable path, but from time to time some crisis or incident occurred to shake us out of our complacency.

McBain was close to the national road – it by-passed us on the far side of the hill about three miles from the turn-off. Not many vehicles turned off at the junction. We were off the beaten track. No one braved the pot-holed driveway to get to our ancient hand-cranked petrol pump.

For years my mother wrote letters to the supplier complaining about the outmoded pump and the fact that there were no signs on the road to indicate that we were there. The petrol company eventually placed a sign at the turn-off, with an arrow pointing to McBain. But it didn't help. Traffic continued to whizz by, preferring to fill up at a service station in town, where other amenities were provided too. Papa said we had become a ghost trading post.

Then, one wintry Saturday afternoon, an unexpected visitor stopped in. It was bitterly cold outdoors and we were huddled around the paraffin stove in the shop. Papa had stayed in the house, resting in his warm bed. I heard the car coming up the driveway and reached for the keys to the petrol pump. But before I could move, a thickset man with greying hair appeared in the doorway. He stood there for a moment, squinting to adjust his vision to the gloomy interior.

Ma glanced up and a slow look of dawning recognition slid over her face. She half rose out of her chair.

Nana scowled.

Hermanus Steyn, retired Member of Parliament for our district, hesitated on the threshold, his gaze slowly moving from Ma to Nana, to me and then to Soraya. I waited, the petrol pump keys dangling from my hand.

'What are you doing here?' Ma demanded.

Hermanus Steyn looked at her and then at Soraya again.

'Take Soraya to the house, Meena.'

Ma's eyes were like slivers of polished granite as she glared at Hermanus Steyn.

Soraya, reluctant to leave, resisted, curious about the newcomer. She had sensed the undercurrents and was trying to squirm out of my grasp.

Hermanus and Cobus Steyn had created more havoc in our lives than all the storms gathered along the horizon. He was the last person any of us had expected or wanted to see again.

I took Soraya to the house and left her with Papa while I returned to the shop to hear what Hermanus Steyn wanted. When I got back he had already left.

'What did he want, Ma?' I asked.

'To make trouble of course,' Nana said.

'He didn't say,' Ma said, adding, 'but it's obvious he was here to make trouble.'

'Why would he do that?' I asked. 'What does he have to gain?'

'I know more about these things than you do!' my mother said, irritated with my questions.

'Do you think he came to see Soraya?' I asked.

'How would I know!' Ma snapped.

Hurt by her tone, I fell silent.

'The cheek,' Ma muttered, her face still flushed with anger. Her hair had come loose and tumbled down the side of her face.

'Good thing you gave him a piece of your mind, Delia,' Nana said. 'Let's hope he never sets foot here again. If I'd been a man, I'd have given him and his son the thrashing of their lives.'

'What did you say to him?' I asked.

'I told him to stay away from us,' Ma said grimly. 'Better not tell your father he was here. No need to upset him as well.'

The visit in itself was disconcerting, but more worrying was the fact that he had come and gone without stating a reason for his visit. I wondered if he had come solely for the purpose of seeing Soraya, or was there some other reason – perhaps to see if Yasmin was there?

For us, though, the Steyns had done their damage and Hermanus Steyn's dropping in to disrupt our lives was not what we wanted. We wanted to be left alone now. The visit became a nagging concern. Anything related to the Steyns was cause for worry. But nothing further was heard from Hermanus Steyn and our anxiety slowly diminished.

That spring Sandile, who had completed his matric at a mission school in the Transkei, returned and one Saturday afternoon he walked all the way from the farm to visit me. We had lost contact with each other when I had gone to college, but we quickly picked up the old threads again.

We were sitting on the bench on the shop veranda, and when Ma came out to greet him, Sandile leapt to his feet respectfully.

'You've grown, Sandile,' she said.

He smiled shyly.

'What have you been doing in the Transkei all this time?'

'I was at school there. Now I have finished.'

'And what are you going to do?' she asked.

'I still want to be a doctor,' he said with a wry smile and then added gravely, 'only it is more difficult now. My father has died. My brother Vulani has left his work and wants to become a policeman.' He paused reflectively. 'But it is not a good time for a black man to be a policeman.'

My mother nodded. She understood.

I went into the shop and brought back two bottles of Coca-Cola. Ma left us and Sandile and I sipped our drinks, gazing out into the veld in comfortable silence.

I thought about Sandile for a long time after he left that day. I thought of his tenacity. Anyone else, facing his kind of odds, would have given up long ago.

My father had not been feeling well. So when Sunday came we went to a lot of trouble making some of his favourite dishes, hoping that this would raise his spirits.

But after the effort of preparing the meal, none of us felt much like eating. Papa picked at the food on his plate. I looked at the uneaten food and thought of the time and energy wasted on a meal that was growing cold.

Papa got up from the table, unhitching his braces as he walked unsteadily to the bedroom. Ma and Nana exchanged worried glances. Soraya followed Papa to the bedroom and soon the two of them were fast asleep, oblivious to the rattling dishes and raised voices in the kitchen.

When everything had been cleared away, Ma quietly disappeared. She got into the car and, without a word to anyone, drove off on her own.

I watched the car going down the road. This also used to

happen in the days when we were still living in Soetstroom. Ma and Nana had once had a terrible row about her mysterious excursions. Nana had shouted after her that the house was becoming like a whorehouse. I was too young at the time to understand the significance of that remark.

With Ma out, Nana and Papa resting and Soraya asleep, the house was silent. I read for a while and then lay on my back watching as a bluebottle tried to stun itself against the walls. With the flick of a towel, I put it out of its misery.

Not a breath stirred as the sun beat down on the veld and on the corrugated-iron roof which retained the heat during the day. At night when it cooled down, the roof crunched and creaked as the metal contracted.

Apart from distant sounds, the veld lay heavy and silent, as though it, too, had feasted at the dinner table. Animals waddled off, finding refuge in whatever shade was available. Everything was suspended in a state of aestivation. In the distance a donkey brayed and then a dog barked, but the effort appeared to be too much and it, too, was silenced.

I listened to the sounds, overcome by a vague longing to be loved and to love. A dull ache swelled in a space between my ribs and navel. I flopped around on my bed like a fish out of water, every nerve-ending in my body raw and tingling.

Images of faces drifted through my fantasies. Sandile's face lingered longer than most. I imagined him at the gate, tall and handsome, smiling shyly, his chest oiled and glistening, legs astride, inviting, like the images I had seen in magazines.

A warmth stirred between my thighs. My hands slid down and felt the moistness, the silky erectness outlined against the nylon fabric. My fingers moved discreetly, gently caressing, probing and touching, arousing exquisite sensations.

I dozed off. A slight breeze had sprung up when I awoke. I went out on to the stoep. Nana, feeling restless, joined me. It was much cooler outside.

She stared at the grey ribbon of asphalt that curved out of sight behind the hill. 'Isn't this place pathetic?' she sighed. 'It's a place for fools and baboons.'

'From one God-forsaken place to another!' had been Yasmin's reaction the day she viewed our new surroundings for the first time.

I had shared those sentiments, but was less vociferous about it. McBain defined desolation. Because of our surroundings, we had no difficulty envisaging the moonscape as we listened to the radio commentaries about the Apollo missions.

But McBain – not the moon – was our home.

22

OUR RELOCATION, and later Yasmin's tragedy, only highlighted Papa's helplessness. My mother insisted he had nothing to blame himself for. He had tried to protect his family; that he had failed was not because he was weak as a man or as a father, but because he had tried to seek justice in a country where justice did not exist for non-whites. The political system, Nana said, emasculated men, constantly humiliating them in the eyes of their families.

But, as always, political issues often slipped into the background as the more pressing issues of survival engaged us. We were in another two-year cycle of drought. The ground lay dry and cracked, baked hard as concrete. Business dwindled, farmers pleaded poverty and food prices jumped.

Many children left school. Education for non-whites was not compulsory and was often costly as parents had to pay for books and stationery. When times were hard enrolment waned as children went off in search of work to help support their families. Many of the boys in my standard five class dropped out. Two of the girls fell pregnant and were forced to leave school. Neither Rachel nor Esme had anything to look forward to except more misery.

I drove home in my little Austin, thinking about Rachel and Esme. All around me life seemed to be crumbling to dust. Aloe bushes stood forlorn and scraggy, like weary sentinels, with few flowers.

Most evenings we gathered around the radio. Radio drama,

though, was vastly different from the reality of life at McBain.

The paltry salary I brought home each month didn't seem to make much of a dent in our debts. I calculated that at this rate, I'd still be paying them off, with the accumulated interest, when I was old and grey. I earned very little, but the government considered it adequate. White teachers earned a great deal more than their non-white counterparts. Salaries were scaled according to race and gender.

While we focused on survival, Papa was beginning to ponder his mortality. There was still so much to be done before his death, he told Nana. One of his daughters – namely me – still had to be settled. It was his responsibility as head of the house, he said, to ensure that I was 'settled' before he died.

I should have been wary then as I watched him on the stoep, pretending to rest, but all the while making plans for my future. But no matter what he decided, the old problem of our mixed parentage would always be an obstacle. Yasmin and I were not pure Indian. We were half-breeds. We had a Coloured mother, which in the eyes of the Indian community was a defect. We were spoilt goods and thus of less value.

This purity issue had presented innumerable barriers in finding a suitable boy for Yasmin. In my case it was going to be doubly difficult because I didn't have any of Yasmin's desirable attributes – her beauty or her vivacity.

Although I knew what my father was up to, I was too much of a coward to object. I hated confrontations – unlike Yasmin, I would rather give in and slink away quietly than create a scene.

It took a while for Papa to think of a likely candidate, but he eventually came up with someone – Hamid Khan, who was about my age.

We were alerted to Papa's plans one night at supper when he casually asked me, 'Remember Rashidbhai?'

I looked up blankly, caught off-guard, and for a moment I didn't have the foggiest idea who or what my father was talking about.

'Of course we remember Rashid Khan,' Ma said. 'Why do you ask, Abdul?'

'No reason,' Papa said.

'Doesn't he have a son, Hamid?' Ma asked, her glance darting across the table to me.

'Yes,' I said.

The matter rested there, but it was only a temporary respite.

That night as I lay in bed, the relevance of my father's question finally hit me. Hamid Khan with his pimply face! 'Oh God,' I groaned and pulled the bedcovers over my head.

Papa was being very coy about his plans. After all, it wasn't easy to pick up the phone and say 'I want your son for my daughter'. Besides, he and Mr Khan were not close. The last time Papa had spoken to him was about two or three years earlier at an auction in the city.

Mr Khan was a paunchy, fast-talking fifty-year-old. And on that occasion I had taken an instant dislike to the man. Frequently during his conversation with Papa, he turned to my mother and told her how much he respected Papa because Papa was a man of honour – a dying breed – and all the while his eyes devoured my mother. Ma clearly didn't have much time for him either. She had that telling look on her face, the meaning of which I had learned to decode at an early age.

Papa's plan seemed a bit of a joke to me and unfortunately I didn't take him seriously. I expected the whole matter to peter out eventually and observed with some amusement as he planned his strategy, unobtrusively trying to slide the idea out into the open and then nurturing it for a while.

No matter what he did, I could never remain angry with him for long. Whenever I saw him sitting on the stoep looking lost and vulnerable, my heart went out to him.

At night when I heard my parents moving about in their room, I wondered about the adult world, wondered about my parents and their lives, their needs and their desires.

I'd heard Ma telling Nana that there was no sexual link

between her and my father any more. No affectionate touching. Their relationship had drifted beyond such demonstrativeness. She said that age and stress had rendered Papa impotent. I imagined the two of them lying side by side, silent and resentful. They had become like this in the past few years. Papa indifferent and Ma angry.

Papa had still not given us any clear indication about his plans for me and so we had no reason to tackle him. He regarded this problem as his duty and in his opinion it had nothing to do with the 'women'. Not yet anyway. Not at this stage.

As I lay sleepless at night, thinking about my life, I suspected that Papa, too, was lying awake, thinking about Mr Khan and his son Hamid and how he could connect the dots of our lives.

My recollection of Hamid was of an extremely thin boy, who looked rather like a tuberculosis victim. My initial impression of him was that he was not very bright, an impression enhanced by his appearance, his face pocked with acne scars.

Years before when we were still living in Soetstroom, he and his father had come to visit. Because of his unfortunate complexion, Yasmin had covertly referred to him as Frog-Face. I had felt sorry for him and, since Yasmin had chosen to be mean, I went out of my way to be pleasant. Perhaps he had misinterpreted my kindness. The name Frog-Face rang in my head like a jingle. I was appalled at the ease with which I accessed the cruel tag from my memory.

The issue of appearance would, of course, be of no concern to Papa who had probably already assessed Hamid's suitability. All he cared about was that the boy was from a good, secure family and that I would be taken care of if anything should happen to him.

A few days later, with the issue partly settled in his own mind, Papa waited until Ma and Nana were busy elsewhere before slipping into the shop to make his call.

I was in the office and picked up the extension. Papa and Mr Khan spoke for a long time in their native Gujarati. They got most of the preliminaries out of the way before mention was made of me. Papa tried to toss my name out nonchalantly. Mr Khan, who was no fool, paused. He knew immediately where the conversation was heading.

I imagined Mr Khan on the other end, lighting up another cigarette, taking a puff and smiling as he and my father continued their ritualistic dance of matchmaking over the phone. Furious with my father for humiliating me in this way, I put the phone down and found a quiet corner with *Surrender to Love* and its heroine, Sasha, whose pain I could identify with.

The call from Papa was probably a welcome one for Mr Khan who had obviously also been thinking about his son's matrimonial prospects. He had had Yasmin in mind those days long ago, but because of the vicious rumours of her having loose morals, he had abandoned that plan and had gone to look elsewhere, with little success.

He had no illusions about his son. The boy took after his wife's side of the family. He was tall and lanky, his face covered in unsightly carbuncles, just like his brother-in-law. Mr Khan's main concern, however, was to keep his son, who was running with the wrong crowd, out of trouble.

I'd heard that he was drinking and coming home late at night and that things were a bit dicey at home. Mr Khan probably thought that marriage would knock some sense into him.

No doubt, Papa's call had come at a very propitious time.

I continued to make light of my father's efforts. He was clearly worried about me and what would happen to me if he died. My mother had similar concerns, but for both her daughters. At least my parents shared this one thing – their anxiety.

Papa said there wasn't much he wanted out of life any more, except to see his family settled and secure. With this goal constantly being thwarted, it was like trying to hold a breath of air in a clenched fist.

But I was slowly beginning to realise that the situation was much more serious than I had anticipated and that at some stage

I would have to take a stand. Panic crept over me as I agonised about what I would do and say when the time came for me to confront him.

I rehearsed defiance in front the mirror. Composed. Serene like a madonna, I gestured and dropped my eyes. Yasmin was always able to get away with anything merely by lowering her eyes. But even as I practised and posed, I sensed deep down that none of this was going to work.

'I can't marry him, Nana,' I said, shuddering as I remembered what he looked like. 'He's disgusting. He looks like a frog . . . Yasmin called him Frog-Face . . .'

'Looks aren't everything,' Nana said sharply. 'He might be a nice boy.'

Nana conveyed my sentiments to my mother. 'I think she's right, Delia. Talk to Abdul. He's pushing like he did with Yasmin. Meena is soft, but I doubt she's going to go along with him. She'll probably do a Yasmin on us. Anyway, you wouldn't want grandchildren who looked like frogs, would you?'

The thought that Papa was once again being hasty had occurred to my mother as well. She told Papa about my reluctance, warned him that he was going to have trouble on his hands and repeated the frog story. Papa was not amused.

'What does she know? She's only a child. You, her mother, should know what's best for her.'

'I do know what's best for her, that's why I don't think this'll work, Abdul.'

Papa's expression tightened. He hated to be contradicted, especially by his wife and mother-in-law, both of whom had the tendency to erode his authority.

'She'll do exactly what I say,' he told my mother firmly. 'Last time, too, you were the one who made trouble. Look what happened to Yasmin. *You* ruined her life.'

'What are you talking about?' my mother cried.

'Always it is like this,' he shouted. 'When I say *yes*, you say *no*. When I say *no*, you say *yes*. You have no respect for my traditions. You and your mother! Now you are teaching our children the same disrespect.'

Ma shook her head and walked away.

Papa calmed down, but made his displeasure evident as he and Daniel sat on the stoep. His brows drawn together, expression thunderous, he complained loudly about women. We had all, in no uncertain terms, expressed our opinion about Papa's plans. We had presented a united front against him and now he didn't have the strength to tackle us individually. He was just too tired. The issue of Hamid and my future slowly slipped into the background.

Sandile came to visit again. This time he came to tell me that he had been accepted at the University of Natal Medical School.

'Why do you have to go so far away?' I asked.

He gave me one of his beautiful smiles, his lips parting to reveal his even white teeth.

'My dream is still to become a doctor,' he said.

I looked away, tears of disappointment threatening. I felt like Sasha in *Surrender to Love*, as she and Ricardo were about to part. The same fire burnt inside me. The same agony.

'I don't understand this obsession you have about being a doctor,' I said.

We were sitting on the cement floor of the stoep, his legs dangling over the edge, mine drawn up, my chin resting on them. With a pebble, I absently drew geometric shapes on the cement.

His gaze dwelled on my hand for a long moment then he pulled up the leg of his trousers. 'Remember this?' he asked.

The scar tissue where the torn flesh had been stitched together had thickened into a ridge, defining the shape of the crocodile's jaws. Only it was much bigger now. The scar had grown with him and it was much longer than I remembered.

'I just wish I were more like you,' I said in Sasha's quiet, tormented voice. 'I wish I knew what I wanted to do with my life.'

I continued my agitated scratching on the cement surface.

He reached for my hand and with a light touch, stilled its

movement. 'You're doing what you want,' he said gently. 'You're teaching. I still have a long way to go.'

I had never told anyone how much I hated teaching, especially not after all the glowing comments Mrs Brodie had made about my abilities. Besides, how could I disappoint my parents? I was the one who had insisted it was what I wanted. I couldn't give it up now.

Sandile watched me silently. As I glanced up, I detected something new – a look of tenderness, of adoration.

My pulse quickened as I imagined Sasha's might have done. I averted my eyes.

'How do you know that teaching is what I really want?' I asked sharply, confused and unsettled by his touch.

He looked at me for a long moment and then got up. It was the kind of moment that would have drawn hero and heroine together. They would have been in each other's arms, bodies melting together.

Not me. I just stood there, feeling stupid and inadequate.

I sensed that this might be the last time I'd see him. He would no doubt be swallowed up by his new life. Those who left never returned.

He walked away with his loping stride, turning at the gate to wave.

I wished I had a satin bed to fling myself on to as Sasha did when Ricardo left her, the bed still warm from his body and his scent enveloping her.

All I had was the hard cement floor and I had no intention of flinging myself on to that.

A dull ache gnawed at my insides, hot tears stung my eyes. I knew, though, that a relationship with Sandile would have presented too many problems. He and I were from two different worlds.

A few weeks later, Papa brought home a huge black trunk bought at an auction in town. Inside the trunk, amidst a host of useless items, was a shoe box containing old Irish Sweepstake tickets and several lists of winning numbers.

Papa spent weeks hunched over those tickets, examining them through a magnifying glass. He carefully scrutinised each ticket number and compared it to the list of winners, hoping that amongst them would be a winning number overlooked by the previous owner.

Business had slumped again and we were worried about how much longer we could survive at McBain.

'If it weren't for your salary,' Ma said, 'we would never manage.'

Although I did not complain, there were many problems at school and I was not happy there. The principal and I were at odds about 'Coloured Affairs', a government department established in the sixties to administer 'Coloured Education'.

Other bodies for other races had also been set up at about the same time. 'Indian Affairs' was responsible for Indian education in the same way as 'Bantu Affairs' had, for years already, been administering African education. The latest syllabus was a clear indication of how the quality of education for Coloureds had been eroded.

Ironically, I had finally decided to have myself reclassified as Coloured, in order to keep my teaching post. The process turned out to be much easier than I expected. Nana, always sceptical, thought I was just lucky. We never told my father about what I had done. It would have hurt him too much.

All that trouble – and now I hated being a Coloured, hated being associated with 'Coloured Affairs'. The whole issue was steeped in irony because the Coloured population had always viewed themselves as descendants of the white settlers and as such had expected preferential treatment.

In summer things improved once again.

Some Saturdays the shop was busier than usual with villagers coming to buy small quantities of mealie meal, flour and sugar. Papa disdainfully referred to their purchases as 'penny ha'penny' business. 'It's not worth the trouble,' he declared wearily.

His spirits only lifted at night when we cashed up and told

him what the takings were for the day.

In those days, Saturdays were set aside for shopping. Old men with wrinkled faces and grey beards, leaning heavily on their knobkerries, made their way to the shop at McBain.

They came primarily to socialise and sat outside on the veranda, drinking Coca-Cola and sharing a loaf of bread, often their only meal of the day.

The women also incorporated socialising into their shopping. These were loud and very vocal occasions. Papa, eager to escape the women's chatter, got Daniel to move his wicker chair on to the veranda where he sat with the other men, conversing in Xhosa.

A bond existed between the older men and my father. They were of the same generation. Most of the younger men had succumbed to the lure of the cities and better paying jobs, leaving the old men behind with the women and children.

One Saturday Gladys stormed away from her husband who was sitting on the veranda with the other men. We were convinced then that something was amiss between them. Gladys hadn't said anything to us, but all that week she had been in a terrible mood.

'It's not like her,' Nana admitted when Ma complained.

Not only was she in a fierce mood, but she had dropped two dishes and had absent-mindedly put things in the most unlikely places. When Ma attempted to find out what was wrong Gladys almost bit her head off.

While the men, including her husband, sat smoking on the veranda, the women crowded into the store.

Suddenly the buzz in the shop dropped a few decibels.

The cause of this silent interest was a woman who appeared in the doorway. It was Sis Tandi – 'Sis' being a respectful form of address. She was, after all, the chief's first wife – the grandam, the doyenne of the local community, mother of the chief's three sons. And Gladys's nemesis. When we saw her, we immediately understood the reason for Gladys's ill-humour.

She was a big woman and wore the traditional long skirt, a black fringed shawl wrapped around her chest. Draped over this was an elaborately decorated modesty-bib. A hand-woven choker in brightly coloured beads circled her neck. Her face was coloured with ochre and an enormous black headscarf was wound around her head like a turban. In one hand she held her pipe, its stem at least fifteen inches long. She gestured regally at the other women.

After the formalities of greeting, Sis Tandi settled down to participate in the shopping. Gladys, scowling, came to pay her respects. The two women greeted each other cautiously. Then Sis Tandi, with the assistance of the other women, inspected the bolts of German print.

A decision was made and she signalled Nana with a nod of her head.

Nana who had been waiting patiently behind the counter, asked: 'How many yards?'

The question caused further debate. The women consulted each other. 'Ten yards,' they agreed.

Nana carefully measured out the cloth.

Sis Tandi reached into her turban. Tucked into its folds was a handkerchief in which her money was knotted. Nana cut the fabric, folded it and wrapped it.

Sis Tandi unknotted the handkerchief and carefully opened it. Inside, folded into four, was a five-rand note. It was not enough to pay for the cloth. Nana, unmoved, stared at her.

With a woeful sigh, Sis Tandi loudly declared for all to hear how sad it was that a chief's wife, one who had born him all his sons, could not even afford to pay for a piece of cloth to cover her frail body.

Nana listened to the complaints without comment, quietly standing her ground. Finally, with another exaggerated sigh, Sis Tandi reached in under the top layer of her skirt and removed a pouch. She opened it slowly and deliberately, pouring the coins on to the counter. A few rolled off and dropped to the floor. One of the women helped to retrieve them. Most of the drama appeared to be over now and Sis Tandi leaned her elbow on the counter, carefully counting out the money, separating the coins into piles and then stacking them as she counted them.

Gladys stepped forward with an offer of help, but Sis Tandi waved her aside.

The money was finally counted. Then Nana counted it and found that it was still five rands short. The look of consternation on Sis Tandi's face would have been the envy of the most seasoned actress.

'*Hayi, kaloku*, it should be enough,' she exclaimed loudly. 'I thought it was enough.' She appealed to the others, wondering aloud what to do now. The cloth had been cut, had it not? Was that not the wrapped cloth lying on the counter?

There were nods all around. Nana and Gladys exchanged glances.

Nana raised her eyebrows. 'Five rands short,' she said again.

'What am I to do?' Sis Tandi wailed. 'Am I to be like a beggar?' The statement phrased like a question was tossed with dramatic effect so that it reached the men on the stoep. The volume of their conversation dropped immediately.

Gladys told Nana to put the shortfall on her account. Sis Tandi, looking triumphant, made a regal exit. She knew exactly how to manipulate Gladys and Gladys had been caught yet again. She was in a rage and declared that she was ready to leave the chief.

'Are you going to let that woman bully you?' Nana demanded. 'You'd be a fool to let her drive you away. You've made sacrifices for the children – her children – while she lived like a queen in the Transkei.'

Gladys, head bowed, looked like a chastened child.

'You wanted to be his wife. I warned you about that old fox, but you wouldn't listen. Now when things get tough, you want to run. Oh no, my girl, you get back in there and fight for your rights!'

Gladys returned to the village and stood her ground. Three weeks later Sis Tandi returned to the Transkei and Gladys's disposition improved.

From time to time these small dramas enlivened our uneventful existence at McBain, but I was always happy to get back to my reading.

I had read hundreds of romance novels, burying myself in the escape they offered me. And it passed the time. I was probably becoming a composite of all those hundreds of female characters who loved, lost and in the end triumphed. But my life would probably not be triumphant. It was more likely to be doomed just like Michelle's in *Lost Paradise*. She had loved and lost.

23

SINCE NO further mention was made of Hamid or of getting me married, I relaxed. I should have remembered Nana's dictum about never taking anything for granted because disaster had a way of following closely on the heels of happiness.

But there were signs that my father had given up on his matchmaking plans. Perhaps Mr Khan had not been too keen on the idea anyway. He probably remembered me as a fat little girl who didn't have much to say. Perhaps Hamid had his sights set higher, after all their first choice had been Yasmin. But, whatever the reason, all I could say was 'thank God'. Nana warned me to remain watchful. She said my father was like a sleeping dog. It didn't need much to stir his interest.

Papa spent a lot of his time out on the stoep with Soraya. The two were inseparable. Papa's eyes, opaque with cataracts, gazed short-sightedly at Soraya. He gently caressed her hair as she leaned her head against him.

Whenever I saw my father like that I knew that I could never break his heart the way Yasmin had. Although nothing more was said about Hamid, I worried that the idea might still be rattling around in his head. Occasionally he mentioned it, but when the subject came up I found some excuse to be elsewhere.

Elsa had been away again. This time for longer than usual. After an absence of more than six months, I saw her standing in their yard one day and waved to her. There was no response or acknowledgement but I none the less went over immediately.

With a detached, bored look, Elsa watched as I scrambled down the embankment.

Elsa's mother, who had also been away, had returned with her and had resumed her position at the door.

The eager, welcoming smile froze on my lips. My eyes were drawn away from Elsa's face to her waist. The matchstick figure, with its fragile arms, legs and distended belly, reminded me of a picture I had seen of starving Biafran children.

I waited in astonishment for her to say something.

In response to my unspoken question, she nodded and then turned away. 'I'm five months,' she said quietly.

She beckoned me to follow her. I glanced over at the door and saw her mother's eyes following us.

'Elsa . . . whose baby is it? Where is the father?' I asked as we hurried away.

After a long pause, her eyes darting to and from my face, she said: 'He's in Pretoria.'

I believed her. Because she'd been gone for six months, it was highly unlikely that someone from around McBain was responsible.

'Who is he?' I asked.

Elsa walked away, flinging pebbles at the rails.

In the stillness of the veld, the sharp ping, ping, sounded like gunshot.

I caught up with her and grabbed her arm. 'Elsa, tell me who the father is,' I insisted.

'No!' she shouted.

There was a brittleness about her, a discordance that was terribly unsettling. I held on to her arm, but she winced and so I let go.

She stomped off angrily, her old sandals flapping against her heels, her thin legs pale and bruised.

'What does the doctor say?' I shouted after her.

Elsa paused and waited for me to catch up with her. I was angry with her. It was a stupid thing to do. I thought of Rachel and Esme, my two students, and of Yamin. Their lives ruined.

'I saw a doctor in Pretoria. My mother and I will only be staying a few weeks and then we'll be going back to Pretoria. So just mind your own business.'

'Well, see if I care!' I retorted as I turned and headed back towards the house.

Elsa continued to walk down the rails, swearing at the top of her voice.

'Well, see if I fucking care too!' she called after me. 'You miserable bitch!'

A contrite Elsa came to see me a few days later. At first I didn't want to have anything to do with her, but when I saw how gaunt and wretched she looked, my anger vanished.

Ma and Nana, who both saw her, agreed that she might be much more advanced than five months. It had obviously happened at McBain and they speculated about who the father could be.

I told them what she had said about seeing a doctor in Pretoria, but Nana still maintained that Elsa was lying about being five months.

'Why would she lie?' I asked.

'A girl with a filthy mouth like hers would lie about anything and everything,' Nana said.

'I wonder how she's going to manage,' I said.

'Don't worry, the government looks after its own,' Nana replied.

'They'll get some kind of assistance,' Ma added. 'Afrikaner women are encouraged to have children.'

After a thoughtful pause, Nana said: 'I hope it's not what I think it is.'

I waited to hear more, but Nana didn't say what she thought it might be. Apart from a quick exchange of glances between her and my mother, nothing more was said.

In the mean time the mystery deepened. It was a sad distraction in the dull routine of our lives. We pondered and analysed everything about Elsa. It was not like one of my romance novels, it was more like a mystery story, a 'whodunit'.

In this case, it was 'whodunit' to Elsa.

Four weeks later, on a Sunday morning, Elsa went into labour.

Around eleven o'clock, Mabel called from the hollow near the tracks: 'Come quick! The baby is coming.'

Gladys relayed the message.

'Where's her mother?' Ma called.

'She's there, but she's drunk again,' Gladys said. 'You'd better go quickly.'

'Dammit, she should've been taken to hospital,' Ma shouted as she rushed out. 'What if there are complications? She can't be giving birth now!'

Half an hour later Mabel came to call me and Nana. Papa told me to take the car in case we had to drive Elsa to hospital.

Nana and I drove around to the crossing and then took the dirt road which led to the cottages.

Mrs Botha was sprawled on the sofa in the front room, an empty brandy bottle on the floor next to an upended ashtray. In the next room Elsa was lying on her mother's double bed, writhing and heaving in agony. The sheets had crept up, exposing a dirty stained mattress.

Ma sat on the edge of the bed, holding her hand. Elsa's eyes were like saucers. She was in so much pain that she was drooling, her eyes glazing over with each wave.

'I don't know what to do,' Ma whispered to Nana.

'Let me see,' Nana said.

Ma moved aside. Nana ran her hands over Elsa's abdomen, gently probing.

'It feels like the baby's not lying right. Dear Jesus, her pelvis is so small . . .'

'What can we do?'

'Call an ambulance quickly!'

'There's no time, Mum!'

'I'll try to turn the baby,' Nana said.

I stood gawking.

'Dammit! Go call a doctor, Meena. Hurry!'

Galvanised, I bolted back to the house and with trembling fingers dialled the hospital for an ambulance. I was told that both the ambulances were on calls and might not respond for two hours or more. I asked them to send an ambulance to the McBain siding as soon as possible.

I reported back to Ma and Nana, who were both looking frantic.

'Can't we drive her to the hospital?' I asked.

'No, it's too risky,' Ma said. 'We have to do what we can for her here.'

'Where the devil is her father?' Nana asked. 'Go see if there's anyone next door at the Jouberts' house.'

Mabel, who was standing in the doorway, shook her head. 'They have all gone into town. They won't be back until tomorrow.'

Elsa screamed. A long piercing scream ripped from the very depths of her soul. Alarmed, I fled.

There were no towels at the Bothas' house; I volunteered to fetch some. Gladys arrived. She was carrying a bottle of mud-coloured liquid.

Elsa, distraught and exhausted, was made as comfortable as possible. Now and then her eyes opened and with a demented look she'd clutch at the air, her eyes rolling back. Three hours passed and still we waited for her to dilate.

'Any sign of the ambulance yet?' Ma asked.

I shook my head.

'I have to help her,' Nana said. 'She can't suffer like this. Give her some of that mixture Gladys brought.' Gladys had told Nana that they used it in the village when there were problems with childbirth. It helped with the pain. 'She's going to need it.'

Ma hesitated only for a moment and then propped Elsa up, urging her to drink from the cup. By this time Elsa was in so much pain she would gladly have done anything for relief. Her eyes, ringed with blue, met mine over the rim of the cup.

There was nothing more I could do. I couldn't stand watching Elsa suffer so. This was where I lacked the toughness of Jessica in *Sudden Storms*. Isolated by the storm, she was the only other person there with Stephanie. Even though the baby was Eric's and both women were in love with him, Jessica had saved mother and child.

I left the room and waited in the kitchen, hands clamped over my ears to shut out Elsa's screams.

Anna Botha had passed out by then and knew nothing about her daughter's suffering.

Finally, hours later, there was one more loud scream and then silence. I opened the door a crack.

Ma was holding the baby in her arms. The exhausted Elsa was lying very still. For a moment, seeing her like that, I was sure that the ordeal had killed her.

Ma smiled at the bundle in her arms. Elsa's eyes flickered open and then she drifted off again – either into the oblivion of sleep or unconsciousness.

I reached into the towel to take the baby's hand. Startled I jerked my hand away. I stared at my mother in horror. She gently shook her head, signalling me not to say anything.

I stayed at Elsa's side until the ambulance arrived hours later. It was almost dusk when they pulled up in front of the house. Elsa and her baby were taken to the hospital.

Her mother stirred as though awakening from her stupor, but the effort was too great and she slumped back against the chair again.

When we got home we discussed the situation.

'I thought it better not to say anything to her,' Ma explained. 'Poor thing, she has enough to cope with.'

'Why didn't the baby have hands?' I asked.

'It's one of those things,' Nana said. 'The hands just never developed.'

'I wonder why they didn't develop? Have you ever seen anything like it before?' I asked my mother.

Ma shook her head and turned away from me.

Elsa returned home rejecting the child. The responsibility for his care fell on Mabel.

It took a combined effort from all of us to persuade Elsa to take an interest in her baby. It was a long process. At first it looked like a hopeless cause, but in the end, perhaps out of loneliness and a desperate need to be close to another human being, she did.

One day as I was looking out the kitchen window, I spotted Elsa in the yard, cradling the infant in her arms.

Many of Soraya's old baby clothes found their way to Elsa's baby. Ma and Nana helped out as much as they could. We felt terribly sorry for Elsa. Her mother was not in the least bit concerned about her and we all thought it very strange that Mr Botha never came near the shop.

Ma and Nana speculated about the paternity of the child. An ugly suspicion had reared its head in both their minds.

'Remember old Marie Steenkamp, and her daughter?' Nana asked Ma. 'Poor woman, she carried that cross to her death.'

'What does that mean?' I asked curiously.

'Never mind,' Nana said quickly. 'It's not something one wants to talk about.'

It seemed that Nana, like my father, was constantly engaged with the past, trying to find comfort and reassurance in simpler and happier times. She had often mentioned the Steenkamps who were her neighbours in the days when she lived on the banks of the Orange River.

Her preoccupation with those nostalgic reminiscences was quite peculiar. 'Remember how you fell into the prickly pear bush at the bottom of the old *krans*?' Nana said to my mother. 'Remember how the other children brought you home and we had to smear fat on your bum so the thorns could be removed easily? Remember, you couldn't sit for days afterwards?'

Ma merely nodded, but never elaborated on the stories about her childhood. She never in any way committed herself to their veracity.

At times when I watched my mother and saw that faraway

look in her eyes I wondered about her, wondered what secrets from her past she was guarding so determinedly.

Nana had once let slip that Ma had been in love with a young man in the days before she met Papa. The man's name was Nathaniel Basson. I had tried to question my mother about him, but she became quite irritated with me and walked away without answering. I wondered what had happened to him.

Nathaniel Basson captured my imagination. Perhaps he was my mother's great love, just as Hunter Ashworth was Helena Simpson's in *Blossoms in the Dust*. Like Helena, a sadness sometimes seemed to gather in my mother's eyes. At other times her eyes would light up nostalgically at the whiff of a familiar perfume or the sound of a familiar tune.

But for my mother the pain of making the wrong choices had long since eased. She never complained about her life or the decisions she had made.

Months passed.

One afternoon I went to visit Elsa. I hadn't seen much of her since the baby was born. She was sitting on the back steps, vacantly staring at the ground while her son crept around, propelling himself on the stumps that were his arms.

'Hello, Niels,' I said.

The child sat down with a thump and smiled. He was a beautiful boy with all Elsa's best attributes. He had her long lashes and the same sweet smile. He was an adorable child and apart from his stunted arms he was normal in every way.

I sat on the step next to Elsa.

'How've you been?' I asked. 'I haven't seen you in ages. Gosh, he's grown,' I said, looking at Niels. 'One of these days he'll be walking.'

Elsa did not respond.

I picked Niels up. He was soaking wet.

'You'd better change him. You can't leave him wet all day,' I said. 'He'll get sores, just like Mannetjie did.'

Elsa did not answer.

I got up off the step, slapped the dust from my dress and headed back home. At the gate I turned and saw that Elsa was crying.

Pretending not to notice, I shut the gate and walked away, climbing back over the tracks.

From the kitchen window I saw that Elsa, motionless as a stone Buddha, was still sitting where I had left her.

24

I RECEIVED my first salary increment. A small one. Hardly noticeable on my pay cheque. The increase had depended on the inspector's report and I, like the rest of the teachers, had played the game – capitulating, selling out to 'Coloured Affairs'. But what else could we do? It was either sell out or ship out, as one of the older teachers had remarked.

I was on the stoep with Nana, complaining about the government. Ma joined us.

'Things can't remain the way they are,' Nana said. 'It's got to change. I hear there's this new fellow – what's his name?'

Ma and I looked at each other blankly.

'A young man. He comes from around here – King William's Town way.'

'Steve Biko?' I asked.

'*Ja*. That's the one.

'What about him?' Ma asked.

'He's someone to watch out for. He's leading this Black Consciousness movement. I hear he's very popular.'

'I wonder where we're going to fit into the scheme of things,' Ma mused aloud.

There was a long moment of silence and then Ma said: 'This Biko fellow probably won't be around for long either. Our jails are full of black leaders.'

But our discussion was curtailed by Mr Joubert, the siding master, who stopped by and expressed an interest in buying two bikes for his girls who were living in town with their grandmother.

The bikes in the shed were now almost ten years old, bought for Yasmin and me when we were still in Soetstroom.

It was time to get rid of them, Ma said. But Papa was reluctant.

Ignoring my father, Ma instructed Daniel to dig the bikes out from under the mound of rubbish that had accumulated over the years. Daniel inspected the bikes and reported that they were badly rusted; they also needed new tyres and some of the spokes would have to be replaced.

'What if Yasmin returns? What if she asks for her bicycle?' Papa wanted to know.

'Please get rid of those bikes while you can still get a price for them, Abdul. There's no use hanging on to the past and a load of rubbish.'

'But if Yasmin comes . . .' Papa insisted.

'When are you going to get it into your head, Abdul, that Yasmin is gone. She may never come back. She might be dead for all we know.' Ma choked back the tears as she put into words what all of us secretly dreaded.

'And even if she does come back, the day she gets on that thing will be a cold day in hell,' Nana added, casting a critical eye at the bikes.

'She preferred horse riding. She said it was a lot more dignified,' I added, remembering how Yasmin had dreamily said, 'Equestrienne'. That was what Yasmin had said she wanted to be.

'Equestrienne', enunciated so elegantly by Yasmin, just as I imagined Elizabeth Farnsworth might have done in *Castles in the Sky*, was what might have been responsible for her tragedy. Had she not gone to the village to return the horse that night, things might have turned out differently.

We watched as Papa and Daniel worked on the bikes. They were engrossed in their new project and paid no attention to us.

Nana said: 'Remember Albert Makalima?'

'Are you going to tell that story again?' Ma asked.

'I'm not talking to you, I'm talking to Meena,' Nana said. Although I'd heard most of her stories already, I feigned interest.

'*Nou ja*,' Nana continued. 'He was with the African Corps in North Africa and do you know that all he got for his trouble was a stupid bicycle exactly like yours. A Raleigh. A girl's bike.'

I nodded absently.

'Just shows you the value they placed on the lives of our men,' Nana added. 'All they did was drive, clean and cook. All the dirty work to make the lives of the white soldiers easier and more comfortable.'

'At least they saw countries and places they would never otherwise have seen,' Ma commented.

Nana nodded. 'I suppose if you look at it that way. Some of them went all the way to Tunisia and Algeria.' After a thoughtful pause she continued. 'Anyway, when Albert got back, he named his first daughter Tunisia. He wanted to name his son Tobruk, but the clerk at the registry office couldn't spell, so Albert's son ended up with the name *Taaibroek*.'

Ma and I burst out laughing. *Taaibroek*, translated, meant Stickypants.

My father was still in the yard with Daniel, the two of them fussing with the bikes. He had a defeated look, as though the act of giving up the bikes had brought home the realisation that he would never see Yasmin again.

He left Daniel to clean the bikes and went to sit on the stoep. Sometimes it was painful to see him sitting alone, his gaze turned inward, mumbling to himself.

I dreaded the day my father would no longer be there. I didn't even want to think about this eventuality. When I was younger and in some of my more desperate moments, afraid of losing the people I loved, I resorted to prayer, praying first to Allah and then to the Christian God, hoping that one of them would heed my prayers.

This dichotomy in my religious convictions had always existed – torn between Papa, a staunch Muslim, and Ma and Nana, who were Christian. Papa had given both Yasmin and me religious instruction and had taught us the Koran in Arabic. He believed that he had raised us in his tradition. But at times the pull of the other was equally strong.

When we were at primary school in Soetstroom, Yasmin and I used to sneak off to participate in Christmas concerts, belting our little hearts out in the choir.

'*Oh, come all ye faithful . . .*' our angelic faces as devoted as those of the Christian children. Papa, of course, never found out about this. He would never have approved.

'The Christians have all the fun,' Yasmin complained. 'Muslims have nothing like this.'

On concert nights Ma and Nana stole away to see us on stage. We were given minor roles in the pageants.

'Always the damn shepherds,' Yasmin complained. 'Why can't I be Mary?'

It never happened.

I was quite satisfied with my part, but Yasmin whined constantly that the reason we were given the worst roles was because the teacher didn't like her.

Neither of us, of course, could ever have begun to imagine the trouble we would have been in had Papa found out what we were up to.

We weren't always strict about eating halal foods either, though Papa made such a big issue of it when Yasmin went to private school. Our religious convictions often depended on where and with whom we were.

This inconsistency presented itself in all aspects of our lives: whenever I thought of my father dying, I prayed that if he was spared to live for a long time, I would become a good Muslim.

I had tried in every possible way to make up for the loss of Yasmin. But I knew that when my father was sitting on the stoep gazing out into the distance with longing eyes, it was not me he was thinking of.

I went to see what Papa and Daniel were doing with the bikes.

'This time *I* . . . will teach her to ride the bicycle,' Daniel said, emphasising the 'I', his thin face contorted into a smile as he vigorously polished the saddle. Daniel had once tried to teach Yasmin to ride her bike, but Yasmin was not the biking type. She was an 'equestrienne'.

'Daniel, maybe when Yasmin comes home she'll help you get your licence, eh?' Papa said. He believed that Yasmin was safe. He had to. In all the years since she had left he had never allowed himself to explore the unspeakable possibility of its being otherwise.

'I've got my licence, sir,' Daniel said.

'Where? When?' Papa demanded, momentarily fooled by Daniel's grave tone.

Daniel reached into his inside pocket.

Papa, realising what was about to happen, said: 'That stupid piece of paper again! How many times do I have to tell you that it is not your licence? It is nothing! It is just a piece of paper with nonsense written on it. How many years have you been working for us, Daniel?'

Daniel shrugged his bony shoulders.

'Maybe eighteen or twenty years, eh?' Papa said, massaging his head. 'For all those years you've had that piece of paper. It is nothing. I keep telling you it is not your identification. Why do you behave like a fool, Daniel?' He paused, looking at Daniel through his thick glasses. Daniel looked miserable and Papa's expression softened. 'We must get papers for you, Daniel. One of these days the police will ask you for papers and when they see that you don't have any, they'll put you in jail. Then what?'

Daniel said nothing.

'When Yasmin is home, I will teach her to ride this bicycle,' he eventually responded. He hadn't taken in a word of what my father had said.

'Listen to Papa telling Daniel Yasmin's coming home,' I said. 'I can't believe it. When is he going to accept that she's gone and will never come back here?'

'Oh, leave them alone. If it makes your Papa happy to think that she is coming home why bother to tell him otherwise,' my mother said.

'It's tough to get old, you know,' Nana reminded us. 'I should know.' She went to the door and watched Papa for a few thoughtful moments. Sighing, she turned back to Ma and me. 'Maybe he's becoming senile,' she said.

Later Nana went to speak to Papa. 'Abdul, why are you telling Daniel that Yasmin is coming home?' she asked.

'So he will fix the bicycles quickly,' my father said. 'Joubert is waiting for them.'

Nana grinned. She was relieved. She had feared the worst, that Papa was becoming senile. She was measuring her own progress against his.

I went to see Elsa.

She was sitting on the stoep.

'How are you? How's Niels?' I asked, looking around for him, but he was nowhere in sight. 'I heard from Mabel that he'd been sick.'

'He's all right now,' she said.

There was a long, awkward pause. We had grown apart. There wasn't much for us to talk about any more. My work no longer seemed to interest her, especially when all I could do was complain about the government. Her government. That was not what she wanted to hear.

Lying in the pathway near the gate was a doll with its head ripped off.

'My child is broken too, just like that,' Elsa said, bitterly.

'Niels is lovely,' I assured her. 'He has your eyes.'

'He has no hands.'

Elsa picked up a stick and absently drew designs in the sand. She looked gaunt and wasted. The silence hung between us like a curtain. I groped for something to say, but could think of nothing that might ease her pain.

I got up to leave.

Elsa's eyes, full of desperation, held mine. She followed me to the gate.

I stepped over the headless doll lying in the pathway.

'I'm going away,' Elsa said dully.

'Where to?'

'Pretoria.'

'Oh,' I said and turned to go.

'I'm going to stay with my aunty. I can't stand being here any more. I hate this place and I hate them.' She looked back at the house as she shut the gate behind me.

I paused, uncertain about what to say to her. She'd always been an enigma.

Elsa stood with her head bowed as I walked away. I reflected on the way things had changed from those early days when we were growing up, walking the rails and flinging obscenities into the wind.

25

ELSA RETURNED from Pretoria with a husband. Johan Bezuidenhout was a young Afrikaner about two years older than her. Like Elsa, he was tall and slender and – I couldn't help noticing as Elsa proudly paraded him around the backyard like a trophy – he was quite good looking.

'I wonder where she got hold of him,' Nana said, as she watched Elsa and Johan from the kitchen window. 'That family has more than one screw loose.'

Elsa had her arm linked in his. Conscious of being observed, she tossed back her blonde shoulder-length hair and posed affectionately with her new husband.

Niels tottered over to his mother and threw his stumpy arms around her leg. She was impatient with him and pushed him away, but he persisted, determinedly hanging on to her leg. Johan picked him up and took him into the house. Elsa wrapped her arms around herself and turned her face to the sun, basking in its rays and our attention.

I had spoken to Elsa only once since she had returned with her new husband.

'Is he Niels's father?' I asked.

Elsa's expression changed. Like twin trap-doors, her eyes snapped shut. She swung away.

'Wait! Don't go,' I called. 'Are you going to be staying here now?'

'I don't know. Johan must see if he can get a job.'

'Here?' I asked.

'No. We'll go into town,' Elsa said. 'My mother is in hospital there.'

'What's wrong with her?' I asked, surprised, but noticing for the first time the absence of her mother's eyes at the screen door.

Elsa wouldn't say.

I heard later from my mother that Anna Botha had been admitted to the mental institution.

Mabel said that the Bothas were in town most of the time now, and that Mr Botha was going to retire soon and would put in a word for Johan to be hired as his replacement.

'It's all quite strange, isn't it?' Nana said. 'Don't you think it's strange, Delia?'

Ma didn't say anything.

'I wonder what's going on with that family,' Nana continued.

Nana asked Papa if he knew what was going on across the tracks, but he didn't know any more than we did. He did, however, confirm the story about Mr Botha taking early retirement so his son-in-law could take his job.

'He doesn't look old enough to be pensioned off,' Nana said.

'Who knows,' Ma shrugged. 'It really isn't any of our business. We have enough of our own problems to worry about.'

One afternoon Ma and I were sitting in the yard watching the children splash in the old blue plastic pool which we'd had for ever. Ma had invited Florence and Niels to join Soraya.

Mabel, who had brought Niels, was enjoying having time to herself. She and Gladys sat outside, gossiping about their respective employers.

'Ma,' I said tentatively, suddenly realising that I was about to plunge into hazardous territory.

My mother glanced at me questioningly.

After a brief hesitation, I said: 'I've been thinking about going away.'

Startled, Ma's eyes widened. She studied me for a moment as if processing the information.

'Go where, Meena?' she asked finally in a voice which belied her anxiety.

I had wanted to discuss this with Nana first, but the words were out before I had time to consider the consequences.

Now I struggled to find other words that would complement them and convey my dread of spending the rest of my life at McBain. I didn't want to sound ungrateful, but how else was I to tell them that I could no longer stand the isolation and that I needed a life of my own?

How would any of my companions in the romance novels have phrased it, I wondered. I quickly dismissed these thoughts. Now was not the appropriate moment to lose myself in fantasy.

Not wanting to sound like Yasmin, I hesitated. After all, it was Yasmin's restlessness that had caused all the problems in our family. I had castigated her, yet here I was, five years later, in the same boat. It seemed that history had a way of repeating itself in our family.

I felt as though I was suffocating at McBain. Work was no escape. The stress at school was merely compounding the problem. Everything was building up inside me, like a dam about to burst. My wishes seemed so small and inconsequential in the larger scheme of our lives. All I wanted was to explore the world beyond McBain. Perhaps not all at once the way Yasmin had, but cautiously, in small chunks. Nana had once told me that one could be as restricted by space as by the lack of it. I thought of Sandile and Yasmin, both of whom had escaped. I now understood their desire to expand their horizons.

'So, you want to follow your sister's example,' my mother said.

'No, Ma. Not like her . . . not the way she left.' I studied my hands, conscious of my mother's eyes on me.

'It certainly looks like it to me.'

'Ma, I can't spend the rest of my life in this place.'

'What's wrong with this place?' she asked scathingly, her eyes fixed on mine, trying to draw out more than just the words that had tumbled from my lips. 'It's been good enough for us. It helped to put you and Yasmin through school. Thanks to "this place" you have a profession. You can support yourself.' She paused for breath. 'You and your sister are equally ungrateful!'

'That's not true!' I cried indignantly.

'Well, that's the way I see it.' Ma wet her lips, her attention returning to the children in the pool.

After a while she asked: 'Where will you go?'

'Johannesburg . . .'

'What's so special about Johannesburg?'

'Nothing . . . nothing special. But I know I'll be able to find a teaching job there.'

'You've got a teaching job, Meena.'

Getting away was going to be a lot more difficult than I had anticipated.

'This is all very sudden,' my mother said.

I shook my head. It wasn't sudden. It had been brewing for years.

'All we have left is you and Soraya,' Ma added quietly. 'I don't want you rushing into a decision you may regret later. Soraya needs us all. We're a very small family. We have to stick together.'

'But it would have been all right for me to leave if I had married Hamid,' I snapped, angry with my mother for expecting so much from me. Wasn't it my turn now? Hadn't I earned it? Like Olivia, who had sacrificed herself to care for her invalid mother in *Broken Hearts*, I'd stayed home all this time, playing the good daughter.

Ma was silent, searching for answers which lay buried in her own experiences.

Eventually she said, 'I suppose if you really want to leave, I can't stop you.' There was a long pause as though she was trying to reach some momentous decision before she said: 'All right, I'll speak to your father.'

Ma spoke to Papa. She told him that I wanted to go to Johannesburg.

'Never!' he cried, his eyes blazing. 'Are you mad? Are you forgetting what happened to your sister? Never! I will never let you go to the city to be swallowed up there . . . You stay home – here with us!'

I couldn't believe my ears. I had expected resistance, but nothing like this. I glared at my father, my lips quivering, my body rigid with defiance. 'I won't have you run my life the way you tried to run Yasmin's!'

'Yes and look what happened to her! She didn't listen. She wanted to hurry-scurry with her life and look how she broke our hearts!' Papa gesticulated wildly, almost apoplectic with anger.

Ma watched anxiously as Papa and I unleashed our fury.

'Yasmin would have left this house, no matter what you did!' I shouted.

Hurt and bewildered, my father looked at me through his thick glasses, his eyes magnified to almost twice their size. 'You're trying to force me into doing what she wouldn't do!' I yelled. 'It won't work, Papa!'

'Shut up!' he shouted. 'I will not have you speaking to me so disrespectfully! I will not have you disgracing me the way your sister did. What is wrong with you girls? Is it so hard to be honourable? Do you have to be cheap? Muslim girls don't run around the country – they stay home with their families. They know what's right and wrong!'

'So what are we? It's not our fault that we're not what you wanted us to be!'

'Meena!' my mother cried sharply.

'I have done everything for you. I went to a lot of trouble to find a suitable boy for you, but like your sister you are going to disgrace me again. What will Rashidbhai think of me? First your sister and now you . . . My name will be dirt! You and your sister have damaged our good family name.'

'I don't care! I would not have married Hamid if he were the last man on earth!'

Soraya heard the commotion and came to investigate. She stood watching, her eyes wide. All the ugliness was laid bare in our voices, our emotions raw and exposed.

'Well, it's true!' I sobbed as my mother approached. 'Papa

talks as if we don't have any of his blood. What are we? No one wants to have anything to do with us. Papa has to go around begging for our acceptance. And you, Ma, you have to force us on to your people!'

'Get out!' my father yelled furiously, his voice breaking. 'You ungrateful child!'

'I'll go!' I tossed back defiantly. 'You never cared for me anyway. It was always Yasmin!'

We were both beyond reason. It was too late to retract.

I had lived in Yasmin's shadow, second best in our father's affections. The anger and feelings of rejection had festered. In that moment they exploded and I couldn't stop myself. Words tumbled out of my mouth. Angry words, accusatory words, hateful words.

'I love both of you equally,' my father said in a calmer voice.

'You never loved me!'

'Meena!' my mother cried, shocked.

'Go!' Papa cried, pointing to the door.

Soraya screamed at us to stop. She had her arms wrapped around my legs and I couldn't move.

'You're upsetting her,' Nana said, drawing Soraya into her arms.

Soraya's reaction forced restraint from us.

Stunned into speechlessness, I stared at my father. He glared back at me. I realised then that I didn't want to go like this, not with all this acrimony between us.

Ma put an arm around me. 'Go wait outside,' she said. 'I'll talk to your Papa.'

I turned to leave, hesitating in the doorway. My mother waved me out of the room. Still, I hesitated.

Eventually, my own anger spent, I saw how ugly all of this had been. In a frantic appeal, my eyes turned from Ma to Nana.

'Come, Meena,' Nana said gently.

I went with her.

26

IN THE days following our confrontation, I often thought about killing myself. Slashing my wrists was one of the more dramatic options, like Melanie in *Second Chance*. But at the last moment, as her life hung by a thread, her lover, Harrison James, rushed to save her.

It was highly unlikely that someone like him would be there to save me. Besides, I had never been able to stand the sight of blood – my own or anyone else's. I even considered hanging myself, but that was not the grisly ending I had envisaged for myself, limp body twisting and turning at the end of the rope.

Fortunately such drastic action was not necessary. After moping around the house for a few days, feeling totally miserable and sorry for myself, I patched things up with my father.

We had both been hurt by the exchange and were both anxious to put it behind us. Papa must have remembered what the consequences had been of pushing Yasmin too far.

I made no further mention of going away and my father assumed I had come to my senses.

'You're silly to give up so easily,' Nana told me. 'You can't lock yourself away here, Meena. You have a right to your own life.'

'I have to help while I can,' I told her.

'We'll manage. There's no need to sacrifice yourself.'

Nana subsequently told my mother what I had said.

Ma didn't say anything. My salary, small as it might be, was what kept us afloat. Especially when business was slow.

My father no longer talked about getting me married.

Nana had assured him that there was nothing to worry about. I had a job and was more than capable of looking after myself – and the rest of them.

Ma had also persuaded him that I was sensible and would do what was right and proper when the time came.

In this way the issue was ultimately settled.

Mr Khan still phoned to keep the pot boiling, as it were, but Papa talked about other things: the state of the country and why the government wanted Indian businesses to fail.

The letter from Uncle Ewin came as a surprise. It was the first Nana had heard from him in the fifteen years since he moved to London.

He and his stepson Jonathan would be visiting South Africa over Christmas and wondered if they could call at McBain. They were planning to fly to Johannesburg and then drive a rented car to Cape Town.

Nana wrote back promptly to say that she was looking forward to seeing them. We were excited about their visit, even though it was still seven months away.

Papa was the only one who remained indifferent. Even Daniel was enthusiastic. Any small change in the routine at McBain was cause for celebration.

'It's time,' Nana declared, 'to give McBain a facelift.'

Papa looked dismayed. 'We have no money for such things,' he protested.

'No need to worry,' Nana said. 'It won't cost you a penny. I'll pay for it.'

'With what?' Ma asked caustically.

'I have a few pennies saved from my pension,' she said. 'We've been meaning to paint the place for years now. Look what the buildings look like.' She pointed to the walls as she took us on an inspection of the property. 'That's the mud from the very first storm we had here at McBain. Remember?'

The shop roof had been damaged during that storm and had still not been repaired. Nana thought there would be enough money for a few new sheets of corrugated iron as well.

Papa considered it a waste of money. 'It'll look like this again when we have another storm,' he said sullenly.

But Nana's mind was made up and she ignored all his protests.

'This is our home. It is where we will be spending the rest of our lives,' she told him.

Ma reminded us of the furore over the installation of the flush toilet at Soetstroom.

At McBain our toilet was like a bottomless pit with a seat over it. It was responsible for one of my phobias, the terror of falling into it. When I was younger I feared that a hand would reach out from the bowels of the earth to grab my bottom. My terror of this toilet was real enough because both Yasmin and I had encountered a mamba sunning itself in the doorway.

My mother rolled her eyes at Nana's insistence on renovating but she surrendered in the end. She said that once Nana had her mind set on something, all the wild horses in China would not make her change direction.

Both Ma and Nana had a cache of sayings which they drew on as the occasion demanded.

The yard around the house where thorn bushes sprouted like prize roses was cleared by two villagers brought along by Gladys. We had never bothered to cultivate a garden because goats clambered over the low stone wall around the property and devoured everything in sight.

Papa's resistance was eventually worn down and he also got into the spirit of the clean-up, directing operations from his chair on the stoep.

'Typical, isn't it?' Nana said. 'On his throne, directing his subjects.'

Ma laughed. 'Let him think he's in charge – it makes life easier.'

'Reminds me of the story of the old Afrikaner and his ox-wagon,' Nana said. 'His little dog, running alongside the wagon, head up, tail proudly wagging, convinced that he and not the ox was pulling the wagon.'

Ma snorted with laughter.

McBain was eventually spruced up. It took ages, but when it was done, we agreed that a few coats of paint – whitewash in fact – and some cleaning up had made an enormous difference.

In the evenings when Ma and Nana sat outside on the stoep talking, the subject often turned to family topics. With Uncle Ewin coming soon, Nana talked about her family – brothers and sisters, all of whom had died. She spoke about her parents, whom I had not known.

She immersed herself more than usual in the past. Nana's brother Patrick, Uncle Ewin's father, had died of alcoholism. This was Nana's abiding disappointment. For the first time she admitted openly to having been ashamed of her brother. She said that he had stooped so low that he would steal food money from their mother's purse to buy drink. Her admission surprised me because she had always told me that her brother had died of cancer.

Later, when the initial euphoria induced by Uncle Ewin's letter had faded and when Ma and Nana watched the sun set over the veld, a look of longing came to Ma's eyes.

'London,' she sighed. 'I always wanted to travel. I don't suppose that will ever happen.'

'Don't talk like that. Your life is far from over, Delia. Sometimes the good Lord takes with one hand and gives with the other.'

While the women were preoccupied with the past, Papa became increasingly obsessed with restoring his sight. Although Ma and Nana both thought it was madness to have an eye operation at his age, Ma drove him to the city for an appointment with a specialist. As was usual on our trips to the city, we stayed with our old friends Cassimbhai and Aishaben.

Soraya loved visiting them because the family doted on her. And since schools were closed for the June holidays, I decided to go with them.

Nana stayed at McBain to look after the store.

We arrived the day before the appointment. Papa and

Cassimbhai, who had not seen each other for months, spent the entire afternoon on the veranda conversing in Gujarati.

They talked about life in their ancestral village and the family they had not seen for more than fifty years, some of whom were long gone. Papa paused often in his conversation to sigh and draw a hand across his smooth head, retreating to some distant place as he searched for images of his home in India.

Cassimbhai had once suggested that the two of them make the trip back home together. It was an idle dream they shared. Neither was capable now of making the journey. They were too old. It was too late. There was no money.

I stood in the shadows listening to their desperate yearnings.

Early the next morning, Ma took Papa to the eye specialist and arrangements were made for him to be admitted for surgery the following day.

When they returned Papa and Cassimbhai sat on the veranda for a while and then Cassimbhai took him for a long drive along the beachfront.

Papa admired Cassimbhai's independence and looked forward to having his eyesight restored so that he, too, could be independent.

'If Papa's going to be home the same day, like he says, why does he need all these things?' I asked as I watched my mother packing my father's overnight bag.

'The doctor said quite clearly that your Papa will probably be in hospital for three or four days. I don't know where he gets the idea from that he'll be home the same day.'

Anxious to get started, my father was up and ready early the next morning, but he dozed off while waiting for us on the veranda. I touched his arm lightly. Startled, he sat up, blinking at me through a fog of vague recognition. When he realised where he was, he rose eagerly.

Aishaben and Cassimbhai joined us and Papa said a few words to Cassimbhai in Gujarati. We walked to the front gate where the car was parked. Papa's step faltered a couple of times, but none of us noticed that anything might be wrong.

At the gate Aishaben embraced him. Soraya wanted to go with him.

'I'll be home tonight,' Papa assured her as he hugged her.

'Where are you going, Papa?' she asked, tightening her arms around his neck. Papa smiled and gently disengaged himself.

Aishaben told Papa that she'd visit him in the afternoon, after the operation.

'Not to worry,' he said cheerfully. 'I'll be home for supper tonight.'

Cassimbhai and Aishaben stood at the gate with Soraya and waved as we drove off.

Papa was admitted to the general ward. Ma knew the nursing sister on duty.

'Don't worry, Delia,' the sister assured her. 'We'll take good care of him.'

We waited until the staff had settled Papa into bed and then prepared to leave. Ma patted his hand and I kissed him lightly on the cheek. We paused at the door and looked back at him. His eyes were closed. He had dozed off already.

That was the last time we saw him alive.

The sister phoned to say that Papa had died under the anaesthetic. The doctor explained that the strain of the general anaesthetic had been too much for his heart. He had died of heart failure.

I blamed everyone for Papa's death: the doctors, the hospital, my mother. I could not accept that a perfectly healthy man had entered the hospital and was now dead.

Had I not left him in the hospital room, lying in the bed, seemingly fine? I demanded. How was it possible that a few hours later he would be dead? And in a *hospital*?

I prayed desperately, willing my father to come alive, to sit up and look at me, but he lay motionless, beyond my reach.

Ma took me in her arms and comforted me.

In death my father seemed much taller. He looked younger too; in that face I glimpsed the shadow of the young man I had never known. My mother eventually coaxed me away.

The Islamic Society was called. He was no longer my father or Abdul Mohammed. He was the *Mayet* – the deceased, which was the way they referred to him. Heart-broken, I watched as the men from the Islamic Society came to remove his body for the ritual ablutions.

I cried, hanging on to my mother who remained strangely detached, as if removed from the grieving around her.

Since no older brother survived to arrange the funeral, the Imam called together members of the community. It was night already.

It was too late to bury him the same day, and so the burial was planned for the following day after prayers.

Ma telephoned Nana to break the news. But it was much too late. Nana said there was no point in her coming. The funeral would be over by the time she got there.

Ma understood, but I yearned for my grandmother's comforting presence.

The men from the Islamic Society prepared Papa's body at the hospital, praying as they performed *Ghusl* – the cleansing. At Aishaben's house, a room was emptied of furniture and all pictures with human and animal forms were removed. A carpet was spread on the floor and covered with sheets. My father's shrouded body, only the face exposed, was placed on the floor in the centre of the room.

Dazed by the swift unfolding of events, I joined the women who arrived to keep vigil. We sat on the floor around the shrouded body, reciting the Koran. My grief had numbed me and I was only vaguely aware of people coming and going throughout the night.

In the morning the hearse arrived and the men entered the house and covered his face, securing the shroud around his head. It was then, with that sense of finality as they lifted his body on to a bier and placed it in the hearse, that the reality of his death finally sank in.

The drive home to McBain after the funeral seemed endless. It might also have been silent, had it not been for Soraya's questions. She was still puzzled that Papa had gone so suddenly. The last time she had seen him alive was when she waved to him from Aishaben's gate. The next time she saw him, his shrouded body was lying on the floor surrounded by praying women.

Ma had explained to her that Papa had died. But death was a difficult concept for someone as young as Soraya. It was difficult enough for adults.

'When is Papa coming back from death?' she asked.

Startled, Ma looked at the earnest little face, her brows quizzically drawn together as though she had given the question a great deal of thought.

'Papa's not coming back,' Ma said, her voice catching. 'He's gone to heaven. Remember, we talked about all of this, Soraya?' Ma had found the Christian concept of heaven easier to explain.

'Where's heaven?'

'Up there,' my mother said, pointing to the sky.

'I don't see it.'

'You can't see it, but it's there.'

Soraya gazed at the sky, frowning.

'You can't see him, but he can see you,' Ma added.

Soraya thought about this for a long time. Ma and I exchanged glances and I felt tears stinging my eyelids.

'I saw Mr Khan and Hamid at the house after the funeral,' Ma said.

'I saw them too.'

'I made certain they understood that you had no intention of marrying anyone.'

'Thanks, Ma,' I said listlessly.

When we arrived home, Nana wrapped her arms around my mother, who only then wept. Only in the privacy of her own home would she give way to her sorrow.

In the following weeks we clattered around the house, feeling its emptiness without Papa. We often caught ourselves forgetfully referring to him as if he were still with us.

Daniel felt the loss too and for a few weeks his eccentric behaviour was worse.

In the past Papa's monologues had merely been punctuated with perfunctory nods from Daniel. Now it was Daniel who spoke constantly, conjuring his words almost perfectly from memory.

I returned to classes after two weeks' leave of absence. By then everyone at home had settled down and accepted the loss. Soraya was the only one who still looked for him, running into the room, calling 'Papa, Papa!' Then she'd turn her bewildered eyes on one of us. It broke our hearts to see her so lost.

'I miss your father,' Daniel said quietly, his eyes fixed on the veld. A sadness had settled over him. It seemed that Hitler had retreated. He seemed more sane now than he had ever been.

'I suppose he's grieving too,' Nana said.

For Soraya and Daniel the adjustment was harder than for the rest of the family.

As winter approached I quietly turned twenty-two. Ma baked a cake and we had a small party, but it was more like a wake than a celebration.

Life at school was becoming intolerable. I was expecting another inspection. We had no textbooks and I often supplied writing materials to students who could not afford their own. There was no relief in sight.

The teachers, fearful of losing their jobs, were muzzled. We all complained, yet tried to do our best under difficult circumstances. At the beginning of the year when I received a new crop of students, I discovered that only a very small percentage of them were able to read. They had been pushed along from one year to the next, minds frozen in ignorance. We carried on regardless of how students would be affected because there was no one to appeal to.

Seven months later they were no further than they'd been when I received them. I hoped for a glimmer of light in all this darkness, but there wasn't even a spark.

Sergeant Klein came to see Ma after Papa's death and offered his condolences. He looked sadly at Ma, not knowing how to comfort her.

I saw the expression in his eyes and wondered about it. It was an awkward moment and it struck me then that Ma was more than just my mother; she was a beautiful woman whom men observed with more than just passing interest.

27

THE WINTER that year was bitterly cold. The students sheltered in the school yard, building small bonfires to keep warm. Some of the younger students in the lower standards arrived barefooted, wearing only flimsy garments. They were much too cold to concentrate on school work and huddled together to keep warm. I brought old clothes from home and wrapped them in these. Their heels and lips cracked and bled from contact with the frost, but they came to school because conditions at home were no better.

On weekends, bored and lonely, I lost myself in the exotic lives of the romance characters.

Even though I hoped Sandile would return, I knew deep down that he was lost in the city, lost in his life and his work. He had promised to write, but there had been no word from him. It was as though he had dropped off the face of the earth, existing only in my imagination.

Sometimes I was angry and disappointed, but I had known from the beginning that nothing would come of our friendship. The gulf between us was too wide.

One Sunday afternoon I heard my mother driving away. She was gone for much longer than usual.

'Where were you, Ma?' I asked curiously when she got back late that afternoon.

'Out for a drive,' she said. 'Out by myself to think.'

Nana had heard her coming in and followed her into her

bedroom. She shut the door behind her.

'Where were you, Delia?' she asked. 'Why are you taking such risks?'

'Leave me alone, Mum,' Ma said.

'Has Yasmin not done enough already?' Nana demanded. 'Are you trying to ruin us completely?'

'Don't be ridiculous!' Ma shouted. 'I'm trying to fix things – trying to solve our problems.'

'Hah! Fine excuse. With Abdul out of the way you think you're free to act anyway you choose. Well think again, my girl! Don't forget what happened before. I warned you then too, but you wouldn't listen!'

'Stop it!' Ma cried. 'Stop telling me what to do.'

'You didn't listen to me before either,' Nana persisted.

'I went for a drive, Mum. That's all.'

'And you expect me to believe that?' Nana said.

Alarmed at hearing the raised voices, Soraya ran to the bedroom door.

'Ma! Nana!' she called. 'What are you doing? What's wrong?'

Nana came out smiling grimly. 'Nothing, baby. Your Ma and I were just talking loudly.'

'You were shouting,' she said.

'Not really, sweetheart,' Ma said.

Soraya knew better and her reproachful glance included both Ma and Nana.

There was lots of snow on the mountains that year and the icy wind seemed to find every crack in the house. At night we huddled around the fire as temperatures fell well below zero. We all came down with coughs and chest colds but Soraya, who had been ill before, had no resistance. She started a fever which Ma tried to treat with home remedies. Nothing helped. Soraya was burning up. Her cheeks and lips were cracked and at night she gasped for breath.

Ma took her to the doctor in town. He diagnosed whooping cough and prescribed medication to bring down her fever. None of the medicine seemed to have any effect. Her fever continued, raging through the night.

Ma cradled her in her arms. Soraya's eyes glittered like glass, her hot cheeks pressed against Ma's breast. My mother's eyes were dull with anxiety.

We tried everything to reduce the fever, taking turns to sit up with Soraya through those terrifying nights. Children died of whooping cough. And for the first three days of our ordeal, Ma was on her knees next to the bed, praying that this would not be Soraya's fate.

Soraya continued to burn up, coughing until she vomited huge amounts of phlegm. Nana thought this was a good sign, but there was no other indication of improvement. It seemed to me, as I gazed at her red cracked cheeks and burning eyes, that she was getting worse.

We were at our wits' end. We'd tried everything from steaming to poultices and continued to give her the doctor's medication. We wanted to take her back to the doctor but feared that taking her out in the cold air might compound the problem.

The three of us crouched around Soraya's bed, desperately watching for some sign of improvement.

'She's breathing a lot easier,' Nana observed on the third day, her desperate eyes appealing for confirmation.

Soraya hardly cried, except at times when her body was convulsed by the racking cough. Mostly she just lay there quietly gazing at us, eyes mutely pleading.

She looked so small, so vulnerable.

Ma managed to get her to take some soup, but nothing would stay down.

Fearing she might become dehydrated, we resorted to bottle-feeding her, and for the first time fluids stayed down.

Both heaters were lit. The paraffin heater had a pot of water constantly boiling on it and the room was warm and humid. Using camphor, Ma steamed her at least twice a day.

We waited, talking in whispers. Terrified that Soraya was going to die, I repeated over and over again, like a mantra, 'Please

God, let her get better'.

On the fourth night, at around ten-thirty, Ma suggested I take a nap while she sat with Soraya.

Exhausted by the constant vigil, I fell asleep at once. But I was soon woken by someone roughly shaking me by the shoulders. I opened my eyes. My mother was standing at my bedside. 'Meena, come quickly!' she cried.

I was awake instantly. I leapt out of bed and rushed to the other room, expecting the worst. It was morning and Soraya was sitting up in bed. Her eyes were wide open and although she had a lingering cough, her colour had returned to normal.

Overwhelmed with relief, I sat on the edge of the bed and wrapped my arms around her.

Soraya's recovery was slow, but her persistent cough eventually eased.

Ma did not think she was well enough to go outside yet. Only when the doctor had confirmed that Soraya's lungs were clear, did Ma relax her vigilance.

Even though our lives had returned to normal, we would remember those terrible days and nights for a long time.

A few weeks after Soraya's recovery, Hermanus Steyn surprised us with another of his visits.

'I thought I told him to stay away from us,' Ma said.

We watched as Hermanus Steyn got out of his car and, sensing our hostility, stood in the doorway.

'Don't get upset,' he said, addressing Ma. He spoke in English out of consideration for us, but with an awkwardness that suggested an unfamiliarity with the language. 'I've brought something for the child.'

'*The child*'s name is Soraya,' Ma said coldly.

He hurried back to his car. We went to the door and watched as he reached into the back seat and carefully lifted out a small cardboard box.

Soraya, who had heard the car pulling into the driveway, came to investigate. When she saw the stranger, she stood aside, quietly observing.

Hermanus Steyn returned and paused on the top step. He put the box down. A puppy poked its nose out sleepily. Soraya inched towards the box.

'I heard about your husband,' Hermanus Steyn said to Ma. 'I'm sorry.' He gazed at Soraya, a small smile forming on his lips.

Ma was silent. Soraya discreetly tugged at her dress, glancing up into her face, waiting for permission. The puppy started yapping. Hermanus dropped to his haunches next to the box and stroked it.

Soraya, barely able to control her excitement, waited for approval, her eyes fixed on Ma's face.

Ma narrowed her eyes and looked disapprovingly at Hermanus Steyn.

Soraya monitored every shifting nuance, waiting for the smile that would say 'yes'.

Hermanus Steyn stroked the puppy's head and looked back at Ma. Suddenly Ma's expression softened. She questioned him without speaking.

'I have no one now,' he explained, his voice catching. 'Cobus . . . my son was killed in Mozambique . . . guerrilla fire . . . last month.'

Ma and Nana exchanged glances. A curious glint flashed briefly in my mother's eyes. But she uttered no word of sympathy or condolence, she just stood there staring down at the man she had detested for years. Any words of sympathy would have been hypocritical. Cobus was dead. It was a relief. A festering abscess had finally been excised. None of us spoke.

Hermanus Steyn's eyes clouded briefly. I found myself feeling sorry for him and had to force myself to remember what his son had done to us.

'I hope you don't mind me bringing the child . . . So-reeja . . . the puppy,' he said, smiling as he stumbled over the name. 'A child needs an animal to love. It must be lonely out here for her.'

'She doesn't need an animal to love,' I said. 'She has us.'

His eyes turned to me, flickered briefly, but there was no hint of recognition.

Ma took a deep breath. 'Thank you,' she said to Hermanus Steyn. She nodded at Soraya who dropped to her knees next to the box. She carefully removed the puppy, which promptly slobbered all over her face. Soraya smiled ecstatically.

'What do you say, Soraya?' Ma asked.

'Thank you,' Soraya said and smiled, her eyes full of love and wonder for the four-footed miracle that had arrived in a cardboard box.

Hermanus Steyn got up off his haunches, touched his hat and walked to his car.

We watched as he turned the car around and drove off the property.

Nana shook her head. 'Well, I never,' she said, her hands on her hips as she watched the car disappear down the road. 'So Cobus got what was coming to him. I told you something would happen.'

Soraya played with the pup, too busy to pay attention to the adult currents eddying above her head.

'What are you going to name the dog?' I asked her.

'Yasmin?' she asked, in a tremulous voice.

'No! Yasmin is not a dog-name. Anyway,' I added, 'it's a boy-dog.'

She considered this for a moment as the puppy licked her face. It had two black paws and the rest of it was light brown.

'It looks like a German Shepherd,' Nana remarked.

None of us knew enough about dogs to confirm or deny this.

'I want to call it Birdie,' Soraya said gravely.

'Birdie! Why Birdie?' I cried in mock-horror.

'Well,' she said, 'it made all the angry faces fly away.'

We exchanged amused glances.

'And you think she doesn't pay attention,' Nana laughed. 'You'd be surprised what goes through that little head.'

'Pity Abdul isn't here to share in this,' Ma said sadly. 'He so wanted to be around to see her growing up.'

Nana believed that we had not heard the last of Hermanus Steyn. The spectre of his subdued, defeated figure haunted us. Not only had he lost his wife, but now his son as well. Although none of us would shed any tears for Cobus, I couldn't help feeling sorry for his father.

Because our lives were so uneventful, we occupied ourselves speculating about the Steyns.

The Steyns' maid Maria was a relative of Gladys's, and she sometimes brought little tit-bits of news.

There was no doubt that we were relieved that Cobus was dead.

A few days after Hermanus's visit, Nana said: 'It's not right to rejoice in the misfortunes of others. Bad luck boomerangs, you know.'

'You were the one who put a curse on the boy, remember?' Ma said.

'I never wished him dead.'

'You said . . .' I interjected, eager to remind Nana of what she had said.

'I was just saying . . . ' Nana protested.

'We're not rejoicing, Mum,' Ma said. 'We're relieved. He was a monster. Who knows what else he might have done? Remember how he tormented the girls when they were growing up and then look what it all resulted in. How can one forgive what he did?'

'I know,' Nana said. 'That boy has been a curse to all of us. From what I hear he was a curse to his father as well.'

The full story of Cobus's death was revealed later. He had joined the South African Defence Force. He'd been in and out of trouble while in the army and his father had had to bail him out several times.

'What did he do?' I asked curiously.

'Who knows?' Nana said. 'The army protects its own. It gives refuge to misfits like him. Murderers and psychos . . .'

'One day the history of the South African army will be written in blood,' Ma said.

'Too late then. Like Hitler's armies. The damage will have

been done.'

'Poor man,' I muttered, unable to dispel the image of Hermanus Steyn with the puppy.

'Don't you ever feel sorry for him,' my mother snapped. 'Hermanus Steyn is a bastard. He humiliated your father. There are things I can never forgive him for.'

'And we thought they'd got off scot-free,' Nana said. 'We thought there was no justice. Well, look what happened. Life is strange, isn't it? One must never doubt Him for a moment.'

I listened to this exchange between my mother and grandmother and wondered, not for the first time, about Nana's attitude to religion. One moment she scorned it, the next she vehemently defended it. She explained her apparent inconsistency as a differentiation between 'faith' and 'organised religion'. She decried the latter as an instrument of control, a perfect example of which, according to her, was the Dutch Reformed Church.

The Muslim/Christian dichotomy in our lives and the way Nana saw things was puzzling. It wasn't until years later when I was old enough to recognise the complexities of our situation, that I managed to make a little sense of the puzzle.

28

UNCLE EWIN and Jonathan arrived the first week in December. They wanted to spend Christmas in Cape Town with family there and intended to spend ten days with us at McBain. Fortunately for me, schools were closed for the Christmas holidays.

I was thrilled at the prospect of meeting Jonathan – someone my own age and with whom I would have things in common.

My thoughts still lingered on Sandile, even though nothing had ever developed between us. He was just a figure inhabiting my fantasies. But Jonathan was real. Because he had grown up in London, he was worldly and sophisticated. I was sure he would have all the qualities I coveted.

I, of course, was twenty-two and still a virgin.

There was an instant chemistry between us. I could feel it and so could he. I understood, for the first time, what it was like in *Cast Adrift* when Quatrain had attracted Waneta's eyes across a room full of noisy guests. The moment their eyes met, everything else had faded into the background, as if the two of them were castaways, alone on a desert island.

Ma and Nana were too engrossed with Uncle Ewin to notice what was happening between Jonathan and me.

We spent every single moment together: walking, talking and enjoying each other's company.

He told me all about his life in London. I learned that Jonathan's mother, Aunty Kate, was Uncle Ewin's third wife. Jonathan was a son from his mother's first marriage. It was confusing trying to understand the relationships and it didn't matter anyway. Jonathan told me that Uncle Ewin was drinking again and that his previous two wives had left him because of this. He said that his mother was visiting relatives in Australia and that she, too, was thinking of leaving Uncle Ewin.

We explored the veld together, going out early in the morning when the light was soft and gentle, and late in the afternoon when long shadows turned the brown veld into shades of indigo.

Lonely and hungry for affection, and with the two of us tossed together like twin zygotes trapped in the same egg, our relationship was transformed from friends to lovers.

When we were alone nothing mattered except the moment – each of which, like a snapshot, was arrested and preserved in time.

Every afternoon we drove out to 'our' secluded spot, far from prying eyes. The old blanket which I kept in the boot of my car was carefully spread on the bare ground. Quietly and with a sense of belonging, we lay together.

On the first occasion we were both stiff and awkward, painfully aware of the way events would unfold.

Then he touched me, tentatively at first. I could feel my skin tingling under his fingers. I became both participant and observer as I responded. We were one. Exploring, discovering, marvelling.

My fingers moved over his body, over the smoothness of his chest, his belly, caressing the softness of his skin, of his sex. He moaned and writhed beneath my touch and then, the pleasure unbearable, he rolled on to me.

The initial pain drawn away, our union became pleasurable and we were both transported by it, embracing it.

Afterwards when he saw that I was bleeding, he asked if he had hurt me. I assured him that he hadn't.

He carefully wiped my blood from his body.

As I watched he turned to me, smiling.

We lay under the darkening African sky, wrapped around each other, the blanket crumpled beneath us.

The days I spent with Jonathan were unlike anything I had

read about in romance novels. None of the books did justice to those moments of absolute bliss. I wished it was possible to freeze them. The tenderness, the passion, the desire . . . I didn't want to think about him leaving, tried to put it from my mind, but the thought always intruded. I didn't want to fall in love, tried to stop myself from hurtling headlong into hell.

We were so wrapped up in each other that neither of us noticed problems developing between Nana and Uncle Ewin.

Uncle Ewin was drinking himself into a stupor. At the end of the week when his supply of liquor ran out, he quietly slipped away and drove to the liquor store in town.

That afternoon Nana waited on the stoep with Jonathan for him to come home. They waited until it got dark, but there was no sign of Uncle Ewin.

Nana was furious and Jonathan admitted to her that Uncle Ewin had been drinking like that for years.

When he was still not home at ten o'clock that night, Nana gave up and went to bed. Jonathan and I stayed up all night, making love on the veranda while Ma and Nana slept.

Around mid-morning the next day Uncle Ewin arrived looking sheepish. Nana would have none of his excuses or his promises. She marched to the car and searched it, finding several bottles hidden under the seat and in the boot.

Opening the bottles of liquor she emptied their contents on to the ground. The liquid trickled along the dry ground in little streams like brown tears.

I had never seen Nana so angry. 'I never want to see you again,' she said to Uncle Ewin. 'You are a disgrace! I wish you'd stayed in England. What kind of example are you to the boy?'

Jonathan was standing to one side, an uncomfortable spectator.

'What a damn shame that a man like you, with intelligence and a good family, threw it all away.' Nana's lip curled contemptuously. She spat on the sand. 'You disgust me. Here, take the keys. Get into your car and go. As far as I'm concerned I don't know you.'

Uncle Ewin took the keys. He couldn't look at Nana. He glanced at Ma, mutely appealing to her, but her face was expressionless. She turned her back on him and went into the house.

For a moment Uncle Ewin seemed uncertain about what his next move would be.

Nana was unrelenting.

'Fine,' he said. 'I'll go.' He went into the house to pack his bags.

While he was packing, Nana took Jonathan aside. He looked at her with large brown eyes, eyes that reminded me of Sandile.

I was angry and disappointed that they were leaving.

'Why do you have to go with him?' I demanded when I managed to corner Jonathan.

'I have to go with him,' he said. 'Things will get even worse if he's alone.'

'I can't believe this is happening,' I said.

'I hate leaving too, Meena. I'm going to miss you terribly.'

'Of course you are, you can hardly wait to get away,' I said sarcastically.

'That's not true,' he muttered.

But I was too angry to listen to him and walked away.

'Don't let him drive, my child,' Nana pleaded with Jonathan before they left. 'Please, I beg of you.'

'He'll be all right, Nana,' Jonathan said.

'I don't know why you came with him. It was a big mistake,' she said.

Jonathan was silent. His eyes, pained and anxious, sought mine. But I was still angry and in no mood to be sympathetic. All I could focus on was my own pain.

'Why don't you stay here with us, Jonathan? Let him go to Cape Town on his own.'

'Yes, why don't you, Jonathan?' I added bitterly.

Jonathan hung his head miserably and looked away.

'You're a good boy, Jonathan,' Nana said.

Jonathan shrugged self-consciously. 'I think he's trying to work things out. I'd like to help him. Everyone has turned their backs on him.'

'But he won't listen,' Nana said.

'These things take time.'

'What does your mother say about all of this?'

'She's tired of it.'

Nana gently touched his cheek and sighed. 'I wish I knew what to do,' she said. 'I went through this once before with my brother Patrick.'

While Uncle Ewin packed I had a last few moments with Jonathan.

'I'll see you on the way back. We may pass by here again on our way to Johannesburg in January.' He paused. 'I'll miss you, Meena,' he said quietly.

'I'll miss you too,' I said. 'I'm sorry about the things I said earlier. I hope you come back this way, but it looks as though your father and Nana are no longer on speaking terms.'

'They'll make up. They're family, aren't they?'

'I hope you're right.'

Uncle Ewin was ready to leave. Ma and Nana stood on the stoep in silence as he got into the car. Jonathan said goodbye. My chest tightened, already feeling the loss, as he walked to the car.

Uncle Ewin drove to the gate without looking back. Jonathan waved. Soraya held on to Birdie who was straining to run after the car.

My aching heart bumped over the rocks like an old shoe tied to a wedding car. Long after they had gone I remembered how I had given myself in the veld. Raw and uncluttered amidst the lizards, ants, the sand and the prickly karoo bush.

The rains came late that December. Not the usual heavy storms that precipitated the summer rains, but steady showers that fell every afternoon for three weeks. Farmers were jubilant. Instead of rampaging floods which washed away the top soil, the rain seeped into the earth and replenished the diminishing ground water levels.

After the rains the air felt fresh and clean. Nana said it was like champagne. We teased her, asking where and when she had tasted champagne. She just smiled and said there had been a time during her youth when her life had been vastly different from what it was now.

I moped around the house, missing Jonathan. Christmas passed uneventfully. Soraya opened her gifts and tore around the house excitedly. For me it was a day like any other day. I tried to read the new book I had picked up at the library, *Summer Paradise*, but found it hard to concentrate. I was getting bored with romances. They had become predictable. I knew now that there was no such thing as a happy ending. Reality was vastly different from the diet of fiction I had been feeding on.

I became depressed and ever more conscious of my loneliness. I paced around restlessly. Nana seemed to understand, but my mother became impatient with me.

'What's wrong with you?' she asked irritably.

Nana didn't say anything, but I could tell from her expression that she knew about Jonathan and me. She had obviously not said anything to my mother . . . yet.

I had known this would happen. I had dreaded the misery that follows in the wake of falling in love. It had been so well documented in the romance novels. The writers obviously had all experienced the angst of falling in love and then parting.

How was I going to exist without him? He had opened the sluice gates, peeled away the lid, leaving me raw and exposed.

I got through the days, one hour at a time, one day at time, one week at a time.

About a month after Uncle Ewin and Jonathan left, we received a letter from Jonathan to say that they had returned to London much earlier than planned.

Uncle Ewin had rolled the rented car in Cape Town. Fortunately neither of them had been injured, but the shock had brought Uncle Ewin to his senses. He had agreed to go into a rehabilitation centre on their return to London.

Nana was relieved. She hoped it was a decision he would stick to.

While I was struggling to untangle myself from my web of misery, McBain was struck by a plague of frogs. They arrived, or hatched, a few days after a light summer's rain.

They were everywhere, hopping around the backyard, congregating in ditches and gullies. The birds swooped and crows assembled for the feast. None of us had seen anything like this before. Soraya was terrified of going outside. But the frogs' life-cycle was short and they were soon gone. Daniel cleaned up, shovelling dead frog carcasses into a hole.

Then he quietly disappeared. Because this had happened before, we were not unduly concerned.

A week later he returned and though Ma questioned him about where he had been, he wouldn't give any explanation.

We would have forgotten about his few days' absence but the police arrived at McBain to question him. It was then that we discovered that Daniel had gone into town to apply for his driver's licence. When he could not produce any identity documents, the licensing officer reported the matter to the police.

We expected him to be arrested and carted away, but the police officer seemed preoccupied. Eventually he left, threatening to be back soon. Ma promised that she'd have all Daniel's papers in order.

We were nervous about Daniel's situation. Although he had his sane and rational moments, most of the time he seemed to be in his own world. We were concerned that he might say or do something stupid and draw attention to himself. One of his fantastic claims to be working for the FBI was all the excuse a paranoid official needed to lock him up and throw away the key.

'Thank God they talked to him during one of his lucid moments,' Ma said as the police left.

That seemed to be the end of the matter. We had no idea what Daniel had said to the police, but whatever it was they appeared to be satisfied. For the moment.

Sitting on the stoep with my mother, I watched Soraya and Birdie playing in the yard. They were inseparable. Birdie had been sleeping on her bed until Ma put a stop to it and the dog was relegated to a box at the foot of the bed.

'This is not a person,' Ma told her. 'It's a dog. And it's not healthy to have a dog sleeping on your bed. He has ticks and fleas.' In spite of Ma's admonishments, when Birdie whimpered at night, Soraya invited him back on to the bed.

Ma's eyes followed Soraya and Birdie as they played in the yard, but her attention was clearly elsewhere.

After a while she turned to me and asked: 'Are you still thinking of going away?'

Surprised, I hesitated. Then I shook my head.

'I appreciate the sacrifice you've made, Meena,' she said. 'Unlike your sister, you've always been obedient. You stuck by us, even when the going was tough. Despite what you might think, your Papa loved you very much. He had a small life insurance policy. It's not much, but it'll be enough to make our lives a little easier. At least I can stock the shelves again and there'll be a little bit left for an emergency. It'll ease the pressure on you.'

I didn't say anything.

'If you're still thinking of going away,' Ma said, 'I won't stop you.'

I thought about what my mother had said. Although the desire was still there to explore the world beyond McBain, I knew that I could not and would not abandon my family while they required my help. Besides, I had never been away from home for any extended period, let alone gone beyond the borders. Much as I wanted to venture off, I wasn't quite as ready to leave as I thought. Papa's life insurance was very small and would not be enough to solve our problems. My salary was still needed.

Elsa and Johan returned to the McBain siding. Gladys told us that they had moved into the same cottage. Niels was staying with an aunt in town while Elsa and Johan settled into their married life. Elsa's father had retired from his job with the railways and Johan had taken over as the engineer, inspecting the lines ten miles on either side of McBain.

On the day he started I saw him with the labourer, scooting along the rails on the small inspection trolley. I still occasionally walked the rails, but not as often as I used to. There were too many reminders of Jonathan. Places we had explored together. Each time I saw one, there was a tug at my heart and an unbearable ache, a longing that could not be assuaged.

School was opening soon and I tried to work up some enthusiasm for the event. But my heart was no longer in my work.

The day after schools opened, Niels returned to his mother. Nana was more convinced than ever that something strange was going on at the Bothas. Niels was home for a week, running around in their backyard. Soraya, sorely tempted to join him, remembered Ma's warning that she was never to cross the railway tracks on her own.

Later that afternoon Nana saw Mr Botha arrive at the cottage. Her suspicions aroused, she remained at the kitchen window, watching as Mr Botha played with Niels, then picked him up and carried him into the house.

An hour later when Nana went back to the kitchen, Mr Botha's car was still in the yard. She went about her business, pausing now and then to peer out across the tracks.

At about five o'clock Nana was at the kitchen sink filling the kettle for tea. Niels was outside, playing next to Mr Botha's car. He was engrossed in his little game, paying no attention to his mother and grandfather on the stoep.

As Mr Botha got into the car Nana looked out and realised that he hadn't seen Niels behind the car. She dropped the kettle and ran outside screaming at Mr Botha to stop. It was too late. Niels had already disappeared under the wheels.

Mr Botha stopped the car and got out. Niels was lying in the sand, his little body crushed.

In those terrible moments of paralysis no one moved. Nana screamed and Ma rushed out to see what was going on. Unable to speak, Nana gestured across the tracks. Ma saw Elsa and her father at the car. Then she saw the tiny body.

'Dear God!' she exclaimed and rushed towards the tracks, followed by Nana. I was in the shop with Soraya.

'Meena! Meena!' Ma called as she half-walked, half-ran to the tracks. I heard the desperate note in her voice and came running.

'Call an ambulance!' my mother cried. 'Hurry! Tell them it's an emergency!' With that, Ma was down the embankment and across the tracks.

'What's wrong?' I called.

'Hurry!' Nana shouted, giving me a little shove. 'It's Niels, he's been run over.'

The police arrived. The ambulance was there soon afterwards. But it was too late. Niels was dead. Elsa was white with shock. She couldn't speak. She stood there uncomprehending, staring at her child's lifeless body.

Ma had her arm around Elsa. The rest of us watched – too stunned to speak. Mr Botha was sitting on the edge of the stoep holding his head in his hands.

'I didn't see him,' he said as the police questioned him.

Nana said that she had seen it all from the kitchen window. She confirmed Mr Botha's story about not having seen the child.

Ma and Nana sat up late into the night. Nana was still in a state of shock. 'If only I'd got to the window earlier, I might've been able to warn him.'

'No, Mum. It's no use blaming yourself. You couldn't have done anything.'

Niels was buried a few days later after the district surgeon had performed a post-mortem. The undertaker had tried to restore his face as best he could, but it was horribly disfigured. At the service the casket was closed.

We stood to one side at the cemetery, away from the white congregation.

Elsa left a few weeks later. Left her husband and the horror of her life behind her. No one knew where she'd gone. The police telephoned her aunt in Pretoria, but she hadn't seen her.

Nana said it was all too much for a mother. Poor Elsa, she said, as she recalled how Elsa had at first rejected the child, then accepted him and in the end lost him.

'It's too much for a mother's heart to bear,' she said.

About two weeks after Elsa left, the police came to investigate her disappearance. They came to the shop to question Ma and Nana and also wanted to talk to Daniel again.

We were in the shop when the two constables arrived, chests thrust out, holsters clearly visible.

I went cold when I saw them. The police, like gods, had power over life and death. They could summarily dispense justice without the benefit of a court of law.

One of the pair, the bigger of the two, had dark hair and a moustache and was wearing a pair of cheap sunglasses. The other was a slender fellow, blond and very fair – almost albino-white.

'Where's the boy who works here?' the constable with the sunglasses demanded.

Ma didn't say anything at first, her resentful eyes shifting from one policeman to the other.

The dark policeman's face twitched impatiently.

The other policeman looked around.

Ma's expression tightened.

'He's outside,' I said, fearing what they might do under provocation.

'What do you want with Daniel?' my mother asked, addressing the sunglasses.

'We want to question him,' he said.

'But you've already questioned him.'

The policeman removed his glasses and polished them, his gaze appraising. 'We'll want to talk to you, as well, about his papers.'

'And about failing to register your servant,' the other said.

'All the people who work for us are registered.' The lie slipped from Ma's lips, smoothly and easily.

'We'll see, won't we,' Albino said, his eyes narrowing as he looked first at Ma and then at me.

Although outwardly calm, I could tell Ma was quaking. A second visit from the police did not bode well.

I went outside. Daniel was trying to fix a fence at the far end of the yard. The police followed me on to the veranda and waited in the shade while I called Daniel. Daniel was confused by all the police attention, especially since they were bent on conducting their interrogation in Afrikaans. He did not understand a word they were saying.

'Where do you come from?' they demanded. 'Why don't you have papers? Where is your passbook?'

Daniel waited, wide-eyed and open-mouthed, too shocked to speak.

He looked at Ma, appealing to her, but before she could react, the policeman grabbed him by the collar as if to shake a response from him. Daniel quickly thrust his hand into his inside pocket and withdrew a folded scrap of paper. He handed it to the policeman.

My heart sank. I recognised the dirty piece of paper, taped along the folds where it had fallen apart. I'd seen it often enough over the years, produced with a flourish in a parody of Elliot Ness in the film *The Untouchables*.

The two policemen exchanged glances. '*Ja*, old pallie, we've got him now for sure,' Sunglasses said in Afrikaans, handing the paper to his partner. He made a twirling motion at his temple.

His partner chuckled as he scanned the sheet of paper.

They marched Daniel to the van, pushed him up against it and continued their interrogation.

'Ma, where is Daniel going?' Soraya asked.

None of us dared tell her.

They shoved Daniel into the back of the van. The van roared away, Daniel's frantic face pressed up against the back window in mute appeal.

He looked so terrified, so abandoned, that I ran after the van, vainly trying to stop it. It spun out of the driveway in a cloud of dust, bumping over the rocky patch at the gate. With a squeal of tyres, it took off down the main road.

Ma raised her fist at the departing van. 'Surely they could see that Daniel isn't all there?' she cried.

'Why did he have to show them that stupid piece of paper?' I asked.

'He's completely harmless. Why couldn't they leave him alone?' Ma stood with her hands on her hips, staring down the road where the van had long since disappeared from view. 'I'd better go into town to see if Sergeant Klein can help us,' she said at last.

'It's out of his district,' Nana reminded her.

'At least he can advise us,' Ma snapped impatiently.

'The way those devils question people, we may never see Daniel again,' Nana said grimly.

'Poor Daniel. If they keep him locked up, he'll go berserk,' I remarked.

'Mum, what are we going to do?' Ma asked.

But even Nana was at a loss.

29

THEY NEVER found Elsa.

Gladys told us that Mabel had some nasty things to say about the Botha household. It was obvious that there had been more going on than any of us had suspected. I was reluctant to believe the stories about Elsa and Mr Botha. Mabel couldn't be trusted. She had a reputation for lying.

Ma and Nana had considered some of these issues too – not the killing of the child, but the fact that Mr Botha and Elsa might have had an incestuous relationship.

I began to think of Elsa's strange behaviour, her secretiveness. Did her mother know? Was that why she always used to watch Elsa? Was the burden of the secret too much for her? Was that why she drank so much?

It was difficult, though, to see Mr Botha as a child molester. He had always given us the impression that he was a decent, civil man.

Nana listened in silence when I told her about some of my thoughts.

'Life is not always straightforward, Meena,' she said. 'You can't always judge a book by its cover.'

I still peered out of the kitchen window to the cottages across the track, expecting to see Elsa in the yard.

Her husband Johan, totally traumatised by events, had left as well. He'd obviously also heard the rumours about Elsa and her father. We heard that he had found a job in Bloemfontein.

Sergeant Klein telephoned to say that Daniel was being held

in jail. Because of all his talk about the CIA and FBI, the police suspected that he had terrorist connections.

We laughed at the outrageous notion of Daniel as a terrorist. Sergeant Klein, who had known Daniel for many years, agreed that the charge was a ridiculous one, but said there was nothing he could do because it was out of his jurisdiction.

'What do we do now?' Ma asked.

'Nothing,' Sergeant Klein said. 'Let matters take their course.'

'That probably means he'll be shot, and the police will claim that he was trying to escape,' Nana said.

We were only beginning to grasp the seriousness of Daniel's situation.

One afternoon after school, Ma and I met in town to visit Daniel in jail. But gaining access to him was not as easy as we thought it would be.

'He's in solitary,' the sergeant at the charge office barked. 'No visitors allowed.'

Ma, having had some experience with the police, had come prepared. She discreetly produced a bottle of brandy, wrapped in a nondescript brown paper bag. It had been bought specifically for this purpose.

'*Ag*, never mind, Sergeant. I brought this for you anyway,' she said sliding the bottle across the desk.

The sergeant's furtive eyes swept the room and in one movement he had scooped the package into his desk drawer.

'What are the charges?' Ma asked, all wide-eyed innocence.

'You'll know soon enough,' he said with a dismissive flutter of his hand.

'Please sergeant, could we see him . . . just for a moment?' she wheedled. 'What harm can it do?'

The sergeant shook his head. Ma did not move. She sat across the desk, her gaze fixed unwaveringly on him. He capitulated, perhaps out of sympathy, but more likely encouraged by the bottle in his desk drawer. He instructed the duty constable, who had just entered the office, to phone the jail.

'*Dis vir die mal jong,*' he said in Afrikaans – it's for the crazy one. 'Just fifteen minutes,' he shouted, as we hurried out of his office.

At the jail we were ushered into a waiting-room in the African wing: a dingy room, painted dark green and layered with the accumulated grime of years. An overpowering stench of urine permeated the building from the open urinals. Suspended from a frayed electric cord, a single light bulb with a dirty, fly-speckled green shade, illuminated the room. A barrier of chain link and wire mesh separated the prisoners' area from the visitors.

We waited for Daniel, feeling totally out of place. Just as we were about to gag on the foul air in the small room, Daniel was ushered in. He approached slowly, dragging the shackles which bound his ankles. The left side of his face was swollen; his left eye was shut. His lips looked like sausages, the upper one split down the middle. He was barely recognisable.

Appalled, Ma and I stared at him. He had lost weight and his bony shoulders protruded grotesquely from a dirty khaki shirt that was much too big for him. He was obviously having difficulty seeing through the injured left eye and lowered his head. We dreaded what might still lie in store for him as he stood on the other side of the mesh barrier, his hands clasped in front of him and his head bowed.

'My God . . .' Ma whispered.

Daniel glanced at the guard standing at the door.

'Who hit you, Daniel?' she asked.

Daniel turned away, fearful of the guard.

Ma was concerned about his injuries. He needed medical attention, but we knew he would receive none.

'Are they giving you food, Daniel?'

'Yes, Madam,' he said, speaking with great difficulty through his swollen lips.

There was nothing else to say.

'I will come back again when I have some news, Daniel,' Ma promised.

He said nothing.

'Do you understand, Daniel?'

Daniel gazed at her and then slowly nodded his head.

For a moment his face brightened. 'The bicycles. Are they still there, Madam?'

'Yes, Daniel. They are still there.'

Daniel tried to smile, but it was obviously too painful.

'Daniel,' Ma said gently, 'they may send you back to Rhodesia – to your home. It might be better that way.' She was lying, trying to give him some hope, something to cling to. But Daniel didn't want to go back home.

He put his hand out against the wire mesh, his broken face pleading. 'This is my home, Madam. My home is with you.'

Tears slid down Ma's face. She brushed them away quickly.

'Time up!' The guard stepped forward, roughly taking hold of Daniel's arm. We watched for a moment longer, looking at each other helplessly as the guard led him away. Then we left, relieved to step out into the sunlight and fresh air.

When we told Nana what we had seen she was furious. She said one could expect no better from a system designed to destroy our men. Gladys stood to one side, listening, shaking her head and clucking.

'*Yini*, I told you,' she said, reproachfully. 'They are bad men, the police. They will kill him.'

'I don't think it will come to that,' Ma said. 'They'll send him home to Rhodesia.'

'They will kill him,' Gladys said emphatically.

'Dammit, can't they see that Daniel is harmless?' I cried. 'He's a bit dilly, but he's harmless. There must be something we can do!'

A few nights later we were awakened by frantic knocking at the front door. Birdie went into watchdog mode and barked furiously. I went to the window and drew the curtain aside. Illuminated in the light from the stoep was Daniel. Startled, I let him in. The knocking had woken Ma and Nana and they came to see what was going on.

Daniel was panic-stricken. A thin thread of mucus dribbled from the corner of his mouth.

'Daniel! What on earth are you doing here?' Ma asked. Then it dawned on her. 'My God,' she said, as she shut and locked the door. 'He's escaped. How did you get away, Daniel?'

But Daniel was too terrified to speak. We pulled him into the kitchen towards the back door.

'You must go back, Daniel,' Ma urged. 'The police will kill you if they find you. Give yourself up.'

Daniel shook his head.

'What are we going to do?' I asked fearfully as I remembered the threatening presence of the police when they came to arrest Daniel.

'This will be the first place they'll come to look,' Nana said.

My mother opened the back door and peered out. Daniel stood in the middle of the kitchen, his head lowered, quivering with fear. There was no fight left in him.

'Dear Jesus, please help,' Nana muttered as she took Daniel by the arm and led him to the back door. Daniel went meekly. 'Daniel, you must find a place to hide. Go now.'

But Daniel didn't want to leave. He jerked his arm free.

'What are we going to do?' Ma asked anxiously, the three of us gathered around Daniel.

'Daniel, how did you get away?'

Daniel gazed at us, bewildered.

'Daniel!' Ma said sharply. 'Talk to me.'

Finally he stammered: 'I jumped over the wall.' He wrung his hands. 'They will kill me. They will kill me, Madam,' he cried.

'I'm sure the police will be here any minute,' Ma said. 'I've got to find a place for him to hide. Bring the flashlight,' she called after me as I ran to my room to get my robe.

'I'll go with him,' I said. 'You wait here in case the police come.'

'No,' Nana said. 'It's too dangerous. Stay here. I'll try to make him understand that he has to hide somewhere.'

'It's too late,' I said.

'You'll be shot along with him. You know what the police are like! You're not setting foot outside this house.' Nana barred my way.

While the two of us argued, a police car pulled up at the front of the house. Nana pushed Daniel out the back door and slammed it shut behind him. Daniel scrambled down the embankment towards the tracks. Nana turned off the stoep light, plunging the yard into darkness.

Awakened by the commotion Soraya appeared, rubbing her eyes sleepily.

The police were about to beat down the door when Ma opened it.

'What do you want?' she demanded as one of them burst in through the open door.

There were two vans parked in the driveway. Three policemen remained on the stoep while the others searched the property.

One of the policeman, the young constable with the dark glasses whom we had encountered before, pushed his way into the house. 'Where is he?' he demanded.

'There's no one here,' Ma said.

The policeman glared at her and without another word marched into the house and began turning the beds over and pushing furniture around, leaving chaos in his wake. We could do nothing, except watch as the police tore our house apart.

Satisfied that Daniel was not hiding in the house, the policeman signalled to the others. He scowled at us and strode away.

Ma flung the door shut. We went to the kitchen window. Birdie had taken off into the darkness. There was no sign of either Daniel or Birdie.

Ma opened the back door and called quietly. 'Daniel! Daniel!'

Birdie barked in the distance. Soraya started to cry.

'I hope Daniel's found somewhere to hide,' I said anxiously, peering out into the night.

'He took off like a jackrabbit when the police arrived,' Nana said. 'He must be down at the tracks by now.'

'I hope he made it,' I said.

'I want Birdie. Where's Birdie?' Soraya whimpered.

'For God's sake!' Ma said impatiently. 'Meena, see if you can find Birdie.'

Knotting the belt of my robe, I went out on to the back stoep. I could still hear Birdie barking, but of Daniel there was no sign.

'Daniel, Daniel,' I called softly, in the hope that he might hear me, but there was no answer. Nothing moved in the backyard.

'Birdie! Birdie!'

Birdie's responsive bark came from the direction of the cottages. I went back inside.

'Birdie's across the tracks,' I told them.

'I wonder where Daniel is,' Nana said.

'Long gone, I hope,' Ma replied.

We stood at the window for a while. Birdie came running back towards the house. I went to the back door and waited for him. He came all the way up to me and then just as I was about to grab his collar, he took off again, running half-way down the embankment and waiting, as though expecting me to follow.

Soraya was at the door in a flash, eager to run after him. Nana pulled her inside. She started crying, loud heart-wrenching sobs.

I took the flashlight and pulled the back door shut. As I hurried after Birdie I noticed several sets of headlights approaching the railway cottages from the direction of the crossing.

'Come back, Birdie! Get back here this instant! Damn dog!' I muttered, hitching up my robe as I leapt across the tracks. Except for the occasional goods train carrying a special load like coal or petrol, there were few trains at night.

As I scrambled up the other side of the tracks I could hear the policemen calling to each other. There was the sound of voices and dogs barking and I suspected that Birdie was in the middle of the furore. The police had stopped further down the track. The beams from their flashlights moved around in eerie, disembodied arcs. Fearful of being shot, I stepped behind a tree and turned off my flashlight. Fortunately I knew the area well and could find my way in the dark. Lights began to go on in the cottages.

'Birdie, Birdie,' I called. Something rustled behind a tree in the Jouberts' yard. Thinking it was Birdie, I crept forward. But instead of Birdie, I found Daniel.

'Run, Daniel!' I pleaded. 'For God's sake, run! The police are here.'

He hesitated. I gave him a small shove and he scuttled away. Something wet moved against my leg. I reached down and located Birdie. Grabbing his collar, I dragged him off roughly and he whimpered in protest. I moved forward determinedly but cautiously, aware of the danger I was in.

There was no sign of Daniel now and I assumed he'd got away. His only hope was to get into the hills before daylight because by morning the place would be swarming with police. I slithered down the embankment, dragging Birdie with me. When I reached the tracks, Birdie pulled free and bounded off. Again I went after him, grabbing his collar and cursing under my breath.

As I turned back my foot touched something soft.

It was Daniel, lying prostrate, his leg twisted grotesquely. He was moaning quietly. He cried out in pain as I tried to help him up and I realised that he was badly injured. I needed help.

I cast an anxious glance at the swaying lights in the distance. I wondered if I'd have enough time to get to the house and back before the police thought of searching the tracks.

'I'll be back, Daniel. I'm going to get help.'

I took a firm hold on Birdie and dragged him home. He no longer resisted. It was as if he knew something would be done about Daniel.

It took only a few minutes to get back to the house.

'Quick,' I told Ma and Nana. 'Lock him in a room. I've got to go back. Daniel has a broken leg. Ma, you've got to help me. We've got to drag him clear of the tracks.'

'Oh God, what else can go wrong?' Ma moaned. 'How did he manage that?'

'I don't know. But we've got to get him to safety.'

But when Ma and I reached the spot where I had left Daniel, there was no sign of him. The police were getting ever closer.

'Maybe he's managed on his own,' Ma said. 'We must get

back to the house.'

I realised that I had lost one of my shoes only when I felt a slight tremor beneath the shoeless foot on the rail.

'There's a train coming,' I said as we turned for home.

We continued to observe the police from the kitchen window. Three of their cars were parked in the veld, their lights illuminating the surroundings. The cottages were lit up, the occupants curious to see what was going on.

'Thank God Daniel got away,' Ma said.

The train approached, its bright beam slicing through the darkness. We heard its whistle at the crossing, saw its light. And saw Daniel trapped in its beam. He tried to push himself up on his broken leg. But it was too late. Transfixed, he huddled on the tracks as the train barrelled towards him.

The engineer claimed that he had felt a bump and realised he had hit something – an animal, he thought. A sudden stop would have been impossible because the cars would have jack-knifed and derailed, and the cargo of petrol would have become an inferno.

Daniel was dragged three hundred yards before the train stopped. The medical report suggested he had died instantly.

There wasn't much left to identify. Ma arranged for his remains to be buried in the small cemetery near the village.

We heard later that the day after we had visited Daniel in prison, his shackles had been removed because of an infection around his ankles. That same night, Daniel got away and scaled the prison wall. His escape went undetected until later that night. He had managed to get to the station and hid in a cattle cart on one of the goods trains that just happened to be going by McBain.

30

FOR THREE days the merciless berg winds continued to sweep across a veld already scorched by two years of drought. We stood on the stoep scanning the horizon, searching for relief, each blistering breath gritty with dust.

Above us the blanched sky, leached by heat and dry winds, remained clear and cloudless. Birdie chased dust-devils across the yard, pausing intermittently to look at Soraya for approval.

One evening, in the midst of this discomfort, the phone rang – two short rings and a long one, our signal on the party line. I answered it and heard Henrietta le Roux's wheezing voice.

'Person-to-person call from London for your mother,' she said.

There weren't many international calls on Henrietta's switchboard. On the rare occasions when a foreign operator came on the line, she struggling to understand them and they trying to make sense of her Afrikaans accent, her breathing became even more laboured.

She remained on the line while I called my mother. I returned to the phone. Henrietta and I were both eager to know who the caller was.

The word London had triggered thoughts of Jonathan, who had swept into my life and taken my heart and had then returned to London. Now as I waited on the line listening to Henrietta's strained breathing, I wondered if something had happened to him. Perhaps he had been killed in an accident. My heart, swollen with the anticipation of grief, tightened painfully.

My mother's arrival at the phone ended my fantasy of a lonely, grief-stricken figure standing on the English cliffs, hair whipped by the wind, inconsolably mourning her lost love. The image was from a romance I had recently read. The line crackled with static electricity, snapping me back to reality.

Out of breath and slightly alarmed about a long-distance, person-to-person call, Ma took the phone from me.

A few moments later I watched the colour drain from her face. Her free arm flailed for a chair and, looking stunned, she sat down. Nana and I crowded around her.

Ma didn't say anything to us. She listened, uttering endearments and words of comfort. I wondered who she was talking to.

'Who is it?' Nana and I demanded, almost in unison.

Ma put her hand over the receiver, eyes glittering with tears.

'It's Yasmin . . .' she whispered.

My grandmother didn't say anything. She didn't have to. The relief in her expression was all too evident.

I hopped around, reduced to childish behaviour as I waited with outstretched hand for the receiver to speak to my sister. But Ma ignored me, said goodbye and put the phone down. Disappointed and hurt, I watched as she leaned forward in her chair, succumbing to the anguish she had contained for such a long time. Nana put an arm around her. She cradled Ma's head against her breast as she might have done when Ma was a little girl.

'What does she have to say for herself?' Nana asked eventually.

'She's coming home . . .'

'When?' I cried.

'I don't know. We couldn't talk for long. It was a long-distance call,' was all she said by way of explanation.

'What else did she say?' Nana asked.

'Not much. She'll phone again.' My mother seemed tired.

'Ma, what else did she say?' I persisted.

'Enough with the questions.' My mother had said all she was

going to say. She withdrew, blew her nose loudly and went to the door. With the crumpled tissue pressed to her nostrils she gave a dry, shuddering sob. Above her the sky was like a vast canvas on which the image of my sister Yasmin was etched.

After almost seven years of complete silence, all of us fearing the worst, Yasmin had resurfaced and had deigned to call.

In the hours following the telephone call my mother retreated from us, escaping to a safe place in her head.

I remembered all too clearly the way things had been when Yasmin ran away from home. I was thrilled that she was coming back. For Nana and me, the news provided a diversion, a crack in the dull routine and monotony of our lives. We flitted around the house, laughing and joking, reminiscing about Yasmin.

Soraya had never known her mother and showed little interest in our talk about Yasmin. As far as she was concerned Ma was her mother and none of us had bothered to correct her.

When our excitement died down, Nana began to remember all the disappointment and heartache Yasmin had caused. Perhaps she wasn't really coming. We hadn't heard a word from her in all these years, why would she return now?

'I don't think we should get too excited. Let's just wait and see,' she declared.

The atmosphere was thick and muggy. The wind had died down and the air had become oppressive. An ominous stillness settled over the veld – a deathly, stagnant calm which lasted for two days.

On the third day we watched with mounting anxiety as the sky turned into a churning leaden cauldron rent by slashes of lightning. The first huge drops of rain pelted down, pocking the dry earth with craters.

Terrified, yet fascinated, we watched as the storm played out its fury. Thunder rolled over the landscape like cannon shot. Soraya clung to Ma, her face buried against her shoulder, her hands pressed to her ears. Ma took her into her bedroom, covered her with the eiderdown and sat with her.

In the vastness of the open veld the cluster of buildings at

McBain huddled together like tired old women, defenceless against the elements.

The storm raged all through the night. Nana left the lamp burning in the window. In that expanse of veld and in a darkness lit only by flashes of brilliant lightning, the lamp was like a beacon.

All the mirrors and glass surfaces were covered as we waited out the storm. And in the morning we emerged. Nana, grey hair unfurling from its knot, expressed amazement that we had not been drowned by the deluge.

The rain had turned the yard between the house and the shop into a lake of mud. The stone wall near the shop had withstood the pressure of the water dammed up behind it. Had the wall broken everything in the shop would have been swept away.

The water continued to run off the roof long after the storm had ended, forming pools on the stoep. The river down the road from us, so recently a dry creek bed, had swollen and broken its banks. Two thorn trees, plucked up by the storm, were lying up-ended on the far bank, their roots grinning at the sky. A bloated goat carcass was wedged between the pylons of the small bridge where bluebottles had converged to feast on the carrion.

A few days after the rains, masses of white butterflies appeared like snowflakes from a cloudless sky, wings sparkling in the sunlight. Then they were gone. The heat returned. The sun bleached the grass and shrivelled the sweet young shoots.

The rains were once more relegated to history.

On the morning of Yasmin's arrival Gladys, having walked the two miles from the village, was at McBain by half past five. She had never had children of her own. Abandoned by her first husband for another woman years before, she had taken care of first Yasmin, then me, and finally Soraya. Part of our family for more than twenty-five years, she had been present at every major event in our lives, including the crises. And now, along with the rest of us, she awaited the arrival of my sister.

At six o'clock Ma, Nana and I were ready to leave for the station. It was much too early, of course. The train was only due at eight o'clock. The station was barely a thirty-minute drive away, but we were like ants on a hot tin roof.

Gladys locked Birdie indoors to stop him from chasing after us. Soraya dragged her feet reluctantly, pausing on the stoep, torn between the mournful sounds of Birdie's wailing and Ma's stern expression.

'I don't want to go with you,' she said, her face screwed up stubbornly. 'I want to stay here with Birdie.'

'Get into the car, Soraya,' Ma replied tersely.

'No,' Soraya shot back, scuffing the toe of her shoe on the cement.

Birdie heard her voice and scratched frantically at the door.

'Get into the car,' Ma snapped, losing patience.

Soraya stared at her defiantly. 'No. I'm staying with Birdie.'

'Soraya, we'll be home soon,' I said, trying to reassure her. 'We'll only be gone for a little while. We're going to the station to meet Yasmin.'

'I don't want to go!'

'Leave her here,' Nana said.

'No.' Ma's eyes narrowed.

Soraya saw the look on Ma's face and moved with deliberate slowness while Ma waited impatiently to shut the car door.

'It's all right,' I whispered, taking Soraya on to my lap. 'When we get to the station, I'll buy you a comic book.' My arms tightened around the child. I knew well enough what it was like to have my own desires ignored because someone else had higher priority.

It had always been Yasmin, even after she had left, our lives wrecked by her thoughtlessness.

Preoccupied with her thoughts, Ma drove slowly. She and Nana were both silent, their eyes fixed unseeingly on the landscape unfolding in the soft morning light.

'It's still fresh after the rains,' Nana remarked as we passed

Miss Myberry's farm with its long avenue of cypress trees.

Ma remained silent. The old anger, lying dormant for all those years, had resurfaced. It was an anger which had cocooned her in silence – a silence that had wrapped itself around her heart the day Yasmin ran away from home.

The turn-off on to the gravel road came into view. There was not another car in sight. It was still too early, even for churchgoers.

The road into Soetstroom was a familiar one. We could have driven it blindfold. I shut my eyes as we jogged over the cattle grid, followed the curve in the road to the bridge and then, three blocks down, turned into the main street. We bumped over the concrete ditch and slowed down as we neared our old home. I opened my eyes just as we reached the house of our former neighbour, Mrs Olivier.

For a brief instant Ma hesitated as though to stop, but then she changed her mind.

Our house stood vacant and abandoned. There was no one there now to reflect on its former inhabitants. No one to smell the cooking odours embedded in the walls, the scent of Yasmin's cologne, or Ma's *Evening in Paris*, or the smell of age on my father's breath. No one to hear the echoes of laughter or tears. No one to wonder about the history of the previous occupants or their secrets.

The beautiful garden lay in ruins, the shop windows barred and the doors padlocked, just as we had left them – the Coca-Cola billboard still tacked to the side wall. In the rear-view mirror I caught a glimpse of my mother's image and the sadness in her eyes. She accelerated past the house and then slowed down again.

I thought about my father as we drove past the house and how his despondency had grown in the years following our relocation. It was as if he had lost his will to carry on. For our sakes, he had gone through the motions of settling at McBain. I had never been able to ease his anguish and although I was too young at the time to grasp the depth of his pain, I witnessed his slow deterioration.

He used to sit on the stoep at McBain for hours on end, making mounds of funnel-shaped packets out of pages from the *Farmer's Weekly* or *Indian Views*. Using his thumb and ring fingers, he deftly twisted the narrow end of the funnel. His index finger, injured in the incident when he was jailed in his youth, was so stiffened by arthritis that it had taken on a permanent attitude of accusation.

I had found solace in my father's company, enjoying the stories he told when we sat together. I was almost four years younger than Yasmin, and by the time I was born Papa was already an old man. I had no memory of him being playful or demonstrative. The distance between the two of us was underscored even further whenever he referred to me by my formal name, Amina.

On the rare occasions when he lapsed into calling me Meena, which was what everyone else did, I used to feel an inexplicable bond with him. Although I had not participated in his experiences, I listened eagerly as he recounted incidents that were part of *his* history. In later years when I reflected on our relationship, I understood how this distance between us had shaped my life.

Most of the stories my father told had their origins in his ancestral village in India where babies were snatched by pythons with girths as wide as a man's trunk. The expression on Papa's face as he related these episodes had always suggested a yearning for that long-ago life.

My father had never recovered from the shock of losing Yasmin. He had waited in vain for her return.

31

WE PASSED the town square and the shops: the post office, the hotel, the café, and then drove down the road to the station. All of it familiar. A big chunk of our history had played itself out there. It was not something that could easily be swept aside.

Despite having been wrenched from our home under such terrible circumstances, Nana believed that, through our strength and endurance, we had left our personal stamp on the town.

At the station we turned off the main road and bumped over the short coal-blackened track to the entrance. The familiar segregation signs had recently been repainted and were brilliantly eye-catching.

Ma and Nana ignored the signs and marched straight through the 'white' entrance. Soraya and I followed. Those who knew us from the old days weren't at all surprised at Ma's impudence. She had never been cowed by petty apartheid laws.

Eddie, one of the students at the school where I taught, had been visiting his aunt in Soetstroom. They were both waiting on the platform and waved when they saw me.

We were much too early. I paced impatiently, gazing along the tracks for signs of the approaching train.

In the early days the station had been one of Yasmin's favourite haunts. She spent endless hours there, staring into space, dreaming of being whisked away to some exotic and exciting destination. For her, the isolation at Soetstroom and then at McBain had been unbearable. She hated being cut off from the rest of the world, knowing that out there, in territories unexplored by her, mystery and excitement lurked.

Increasingly agitated, I peered down the line as though willing the train to arrive, constantly glancing at my watch and then at the station clock.

At last we heard the familiar blast of the whistle as the train approached the crossing a kilometre away. Ma grabbed hold of Soraya's hand.

The train drew into the station, pulled by one of the new diesel engines. Steam was being phased out.

The non-white section was at the rear of the train and we ran to the far end of the platform. Yasmin was leaning out of the window and she smiled when she saw me.

'Hi, Meena!' she called. Then her glance darted along the platform to Ma and Nana. For a moment, as her eyes alighted on Ma, they were bright with anxiety.

Ma arrived out of breath, clutching Soraya's hand.

'Yasmin!' she cried.

Yasmin leaned out of the carriage window and touched Ma's hand. 'Just a sec,' she said. 'I'd better get my stuff before the train pulls out.'

There was no platform alongside the last carriages and it was a huge struggle to get her luggage off the train. She had two enormous suitcases, both of them too heavy for either of us to lift. A steward saw us struggling and came to our assistance. Together he and I dragged the suitcases off the train while Yasmin collected the few loose items lying in the coupé.

Yasmin disembarked and hugged Ma and Nana tearfully. Then her eyes lit on Soraya who stood aside, shyly watching. She disengaged herself from us as Soraya pressed herself against Ma's leg, apprehensive eyes fixed on Yasmin.

'Soraya,' Yasmin whispered.

She knelt and Ma gently urged Soraya into her arms. Soraya, looking quite frantic, backed away, retreating to Ma's side. Yasmin got up off her knees, brushed away her tears and hugged us all again.

'Why's everyone crying, Ma?' Soraya asked.

The steward who had helped us with the luggage caught Yasmin's eye and smiled. She went towards him, holding out her hand. With a look of adoration, he took it.

'Thank you so much for your help, Oscar. And good luck!' She reached into her purse to tip him.

Oscar shook his head emphatically. 'No, no, please. It was my pleasure. Entirely my pleasure. Thank you.' He backed away, going through all sorts of contortions to avoid turning his back on her.

Yasmin soaked up the admiration like a sponge. This was the Yasmin I remembered. Yasmin the *ingénue*, the conqueror of hearts.

We crowded around her, but she could not take her eyes off Soraya.

'Isn't she gorgeous, Ma?' she whispered.

Ma nodded, smiling proudly.

'You're absolutely lovely,' Yasmin said, reaching to touch Soraya, but Soraya ducked away. Yasmin knelt beside her again. 'May I give you a hug?' she asked.

Soraya was reluctant, but Ma smiled encouragingly.

With a conspicuous lack of enthusiasm, Soraya allowed Yasmin to embrace her.

I reached for Soraya's hand, sensing her confusion.

'Where's Papa?' Yasmin asked, glancing around and noticing his absence for the first time.

Her question fell into a vacuum. She looked first at Ma, then Nana, then me. Realisation slowly set on her features.

Ma took her hand.

Yasmin paled, looking at me for confirmation. The expression of shock and pain on her face rekindled all the old grief about Papa's death.

'How did it happen?' she asked, in a voice quivering on the brink of tears.

'A minor eye operation. He died under the anaesthetic,' Ma said.

'Oh, Ma,' Yasmin choked, putting her arms around her.

'We'll talk about it at home,' Nana said.

Eddie, who had witnessed our struggle with the luggage, came over and offered to help, grimacing as he dragged the larger of the suitcases to the car. Eddie was sixteen and still in standard five. He had failed in two consecutive years and I suspected that his aunt would take him out of school if he failed again.

'Thanks, Eddie,' I said as we heaved the suitcase into the boot. 'See you at school on Monday. Make sure your homework is done.'

'*Ja, Juffrou* – Yes, teacher,' he said as he went off to join his aunt.

'How was your flight from London?' Ma asked, as we got into the car. Despite the excitement of having Yasmin home again, there was an undercurrent of awkwardness. There were so many questions hanging in the air, questions that would have to wait until we got home.

'Fine,' Yasmin said as she settled into the front seat. 'But I'd forgotten how long the train trip from Johannesburg took.'

We drove back the way we had come.

'I see the house is still vacant,' she remarked as we once again passed our old home.

'It's been vandalised,' Ma said.

'They've destroyed everything inside,' I added.

'Ripped its guts out,' Nana confirmed.

Soraya nodded, her large blue eyes pensive, as if she knew what all of this meant. Yasmin reached over the seat and ruffled her hair.

'Come sit here with us,' she said. She helped Soraya move over to sit between her and Ma. Yasmin put her arm around Soraya who sat very still and rigid as though the embrace was a trap from which she could not escape.

Yasmin sighed. 'Poor Papa. I'm so sorry, Ma, that I wasn't around.'

Ma found her hand and squeezed it.

Soraya's eyes were riveted on Yasmin. She reached up and gingerly touched Yasmin's hair. From the back seat I studied my sister's profile. All my questions would have to wait.

Yasmin gazed out at the desolate veld. In the distance a windmill turned slowly and sheep grazed on the sparse vegetation in the shade of a thorn tree.

'We had a lot of rain, but it's all dried up again,' Ma explained.

The drive home was filled with small talk and sadness about Papa.

'How long are you staying, Yas?' I asked.

'Until after New Year.' She turned to me as she spoke, her eyes softening and her smile almost apologetic. 'I'm sorry about Papa, Ma,' she said again. 'I'm sorry I wasn't here for you.'

Ma glanced at her. She was obviously battling to repress the desire to admonish Yasmin for not having been in touch.

Nana practised no such restraint. 'He waited for you,' she snapped.

Yasmin winced. Soraya looked from one face to the other unable to gauge the reason for the sudden shift in tension.

'I have a dog,' she announced to Yasmin. 'His name is Birdie.'

'Birdie?' Yasmin laughed, a little too loudly.

Soraya nodded. 'I love him.'

Yasmin grinned.

'Are you going to stay with us now, Yasmin?' Soraya asked.

The old Yasmin smile reappeared. She ruffled Soraya's hair and avoided the question. 'I must have your hair cut nicely,' she said. 'So it will grow out evenly.'

'What's wrong with the way her hair's cut?' Nana asked.

'Nothing, but I'd like to have it styled. It's such a lovely colour. I didn't think it would be so light.'

Nana rolled her eyes at me. It was just like the old days again.

Birdie was lying on the veranda when we pulled up in front of the shop at McBain. He yapped ecstatically, leaping up against everyone as we climbed out of the car.

'Down, Birdie,' Ma said sharply. Birdie looked dolefully at Ma and then at Soraya.

'Come, Birdie,' Soraya said.

Instead of obeying, Birdie jumped up against Yasmin. Over-excited, he peed on the ground right at her feet. She stepped aside quickly.

'Really,' I muttered in disgust. 'That animal should be trained.'

'Where did she get the dog?' Yasmin asked.

There was silence. None of us wanted to tackle this question. Gladys came to the rescue as she rushed out to greet Yasmin.

'*Yini*, Yasmin. You are a woman. Look at you!' she cried, holding Yasmin's shoulders and subjecting her to her loving scrutiny. Yasmin threw her arms around Gladys's neck. Then Gladys stepped away from Yasmin, shaking her head and clapping her hands.

'*Kaloku*, you are beautiful,' she said. 'You are so beautiful.'

Nana and I exchanged glances, wondering whether anything had actually changed in the years Yasmin had been away . . .

32

YASMIN STOOD on the veranda surrounded by her suitcases and gazed around her. Aware of our eyes on her, she took a deep breath and smiled.

'What about the suitcases?' I asked my mother. 'They're much too heavy to carry up to the house.'

'We'll leave them in the shop. Drag them into the corner over there,' she said.

'Why can't Daniel take them up to the house?' Yasmin asked.

Ma shook her head.

'Where is he?'

None of us said anything.

'Has something happened to him?'

'He's dead. . .' Ma said.

'How?' Yasmin asked.

'It's a long story,' Ma said. 'I'll tell you about it later. Let's all help to get the luggage into the shop. We'll leave it there until we can find help.'

Ma tested the weight of one of the suitcases. 'What on earth have you got in here, Yasmin? Rocks?'

Yasmin grinned sheepishly as she and I dragged the suitcases into the shop.

'Tomorrow, Gladys, send two of your boys, strong ones, to carry the suitcases,' Ma said.

We carried the smaller parcels to the house. Even Soraya had her arms folded around something.

'I'll make the tea,' Nana said, dropping her parcel on a chair and heading straight into the kitchen as though anxious to escape the clamour.

Yasmin inspected the house then came to sit down at the table with us. 'Ma, tell me about Papa. I can't believe that he's gone.'

'All his old friends were there,' Ma said. 'Aishaben and Cassimbhai were very good to us. They made the arrangements. Cassimbhai and your Papa were as close as ever, right to the end.'

'Poor Papa,' Yasmin said, her expression saddening.

Ma took her hand and squeezed it. 'I know that you'd have come if you'd known.'

Nana scowled as she watched the two of them.

I felt the old anger pushing up, threatening to choke me. I watched my mother and sister, remembering how Yasmin used to turn on the tears at will. She was an expert manipulator. She wore her uncaring glamorous exterior like a plate of armour, hiding her soft underbelly of vulnerability. She never wanted to give the impression of weakness.

Yasmin was like an onion with all its various layers. On the surface was the tough businesswoman, below that lay the insensitive manipulator. Deeper still, was the dewy-eyed innocent and yet deeper lay the child-like vulnerability, so rarely exposed.

Much as I wanted to, I couldn't hate her. Despite everything, the old feelings of affection returned to me, overwhelming me. Yasmin put her arms around my mother.

Soraya watched, looking resentful that Yasmin had usurped her place in Ma's affections. Ma glanced over Yasmin's shoulder, saw the look on Soraya's face and quickly released her.

She took Soraya into her arms. 'It's all right, Soraya. You are all three my babies and my sweethearts. I love all of you.' My mother caught my eye and I turned away.

Soraya, not at all convinced, withdrew from her and went to Nana. She had known almost from birth how to play one off against the other.

'So tell me about Daniel, Ma,' Yasmin said as she went to the kitchen window to look out at the siding.

Ma joined her at the window and began recounting the story.

I went into our room where Yasmin had started unpacking. The smaller bags were on the bed, her belongings strewn everywhere.

She had carelessly tossed her handbag on to my bed and its contents had spilt out. I could not help noticing a photograph of Yasmin with a handsome older man. His brown hair, lightly peppered with grey, was receding slightly. He had a small beard and laughing eyes. I turned the picture over but there was no inscription on the back. I put everything back into Yasmin's bag and shut it.

'It's terrible about Daniel, isn't it?' Yasmin said later as she joined me in the room. 'Poor Daniel. He was so gentle. He wouldn't have hurt a fly.'

I watched her kick off her shoes. She rummaged in her hand luggage and then sat down at the dresser to brush her hair with the long, regular strokes I remembered so well. When she was done, she swept everything off the bed and stretched out, hands behind her head. She looked at me questioningly.

'What about you, Meena? What've you been up to?'

'Nothing much.'

'Still a virgin?' she teased as she would have done in the old days.

'None of your business,' I said, tossing a pillow at her.

'Does that mean you're *not* a virgin?' Yasmin said, continuing to tease me.

'No, I'm not.'

'Who's the boy?'

'None of your business.'

'I heard about your big spat with Papa,' Yasmin said.

'Who told you?'

'Ma, of course. What else happened?'

'Nothing. I'm still here, aren't I?'

Yasmin lowered her eyes and studied her fingernails. 'I know it was difficult for you,' she said. 'I'm sorry I had to desert you.

I just saw no sense in both of us sacrificing our lives.'

'Nothing seems to have changed,' I said drily. 'You're still as selfish and self-centred as ever. When will you stop thinking only of yourself and start considering others?'

Yasmin continued to study her nails. At length she glanced up. 'I'm home now and I promise I'm going to make it up to all of you.'

I didn't say anything.

'Come back to London with me, Meena. There's nothing here for you. I'll help out until you get on your feet.'

'Where were you when we needed you, Yas?' I asked.

She winced as if I'd touched a raw nerve.

Soraya materialised in the doorway. Yasmin smiled affectionately and beckoned. 'Come here, chicken. Let me hug you.'

'I'm not a chicken,' Soraya said indignantly. 'And I don't want a hug. Ma says I must tell you the table is set.' She vanished as quickly as she had appeared.

'I'm sorry,' Yasmin said quietly, obviously hurt by Soraya's hostility.

'She didn't mean it that way . . .' I started to explain. 'She's just not used to . . . strangers.'

Yasmin got up off the bed, went to the mirror and examined her face. She caught my eye in the mirror. 'Think about my offer. I'd love to have you.'

If only Yasmin knew what a temptation the offer was. I thought of London and Jonathan. Remembered his body pressed against mine. Yasmin was watching me and I shrugged away the memory.

We went into the kitchen. Ma, still overwhelmed at having Yasmin home, hugged her. Soraya interposed herself between the two, easing them apart.

Once we were seated around the table, the discussion turned to Papa.

'My poor father,' Yasmin said. 'All he ever wanted was to make that trip to India. I was so hoping I could help.'

'How?' Nana asked.

Yasmin studied the faces around her. 'I wanted to take him.'

'You!' Nana scoffed.

Yasmin looked hurt. 'Yes . . . Me! I was setting aside some money for it. Saving up, you know.'

'We know nothing,' Ma said. 'You've told us nothing. Not a word about what you've been doing these past years, or why you've come home now. But I suppose I can guess the reason for that.'

'For all we knew, you might have been dead,' Nana added.

Yasmin looked down. The noose was tightening. She toyed with her cup.

Yasmin and I had already talked about some of her missing years. I knew part of the story and I waited now to see what she would say.

Ma scraped some leftovers out of the pot for Birdie.

No one spoke. Soraya had gone outside to play.

Yasmin took a deep breath. 'I don't want you to get upset, Ma,' she began.

Ma put the pot down. She still had the big wooden spoon in her hand.

Yasmin hesitated and glanced at me. I looked away.

'I've come to fetch Soraya,' she said.

'What did you say?' Ma asked. She approached Yasmin with the spoon gripped like a club.

'I said . . . I've come to fetch Soraya.'

'Over my dead body,' Ma hissed. She leaned on the table, her face close to Yasmin's. 'Isn't it enough that you've messed up your own life? Do you think I'll let you ruin Soraya's as well? Never!' Her face was white with anger. 'Never!' she cried again.

I put a calming hand on my mother's shoulder. She shrugged it away.

'Leave me alone!' She turned back to Yasmin. 'You gave up any right to Soraya when you walked out on her.'

Nana listened, uncharacteristically silent, her eyes moving from Ma to Yasmin.

'Soraya is my child!' Yasmin said, leaping up.

Ma brandished the spoon at Yasmin. '*Your* child! Who sat up with her, night after night, when she was sick? Who loved and cared for her? Not you! Where were you when she was growing up? Where were you when she needed a mother? As far from her as you could get!'

'I was trying to make a life for myself!' Yasmin shouted back at Ma.

'Some life!' Nana muttered.

'You stay out of this,' Yasmin snapped.

'Watch your tongue,' Nana said.

'You're always interfering,' Yasmin said. 'This has nothing to do with you!'

'It has everything to do with me!'

'Tell me about the life you've made for yourself,' Ma said with a touch of sarcasm as she struggled to regain her self-control.

'Why should I tell you anything? You won't understand anyway!'

'Calm down, everyone!' I pleaded. 'Let's talk about this sensibly, for Soraya's sake. Yasmin, tell us about England.'

Yasmin paused.

'Tell them about the boutique,' I urged quietly.

Ma and Nana waited, Nana's expression cynical.

'I have a small dress-design boutique in London,' she said almost reluctantly. 'It's called Soraya.'

I nodded, encouraging her to go on. 'It's in a posh part of London. She sews for all the rich women. She even sews for royalty.'

Yasmin got up out of her chair and walked to the door. Then, turning back to us, she said: 'Ma, I make a good living.'

Ma and Nana quietly absorbed this information.

Nana was the first to respond. 'So . . . you're a seamstress.' The tone of her voice said it all.

Yasmin threw her arms up in exasperation. 'See what I mean?' she said to me. 'What's the point of trying to have a normal conversation with any of you?'

I went outside to see where Soraya was. She was playing with

Birdie. Gladys raised her eyebrows quizzically at me. 'Gladys, take Soraya for a walk,' I said quietly.

Gladys understood.

I watched them walk off and then returned to the kitchen. Ma was calmer now, but distant and cold. I hated it when she was like this. Reaching her was like trying to cut through a block of ice with a steak-knife.

'I'm sorry about everything,' Yasmin said, tears trailing down her cheeks. 'I'm really sorry I hurt you. I never meant to. How much more can I say? I went through hell, but it's done now. It's all over. In the past. Can we please forget it and get on with our lives?'

'What do you think *we* went through?' Ma snapped.

'I know, I know . . . But I just want to start a new life, Ma. And I want to get on with it. I can't hide in the past. Please, Ma.' Her voice broke. She stood at the door, toying with her hanky, mutely appealing for understanding. 'When I left here, I went to Cape Town. I found a job as a nanny. My employers were from England. Six months later when they decided to return there, they took me with them.'

'You abandoned your own child so you could care for a white man's children?' Ma asked in disbelief. 'What was going on in your head, Yasmin? What?'

Yasmin turned away.

I felt sorry for both of them.

'Go on,' Ma said.

'In London I worked for the family during the day and took a dress-designing course at night school. A year later I went into business for myself.'

'Where did you get the money to open your own business?' Nana asked.

'The people I worked for lent me the money.'

'And then . . .?' Ma asked.

Yasmin straightened her shoulders. 'I've paid back every penny of the loan with interest. The business is doing well. It's small, but it's in a good area. I have a workshop close to the boutique.'

She became enthusiastic. 'I have a cutter and two seamstresses in the workshop and another seamstress in the boutique for alterations. We'll be running out of space soon, but I'm looking for another place.' She spoke proudly, the tears gone. 'I'm doing well, Ma.'

'How long are you staying?' Nana asked as if she hadn't heard a word.

'I can't be gone for longer than six weeks. My cutter is managing the business while I'm away but I mustn't be away too long. I only came because . . . because . . .'

'Because of Soraya,' Ma said. 'Why now, Yasmin? You never showed any interest in her before. You never wrote or phoned – not one word to ask about a child that you now want to cart off to the other end of the world.'

'I didn't want to disrupt her life, Ma. I knew she'd be better off here with you. What she needed was stability and she got it with you. I wasn't ready.'

'And you're ready now, I suppose,' Nana said coldly.

'Yes.' She hesitated, lowering her eyes. Then she continued. 'I may be getting married.'

'*May* be?' Nana asked. 'Don't you know?'

'I have too many things to consider right now,' Yasmin said.

'Who's the man?' Ma asked.

'All in good time,' Yasmin said tiredly. 'I'll tell you about it later.'

'Yasmin, you can't turn feelings on and off like a tap,' Ma said. 'Think carefully about what you're trying to do. You're not going to drag Soraya off into a situation that you're not sure about. I won't have it!'

'She's my child!' Yasmin said.

'I raised her,' Ma said. 'You dumped her. As far as Soraya is concerned, I'm her mother.'

'Well, it's time to correct that misconception!' Yasmin cried, her voice shrill and thin. 'It's time to tell her the truth – that I am her mother!'

'Some mothers eat their young!' Ma said, chest heaving.

Yasmin glared at Ma and stormed out.

Nana shook her head. 'You can't stop her from taking the child, Delia. You know that.'

Ma's breathing was still ragged. She made a conscious effort to compose herself.

'I know, Mum,' she said. 'I know. I must make sure that she's not messing around again. If and when she takes Soraya, it has to be into a stable home. I won't let that child be shoved around like a piece of furniture.'

Ma went to the stove and distractedly moved the pots and pans around. 'We'll see how things go in the next few weeks,' she said.

'Be careful, Delia,' Nana said, 'that you do what's best for Soraya.'

Ma glanced at Nana and then turned back to the stove. But the issue remained with us, troubling us.

The mushrooming hostility between Yasmin and Soraya was quite evident. It was as if Soraya was trying, in her young mind, to work everything out. Her anger at Yasmin was palpable, almost as if she knew the truth about Yasmin and resented her for it.

We had often talked about Yasmin. Soraya had known she was coming. But the moment Yasmin stepped off the train Soraya's behaviour changed noticeably.

One afternoon Soraya was standing at the table next to Ma. No one was paying attention to her. All attention was on Yasmin. When she thought that no one was watching her, Soraya slid one of the plates to the edge of the table and then, leaning against the table, she nudged the plate. It crashed to the floor.

'Soraya!' Ma cried. 'My good china!'

Soraya's eyes darted to me. Like little twin spikes they nailed me, daring me to say something. I looked away.

Ma picked up the pieces and sighed. 'My best plates. Oh, Soraya!'

Soraya lowered her head and scuffed the toe of her shoe on the floor.

'Never mind,' Ma embraced her. 'It was an accident. It couldn't be helped. But you must be more careful, darling.'

Yasmin looked on. She smiled knowingly. 'Come Soraya, let's go for a walk.'

Soraya refused. She disengaged herself from Ma and went to look for Birdie who was in the backyard. There was a loud disturbance from the back stoep as the hen, chased by Birdie, squawked its head off.

'That dog,' Ma muttered, going to the door. 'Hermanus Steyn devised this plan to drive me mad.'

'Here, Birdie!' Soraya called and the dog obediently rushed to her.

'This is a crazy household,' Nana said, walking out on to the stoep to see what was going on. 'There's always something happening. Always ructions.'

Ma was preoccupied with the issue of Yasmin wanting to take Soraya away. The main topic of conversation between Ma and Nana revolved around Yasmin's decision to get married and how Soraya would fit into the scheme of things.

'Neville's very sweet, Ma,' Yasmin said reassuringly. 'You'll like him.'

'And when are we going to meet this Neville?' Nana asked, her eyebrows arched.

'I want all of you at my wedding,' she said.

Nana rolled her eyes.

'How do you suppose we're going to get there?' Ma asked.

'I'll send your tickets.'

'No. I don't think so,' Ma said.

Yasmin looked down. 'I'd like Soraya to be there. I want to introduce her to Neville.'

'We'll have to see . . .' Ma said.

'Who is this Neville? Where is he from?' Nana asked.

I got up and went to the sink to draw a glass of cold water. I watched Yasmin over the rim of my glass as she gathered her thoughts. She looked at Ma and Nana and then at me, silently pleading for help.

'Neville is divorced . . .' She paused and took a deep breath before continuing. 'He's fifteen years older than me.'

Ma's glance flew to Nana.

'Where did you meet him?' Nana asked.

'I worked for him . . .' Yasmin said.

'Where?' Nana persisted.

Yasmin toyed with the edge of the table-cloth while Ma and Nana waited for her response.

Yasmin had told me the whole story, so I knew what was coming.

'Well . . .?' Ma prompted.

'Neville was . . . He and his ex-wife were the couple I worked for here and then went to England with . . .'

Ma leapt up, almost knocking her chair over. 'Are you serious?' she exclaimed.

As though guessing her thoughts, Yasmin said: 'Ma, it's all right. I didn't break up his marriage. When they returned to England they had already decided to separate.'

Ma went to the sink, busying herself there. She needed time to think about what Yasmin had just told her. Then, as though she had come to a decision, she turned to Yasmin, drying her hands on the dish towel.

'He's a good man, Ma. He's kind and gentle. I know I'll be happy with him and I know he'll be a good father to Soraya.'

'What about his own children?' Ma said quietly. 'The children you looked after.'

Yasmin sighed. She furled and unfurled the edge of the table-cloth. 'Their mother has custody of them.'

'This doesn't seem right, Yasmin. Your stepping into a broken home can only bring problems. I don't want Soraya to be caught in the middle.'

'But she won't be!' Yasmin cried.

Ma shook her head, tossed the dish towel on the table and left the kitchen. Yasmin looked defeated.

The issue of Yasmin and Neville was debated often. Ma and

Nana criticised Yasmin at every turn, building a worst-case scenario of her and Neville with Soraya.

I was sick of the gloomy predictions and relieved when Yasmin found an excuse for us to go into town the following Saturday.

She wanted Soraya to come with us, but she wouldn't, not even when I pleaded with her to do so.

33

IN THE early days after Yasmin's rape, crushed under the weight of its consequences, we had tried to gather our strength – to consolidate our emotional and spiritual resources. But when Yasmin ran away and abandoned her baby, she left our lives in tatters.

Nothing, not even the forced eviction from our home by a government implementing its draconian laws, could compare with what we went through in those traumatic months. That fateful night when I found her cowering in the shower, her bloody underwear on the floor, I knew that my sister had suffered more damage than any of us could ever imagine possible.

At the time I had no inkling what the effects of such a brutal act would be on her. We watched helplessly as she came apart. Counselling for situations like hers was unheard of then. Abortion, unless obtained through a backstreet practitioner, was illegal. We lived in a patriarchal, Calvinistic and racist society. And Yasmin, in the bloom of her life, had been brutalised.

How could one ever come to terms with an act of such barbarism? What was there that one could say to a rape victim that would ease the pain and horror? What is it in the nature of a man that craves such savagery against another human being? What was it about our society that engendered such inhumanity? Was it something in our past? Was it something in our history? Was it the way we had been dehumanised by the regime which ruled us?

I could find no answers to these questions. One question

merely led to another.

I thought of our childhood, when our lives were unsullied by tragedy. When I thought I knew my sister well. Those had been carefree and innocent times.

But our lives had changed. Her life had changed. Beautiful, headstrong and independent, Yasmin's life was totally destroyed by a single savage act.

Our parents, fearing that Yasmin would be prosecuted in a system that almost invariably punished non-white victims, did not report the rape. Believing that they would never be able to convince the authorities of Yasmin's innocence, they closed ranks. Our family became united in shame.

Yasmin, who had expected to be able to abort the foetus, was devastated when she learned she had to carry the pregnancy to full term. She did not want the child. She had railed against it from the moment she found she was pregnant.

It was only after Yasmin left that we quietly rejoiced in the fact that we had not succeeded with the abortion plans.

'God works in mysterious ways,' Nana had remarked. 'Look at her,' she said as we watched Soraya, the baby. 'It would have been a tragedy, Delia . . .'

We knew what Nana meant. Fate had played a big hand in events. Despite being rejected by her mother, Soraya was born into a loving environment with three adoring women to fuss over her.

Ma admitted afterwards that had the situation turned out differently, had Yasmin taken the child with her, it might have been an even greater tragedy. Yasmin, Nana agreed, was not capable of loving a child who was a constant reminder of the rape.

'Soraya must never know the truth,' Ma decided. 'It'll break her heart. 'She can never know that she was the product of such a vile act. And she must never know that we tried to get an abortion. My God, Mum. Just think of what might have happened if we'd succeeded? Can you imagine our lives without her?'

'But I suppose she'll have to be told eventually,' Nana said. 'She can't go through life believing a lie.'

'We'll just tell her that her father's dead. It's not really a lie, is it?'

Nana gave Ma a reproachful look. 'The truth always has a way of coming out and when it does, she'll never forgive any of us.'

But Ma had made the decision and the rest of us accepted it and abided by it.

It was ironical that Yasmin was now, years later, fighting to take Soraya back to England with her. I marvelled at the twists and turns of fate.

Ma and Yasmin, angry and confrontational, were locked in a war of wills. To escape the tension, I reverted to walking the rails, sometimes joined by Yasmin.

Soraya was still shutting Yasmin out. But Yasmin, too, was holding back, waging an enormous battle of her own as she struggled to unlock her feelings for the child. Soraya, resisting Yasmin at every turn, was not making it any easier.

Her naughtiness was disconcerting and disruptive. She stayed close to Ma until Ma became impatient with her. She had suddenly turned into a surly, disobedient child.

Nana, the only one who understood what was going on, tried to ease the tensions between the three of them.

'Soraya, please . . .' Ma said sharply, loosening Soraya's grip on her dress. 'Go and play.' As soon as the words were out, Ma regretted them. She knew that Soraya was only reacting to the turmoil that was so obvious in the behaviour of the adults around her.

There was an unfamiliar edge to Soraya's laughter. We never let her out of our sight. There was always someone around to keep an eye on her and to allay her insecurities.

'This has been an eventful year,' Nana said to me one evening when the two of us were alone in the kitchen.

I took my grandmother's hand. 'Next year will be better,' I

assured her.

'I'm getting too old for all these ructions,' Nana complained.

We wrapped the Christmas gifts and decorated the house with crêpe paper and balloons. Soraya became more animated, excited about the many gifts waiting for her, most of them from Yasmin. We knew now why her suitcases had been so heavy.

All we needed was a Christmas tree. We cast around for one and then remembered Miss Myberry at Cypress Farms. It was from her property that Yasmin and I liberated a small tree on Christmas Eve – lugging it to the car under cover of darkness and stuffing it into the boot. At home we planted it in a tub and decorated it.

We sat up half that night talking in the dark. It was like the old days. Much younger then, we had struggled to unravel the mysteries of the human body. What went where? Why there and not elsewhere? Was it painful or pleasurable? What was a 'climax' and how was it achieved? What caused babies? In those days we used to explore the whole puzzling realm of adult sex, picking our way through the minefield of language and ignorance.

Now, from the perspective of maturity and experience, the tone of our conversation was different. We now talked about an 'orgasm' and what made a man either a skilled or a lousy lover.

I told Yasmin about Jonathan. Unburdened myself of every blissful moment. Amused, Yasmin listened as I told her about how we had made love in the veld and on the stoep, under the noses of Ma and Nana.

'So, you've finally grown up and joined the rest of us in the real world,' Yasmin said. 'Do Ma and Nana know about Jonathan?'

'I think Nana does, but Ma hasn't said anything to me.'

I felt a rush of affection for my sister. All hostility forgotten, I got up out of my bed and crawled in beside her.

'I'm sorry, Meena,' she whispered. 'I'm sorry for all the pain I caused. I know I was selfish. I probably still am, but I want you to believe that I'm trying hard to change.'

I squeezed her hand. We fell asleep like that, snuggled up next to each other, as we used to do when we were children.

That Christmas was a special one. Not only because Yasmin had come home, but also because it was possible that it might be Soraya's last Christmas at McBain. No decision about her leaving had been made yet, but I expected that Ma would ultimately relent. She always did where Yasmin was concerned.

Nana disagreed. 'Not this time,' she said.

On Christmas morning we exchanged gifts. I gave Yasmin a silk scarf she had admired in a store window in town. Ma had bought her a silver bracelet and Nana gave her a colourful cosmetic bag.

There were expensive perfumes for Ma, Nana and me from Yasmin. Also, a gold locket for me and smaller pieces of jewellery for Ma and Nana. She had bought a beautiful angora stole for Nana who wondered aloud when she would ever have an opportunity to show it off.

There were many gifts for Soraya – each one individually wrapped. It took her the best part of the morning to open them, discarding the colourful wrappings on the floor next to her while Birdie chewed them up or chased them all over the front room. There were gifts for Papa, Gladys and Daniel. The gifts for Papa and Daniel remained unopened.

We missed Papa on that day. Despite his criticism of the holidays, he understood our excitement and participated to the fullest, pulling Christmas crackers and wearing a festive paper hat like the rest of us. Christmas day gave him as much pleasure as it did us. This was just part of the paradox of living between the Muslim and Christian worlds.

Ma and Nana went to a great deal of trouble with Christmas dinner. Malgas, the old rooster, was too tough or he would have been called on to substitute for a turkey. Instead, they prepared roast leg of lamb with all the trimmings.

The table was set with Ma's best linen and dishes. Beside each plate was a Christmas cracker. In anticipation of Yasmin's arrival,

Nana had made her special Christmas pudding. Soraya and I had scrubbed and boiled the silver coins Ma had saved over the years. They were tickeys and sixpences from the days before the currency conversion to rands and cents.

We split our crackers and read the legends. In our old spirit of competitiveness, Yasmin and I pounced on the coins in the Christmas pudding. Our enthusiasm kept Soraya eagerly competing. Amidst the laughter, I reminded Yasmin that Papa used to pass his coins on to her and that was why she always had more than I did.

We could hardly drag ourselves from the table at the end of the meal.

'It will take me months to lose all this,' Yasmin complained, patting her stomach.

'By now,' Nana said, 'your Papa would have been on his way to the bedroom, sliding his braces off his shoulders, ready for his afternoon nap.'

Ma sniffed a little as she got up from the table. Nana and I helped her to carry the dishes to the kitchen. Yasmin and Soraya were in no hurry. Soraya was laughing.

A shrill edge crept into her voice whenever Yasmin was around. It sounded brittle and artificial, as if she were putting on an act for Yasmin's benefit.

All this attempted good cheer began to depress me.

Yasmin's arrival had given me much to think about. I began to reassess my life. Not much had changed for me. I was beginning to feel ancient. So much of my youth had slipped away quietly and uneventfully at McBain. Other girls my age lived full, exciting lives. I had only my books, living vicariously through those. Second-hand experiences which meant nothing – Jonathan was the only real experience, the only meaningful one of my own. But he had gone. Apart from two letters in the month after his return to London, I had heard nothing more from him.

34

YASMIN WAS anxious to visit Papa's grave and so on Boxing Day we drove to the city.

Nana volunteered to stay at McBain, but Ma insisted that she accompany us. The shop would be closed for three days. If there was an emergency, Gladys would be there. She was staying on the premises to take care of Birdie.

Nana was reluctant. She felt comfortable only in her own surroundings and hated travelling or staying with people.

Soraya sat in the back with Nana and me for a while, but Yasmin coaxed her to move to the front where she sat between her and Ma.

We arrived in the city around lunch time and went directly to the cemetery. Nana had packed a basket of sandwiches and fruit for a picnic on the beach. We had not been to Papa's grave in months and spent a while clearing away the weeds. While we were doing this, Yasmin wept quietly.

We could hear the sound of the ocean from the cemetery. It was a beautiful summer's day and we lingered amongst the graves, Soraya running back and forth, missing Birdie.

'Imagine Birdie here, digging up the old bones,' Nana said.

'He would not,' Soraya protested.

'Yes, he would,' Nana insisted.

Ma ended the argument by pointing to the sign which prohibited dogs.

Afterwards we drove to the Esplanade and took a walk along

the sea wall in an area reserved for whites. Soraya gazed longingly at the children frolicking in the water.

'Let's go,' Yasmin said. 'After the freedom of living overseas, I can't take this.'

We returned to the car.

'It's still early. Let's drive back to the other beach,' I suggested. 'Let Soraya get to the water. We're in no rush, are we?' I looked at my mother who shook her head.

'We can have lunch there,' Nana said.

Ma turned the car around and drove to the far end of the beach front. Yasmin and Soraya ran hand in hand to the water's edge, their differences temporarily forgotten. Seeing them together like that, I felt a little more hopeful that they might yet develop a relationship. Ma watched them exploring the pools amongst the rocks, but it was impossible to divine her thoughts.

'Meena! Meena, come here! Come see!' Soraya called, beckoning excitedly. She and Yasmin were on their haunches, heads together, admiring the crustaceans and the little sea anemones flourishing in the warm rock pools. Even though Soraya had called me, I was reluctant to intrude.

Yasmin held up a small whelk shell. 'Perfect, isn't it?' she said. 'Perfectly preserved, despite the pounding of the ocean.'

I took the shell from her and admired it.

'Look!' Yasmin said. 'There's a crab. Watch your toes!' Soraya leapt up with so much joy and excitement that I began to feel that things would work out between them.

Yasmin's eyes feasted on Soraya. There was something new in her expression, something protective and maternal. She glanced back at Ma, hoping that she had witnessed the exchange.

But Ma and Nana had walked some distance away from us. I watched my mother for a moment as she strolled along the edge of the water, leaving her footprints in the sand.

We had lunch and played at the water's edge until Ma called us back to the car. We packed up and drove to Aishaben and Cassimbhai's house.

Cassimbhai wasn't looking well and Aishaben confessed that

she was worried about him.

'He's so stubborn,' she said. 'He won't listen to the doctors about resting. I worry a lot about him since Abdul's death. You understand, Delia?'

Ma put her arms around Aishaben.

Our time in the city was busy and full of adventure and fun for Soraya, as she and Yasmin took tentative steps towards constructing a relationship.

Eventually it was time to return to McBain. Exhausted, Soraya had taken turns sitting first on my lap and then on Yasmin's. Finally she had fallen asleep, her cheeks rosy pink from the heat, her head on Yasmin's breast.

She awakened as we bumped over the first rut in the driveway. She sat up and rubbed her eyes and then watched through the window as Birdie came dashing towards the car.

'One day that dog will get itself killed,' Ma said, crossly, as she stopped the car. Soraya climbed out and Birdie almost bowled her over. He shivered with delight, his tail thumping against the side of the car. Soraya tore off with her dog after her.

We saw in the New Year quietly at home, toasting each other with hopes for a better future. Yasmin had decided to postpone her departure for ten days. She made several calls to London to explain that she had been delayed.

One of the calls was to Neville. While Ma and Nana were in the backyard, she quietly explained the situation to him.

Soraya and Yasmin were beginning to draw together in a process of healing and bonding. But Soraya still did not know that Yasmin was her mother.

'I have to leave, but I'll be back soon,' Yasmin promised. 'I'll be back to fetch Soraya.' There was a note of determination in her voice and I was sure that she meant it.

Ma tried to begin the process of distancing herself from Soraya, dreading the inevitability of Yasmin's departure.

She was torn between her love for Yasmin and her love for Soraya and the desire to do what was best for both of them.

'You can't stop what's happening,' Nana told her. 'Don't even try. Yasmin is the child's biological mother.'

Yasmin started packing. Her suitcases were much lighter going back than they were when she arrived.

'I'm leaving a suitcase here,' she said one evening as the two of us sat on the stoep watching the sunset. 'I obviously won't be able to take Soraya back with me now. You can see what Ma's like. But I'll be back in a few months to fetch her. Three months at the most.'

Soraya came out on to the stoep to join us and climbed up on to Yasmin's knee.

'Are you ready for your bath now?' Yasmin asked.

Soraya nodded.

'OK, let's go, Chicken. I'll keep you company,' Yasmin said, winking at me. This time there was no protest from Soraya about being called 'Chicken'.

As Soraya passed me, she gave me a peck on the cheek.

'Isn't it a gorgeous sunset?' she said in an adult voice.

'Gorgeous' was the choice word of the week, picked up from Yasmin. Everything was 'gorgeous'. Nana laughed at the affectation, but Ma was irritated.

We were reminded of the days when Yasmin came home from private school tossing out words like 'fabulous', almost driving Nana and me mad.

Yasmin opted to take the train to Johannesburg. She had considered taking a flight from the city, but it would have meant us driving her there again. She told us she was leaving the following Sunday. She would catch the Monday evening flight to London.

On the Friday morning, a week before Yasmin's departure, we were all in the shop. Soraya was in the yard with Birdie. We could hear them outside.

A car pulled up in the driveway and Yasmin went out on the veranda to see who it was. We joined her as Hermanus Steyn stepped out of his car.

'It's all right,' Ma said, coming up behind Yasmin and putting a hand on her shoulder. 'I'll handle him.'

'No,' Yasmin shrugged off Ma's hand. 'I'm not a child.' She looked stonily at Hermanus Steyn.

'I came to see how the dog was doing,' he said. 'It will need rabies shots. There's rabies in the area.'

Yasmin glared at him. He had recognised her immediately.

'Get off our property!' she shouted. 'We don't want you here. Get out of here!'

'There's rabies . . .'

'I don't care. I don't want you anywhere near my child. I don't want you anywhere near us. Leave us alone!'

'Hold on, Yasmin,' Ma said. 'I heard about the rabies scare on the radio.'

'It's just an excuse, Ma.'

'Look, I heard you were leaving with the child . . .'

'So what?' Yasmin demanded. 'What business is it of yours?'

'Are you taking her away?'

'I told you – it's none of your business! Now get out of here!'

'I'm going, but make sure the dog has his shots . . . for the child's sake.'

Ma nodded. 'We will . . . thank you.'

Hermanus returned to his car, his shoulders slumped. Yasmin was still glowering at him as he started his car and pulled forward to swing around in the narrow driveway.

'The bloody nerve!' Yasmin exclaimed. 'Who does he think he is? Ma, you should never have encouraged him with the dog.'

'Don't blame me,' Ma snapped.

None of us noticed that Birdie had run to the gate, or that Soraya had run after him. Suddenly Gladys called out: '*Yini! Yini!*'

Yasmin looked up. 'Oh, God!' she screamed as Soraya and Birdie ran directly into the path of an oncoming car. There was the sound of dragging tyres, the squeal of brakes, and a sickening thump.

I screamed. Yasmin tore down the driveway, the rest of us

close behind her.

The car had stopped. Stunned, the driver looked anxiously at us.

In an attempt to avoid Soraya, he had swerved and hit Birdie.

Soraya was on her knees next to Birdie, who was lying in a pool of blood. He was whimpering. He was still alive, but badly injured. None of us knew what to do. Soraya's face collapsed in anguish. She rocked on her knees, her eyes begging someone, anyone, to do something. The driver could barely speak.

'I didn't see them,' he mumbled, wringing his hands, eyes pleading for understanding. 'I had to swerve to avoid the child.'

Soraya began to wail.

'Please do something,' Ma pleaded with Hermanus as he ran up.

'Take the child inside,' he said.

Ma went to Soraya, but she lashed out, kicking and screaming.

'Come with me, sweetheart,' Yasmin said gently. 'Let's go phone the ambulance.'

Soraya hesitated. Yasmin reached for her hand.

'Please, Baby, come with me. Please.'

Soraya took Yasmin's hand. They returned to the house, Soraya constantly turning to look at Birdie.

Birdie gave a quiet, heart-wrenching whine when he saw Soraya leave.

Hermanus went to his car and returned with a handgun. He waited until Soraya was in the house then raised the gun to Birdie's head.

Birdie turned his gaze on me. I fled as the shot rang out.

Soraya came tearing back down the driveway, Yasmin after her. I caught Soraya at the gate and held on to her. She fought me off, screaming and lunging. She was hysterical.

I picked her up. She screamed and writhed in my arms, pounding me with her small fists. Yasmin took her from me and held her.

Two other cars had stopped. The driver of the car that had hit Birdie fetched an old blanket out of his boot.

Hermanus stood still, his gun-arm hanging limply at his side.

The driver wrapped Birdie's body in the blanket and carried him back into the yard.

'Get me a shovel,' Hermanus said, his voice flat and emotionless.

The driver pulled into the yard, out of the traffic. He and Hermanus dug the hole and buried Birdie. Soraya sobbed inconsolably, her face pressed against Yasmin's leg.

'They had to do it, Soraya,' I tried to explain. 'Poor Birdie was hurting very badly.'

Soraya raised her face. 'You lied to me. You lied to me!' she cried, pummelling Yasmin's leg.

Devastated, Yasmin glanced at Ma. Like the rest of us, she was at a loss.

'Come, Soraya,' Nana said. 'We'll go and pick some flowers and then we'll put them on the grave just like we do when we go to Papa's grave.'

This seemed to provide a temporary distraction. Soraya went with Nana. They picked flowers and placed them on the mound of the freshly dug grave.

'He's with Papa now, is he?' Soraya asked.

'Yes,' Nana said. 'He's with Papa.'

'In heaven?'

'Yes,' Nana said.

Birdie's death and Soraya's pain had a ripple effect which seemed to penetrate all the corners of the house. Everyone mourned with her.

Over tea in our kitchen, Hermanus Steyn had told us there was no point in replacing Birdie with another dog. Soraya had to go through her grieving before she could form an attachment to another animal.

None of us had realised the strength of the bond between Soraya and Birdie. Contrary to everyone's expectations, she did not appear to be getting over it.

'Ma, it's settled,' Yasmin said a few days later. 'I'm taking

Soraya back with me.'

Ma made no comment as she left us and went to her bedroom.

'Where are we going?' Soraya asked Yasmin.

'We're going to London. You're going to love it there.' Yasmin hugged her. Soraya withdrew from her arms and ran to Ma's room.

Through the closed door, we could hear Soraya and Ma talking. Yasmin wanted to join them, but Nana put a hand on her arm and shook her head.

'Your mother knows what she's doing,' she said.

We heard Soraya's high-pitched questioning tone as she asked Ma about London. When the two of them reappeared Ma was smiling and so was Soraya. We knew then that everything was going to be all right.

'I'm going in a train and then I'm going to fly in an aeroplane,' Soraya announced before rushing off to share the news with Gladys.

'Thanks, Ma,' Yasmin said. 'I think we'll leave on Sunday as planned. I've got to get back.'

'I also told her that you were her mother,' Ma added. 'I think she already sensed that there was something different about your relationship with her.'

'What did she say?'

'Nothing.'

'Perhaps she didn't understand.'

'I think she understood perfectly,' Ma said.

'And her father?' Yasmin asked anxiously. 'Did she ask about him?'

'Not a word about him,' Ma said quietly. 'And I'm leaving that to you. You tell her when the two of you are ready to deal with the issue.'

35

WE WENT to see them off at the station. All of us crammed into the car, including Gladys who insisted on accompanying us.

Paralysed with grief, we stood on the platform, waving as the train pulled out. We were still there long after the train had disappeared into the gathering dusk and the station lights had come on.

Ma cried that night. The house seemed dead without Soraya and Yasmin.

Two days later Yasmin phoned to let us know that they had arrived safely. Ma spoke to Soraya who was so excited and thrilled with the adventure that she could barely stop to draw breath.

Ma put the phone down. 'It looks as if she'll settle in nicely,' she said, almost wistfully.

Despite Yasmin having breezed into our lives, once more leaving a trail of disaster, we missed her and Soraya terribly. Gladys complained about how quiet the house was.

Whenever Ma had doubts about her decision that Yasmin should take Soraya, Nana insisted that she had done the right thing.

Yasmin had extracted a promise from me that I would join her and Soraya in London. It was an enormous decision. Not only for me, but for Ma too.

'It all sounds very nice the way Yasmin described it,' Ma said, as we sat around the kitchen table one evening. 'But I think you'd better wait for a while, at least until they've settled down.'

'It might be a good idea for Meena to go for just a few

months,' Nana advised. 'Then she can see for herself what conditions are like.'

Ma sighed. She sat very still, twirling an elastic band around her finger, pondering the problem.

'Yes, but what if she gets there and finds that things don't work out?' she asked.

'Then she can come back,' Nana said.

The two of them were discussing me as though I wasn't there.

'I suppose so. But it is an awful lot of money.'

'I don't have to go,' I interjected.

'She can find a job,' Nana said. 'Yasmin said so. She said it would be very easy because they were always looking for teachers ... supply teaching, she called it.' Nana looked enquiringly at me.

'It's substituting for teachers who are absent. The only problem is I'll have to travel all over London to get to the schools where I'm needed. How will I find my way around?' I was worried about this.

'Don't be such a baby, Meena,' Nana said. 'Other people do it all the time. You'll just have to do what the others do. I'm sure you'll learn quickly. You can't expect just to sit around doing nothing.'

'I know!' I snapped.

Nana gave me a long hard look.

We were silent once more. After a while Nana got up and put the kettle on.

'I know you're scared,' she said, 'but you must go. It's a once in a lifetime opportunity for you. Take it, child. You can worry about the problems when you get there.'

Ma and Nana evidently discussed the issue endlessly while I was away at school. Eventually Ma agreed that it would be the right thing to do. She said that she had been too dependent on me. It was time I broke free.

'But I will miss you terribly, Meena,' she said.

For the first time I felt really close to my mother. I wanted things to stay this way. I was becoming reluctant to leave.

'You must go, Meena,' Nana said, scolding me. 'If you don't

you'll become an old maid here and spend the rest of your life regretting it. And don't worry about us. We'll manage. You don't have to beat yourself up about money.'

'I'll send home as much as I can,' I said.

'That's fine. But don't worry about it too much, Meena. You can't be responsible for us. You must enjoy yourself while you're there.'

It took six months for the necessary paperwork to be completed and my passport to arrive. Finally, almost like a death knell, the ticket arrived from Yasmin and I was packing my suitcase.

I taught right up to the week before my departure. I wasn't sorry about resigning, but I was going to miss my students.

They made a thank-you card for me and I wept when I read it. When they finally came to say goodbye, I wept again as I hugged them.

In the afternoon of that last day at school, I attended a farewell tea arranged in my honour and said goodbye to the principal and the rest of the staff. They presented me with a small farewell gift.

It was all terribly emotional and I was distraught.

It took me a long time to get home that day, my faithful little car chugging along at its own speed. With the wind in my face I slowly began to feel better. Apart from leaving my students, I was relieved to get away from a system of education that had become a burden on my conscience.

If only I could get over my apprehension about leaving my mother and grandmother by themselves. What if they were unable to cope? How would they manage without my salary?

I pulled off the road and parked under a grove of eucalyptus trees. It was so peaceful. The only sound was that of the wind rustling the dry eucalyptus leaves.

Whenever I had had doubts in my life, Nana had been there to nudge me along.

I had looked forward to leaving McBain for such a long time, had savoured it, had fantasised about it, yet now that the time had come I felt a sickening dread. I just could not tear myself away from my family.

Nana assured me that it would be all right. Yasmin would help me and Soraya would be there to ease the transition. 'You'll probably be too busy to miss us,' she teased.

Yasmin had phoned to confirm my time of arrival. I asked her again about the job situation. Despite my anxiety about launching forth in London, I knew that it was important to start work as soon as possible because my salary would still be needed at McBain.

My mother and grandmother went with me to the city. We had decided that it would be best if I flew to Johannesburg and connected there with my flight to London. Aishaben wanted to come and see me off as well, and so we stopped at her place first to pick her up.

The wind was gusting quite strongly. The sky was overcast and stormy. My flight was announced.

I embraced my mother and grandmother, crying uncontrollably.

'Don't worry, Meena, you'll be fine,' Aishaben assured me.

After one final hug, my mother gave me a gentle push to get me started.

I took a few halting steps, but Nana waved me along. 'Get going,' she said, 'or you'll miss your flight.'

A bus transported us to the plane which was parked some distance away on the tarmac. My eyes were red and swollen from crying and I avoided looking at the other passengers.

The wind was much stronger now and I had to struggle to keep my balance as I climbed the stairs towards a smiling stewardess.

When I reached the top of the steps I turned and waved at the terminal building, hoping that the three women would see me. My eyes welled up again as I made my way to my assigned window seat.

I suspected that Ma and Nana would still be waving. My stomach churned with anxiety and I tried to compose myself as we prepared for take-off.

I was still gazing through the window when we took off, my hands firmly gripping the armrests. As I took one last look at the airport, I wondered whether I would ever see my mother and grandmother again.

36

URMILA, AN Indian woman in a sari, sat next to me on the flight to Johannesburg. We were soon chatting like old friends about our respective families and our lives.

We were well into our family histories when the cabin attendants arrived with the drinks trolley. We were each given a foil-wrapped styrofoam plate of sandwiches, a tiny bunch of grapes, and a small carton of fruit juice. I peered under the foil and although the sandwiches looked unappetising, I ate them because I had no idea when my next meal would be.

'It'll be a nice flight to London – long, though,' Urmila said. 'I've been there twice. I'll probably be going again soon.'

I told her that this was the first time I'd ever been on a plane. I'm sure, though, that even if I hadn't told her she would have noticed because my hands, on take-off, were so tightly wrapped around the armrests that my knuckles almost popped out of their sockets.

She told me what to do when I got to Johannesburg where I had a four-hour wait before my flight to London. I was glad she mentioned the transfer from the domestic to the international terminal. I wouldn't have had a clue.

This bit of information was cause for more anxiety. My stomach was already in a tight knot. What if I got on to the wrong flight?

'Not much to do at airports,' Urmila said. 'Make sure you have a good book.'

I indicated my bulging carry-on bag stuffed under the seat in front of me.

'It's likely to be a bit of a hassle when you get to London. They always hassle South Africans, especially if you're not . . . white.'

I could feel the knot in my stomach getting tighter. 'I've got all my papers,' I told her. 'It shouldn't be a problem. And my sister will be there to meet me.'

But what if they didn't let me into the country? Would I be sent back on the next flight? What if . . . What if . . . While I struggled with these questions, Urmila told me about the London Underground. She laughed when she saw my expression of sheer terror. 'Don't worry about it. It's not as difficult as it sounds and it's the easiest way to get around.'

Her reassurances didn't help one iota. My anxiety increased, weighing me down like a rock, pressing me down into my seat.

It was all such a far cry from what I was familiar with – Venter & Son, the bus on which I used to travel to and from school, Papa's old DeSoto and my little Austin which was now parked in the yard next to the shop, in its death throes, abandoned while its owner ventured off to new worlds.

The tension was becoming too much and I felt myself being sucked into a whirlpool of anxiety. I felt as though I was sliding into a bath of jelly in which there was no firm base on which to plant my feet.

Before we landed in Johannesburg, I wrote out Yasmin's address and phone number and gave them to Urmila. 'If you're ever in London,' I said, 'come and see me or telephone me.'

'I'll do that,' she said.

I didn't really believe that I'd see her again.

When we landed I went with her to pick up our bags and then she escorted me all the way to the international terminal. It was thronged with people dressed in the long white muslin *ijaar* and *khurta*, commonly worn by Muslims going on Hajj. They were waiting for their flight to Mecca.

Urmila left me at the barrier to the international terminal and in the jostle and press of humanity, we hugged. I clung to her for a moment, reluctant to let her go. Then, with a quick wave, she was gone.

I pushed my way past the barrier and was stopped by a security guard who told me to go back to the proper entrance where my luggage was to be scanned. I pushed the trolley back into the river of bodies, battling against the current.

I presented my ticket at the counter. I was beginning to lose some of my anxiety and felt a little more confident as I requested a window seat. When I told the clerk that I wanted to take the two smaller carry-on bags with me, she hesitated, but then glanced over my shoulder at the long line of passengers growing behind me. Without further hesitation she pressed a button and sent my suitcases off along a conveyor belt into the bowels of the airport.

She handed me my ticket and boarding card and I made my way through to passport control.

Here, again, there were long lines of waiting passengers and I took my place in one of the shorter lines.

I was relieved when all the formalities were finally completed and I could relax in the departure lounge. I settled down with my book, collecting myself and my fragmented emotions. I imagined that Ma and Nana were already on their way back to McBain.

It was only when I was on the flight to London that it really felt as though I was finally leaving for a foreign country. The faces around me reflected this. I was sitting next to a black woman and next to her on the aisle was a white woman.

Now, as we flew through the dark void of international space, I hugged the adventure of my travel to myself. I peered out into the darkness, wondering if the northern sky would be anything like the southern sky. Would the same stars be visible?

Lights on the dark landscape glittered almost as brightly as the stars in the sky and slowly my fear and anxiety fell from me. Like petals from a flower, they fell into the huge swampy darkness through which we, a tiny dot in the vast universe, were winging our way to new lives. New beginnings.

We arrived in London at about six o'clock the next morning.

The passengers, dishevelled and bleary-eyed, disembarked in a rush. I stepped off the plane through the fluted corridor and into the airport terminal. There were so many signboards, none of which made any sense to me. It took me some time to decide where I was going. Finally, I thought that it would be relatively safe to go in the direction of the passport control sign. I walked amongst other passengers arriving from all parts of the world, overwhelmed by the sights and sounds. It was all so *foreign*. I pushed my shoulders back as I hoisted my heavy hand luggage and walked down the long corridor.

There were already long lines of people snaking around the taped areas. Like rivers, they flowed forward, but some of them, looking troubled and anxious, were cordoned off from the rest of the stream. I waited with a bouncing heart as the streams divided into their many little tributaries.

Years of persecution by police and government officials had cowed non-white South Africans, creating an irrational fear of officialdom. It was a fear and an anxiety that remained with me throughout my life.

I studied the passport officials, looking for a sympathetic face. One of them, a youngish, good-looking man with very blond hair, was smilingly engaged in conversation with a passenger.

It took ages for the lines to move. I worried that Yasmin might have given up on me. How would she know that I was being delayed? Would Soraya be there too? All these questions crossed my mind as I waited my turn.

Instead of being directed to the friendly young man, my passport inspector was an older, heavy-jowled man with large goitre-like eyes. He was obviously not a happy man and after the first quick glance he didn't look at me again until he'd finished his interrogation.

'Why are you here?'
'I've come for a visit.'
'How long are you staying?'
'A few months,' I stammered.
'How long . . . exactly,' he demanded, pencil poised.

The fear that had lain dormant during the flight, manifesting in an occasional flutter and tightening of my stomach, now exploded into my consciousness, almost paralysing me.

'Four months.'

'Where are you staying?'

'With my sister.'

'Address?'

I scratched amongst the papers in my handbag for Yasmin's address, found it and handed it to him.

'How much money do you have?'

My hands plunged back into the jumble of my handbag and I pulled out a small wallet. I carefully opened it and showed him my traveller's cheques. He flipped through them.

'Uh huh.' He pushed the wallet back at me.

I didn't know what that meant. Was it enough? Was it not enough?

'Where's your return ticket?'

I retrieved the ticket from the folder. By this time half the contents of my handbag were spread on his desk. He studied the ticket while I waited, my heart pounding like a sledge-hammer.

'Where does your sister work?'

'She has her own business.'

'What does she do?'

I told him. His heavy jowls shook and then moved involuntarily as though he were chewing. I watched his face. He stamped a piece of paper, handed me back my passport, glanced at me with those goitre-eyes as he waved me through. I was so relieved to have this over and done with that I conjured up one of my sweetest smiles. He didn't bat an eyelid.

The little ox-bow lake of people, most of them in middle-eastern dress, was still waiting, cordoned off from the rest of the passengers. I was thankful not to be amongst them.

I recognised two of the passengers off my flight and followed them to a baggage carousel. I saw people armed with trolleys and searched around for one. I found them stacked together in a long shining caterpillar and almost ripped my arm out of its socket trying to free one.

It was a relief, though, to rid myself of the heavy carry-on bags. By the time I returned to the carousel, it had started moving and luggage came crashing down the conveyor belt. I watched carefully for my suitcases. There were several that looked like mine, but Ma had tied a green ribbon around each of the handles for easy identification.

Three-quarters of the passengers had already retrieved their luggage and I was still waiting for mine. I was beginning to panic. What if my luggage was lost? How would I go about finding it?

Then, with the last few bags, mine came tumbling down the belt. I braced my legs and lifted both suitcases off the carousel before they could disappear from sight.

It was almost over, I told myself. The sign in the last hallway indicated two exits, one for passengers who had nothing to declare and another for those who had. I assumed I belonged to the former category and after a brief hesitation, pushed my trolley through the green exit. There were several passengers ahead of me. I had the exit in my sights. The door swung open briefly and for an instant I caught a glimpse of people waiting at the barrier. My heart soared. I was almost there. I felt exhilarated. Free. I was shedding all the old fears, tossing aside the constraints and inhibitions that had limited my life.

I could do anything I wanted to. I could be anyone I wanted to be. No one here knew me. I had left my past behind. This was the future.

My head was so filled with ecstatic thoughts that I didn't hear the customs officer yelling at me to stop.

I was a few feet from the door, almost there, when a hand clamped down on my shoulder. Startled, I swung around, almost driving my trolley into the passenger ahead of me.

'Didn't you hear me?' a blue-uniformed man with steely grey eyes asked.

Shocked, I looked at him and shook my head.

'Over here,' he said abruptly, directing me to a table.

I followed him.

'You don't speak English?' It wasn't a question, more like an accusation.

I nodded.

'Open your bags.'

I heaved the big suitcase on to the table and waited, not knowing what was expected of me.

'Open it. Both of them,' the man said. One of the other men, thin and wily, sauntered over. He obviously had nothing better to do because the number of passengers had thinned out considerably.

With trembling fingers I fumbled with the key, trying to open the locks. I snapped open the latches, unhooked the strap and stepped back.

'This one too,' the wily man said, pointing to the other suitcase. I unlocked it.

'Do you have anything to declare?' Steel-Grey Eyes asked.

'No,' I said, shaking my head.

He glanced at the two carry-on bags and my handbag. 'What's in there?'

'Just my stuff, my clothes and a few other things.'

'Put all the bags on the table.'

I put the rest of my luggage on the table, unzipping my carry-on bags.

The wily man smiled sardonically as he groped in my carefully folded underwear. I wasn't sure what else my mother had packed amongst my clothes. I saw now that there were strips of *biltong*, wrapped in plastic, tucked into the corners. There were sheets and glassware for Yasmin. I understood now why my luggage was so heavy.

The wily man plunged his hands in amongst my panties and came up with a bottle of watermelon preserve. He read the label and set the bottle aside. In the mean time, Steel-Grey Eyes poked around the edges of my other suitcase.

'And what's this?' he asked as he triumphantly detached from one of my half-slips a small bottle of garlic, ginger and chilli paste which Ma had prepared for Yasmin. I almost died as he pulled out the bottle, for there was a sanitary pad dangling from his watch. The thin gauze had hooked itself around the winder and while he struggled to extricate himself, my face turned several shades of red. I didn't know where to look. I'd rolled the sanitary pads into a neat little bundle and now they were lying open and exposed on top of my luggage. I wanted to reach out to help him disengage himself, or to cover up the rest of them, but I didn't dare move. Finally he pulled himself free. I could tell from his expression that he was not amused.

'What is this?' he barked, holding up the bottle of masala.

'M-m-masala,' I stammered, overwhelmed by all the attention my luggage was receiving.

He opened the bottle. Ma had told me that this was a very hot masala. I watched with bated breath as he opened the bottle, brought his nose closer and sniffed. For a moment he blinked in alarm, then he choked, coughing until his steel-grey eyes were drowning in tears.

I didn't utter a word.

The wily man leapt to his colleague's assistance.

I waited. The other customs officers watched Steel-Grey Eyes being led away and then turned their eyes on me. I was like a rabbit trapped in the bright beam of their angry gaze.

One of them, an Indian man with a huge moustache and turban, came over. He looked at the bottle of masala and grinned.

'It's all right,' he said. 'You can go now.'

He helped me to stuff everything back into my suitcases. I struggled to shut them and then hoisted them back on to the trolley.

As I walked away I heard him yelling to the others: 'I've told you guys, don't smell things. Especially if you've got an Indian passenger.' He laughed. 'You guys will never learn.'

At last, I thought. This was it. I headed for the exit door, pausing as it slid open on my approach.

OTHER SECRETS

OTHER SECRETS

37

DESPITE MY ordeal at the hands of the over-zealous customs official, I felt a surge of exhilaration as I stepped into the arrivals hall. I felt like Felicity in *Storm of Passion,* as she walked away from her past to start a new life.

I glanced anxiously around the arrivals hall, searching for Yasmin and Soraya. Suddenly I spotted Soraya waving frantically. She reached me in a few quick bounds and the moment she flung her arms around my neck and clung to me so ferociously that I thought I would choke, I knew that things were not going well between her and Yasmin.

Yasmin summoned a porter to take my wobbly trolley and in a daze of exhaustion I followed them to the parking garage where her car, a late model blue Mercedes, was parked.

Soraya sat in the back, unusually quiet, almost sullen. Yasmin's eyes constantly darted to the rear-view mirror, trying to include her in the conversation. But Soraya remained uncommunicative.

When Yasmin left South Africa with Soraya we had expected mother and daughter to bond, but from what I saw now the tension between them sizzled like water on a hot stove.

In the months away from McBain and under London's dreary skies, Soraya had lost her sun-burnished vitality. She looked pale and wan, her skin almost translucent. Alone on the back seat, she had all the fragility of an injured bird.

It must have been quite bewildering for both of them – Soraya suddenly finding herself in a strange country, amongst strange people, and Yasmin who, until a few months before had had only herself to think about, now had an eight-year-old daughter, an individual with a will of her own, a child making demands on her time and her attention. I could only imagine what an enormous adjustment this must have been for them both.

It was still difficult to understand why Yasmin had taken Soraya from McBain. Nana was convinced that Yasmin's actions were motivated by guilt. But even though I had great respect for Nana's intuitiveness, I gave Yasmin more credit than that – I painted her with an altruistic brush instead of tarring her the way Nana had done.

Nana had laughed at me, calling me naïve, a hopeless romantic. And, as usual, Nana was right.

Yasmin had not yet told Soraya about her father. Both Neville, whom Yasmin was soon to marry, and I warned her that she should not wait too long, but Yasmin felt that Soraya was too young to understand.

I thought that Yasmin was underestimating Soraya's resilience. I knew that inside that delicate exterior was a tenacious and spirited little person.

'An old soul' was the way Nana described Soraya. In her relationship with Yasmin, however, there was none of the old-soul sagacity. Her vindictiveness was surprisingly nasty for a child so young and one who, moreover, had come from a loving home.

'Leave me alone!' she screamed at Yasmin when she tried to correct her about some minor issue. 'You're a witch! I hate you!'

Yasmin, terrified of a scene, looked at me in despair. Although I wanted to shake Soraya, I kept my mouth shut and avoided both sets of eyes.

But when Soraya and I were alone, she was a totally different child. Like two old friends, we talked endlessly about McBain. Her memories of those early years were vivid. She enquired about Gladys and Florence and spoke sadly of Daniel. She remembered Elsa and her son Niels, who had been born without hands. But she never mentioned Birdie.

Puzzled about this omission, I asked her: 'Soraya, don't you remember Birdie?'

Large eyes, the colour of the sky, fixed on me.

'Remember Birdie?' I asked again.

She looked at me in the curious way she had, her expression closed.

I never mentioned Birdie again.

I talked to Yasmin about getting Soraya another dog.

'The flat's too small,' Yasmin said. 'We can't have an animal. Besides, who will look after it?'

She was right, of course, but I still thought that Soraya needed a pet on which to focus her affections.

She obviously missed her carefree life at McBain. And whenever she spoke of Papa she turned her eyes heavenwards, which was where Ma told her Papa had gone. She remembered how he used to hold her in his arms when he wound the wall clock, and how she had bounced with glee when it chimed the hour. He deliberately used to move the hands to noon before setting the time, purely for the pleasure of watching her reaction when the clock chimed twelve.

'Papa was always there for me when I was a baby, wasn't he?' she said in her very adult voice. 'I miss him. I wish he hadn't died.'

'Everyone dies,' I said. 'Plants die, animals die, people die.'

'I don't want to die here,' she said gravely.

'You won't die here, Soraya,' I assured her. 'But, darling, this is your home now.'

'No!' she cried. 'I want to go back to McBain! I hate this place and I hate Yasmin!' Her eyes welled with tears.

I dreaded what might follow because Yasmin had told me about her tantrums. I could see she was teetering on the edge. I put an arm around her and gently drew her towards me.

'Papa loved you very much,' I said.

She didn't say anything for a while and the threat of a tantrum passed.

'I know,' she said.

Her mood changed as though the memories of her grandfather comforted her. It seemed that she had found a safe place in her mind. One she could touch whenever she needed solace. A place to hide or to heal.

We all have our own places. I discovered mine much later – a place which reflected the geography of my soul.

Soraya spoke of her very early childhood with the same clarity she used to describe recent events.

'But you were too small to remember that, Soraya,' I would say, having serious reservations about the veracity of her recollections. Not even I had such clear memories of Papa, and he had been my father.

'I remember,' she said firmly. 'I was a baby and everyone was so sad. It was because Yasmin ran away, wasn't it?' She had Nana's habit of turning a statement into a question.

I nodded slowly, almost anxiously, wondering what other revelations Soraya had in store for me.

One day when we were lying in bed, cuddled up against the cold, she said: 'I used to cry a lot when I was alone, but now that you're here, I don't cry any more.'

I hugged her. I was still sceptical about her ability to remember so far back. Later, though, when I read an article about a young girl induced through hypnosis to recall her experiences in her mother's womb, I was almost convinced.

I mentioned the article to Yasmin.

'What utter nonsense, Meena!' She laughed scornfully. 'Don't you know that the tabloids print the biggest rubbish imaginable? Soraya's a child. She's making it all up. You know what a vivid imagination she has.'

Stung by Yasmin's response, I walked away.

When I was Soraya's age my mother had said exactly the same thing about me.

38

SOME OF my favourite romance novels were set in London and the city had a familiar feel to it. Long before I actually experienced it, I already had some inkling of its energy and its charm.

The loneliness at McBain had fuelled my imagination and I often became one of the beautiful heroines – Jessica or Angelica, ladies born into privileged society, London at their feet. My reality, however, was different.

I came from a rural environment, where the most progressive piece of equipment was an electric toaster. London, with all its sophistication, left me floundering.

The simplest task was fraught with peril. When I tried to use the washing machine I flooded the kitchen. Thank goodness for Soraya who, already initiated into the ways of city life, was much more knowledgeable than I and took great delight in showing me the ropes.

She demonstrated the operation of each of the appliances in the flat and, when there was time, hauled piles of electrical gadgets out of Yasmin's cupboards: bread makers, mixers, can-openers and juicers, some of them still in their original boxes.

Most important of all, she gave me a basic understanding of how to get around London by myself: how to hail a cab and where to catch a bus.

Schools were still closed for the holidays and Soraya guided me through the neighbourhood, excitedly drawing my attention to everything around us. With her help I began to enjoy London.

I had never imagined a city so enormous, so complex and so

totally overwhelming. Each morning as I awakened I sensed the city coming to life. Like a huge lumbering animal, it flexed its muscles, determining the pulse for the day.

We saw very little of Yasmin. Both she and Neville had busy schedules. Neville was a partner in a well-established law firm and Yasmin was putting in long hours to expand her already successful couturier business.

She had been approached by a representative from a Middle Eastern kingdom and invited to submit designs for a wedding gown for the Princess Nabila. A relative newcomer to the fashion industry, she was quite confident about competing with many of the better-known couture houses.

She worked tirelessly to complete the sketches in time for the princess's visit. She was hardly ever home and when she was it was a quick turn-around to change clothes and see how we were doing.

After all Yasmin's hard work, the princess eventually chose the design of her arch-rival Tony Roshton, a Paris-trained designer. She tried to hide her disappointment, but was clearly devastated.

'That's business. You win some – you lose some,' she said as she feverishly ripped up the designs she'd spent so much time on.

I tried to stop her.

'There's no reason to keep them,' she said. 'I'll never use them again.'

'There'll be other opportunities,' Neville said in an attempt to console her.

But Yasmin, emotionally drained, claimed a headache and went to bed.

Much later I heard her getting up. I tiptoed downstairs and joined her in the kitchen. She smiled disconsolately when she saw me. 'Couldn't sleep either?' she said.

'Remember the night of the storm at McBain when you danced in the rain?' I asked.

She smiled, but didn't say anything.

'You can't imagine how terrified I was,' I said. 'I thought if you were struck by lightning, I'd have a hard time explaining why you were out there . . . naked.'

'We were so young,' she chuckled, with a gesture of world-weariness. She opened a cupboard and took out a tin of biscuits. She paused, the tin suspended in mid-air. 'Life was so simple then.'

'I always said you'd be famous some day,' I said.

'Famous?' she asked. 'I couldn't even get my sketches accepted.' Then she smiled wryly. 'It's not what you know. It's who you know in this business.'

'You're already successful,' I said.

'Recognition. Power. That's what it's all about.'

'It'll come, Yas. This is just a little setback.'

'Or divine retribution.'

'For what?' I asked.

'For all the bad things I've done in my life.'

'Rubbish,' I said.

'Remember, Nana said I was nothing but a glorified dressmaker.'

I shrugged. 'She never meant anything by that. You know how the two of you used to press each other's buttons.'

'I suppose . . .' she paused reflectively.

I plugged in the kettle. 'Tea?'

'Thanks.' She drew up a stool and sat at the counter which separated the kitchen from the breakfast nook. I felt a rush of sisterly affection and leaned over to squeeze her hand.

'I'm fine now,' she said, searching the pockets of her robe for a tissue. 'Oh, I meant to tell you. I've found a bigger space for my workshop. I move at the end of next month.'

That was more like the old Yasmin. The kick-arse-ambition-driven-hard-nosed workaholic. Qualities that some admired and others hated. What I admired, though, was what others seldom saw: the sometimes shy, vulnerable, kind and generous Yasmin who remembered birthdays and anniversaries and did countless thoughtful things for others.

The two of us sitting in the kitchen sipping tea reminded me of those days at McBain when Nana used to make the tea, a panacea for everything that ailed us, and we would sit around the kitchen table talking. But the essential ingredients were missing: Ma and Nana.

'So, how are things, Meena?' she asked as we sipped camomile tea. 'We've hardly had time to talk with all this Princess Nabila stuff. How do you like London?'

'I love it!' I said.

She listened with a half-amused smile. 'You've always been such a country bumpkin . . . don't you miss McBain?'

'I miss Ma and Nana. But not McBain. I should have left there a long time ago.'

'What about Jonathan? Any word from him?'

'I've left at least a dozen messages,' I said with a shrug. 'He hasn't called back.' Although I tried to sound indifferent, his rejection was painful.

Yasmin subjected me to one of her long penetrating gazes. Then, 'Forget him,' she said. 'He's not worth the trouble.'

'Don't worry,' I said firmly. 'He won't hear from me again.'

But all my attempts to expunge Jonathan from my thoughts were futile. The image of the two of us lying in the veld surrounded by sunbathing lizards, darting field mice, soaring hawks, and colonies of ants on their interminable marches, was still too fresh, too precious.

In *Obsession*, the heroine Robyn had never given up on her lover Sean, even though he had abandoned her to go in search of his fortune. In the end her love was strong enough to draw him back from an abyss of treachery and deceit.

'Some day you'll find someone who loves you for who you are,' Yasmin said. 'Trust me.'

We talked for ages. I told her that I didn't think Ma and Nana would ever leave McBain.

'Remember, Nana always said we'd have to carry her off in a box.'

'Stubborn old women,' Yasmin grumbled.

'Don't you dare talk about stubbornness,' I said. 'You and Nana *both* take the cake.'

She smiled.

'And don't forget,' I said, 'that Soraya takes after both of you.'

Yasmin's mood changed abruptly. She frowned and looked pensively into her teacup. Finally, she said: 'I'm worried about Soraya. Do you think I've done the right thing, Meena?'

I waited to hear what else was on her mind.

'Should I have left her at McBain?' she asked.

'Yasmin, for what it's worth, I think you did the right thing.'

She drew her hand through her hair in a gesture of despair. Then she got up and went to the fridge. She stood at the open door for a long time, staring absently at the shelves of food. Unable to make up her mind about what she wanted, she shut the door and sat down again.

'I can't tell her about her father,' she said. 'She's already confused. It'll only confuse her more.'

'Give her some credit, Yasmin.'

'I'll wait until she's a bit older.'

'Don't you think she wonders about her father?' I asked.

'The issue hasn't arisen – she's never mentioned him.'

'She probably feels insecure. Telling her the truth might help.'

Yasmin didn't say anything. It was clear that she had too much to cope with and one more thing, like telling Soraya the truth, would only complicate her life further.

'I'm really glad you came,' she said taking her cup to the sink. 'I hope you'll stay. You've made such a difference to our lives, especially to Soraya's. She's laughing again. She hasn't done that in ages.'

'Yasmin, please,' I said quickly, 'you know why I came.'

She sat down again and studied my face carefully, trying to ascertain what lay behind my words.

'I'd like to get on with my own life,' I continued. 'I have to find a job, Yas. I promised Ma and Nana I'd help. Soraya is your responsibility. She's your child. You took her out of a perfectly good home. You were the one who told Ma that Soraya was yours and that you wanted her back.'

I was a bit vexed that she had assumed I would always be there for her. What about me? What about *my* life? Was I of so little consequence that no one cared about what I wanted?

She looked at me with large eyes, eyes that were capable of melting the toughest resolve.

But I was her sister and I was immune to her charm.

Rather her pain than mine, I thought, as I looked away, afraid of being seduced by her mute despair.

I didn't want to be heartless, but I realised that giving in now would only be a harbinger of things to come.

'You can't just back away because things are not working the way you planned,' I said firmly, angry at her for expecting so much of me. 'This isn't some business deal you're backing out of. This is your child's life!'

Her eyes filled with tears. The scene and all its subtext was like a replay of the scenes we had had years ago, just before she ran away from McBain.

'You did it once before, Yas,' I said, determined to set her straight. 'You abandoned Soraya because your life was so much more important than hers. I won't stand by and see you do it again.'

Yasmin paled. The tears spilt over.

'I've given her everything she wants,' she said. 'I adore her, Meena, even though she's become a very unlovable child.'

My resolve weakened. 'Yas, you've got to spend time with her. You can't just palm her off on others.'

'I'd give up everything for her if only there was some indication . . . some sign from her that it was appreciated. I'm not looking for gratitude. All I want is respect . . . some co-operation. But she's a brat, Meena. She's impossible. She's making my life hell. I just can't reach her. Nothing I do for her is good enough.'

Yasmin's face collapsed. She folded her arms on the counter top and put her head down, her shoulders shaking with quiet sobs. I tried to comfort her. I hadn't seen her like this since our row the night before she ran away.

Neville came to look for her. He found her sitting with her head buried in her arms, sobbing uncontrollably.

He touched her shoulder. She sat up and he gently took her in his arms. My anger dissolved and I watched the two of them with a twinge of envy, longing for the same kind of closeness and affection.

39

THE HOLIDAYS were over and Soraya went back to school. She was at a private school because Yasmin believed it was the only facility good enough to provide Soraya with a solid grounding. To my mind, this meant that Soraya would become British, adopting their speech and their culture and before long her connections with McBain would be severed and forgotten.

Nana used to say that people who went to England and became carbon copies of the English were like *brinjals* – aubergines. Dark on the outside and white on the inside. No matter how hard they tried to be white on the outside, they would always just be brinjals. Nana was at her best with food analogies.

With Soraya at school I was left to my own devices. Lost and bored, I tried to amuse myself as best I could.

In an attempt to familiarise myself with the Underground, I sallied forth, determined to unlock the intricate workings of the Tube and to master its secrets. I took the train from Covent Garden to Gloucester Road, sticking to the blue line as it seemed the easiest route. As I waited for the next train back to Covent Garden, I was already basking in the glow of my accomplishment, pleased that my little venture had been successfully executed.

With Neville and Yasmin at work and Soraya at school, I began to feel the occasional twinge of homesickness – mostly for the sun and the open smiling faces of my own people. It seemed so ironical that the people who had the least to smile about, smiled the most. Here people seldom smiled, even though they had a lot more to smile about than people back home. Yasmin said the weather was what made Londoners so grouchy.

With the approach of winter I found myself spending more time indoors. Although comfortable, Yasmin's flat was small and seemed to shrink with each bone-chilling, knee-numbing day.

I didn't mind spending a few hours after school with Soraya, but I reminded Yasmin that I wanted to be independent and that I had come to London to teach.

'It'll only be for a short while,' she assured me. 'When Neville and I are married, we'll move to the country and I'll be able to get a live-in nanny. And if it makes you feel any better, I've been sending money home to Ma each month.'

She just couldn't see my point, I thought wearily. I had promised Ma and Nana that *I* would help them. Ma had told me quite explicitly that she didn't want 'charity' from Yasmin.

Yasmin had once again put me in a spot. I didn't want to let Soraya down, but I also desperately wanted my freedom.

Yasmin was now gripped by a new urgency to get married soon. Plans to move to the country gained momentum. She painted an idyllic picture which convinced neither Soraya nor me.

Neville didn't seem to mind where he lived, as long as Yasmin was there. It seemed as if his life now was entirely dependent on the vagaries of Yasmin's ambitions. He had lost his will. He was a man beaten down by an unsuccessful first marriage. The notion of having failed as a husband and a father was demoralising, and now to top it all, there were Yasmin's head-spinning plans for the wedding.

Neville's children, Allison and Mark, came to the flat whenever he was unable to take them out of the city. Allison was ten and Mark thirteen and they were both sullen and truculent children. When Neville managed to coax them away from the television to take them for a walk in the nearby park, they went without much enthusiasm and seemed so full of resentment that we felt uncomfortable around them. Although I felt sorry for the children, they were not my favourite people.

Yasmin tried to get some response from them, but failed. It was frustrating for her and quite inconceivable to me that she had at one time been their nanny. Yasmin didn't like to be reminded of that time.

Soraya avoided the children when they came to visit, retreating to her room. Although she tried to hide her feelings, she was clearly envious that they had a father and she didn't.

Yasmin enthused about how wonderful life would be in the country, but Soraya was reluctant to leave her school, especially since it had taken her such a long time to make friends.

'It's much better and healthier for her to grow up in the country,' Yasmin insisted. 'It'll be so much easier to make friends at boarding school.'

'But she has friends here,' I reminded her.

None of my arguments swayed Yasmin. Her decision had been made. Yasmin was the one fixated on boarding schools – Soraya hated the idea.

'She'll come around. All young girls want the boarding school experience,' she explained, as though I were some dolt who had no understanding of these things. 'I just hope I can find a place for her. Some children are on the waiting lists from the day they're conceived.'

'Yes, I know, Yasmin,' I said quietly. 'But I don't think it's what Soraya wants.'

'Why not?' Yasmin demanded. 'What has she said to you? How do you know what she wants?'

'I think . . .' I started, but Yasmin had jumped down my throat before I could articulate my view that I probably knew more about Soraya than she did.

'I know what she wants. I'm her mother.'

I shook my head resignedly. It would be best for me not to interfere. Yet at the same time it was difficult to stand by and watch things going wrong.

Yasmin should have known that Soraya was not the boarding school type. She was the kind of child who needed the closeness, warmth and love of her family. The only reason she might have had for wanting to get away from home was to escape Yasmin's authority and the tension that seemed forever present in our lives.

Yasmin was probably just as keen to send Soraya away for exactly the same reasons.

40

NEVILLE WAS a very loving and affectionate partner and had all the potential for being a good father to Soraya. No one was more aware of this than Yasmin and, perhaps because of this, she desperately wanted to keep him in her life.

Yasmin, though, had no more control over events than any of us. We were like leaves caught up in a current, powerless to change course.

Yasmin moved her workshop to the larger premises. She was one of a dozen up-and-coming young designers and the pressure to succeed was enormous.

Nana used to say that Yasmin was like a cat on a hot tin roof. This was more true now than ever before. It seemed that wherever she went, a trail of turbulence followed her. She never entered a room quietly but always seemed to burst in, as if the normal pace of life frustrated her.

In the short while that I had been in London, the relationship between Yasmin and Soraya deteriorated. On a few occasions, Soraya worked herself into such a state that she began screaming obscenities at her mother. My interventions had no effect and Yasmin was at her wits' end.

A friend suggested that Yasmin take Soraya to see a child psychologist. Yasmin, who thought it might be of benefit, accompanied Soraya to her early counselling sessions. She did all the talking while Soraya had nothing to say.

I watched developments with dismay, wondering what my

mother and grandmother would say if they knew what was happening. I carefully avoided mentioning these problems in my letters home.

The only time there was any peace and quiet was when Yasmin was away. Soraya, always soothed by music, sat quietly with Neville, listening to his classical tapes.

Neville and I had become good friends and he seemed to feel more comfortable sharing confidences with me rather than Yasmin.

Once he said, 'My children mean a lot to me. They have been very damaged by my divorce. Allison especially is very hostile and their mother is well on her way to becoming an alcoholic. My children have to live with that . . . and I don't know what to do.'

At times there was an expression of such infinite sadness in Neville's eyes that I was almost tempted to put my arms around him.

I wished I could help. I wished I could give him the reassurance he sought. But what could I say? Yasmin was unable to cope with one hostile child – her own – so how would she manage with two more? And yet if he left them with their mother, they would be damaged irreparably. The most practical solution would be to pack them off to boarding school.

Neville's sadness reminded me of Brandon, the hero in *Destiny*, a man so much in love with the beautiful, desirable, but selfish Sophia that it almost led to his destruction.

In the mean time Soraya and Neville seemed to coexist on the periphery of Yasmin's 'other' life. Like two tiny ripples in a Yasmin-pool, they were drawn together. It was easy to love Neville. He had a warm, generous nature which made one feel totally at ease.

Some evenings Soraya would sit next to him on the sofa, cradled in the crook of his arm, eyes half-closed as he read to her. Long after we had gone to bed, he'd sit up waiting for Yasmin. Eventually he'd give up and go to bed, disappointed that she was late again. I was angry with her. But it seemed as if

Neville was bewitched. In his eyes she could do no wrong.

'You're going to lose him if you're not careful,' I warned Yasmin one day when Neville had taken Soraya for a walk and we were alone. I hoped I could at least drum some sense into her.

She was silent and unresponsive, but I knew she had heard every word.

'He's a kind and gentle man and he's wonderful with Soraya,' I said. 'You're very lucky.'

Still no response.

'He's unhappy, Yasmin. Can't you see it? You've got to pay attention or you'll lose him. He'll go back to his family or find some young girl in his office . . .'

She looked at me askance.

A few days later, Yasmin lit candles after supper and while Soraya and I discreetly crept off to bed, the two of them curled up together, listening to romantic music and reconstructing their relationship. Those gestures meant the world to Neville.

When Neville's mother died ten years before, he had inherited the family estate and its tenants. When the tenants left five years later it had remained unoccupied and had become neglected. Yasmin, who had always known about the property, now expressed interest in it.

About six months before the wedding, we drove out into the country to inspect the place. It was horribly run down. Except for a few exterior walls, the rest of the stone and mortar structure had crumbled like a cake.

The only building still intact was the carriage house with its three bedrooms, dining-room, lounge, kitchen and bathroom. There was still evidence of a garden and a few moss-covered trees stood in a cluster beyond the collapsed stables. Yasmin seemed to shrink into her designer boots when she saw the place. But she was never one to be put off by a challenge and was immediately able to see potential in the carriage house.

She was determined that she was going to live on the estate.

It had the right address. From there, no doubt, her dreams of grandeur were within reach. I could never have imagined that Yasmin might like living in the country, that she might actually enjoy the peace and the solitude. I didn't give her credit for that kind of sensitivity.

I was wrong, though. We were all wrong about her. This was another side of her that we were not used to seeing. Yasmin was willing to tackle the project. Neville tried to dissuade her, explaining that the reason the property had been neglected was because it would cost a fortune to restore.

'The carriage house is perfect,' she said. 'It won't cost so very much to renovate.'

Neville was still reluctant, but Yasmin wore him down.

A contractor was hired to install new plumbing, to rewire the house and to fix the heating. Yasmin and Neville spent every minute of their free time working on the carriage house. A few friends were recruited to assist, but I was amazed at how capable Yasmin was. She had boundless energy when it came to doing things she was really interested in.

'At last she can assume her role as Lady of the Manor, even though it's little more than a ruin,' I wrote to Nana.

When the carriage house was ready, an interior decorator friend of Yasmin's helped to turn it into an elegant space. The work took several months. When it was done, we all sat around a blazing fire in the hearth and celebrated with glasses of champagne.

'Why don't you come and live with us, Meena?' Yasmin asked. 'You'll love it here, I promise.'

'No, thank you,' I said. 'I'd rather stay in London. Besides, you and Neville don't need me hanging around all the time.'

After years of living in the country, I needed the pace of big-city life. The countryside would always be there if and when I wanted to escape.

Yasmin set the wedding date. She wanted an autumn wedding.

'I'd love Ma and Nana to come,' she said as wedding plans

started in earnest.

'Forget it,' I said. 'You don't have a hope, Yas.'

'We'll see about that.'

'It would be nice if they could come,' Neville agreed, putting his arm around her. 'I know they've had reservations about me. It would be good to meet them.'

'Please Ma, come for the wedding,' Yasmin pleaded over the phone.

'Who's going to take care of the business?' Ma asked. 'We'll go to wrack and ruin! And it's taken so long for us to get back on our feet.'

'You don't have to be gone for more than two weeks or so,' Yasmin said.

'Don't be silly, Yasmin, you know we can't come,' Ma said almost regretfully. 'I'm sorry we won't get to meet your Neville before the wedding, but the two of you can come to South Africa, can't you?'

'No, Ma. You know Neville's white.'

There was a pause at the other end. This was something none of us had considered. Neville would have difficulty accompanying his wife into South Africa, and once in the country they would not be able to travel freely as a couple.

'Hello Ma,' I said from the extension phone in Yasmin's bedroom.

'Is that you, Meena?'

'*Ja*. How are you?' I asked.

'You people must be busy with the wedding and all . . .'

'It's getting hectic,' I muttered quietly, so Yasmin wouldn't hear.

'How's my baby?'

'Soraya's fine. Here she is,' I said and handed the phone to Soraya.

'Ma, I miss you.'

'I miss you too, darling,' Ma said, her voice catching. 'Are you being a good girl?'

'Yes, Ma.'

I took the phone from Soraya. Yasmin was still trying to persuade Ma to come, but Ma made it clear that it wasn't going to happen.

With all the fuss about the wedding, Soraya's problems were eased into the background and, like me, she began to miss McBain and her freedom. The walls of the flat closed in on both of us.

I continued to walk Soraya to school in the mornings. She scowled and scuffed the toe of her shoe on the asphalt as the other children jostled past her into the school yard.

Yasmin was totally immersed in wedding arrangements and day-to-day issues were stowed away in some neglected corner of her mind.

Neville had wanted a quiet wedding. He would have preferred to be married in a registrar's office. But Yasmin wouldn't hear of it. She was determined that none of her friends or associates would be slighted. And she was going to design and make her own wedding gown.

There was to be a large bridal retinue, with Soraya as flower girl. I was to be one of four bridesmaids. To escape the turmoil and to avoid being drawn into Yasmin's grandiose schemes, Neville worked late and stayed on the sidelines.

In the weeks that followed Yasmin's announcement, we spoke to Ma and Nana at least once a week, keeping them abreast of the wedding plans. Arrangements for the reception were being handled by Yasmin's friend Louise, whose profession it was to organise lavish social events. The wedding was to be held in a banquet room at the Victoria Hotel. A hundred and fifty guests had been invited. Yasmin was paying for the entire wedding and felt she was entitled to have exactly what she wanted.

The marriage ceremony was performed by Judge Edwin Faber, an old friend of Neville's, in a banquet room decorated with cascades of white roses and lilies. Yasmin looked stunning in her wedding gown of soft cream satin. The bodice was scooped daringly around the neckline and covered in hand-made Italian lace encrusted with seed pearls.

The bridesmaids' dresses were pale burgundy satin, cut in an empire line. The high waist and soft gathers were ideal for me because they concealed the excess weight I was carrying around my hips. Soraya wore a pale pink dress with layers of net and satin bows. She looked so pretty that I was sorry Ma and Nana weren't there to see her.

I was particularly touched by the look of joy in Neville's eyes when Yasmin appeared on the arm of her friend Jeffrey who was giving her away.

Adrian Sheffield, a colleague of Neville's whom I'd met on a few occasions, was the best man. Yasmin suggested that I might want to date him.

'You've got to go out with men. You're not in a nunnery.'

Although I thought Adrian had potential, he struck me as a bit stuffy. My usual quick analysis was always: How would he get on with my friends and family?

He didn't pass muster.

Louise had organised the reception magnificently, her efforts surpassing all our expectations.

It would have been a perfect occasion had it not been for Sharon, Neville's ex-wife. Although Mark and Allison had been invited, Sharon's invitation was an afterthought, grudgingly extended by Yasmin. She feared that Sharon might have too much to drink and create a scene.

That, of course, was exactly what happened.

Sharon, who'd already had a few martinis too many, decided that she wanted to congratulate Neville and his new bride. In her eagerness to get to their table, she stumbled and fell, crashing into one of the other tables. For a moment all attention was riveted on Sharon while Yasmin shrivelled with embarrassment. Two female ushers assisted Sharon to the ladies' cloakroom. Mark and Allison went with their mother and Neville got up and followed them out of the room. He was gone for about fifteen minutes. When he returned I heard him telling Yasmin that he had got a taxi for Sharon and the kids.

Poor Yasmin. No one would remember her wedding or her beautiful gown without stapling to it the image of Sharon making a spectacle of herself.

Yasmin and Neville moved to their country estate after their marriage. There was a feeling of isolation there despite the verdancy – a strange parallel with the barrenness of McBain. Once again Soraya would be isolated – this time without the love and attention she had received from her family at McBain.

I had warned Yasmin that moving Soraya was going to be disruptive, but she was bent on sending her to boarding school.

'Boarding school gave me confidence,' she said.

I said nothing.

'I don't want to go to the country with Yasmin,' Soraya told me, tears close to the surface as she gazed at me with large mournful eyes. 'I want to stay here with you, Meena.'

'You can't, Soraya. I'll be at work all day and there won't be anyone to look after you.'

'I'll look after myself.'

I shook my head in despair. I felt so helpless, caught between the two of them. A dangerous place to be – between mother and daughter.

There was nothing I could do. I had to find a job. I had promised to send money home.

Yasmin and Neville had lived together before they were married but their life in the country was vastly different from the hectic pace of their life in London. At first the adjustment was difficult. But Yasmin was like a cat. No matter where she was thrown, she'd always land on her feet.

The responsibilities of being wife, mother, businesswoman and daily commuter were stressful, but the process she went through in adapting to the change smoothed away some of her sharp edges.

With Soraya away at boarding school and coming home only at weekends, Yasmin had time to concentrate on her marriage and her business during the week. Then when Soraya was home she tried to devote all her time to her.

But Soraya had become adept at pushing Yasmin away. It was disturbing to see her so intent on destroying Yasmin's hopes that the two of them could have a reasonable relationship.

Soraya's behaviour towards Yasmin was becoming problematic. Her coping mechanisms seemed to have collapsed and she became increasingly destructive. I was afraid that by the time Yasmin woke up to the fact that her daughter was bent on self-destruction, it would be too late.

41

YASMIN FOUND peace amongst the rolling hills of the countryside. It was a landscape she became familiar with, a place which connected with her soul. She eased into it like water flowing over a rock.

But the city with its intensity and its loneliness brought me in sharp contact with the side of me that I had repressed most of my life. The anonymity of the city brought me comfort and release.

Yasmin had kept the flat in town, claiming that it was convenient for the occasions when she worked late. In truth, although she would never have admitted it, she kept the flat for my benefit.

The arrangement worked well because it gave me the space to sort myself out. It was the first time since my arrival in London that I had been on my own and free to make my own decisions without having to consult anyone else.

Soraya spent the occasional weekend with me. It seemed to me that she needed some space from Yasmin. Her face was a barometer of her emotions and I always knew when something was wrong.

When she wasn't too busy being Lady of the Manor, Yasmin tried to involve Soraya in other activities. She sent her for ballet lessons, but Soraya was clearly not a ballerina. She hated the lessons and gave them up after a few months. Instead she started music classes. Her instrument of choice was the flute. She devoted herself to her music, seeming to withdraw even further from us. It was apparent to everyone who heard her play that she was gifted. Yasmin and I joked about her musical talent because no one else in our family was musically inclined.

Yasmin said that Papa had once mentioned a cousin who used to play the flute in his village in India.

'He said that it was so quiet that you could hear the flute in the next village,' she said.

'Now you're really reaching Yas. Maybe she gets it from . . .'

Yasmin shut me up with an angry gesture. 'Don't ever mention his name to me,' she said sharply.

'I want to fix the stables,' Yasmin announced one weekend when I was visiting.

She gave me a guided tour, showing me where and how she was going to change things. Neville didn't have much to say. I suspected he was hoping Yasmin would abandon her plans.

Her announcement had struck a chord. I remembered Ma making a similar announcement when she told us she was going to fix the house in Soetstroom. And the house had just been fixed when we were unceremoniously evicted.

Part of the original stables was eventually restored – an area large enough for two horses.

Yasmin still loved to ride. Sometimes she went out with Neville, but much of the time she preferred to ride alone, abandoning herself to the sheer freedom of the open spaces and the wind in her hair.

I remembered the days at McBain with Blitzen and the events that had led to Yasmin's rape. As Nana would have said, a lot of water had passed under the bridge since that time.

Years and miles away from McBain and Blitzen, it was as if Yasmin had been born to this life of style and elegance.

The novelty and excitement of being in London was slowly wearing off, to be replaced by the reality of having to make a living.

I registered for supply teaching. Early each morning the phone rang and I was given the information for my day's assignment. For months I rushed all over London to supervise bad-mannered, illiterate and uncontrollable classes of disrespectful students. All pleasure in teaching was crushed by these experiences. I swore if I could find work elsewhere, I'd give up teaching in a heartbeat.

In December I had a response from an application I'd sent in a few weeks earlier. It was for a position as a housekeeping supervisor at St Martin's Hospital. The hours were long and the wages modest, but it was preferable to what I was doing. At any rate, the wages were enough to cover my needs and I was saving money by living rent-free in Yasmin's flat. I managed to send a good chunk of my salary home to McBain each month.

Despite Yasmin's scornful comments about my job, which sometimes involved cleaning hospital toilets when we were short staffed, I was relieved that I no longer had to go through the daily ordeal of standing in front of a class of hooligans.

My first winter in London was a memorable experience. There was snow everywhere and Christmas lights winked from every window and rooftop. I didn't mind the cold or the snow, but I hated the gloomy skies when it rained for days on end. At times like those I was drawn into a murky pool of depression. It took great effort to force my mind into a positive space and to find the imaginary sun. Some days my mind was in such torpor that I could barely string two lucid thoughts together.

But the second winter was even worse. I was so miserable that I hardly had the strength to drag myself out of bed to go to work in the mornings. I began to miss home. I thought of Nana's ringing aphorisms: *life is not a bed of roses; opportunity doesn't knock twice;* and, *if you make your bed, you've got to lie in it.*

When I gave my phone number to Urmila on the flight to Johannesburg all those months ago I never really expected to hear from her again. And so it was a pleasant surprise when I got a phone call from her one morning as I was getting ready to leave for work. She said that she was in London for three weeks and wondered if we could meet. I was delighted, but since I would only be free at the weekend we arranged to meet then.

On the Saturday evening Urmila and I had supper at a small

bistro around the corner from where I lived. It was a pleasant evening and we spent most of the time talking about South Africa.

We had finished our meal and were getting ready to leave, when Urmila asked: 'Are you all right, Meena?'

Her question took me by surprise. She had obviously sensed my despondency, especially after all the talk about home.

'I guess I'm a bit homesick,' I said.

'One can be very lonely in a big city.' She smiled sympathetically. 'The pace is hectic and everyone's busy. And the weather doesn't help.'

She paused, as if a thought had suddenly occurred to her.

'Look, if you're free tomorrow, I'd like to take you to meet a good friend of mine. A fellow South African.'

'I'll be all right,' I said, embarrassed at having admitted to my loneliness.

'This place can devour you emotionally,' she said. 'You've got to develop other interests.'

'That's what my sister Yasmin says.'

'Well, she's right. It's not always easy to make friends with the English. They can be standoffish.'

'It's just that I don't have a lot of time. I work shifts and I'm often too tired to go out,' I said.

'I'll fetch you tomorrow and take you to meet my friend Sissie.'

I nodded my agreement a little reluctantly, because I knew it would require effort on my part.

Urmila fetched me the next day and we took the Tube to Earls Court. We walked from the station, strolling leisurely through the thronged streets, some of them lined with small hotels and bed-and-breakfast establishments. Eventually we turned into a side street of ramshackle double-storey houses with paint peeling off the exterior walls, broken fences and neglected gardens.

At the end of the block was a three-storey building, and we turned in at the gate. There were six letter-boxes on the wall and six door bells. Urmila knew which bell to press and after a short delay the door snapped open. We climbed three long flights of stairs, the top flight almost vertical. Out of breath, we paused to recover, and then Urmila knocked quietly at the door facing us. The door was opened almost immediately by a tall, smiling woman who had the physique of an athlete.

'This is Sissie Skosana,' Urmila said.

Sissie's flat was small and spartan, but her warmth made up for what the flat lacked.

'I met Sissie through my cousin Tiny Mathur,' Urmila said. 'You'll meet him too, I hope. I haven't been able to get hold of him.'

We talked endlessly about South Africa, about our common bond to the country. From what Sissie said, I gathered she hadn't been home in years. I couldn't get much out of her – she was expert at deflecting questions about herself.

'You can meet some of the others on Tuesday evening, if you like,' Urmila said.

'Tiny will be here,' Sissie told Urmila.

'Unfortunately, I'm off to Scotland for a few days,' Urmila said. Then, to me: 'You'll have to come on your own, Meena.' She was insistent that I should keep in touch with Sissie.

I was free on the Tuesday evening and I took the Tube to Sissie's place, where I met the others.

Clive Faurie was a young Afrikaner draft-dodger who came from a small town near McBain. Tiny Mathur and Joe Ndlovu were both from Natal, and Sissie Skosana was from Johannesburg. They were all exiles and had come to London from various points of the globe.

I was warmly welcomed into their midst and even though I listened to their heated political debates at that first meeting, I didn't know about the extent of their involvement with the African National Congress until much later. It should have been obvious from the beginning – there were enough clues that I could have picked up on.

Lonely and vulnerable, I succumbed to the attraction of being part of their group, seduced by the romance and intrigue of their experiences rather than by any sense of commitment to their ideology. They became my surrogate family, privy to my problems and my small triumphs, but no matter what detours our conversations took, Sissie always managed to steer us back to politics.

Although Clive had not been associated with the African National Congress, he had gravitated towards the group out of loneliness and his hankering for South Africa. Like the others he, too, had made sacrifices – he didn't think he would ever see his family again. Tiny Mathur and Joe Ndlovu came from ANC training camps in Angola and Mozambique. That was the first time I had heard mention of MK soldiers. Tiny bore the scars of his involvement with MK. His leg had been blown off in a landmine accident. The artificial leg he wore was ill-fitting and uncomfortable, but he never complained.

Joe Ndlovu was in stasis. He expected to return to the training camps and was always ready to leave at a moment's notice. That call never came – not while I knew him, at any rate.

Sissie Skosana had studied at a Moscow university. Although she didn't have much to say about herself, she did tell us about a few of her experiences in Russia. I had wondered about the three missing fingers on her right hand. One night when we were complaining about the cold, she told us that she had lost her fingers to frost-bite while in a training camp.

I spent a lot of time with the four of them and yet I always had the feeling that there were things about them that I would never know. There were secrets that they kept from me, and perhaps even from each other. I began to realise that although I considered myself a friend of theirs, I would never truly belong. I was not a cadre.

We usually met a couple of nights each week, sitting around a heater while we talked politics and drank cheap wine. Sometimes we smoked a joint.

I was a recent initiate into the world of politics and I was interested in the long philosophical discussions about sacrifice, death, God, communism and Karl Marx. There was something so romantic about us huddling together in the cold talking about Karl Marx, who I'd only heard mentioned in vague references. In South Africa, the topics which we discussed so freely would have been tantamount to treason. Anyone opposed to the government of the day was, quite illogically, branded a communist. As a consequence, I had never explored any of these revolutionary philosophies. I knew only enough about communism to mention it in passing to my students in South Africa.

From those four friends I discovered for the first time what the ANC meant in terms of its commitment to overthrowing the status quo. I learned more about people like Nelson Mandela, Walter Sisulu and the many others who had sacrificed their personal freedom for their ideals.

As I listened I realised how little understanding I had of the real issues that were at the heart of the liberation movements in South Africa and how lacking in information my education had been. Since Clive and I both came from the Eastern Cape, we frequently discussed the overwhelming poverty in that area. Tiny explained that the government had embarked on a deliberate policy to stunt the region's development, particularly in black areas, because they wanted to punish black communities for their political activity, communities that had produced men like Steve Biko, who had died in police custody, and institutions like the University of Fort Hare which had produced many of the jailed or exiled black leaders.

I learned about communism from Sissie. I learned about Lenin and Stalin, both of whom she admired even though she admitted, after being challenged by Tiny, that Stalin in his later years had become a paranoid despot. Mao also came in for a great deal of analysis. Occasionally the conversation turned to Fidel Castro and Che Guevara, names tossed out casually as though those two icons were old friends of theirs.

At least two of the romance novels I had read during my teenage years at McBain were set in Havana. But in those stories 'Fidel' and 'Che' were merely cardboard caricatures in an exotic backdrop for characters like Manuel and Carmen or Francesca and Ricardo in the glittering days of casinos and mobsters.

I knew very little about post-revolution Cuba.

When it came to discussions about existentialism, I felt that I could at least stand my ground, but my arguments were often defeated.

They were all atheists.

As a child caught between two cultures, I had prayed to both God and Allah. But my knowledge of God was inadequate against the onslaught of their arguments.

They made fun of me. Teased me mercilessly about my naïvety. The only one who remained silent was Clive. He probably believed too, but didn't dare admit it for fear of being mocked.

'People like you are so easily conned,' Tiny said. 'That's what religion is. It's a con-game. Priests and ministers are con-artists. You're programmed to think that your lives are in God's hands. It's a human failing – this need to believe. If you need so desperately to believe in something, believe in Truth and Justice.'

We joined protest marches and handed out pamphlets appealing to the British public to boycott South African products. We were assaulted by thugs and on one occasion a burly passer-by, obviously South African, used his umbrella to batter us. There was no doubt in any of our minds that we were being watched by South African Security Police.

And then Sissie disappeared. We searched all over for her and made discreet enquiries, but she had seemingly vanished without trace.

Joe and Tiny reported her disappearance to the police, but they weren't able to locate her either. We wondered whether she had received her orders and had slipped away quietly to avoid detection by the Special Branch who had their network of informers spread throughout the UK.

With Sissie, the anchor of our little group, gone, we were set adrift and went our separate ways. Joe returned to Angola where South African forces were being used to rout the liberation army. Clive emigrated to Australia, but Tiny stayed on in London. Although he had said nothing, I suspected that he had strong feelings for me. When he realised that those feelings were not reciprocated, we drifted apart and Tiny returned to South Africa, slipping in through the Swaziland border late one night. He was captured soon after and died in prison.

There were other protest groups, anti-apartheid groups, South African exiles working for the ANC but, deep down, I knew that I wasn't a revolutionary, that I couldn't be committed in the same way as Sissie and the others. My brief foray into politics and my flirtation with revolutionary ideals had been motivated more by a yearning for adventure and the desire to belong.

For me, at that stage of my life, anything out of the ordinary had romantic appeal. There was, of course, nothing romantic in what I had learned from Sissie and her cadres. It was harsh reality, much too brutal for me to feel comfortable with. It was only an encounter, something I had enjoyed vicariously through my friendship with them.

42

OVER THE years Soraya's nature had changed from sullen to dispassionate and by the age of twelve she was a much changed child, confident and independent. Yasmin and Neville, their marriage an emotional roller-coaster, separated for a few months and then reconciled. I suspected that this must have affected Soraya, even though she never seemed to show any emotion. I knew, though, that the pain and disappointment was there, all locked away inside.

Yasmin and I took Soraya and her two best friends out for lunch to celebrate her twelfth birthday. Although Yasmin was physically present and punctuated the conversation with the occasional comment, I could tell that she was distracted. While the girls chatted away happily, she became increasingly quiet and seemed almost relieved when it was time to go home. Clearly something was on her mind, but she gave no hint of what it was.

Then, later that day, Soraya and I joined her in her bedroom to keep her company as she culled her wardrobe, discarding any item of clothing that she had not worn for three months.

She asked Soraya to sort out the contents of her jewellery box. Soraya was quietly absorbed in the task when suddenly she gave an exclamation of delight and held up a small gold locket which had been trapped at the back of one of the drawers.

'I've never seen this before,' she said.

'Good grief,' Yasmin said, 'I thought I'd lost that years ago.'

'It's so pretty,' Soraya said snapping the little heart open.

'Who's AJ?'

Yasmin, who had paled perceptibly, seemed taken aback and was silent for a moment.

I had taken the locket from Soraya and was studying the initials. AJ. Andrew Jordaan, the French kisser, I guessed.

Soraya leaned over my shoulder.

'Who's AJ?' she asked again.

Yasmin sat down on the bed next to Soraya, took her hand and gazed into her eyes. 'Allan Johnson,' she said.

I looked up in astonishment.

'Your father,' Yasmin explained.

Soraya smiled expectantly. This was the first time her mother had volunteered any information about her father. On the few occasions in the past when she had asked about him Yasmin had been evasive. She had eventually stopped asking.

Now was the moment of revelation. I, too, was anxious to hear what Yasmin had to say.

'I know how desperately you want to know about your father, darling,' Yasmin continued, 'but I don't have much to tell you, except that we were very much in love. We were young and, like many young people, we made a mistake. I fell pregnant . . .' Yasmin paused. 'We were planning to get married some day, but he was killed in an accident – he died before I had the chance to tell him that I was pregnant.'

'What was he like?' Soraya asked.

Yasmin smiled. 'He was very handsome, and he was a lot of fun. He was a good dancer . . .'

I suspected that she was recalling Andrew Jordaan's qualities.

'I am so sad that he never knew about you.' Yasmin was so caught up in her fabrication that she even managed to squeeze out a few tears.

Soraya had been sitting rigidly, listening intently, but when she saw the tears in Yasmin's eyes she flung her arms around her mother's neck. 'Oh Yasmin,' she exclaimed, holding her tightly.

Yasmin caught my eye over Soraya's shoulder and flashed a warning. I was flabbergasted. Not even I, who thought I knew my sister so well, could have dreamed that she was capable of concocting such an elaborate lie.

'I never met his family,' Yasmin continued as Soraya drew away from her. 'They emigrated to Australia soon after he was killed.'

'Do you have any pictures? Do I look like him?'

'No, I don't have any pictures – but, yes, you do look like him. You're just as gorgeous as he was. And you have his eyes.'

Soraya listened attentively. There was a sadness about her eyes but she was sensitive enough to be concerned about Yasmin's feelings. She squeezed her mother's hand sympathetically.

'Let's not dwell on this,' Yasmin said. 'It's your birthday. It should be a happy day. Let's not spoil it with sadness. Please take the locket. I'd been keeping it for you, but I thought I'd lost it.'

She fastened the locket around Soraya's neck.

Soraya went to the mirror. 'It's very pretty,' she said fingering the locket. 'Thank you.'

It was a rare moment, a tender and special moment between the two of them. I didn't want to intrude and quietly slipped out of the room. And I didn't want to hear any more of Yasmin's lies either.

Later, when I accosted her, she turned on me angrily.

'What did you want me to do? Tell her that her father was a bastard, that he raped me and that I wanted to abort her? How do you think that would have affected her?'

'Some of the truth would have been a lot easier to digest than this lie,' I replied, furious with her.

'The *truth*,' she said slowly and bitterly, her eyes meeting mine. 'What is the truth? How much of the truth is enough? Stop being so goddamn self-righteous. I'm her mother and I'll do what I think is right for her. All I'm trying to do is protect her. I don't want her to be hurt.'

That was the end of the conversation. I knew that it was too late now to change the story. Yasmin had made her decision. Her fantasy was repeated so often that it was eventually accepted by all of us as the truth.

Although I dated, I had lost hope of ever finding someone I could truly love. The invitations from my colleagues to join them on Friday nights stopped, and I was dubbed *Celestial Virgin*. For me, being alone at home on a Friday or Saturday night with a book or a movie was not a hardship. Office relationships, like those indulged in by most of the women at work, were, I thought, dull and tawdry.

I had no inclination to crawl into bed just for the sake of being with a man, or to avoid the use of my nickname. The values inculcated in me by Ma and Nana when I was a child were too deeply ingrained and, if I ever forgot, Yasmin's shame was always there as a grim reminder.

I was lonely, of course, but I had resigned myself to this. I had to hold down a job, I had to send money home, I had other responsibilities. I realised after my association with Sissie and her friends that I was not in a position to make the kind of sacrifices they had made. Perhaps I lacked the strength of character, or the commitment required for such sacrifices. I suspected that *lack of commitment* was my fatal flaw.

I still missed Ma and Nana deeply, but could not afford to return to McBain until seven years after my arrival in London. It took almost three years of severe self-deprivation to save enough money for my fare.

I wanted to take Soraya with me, but Yasmin was reluctant to disrupt her schooling. She said there would be time for such a trip at a later stage, when Soraya had finished school. I couldn't understand her reasoning, but I suspected that Yasmin was afraid that if Soraya returned to McBain Ma and Nana would try to influence her to stay.

But Soraya needed to get away from Yasmin. Yasmin could not seem to come to terms with Soraya's bouts of adolescent moodiness and there was recurring tension between them. The distance that separated them while she was at boarding school was not enough. Soraya needed a respite from her.

I was sure that in the warm embrace of her family at McBain and under the heat of the African sun, she would recover her spirit.

I worked on changing Yasmin's mind and finally wore her down. She agreed that Soraya could go with me, provided it was during the summer holidays. I rearranged my schedule to coincide with Soraya's school holidays.

The trip was almost a *fait accompli*.

All that was left for me to do was have my South African passport renewed. I sent in all the required documents. Two weeks later I received a letter from the Embassy informing me that my passport had been revoked.

In a state of shock and outrage, I went to the Embassy to demand an explanation from the young clerk who dealt with passport applications. She was supercilious, rudely telling me that they owed me no explanation. She dismissed me with a shrug of her shoulders and returned her attention to the papers on her desk.

My phone calls and letters were to no avail. It slowly became obvious to me that my passport had been cancelled because of my association with Sissie and her friends. I learned that we had been under surveillance by the Special Branch, which was as active a force in London as it was in South Africa.

My main concern now was to renew my work permit. The British authorities were sympathetic and extended it. I still had no travel document, and did not qualify for British citizenship. I knew that concessions had been made for me and I was grateful, but it didn't alter the fact that I could not go home.

I had come to London in search of freedom and now found myself trapped and aching for McBain.

Not only had I been deprived of my South African citizenship, but I had encountered right-wing Londoners who had subjected me to every kind of overt racism imaginable. There was also the covert variety executed with typical British grace, just as they had done in India.

I saw now what Papa had meant when he said that the British

had broken the backs of the Indians. He always maintained that you knew where you stood with the Afrikaners, but the British smilingly doffed their hats and then stabbed you in the back.

'Rather the devil you know than the one you don't,' he used to say.

All my bitterness and resentment at not being able to go home became focused on these racist incidents.

Yasmin reproached me.

'The British aren't all like that, Meena,' she said. 'You can't condemn the whole nation because a few idiots have called you names in the street. The government has allowed you to stay. Look at the number of exiles living in Britain.'

I was not that easily persuaded.

Yasmin, however, remained enamoured of anything British, but even she, with her wealth, her suitable addresses, her very British husband and expensive schools for Soraya, was never accepted into the inner social circles.

She would always be on the outside looking in.

43

I WAS restless and unhappy. I felt confined. Marooned.

I developed irrational phobias about leaving the flat and felt as if I'd lost control over my life and my destiny.

The cause of my misery shifted from the British to Yasmin, for whom everything seemed to come so easily. I drove her away from me and then felt forsaken.

That winter was a cold and bleak one and I sank into a black depression.

In the darkest hours of my life when I was so miserable that all I wanted was to die, I could think only of McBain.

And that was the one place I could not return to.

Yasmin, Neville and Soraya made a trip to South Africa in the mid-eighties, but it was a nightmare for Neville who spent the entire time ducking and diving so as not to draw attention to himself. He vowed he would never return. The only consolation was that the visit had given him the opportunity to meet Ma and Nana, who had both liked him immensely.

It seemed so unjust that Yasmin, who had always loathed McBain, should be able to return there quite freely. Their first-hand news of McBain made my heart ache even more.

The realisation that I might never be able to go home and might well have to remain in England for the rest of my life plunged me into utter despair. Finally, persuaded by friends, I went to see a doctor who merely confirmed my depression and prescribed Valium.

But the blackness spread its inky tentacles into every corner of my mind. I could only view my life and future through a narrow shaft, and there was no light at the end of it. I couldn't imagine that it would ever change.

In a moment of utter despair, I decided that I could no longer carry on. It had all become too much and the pain was so unbearable that I couldn't take a minute more of it. And so I swallowed a handful of Valium. It took a while for it to take effect and as I collapsed on the floor I knew what I needed. It was not Valium; it was professional help.

In a last desperate act to save myself, I phoned my neighbour Rosita, a Nicaraguan woman who had become a good friend.

Nana always said that no one dies before their time. It was clearly not mine. I woke up in the emergency room at the same hospital where I worked and opened my eyes to a nurse vigorously slapping my cheeks to bring me around.

'That was a very naughty thing to do, Meena,' she said.

Veronica was one of the nurses who knew me quite well.

'I'm sorry,' I mumbled, feeling sick and sorry for myself. I was also embarrassed because I knew that everyone in the hospital would get to hear about my stupidity.

I ran my tongue over my lips, tasting the residue of the charcoal that had been pumped into my stomach. The whole floor was probably splattered with it.

My staff and I had cleaned up this kind of mess often enough to know what its significance was. I thought of the unnecessary work I had created for the staff and I cursed myself.

'This never solves problems,' Veronica said reproachfully.

I didn't say anything, my throat working convulsively to ease the discomfort left by the tube they had forced into me.

Later that day the hospital psychologist dropped in for a chat.

I'd heard that one had to reach rock bottom first before one could rise out of this kind of hell. That night, wanting to kill myself, was the lowest point in my life.

It took months of therapy and Rosita's encouragement and support to finally start me on the road to recovery.

Rosita taught me, through example, how to survive. She knew more than most people about struggle and hardship. She had lost everything. Exiled from her country, she'd lost her husband, her family and one of her children. All she owned when she arrived in London were the clothes on her back. Her friendship helped to pull me through those dark days and her faith illuminated the way for me. Nana used to say that a darkness comes into everyone's life.

Yasmin was appalled when she eventually heard the full story. She could not forgive me.

'Am I not your sister?' she demanded. 'Aren't we family? Why couldn't you come to me?'

I wept in her arms.

She was hurt that I had turned to Rosita, a stranger, instead of her. But eventually we mended the rift between us. Neville negotiated the truce, but he too was disappointed that I had not come to them.

'I couldn't, Neville. I just couldn't,' I said. 'I couldn't face Yasmin as a failure.'

He understood.

44

I TRIED desperately to put my life together and, after several years' working at the hospital, I decided to look for another job. Most of the positions advertised required office skills, which I did not have. But one position I thought I could manage was that of receptionist at Curtis Jurgens, an advertising agency. I also took a second job, working in the evenings as a proof-reader on a newspaper. I started at six and finished at ten.

Three and a half years later, I was still with Curtis Jurgens but debating whether I should stay or find something else. It had become obvious that I was never going to advance.

Trying to hold down two jobs left me with very little free time. When I got home at ten-thirty at night, all I could think of was going to bed. But I hung on to both jobs because I needed the extra money to send home to McBain.

I had initially enjoyed the work at Curtis Jurgens. The comings and goings of clients and employees at least allowed me to meet new people. My job at reception included acting as a buffer between the executives and clients. The hours were long and whenever I had to stay late it meant rushing to my second job without supper. I had no social life and at weekends, when there was the time to go out, I was usually too exhausted.

I had fallen into a rut, doing the same repetitive tasks day after day and with no prospect of promotion.

At thirty-five, I wasn't getting any younger and I didn't want to squander my good years with a company that clearly did not appreciate my dedication. It seemed that while I was anchored to the reception desk, younger, less experienced women were moving ahead of me.

They were white.

I was reluctant to make race an issue, but it was pretty obvious.

I now had skills and experience and knew that I could be an asset to any company that hired me. It was definitely time for me to move on, but there always seemed to be more important considerations than job satisfaction.

There were practical issues – like paying the bills. My day-to-day living expenses ate up my entire month's salary. Travel and clothes were expensive items, and there was also the cost of heating the draughty old flat I had moved into when I started work at Curtis Jurgens. The work at the newspaper paid minimum wages, and even with a second cheque there just never seemed to be enough money. I waited in vain for that magical moment when my life would open up with the promise of better prospects. But in the mean time my frustration grew.

Then one day a small, insignificant incident catapulted my life in a new direction.

While I was trying to placate a difficult client on the phone, I glanced up to see a man waiting at my desk. I had been so engrossed in my phone call that I hadn't noticed him come in. But that moment when I looked up and saw him was my moment of revelation.

No doubt in *Forsaken Dreams* Christopher Carpenter had stood at Justine's desk in similar circumstances, catching her off guard just as this man had caught me off guard.

He was young and gloriously handsome, with the devastating good looks – dark hair and brooding eyes – of an Anglo-Indian. He was immaculately attired, as if he had just stepped out of the pages of GQ.

I took all of this in while still talking on the phone. I looked at him questioningly. He smiled and mouthed his name. Matthew Singh. I ran my finger down the list of appointments for the day and located his name.

'Would you please hold, Mr Gray,' I interrupted the client.

I put my hand over the mouthpiece and said: 'Mr Forbes is expecting you, Mr Singh. Please go straight in. Through the door to the right.' I leaned forward to indicate the way. He smiled politely and I watched him walk away.

I saw Matthew Singh on two other occasions – once with a beautiful young woman and the second time as he was getting into a taxi.

Of course, nothing personal developed from my brief meeting with Matthew Singh. There was no wild love affair; there was no love affair of any kind. The Matthew Singhs of the world were far beyond my reach.

After the few words exchanged on that first day, Matthew Singh, who never knew what kind of effect he'd had on me, and probably would never even have recognised me had he seen me again, slipped out of my life. But my encounter with him changed my life.

Matthew Singh became the hero of *Saffron Sunset*, my first romance novel.

I was still addicted to romance novels and it occurred to me one day that I could actually write one. I'd read enough of the genre to be familiar with the formula.

It took me almost a year to finish the manuscript of *Saffron Sunset*. And only when I was totally satisfied with it did I send it to a carefully selected publisher. I heard nothing for more than a year. In fact I had almost forgotten that I had sent the manuscript in when the letter from the editor arrived to say that she had finally read *Saffron Sunset*. The gist of the letter was that she had liked it . . . 'loved it' were her exact words. She commented on my 'excellent character and skilful plot development'. How I savoured those words! They wanted to offer me a contract.

Soraya, who was staying with me for a few months while studying at the Royal College of Music, was even more excited than I was.

Yasmin thought it was all a waste of time. 'Who reads that trash? Don't do anything silly like give up your day job,' she added. Always the pragmatist, she would never have indulged in the kind of fantasies that filled my mind.

Although Yasmin's attitude was hurtful, I was over the moon about the money. What I earned in advances for that first book was almost equivalent to three months' salary. I immediately quit my job at the newspaper but continued working for Curtis Jurgens.

Soraya was now twenty-one and was hugely excited about my publishing contract. She had grown into a dauntingly beautiful young woman. She confessed that she too had spent her childhood reading romances, purely for the escapism they provided. She confirmed what I had always known – that an inordinate number of young girls read romance novels.

It was what I had read most of my life. I always had a pile of new novels stacked in a corner. Who would have imagined that one day I would actually profit from reading those books and that they would provide me with a career?

When the book was launched I was overwhelmed by all the attention I received. What if I couldn't write another book? What if I was only a one-book wonder?

At the launch of *Saffron Sunset* my editor Elise introduced me to Sayeed Farrah, a film maker from Morocco who lived in Paris.

He was not a handsome man – not in the conventional or romantic sense, like the heroes in my novels. He was short and stocky, a few years older than me, with slightly greying hair, but he had an overpowering presence. He was worldly, poised and charming. He had dark, moorish looks with eyes which seemed to glitter with a sense of irony. He was the most charismatic man I had ever met.

His eyes, which held such promise, such endless possibilities, captivated me and beckoned me. He was a strong man, unlike any of the other men I had known. I was not deterred by the fact that he'd been married three times, or that he was still married to his third wife.

He sent me flowers the day after we met. The accompanying card was an invitation to lunch. I must have read and re-read the card at least a dozen times. Every word was etched on my mind. Soraya wanted to know what was wrong with me. Why had I forgotten the pot on the stove, she asked, indicating its blackened contents. It was not like me. Her eyes were full of suspicion.

I didn't think she'd understand. How could I justify an affair with a married man? What kind of example was I setting her? I don't suppose she could ever have imagined that a man would give me a second glance. Sex was for the young – or so they thought. At my age I was supposed to be emotionally dead, sexless, of no interest to any man on earth.

I needed Sayeed, needed a man in my life. I needed to be loved, to be adored, and I needed strong arms around me. The sex would come afterwards. I had never been able to go to bed with a man on a first date, anyway. Not that I had a wealth of experience – the struggle to survive has a tendency to diminish the libido. But the lack of romance in my own life never affected the characters in my novels. Theirs were ideal lives that had nothing to do with reality. Through them I lived out my wildest fantasies. I created a world totally apart from my own. My involvement with my characters was as gratifying to me as it was to the women who read my books and whose lives were much like my own.

I arranged with Curtis Jurgens to take the day off. I made an excuse about having to attend to urgent personal business. One of the temps would fill in for me. I wanted the whole day free to prepare for my tryst.

I lounged around in my robe after Soraya had left for her classes. For the first time ever I felt no guilt about staying away from work. Soraya had wanted to know why I wasn't going to work. I told her I had an appointment, but didn't elaborate. She would have been shocked had she known that I, someone to whom she looked up, was capable of such subterfuge.

I had my own assignation. Like Maxine in *Diamonds For My Love*.

I selected my clothes with care and laid them out on the bed. I had never done this before. There had never been time to focus on something as banal as what to wear. Work always came first and the clothes I wore were always practical – shifts and trouser suits bought on sales. In fact, I hated shopping for clothes – I would rather have spent the time writing.

I chose a fitted burgundy silk dress. It was a new addition to my wardrobe – one of the few extravagances I had allowed myself since I had gone from a size thirty-eight to a thirty-four. I had bought it a few months before at a sale but had never had an opportunity to wear it. I studied the dress and wondered if the newness was obvious. I didn't want him to think that I had gone out to buy a dress especially for the occasion.

I ran a bath and added some perfumed bath beads. A gift from one of the girls at work, they had been sitting in my bathroom cabinet for years.

Allowing my robe to slide off my shoulders, I lowered myself into the bath as one of my characters, Sasha or Yvette or Tiffany, might have done – their figures perfect, their backsides firm and their breasts perky.

I stayed in the bath for ages. I had to force myself to relax, to clear my mind of the chores that were always waiting. Work and the fact that I was a fastidious housekeeper meant there was never an opportunity for such luxury.

My cat Muffin nudged the bathroom door open and after exploring the pile of clothes on the floor, curled up on top of the laundry basket. She watched me, yawned and then started grooming herself. I wondered what sardonic thoughts were going through her mind as she fixed her unblinking gaze on me.

I finally disengaged myself from the real world, from Curtis Jurgens, from my life. I lay back, eyes closed, imagining myself in Sayeed's arms.

The phone rang. I listened for the answering machine to pick up, wondering if it was him or someone from work.

Eventually I got out of the bath. I gazed at myself in the mirror. Water and oil from the bath beads glistened on my skin. The bathroom mirror, like the mirrors in the fitting rooms at stores, was brutally honest and I saw myself for what I was: a woman of almost forty, who had not taken good care of her body, a woman with sagging breasts and buttocks, thighs pocked with cellulite and lined with spider veins. What man in his right mind would want this when he could get any young woman he wanted?

Even as those thoughts crossed my mind, I cursed myself for my lack of confidence and self-esteem. I had been working on regaining both for a long time.

What if we were in bed and he saw what I had seen in the bathroom mirror? What if he had second thoughts? Suddenly I was filled with anxiety.

I decided that everything would be fine as long as we didn't get into bed. But then, what if the chemistry between us was so strong that I couldn't put off the inevitable? What then?

There was no point to any of these questions. It was foolish to anticipate something that might never happen.

For the first time in years I was forced to think about underwear. I opted for something totally impractical. Something slinky. Lingerie instead of the warm, sensible underwear I usually wore. I fussed about this, searching for something suitable.

Then I remembered the gift of lingerie Yasmin had brought me from one of her trips to New York. At the time I could see no use for it and had tossed it into one of my drawers, never dreaming that I would ever want to wear it.

I tried on the lingerie, relieved that it still fitted me. My bedroom mirror offered a more flattering image of myself, boosting my confidence.

Finally I was dressed and satisfied with my appearance. I went downstairs to listen to the message on the answering machine. It was from Yasmin, wondering why neither Soraya nor I had been in touch. I made a mental note to phone her when I got back. I had to be home before six o'clock. I had persuaded Soraya to go out for supper with me – our belated celebration of the publication of *Saffron Sunset*.

I didn't feel like taking the Underground. In my silk dress it just didn't seem like the appropriate thing to do, and so my other extravagance was paying for a taxi. I would probably regret my capriciousness when it was time to pay the bills. For the moment, though, I wanted to spoil myself. Gripped by this hedonistic feeling of irresponsibility, I was determined that for the next few hours I would not consider anything or anyone but myself.

But old habits die hard and even the advance on my book, deposited in my savings account, was no consolation. Five thousand pounds didn't go very far those days. Still, just a bit for myself wasn't that unreasonable – provided there were no emergencies.

But in the taxi all I could think of was that I needed a new geyser. I'd have to pay for it myself because the landlord had refused to. I also needed expensive dental work. I tried to put these thoughts out of my mind, but they kept intruding. As I stepped out of the taxi at Chez Philippe and paid the fare, I realised that it was the equivalent of half my week's grocery money.

Sayeed was waiting for me at a secluded table. His face lit up when he saw me and I understood why women dropped their lives for him.

He courted me at lunch. Courted in the old-fashioned sense of the word. He was thoughtful and attentive and focused on me as though he and I were the only two people in the restaurant, or in the world, for that matter. We dined leisurely. The waiters all knew him – 'I come to London quite often,' he said – and lavished attention on us.

Enthralled, I listened to him recounting his experiences, his voice with its charming French-Moroccan accent captured my imagination and transported me to other worlds.

'I love London, but also I love Paris and Morocco. I am a true cosmopolitan.'

The story of my life was nothing compared with his, but he listened to me with keen interest. I found myself telling him much more than I would normally have told anyone at a first meeting.

The only subject we avoided was my writing. Writing was my secret world and I was not prepared to share it – not even with him. It was my private place, where I went to find solace and comfort. Besides, I had only one book to my credit and I didn't want to make a big deal of it.

'I'd rather not talk about my writing,' I said, quietly, when he asked me a polite question about my work, hoping that my response had not offended him.

He never mentioned it again.

After lunch we strolled to his hotel. He told me that whenever he came to London he stayed at the same hotel, just around the corner from the restaurant. He didn't invite me to his room. He didn't have to. Words were not necessary. We were like two old souls who had lived through many lifetimes to find each other.

I have no recollection of how I got to his room, and nor do I recall the sequence of events, but I do remember that being in his arms felt like the most natural thing in the world to me. I remember kissing him slowly and carefully, as though re-acquainting myself with lost skills.

Swept away by forces beyond my control, my earlier self-consciousness about my body completely forgotten, I slipped into bed with him. His hands moved over me, touching, exploring, as if responding to the yearning he sensed within me: a longing, a hidden hunger. He met my hunger with his own, entering me and moving towards my centre. In *September Sonata*, Shawna had felt the same explosion of passion.

It was a lovely flowing, an unfolding of my being, my body arching with sheer pleasure. He met me eagerly, with fierce, passionate desire. And I shattered into a million fragments, every particle of myself electrified, leaping and probing.

For a long time afterwards I lay in his arms, terrified of moving, not wanting to break the spell as the pleasure slowly and sweetly ebbed away. It was every bit as intoxicating as the moment Shawna curled up in Jarrod's arms. But this wasn't fantasy, this was reality – it was me lying next to Sayeed, every nerve in my body tingling as he gently caressed me and I turned to him once again.

That was the beginning of our love affair. I never took him home to my flat. I wrapped our relationship in an aura of mystery, but the truth was that I was embarrassed about my living conditions. The only improvement I had made was buying a new sofa. It was not the kind of setting I wanted him to see me in.

We met whenever he was in London. I relived the same anticipation I had felt at our first meeting – like a young girl on her first date. He was a marvellous and considerate lover and spoilt me for other men because my expectations were now so high.

What I particularly loved was that we had a different level of commitment. He wasn't underfoot all the time, intruding and demanding. Our relationship had nothing to do with the tedium of daily life. It was always exciting, always new and challenging, and I grew as I might never have grown in any other relationship.

I started writing again, filling the void when he was away. I found an agent for my next book, *Palace of Dreams*, which fetched almost four times what the first book had. When I was finally confident enough, two years and three books later and encouraged by Sayeed, I gave up my job with Curtis Jurgens and took the biggest risk of my life.

Sayeed and I continued to see each other for another year after I left Curtis Jurgens. Then he suddenly stopped phoning. For two weeks there was an ominous, almost frightening, silence.

I resisted the temptation to contact him. I had promised never to do so. But I must have picked up the phone a thousand times to dial his number before having second thoughts and putting it down again. Difficult though it was, I refrained from calling him at home. Our agreement was sacrosanct.

Dear God, I was falling apart again. I had sworn never to feel that way about him, or any other man, but I couldn't seem to control my emotions.

I had accepted that I shared him with another woman – his wife. We never spoke about his other life. I didn't want to know about it. Our personal lives were private. There were boundaries which neither of us crossed. There was no need to tie ourselves to each other. I was confident of his love for me. He never asked me for more than I could give. It was an almost perfect relationship. And now all that confidence wavered as the doubts and nagging fears found justification in what I imagined were hints dropped the last time we were together.

As I waited I became certain that our relationship was over. The silence was uncharacteristic of him and left me sick with anxiety. In desperation, I phoned Elise. She hadn't heard from him either but promised to make enquiries. Elise knew the truth. She had once advised me not to become too serious about him, but by then it was too late.

She phoned back that same afternoon to tell me that Sayeed had been killed in a car crash on his way from Paris to Nice.

I became physically ill. It was as though my soul had been ripped out of me. How would I ever recover from such a loss? I had loved him so completely, so unconditionally.

I could feel myself coming apart. I hadn't felt this way since those dark days when I had tried to take my life. I might have done so again, but I remembered the guilt and the remorse, not to mention the embarrassment, of that incident. It was not something I wanted to repeat.

In a way I was relieved that Soraya was travelling in Europe and not there to witness my breakdown. No one in my family knew about Sayeed, not even Yasmin, although I knew that she had her suspicions.

Rosita was there for me again, helping me through the pain. The nights were the most difficult, because I couldn't sleep. Rosita warned that it would take me a long time to come to terms with Sayeed's death because there had been no closure. It would have helped, she said, if I had gone to his funeral. I couldn't tell her that the funeral was part of his other life, the life that had been separate from mine. Not even in death could I intrude.

Elise tried to comfort me, worried that my writing might suffer. Eventually she coaxed me back to my computer and I started writing again, forcing myself to step outside my pain. Sayeed would not have wanted me to spend the rest of my life mourning for him.

The hole in my universe had grown larger, torn all the way through. There was nothing left except tattered pieces and emptiness.

But there is more resilience in the mind and spirit than one can ever believe possible.

In time I began to heal and my life regained its tempo. It was something I could look back on. Something precious. Something that was mine alone, something I didn't have to share with anyone else. No one suspected that for more than three years I had lived another life. When the pain eased, I immortalised Sayeed in *Sometime This Summer*.

45

NINETEEN YEARS after I had left McBain, Soraya and I departed for South Africa for Nana's funeral.

My mother had called on a Friday evening with the news of Nana's death. Nana had complained of being tired and had gone to lie down.

'She just never woke up again, Meena.'

Although I immediately detected the anguish in my mother's voice, it took several moments for me to grasp the significance of her words.

'She must have died earlier in the afternoon,' Ma said, struggling to control her grief. 'I didn't even know... I thought she was resting. I've tried to get hold of Yasmin. She's not home.' The shock of my grandmother's death had clearly drained my mother.

Another loss, another hole in the fabric of my life. Two holes now in the collective soul of our family.

Ma's voice sounded hollow, as if it had travelled through an enormous void. 'I've got to go now, Meena. I'll talk to you later. Get hold of your sister, will you?'

After several attempts I finally reached Yasmin who was about to leave for a dinner engagement in London.

'I'm on my way out. I can't talk now,' she snapped impatiently.

'Nana died this afternoon,' I said tersely.

There was silence at the other end of the line. I heard Yasmin whisper, 'Oh, God.'

There was another pause. I could hear her drawing in her breath.

'Meena, I can't cancel this meeting now. It's too late. I've got to go,' she said quietly. 'Please make arrangements for us to fly out as soon as possible.'

I could feel the anger rise, fluttering inside me, beating its wings like a moth against a light.

How could she? How could a dinner engagement be more important than the news of Nana's death?

'The funeral's next Sunday,' I said.

'Meena . . . please . . . I'll talk to you later tonight. I have to go now. I know how you feel. I'm devastated too. Just . . . Oh damn . . . look, I'll call you later.' She put the phone down before I could reply.

Much as I wanted to rush to my mother's side, I had things to organise, arrangements to make. I phoned the airlines. There were two seats available on the Wednesday flight to Johannesburg.

Yasmin called later that night. We spoke for almost an hour and arranged to meet on the Tuesday evening. She would stay overnight at my place.

But at the weekend Yasmin went riding. Her horse threw her and she broke a leg. I refused to change my plans.

I could imagine Nana shaking her head. This was 'classic' Yasmin.

I was quite prepared to go by myself, but Soraya offered to come with me. It was actually a relief that Yasmin was not with me. I could do without the drama which always seemed to surround her.

Soraya and I were both preoccupied on the flight to Johannesburg. Lost in her own private world, she spent most of her time staring through the window, earphones firmly plugged in. After several attempts to engage her in conversation, I gave up and returned my attention to my book.

She was twenty-seven now and a lot more mature and less

rebellious than when she had first visited McBain in the eighties. I wasn't sure, however, that the change was an improvement. She had always retained a charming childlike quality, but a dramatic change had come over her in the past few months. She seemed aloof, almost indifferent. I tried to get to the bottom of her attitude of detachment, but she had withdrawn even from me.

I mentioned my concern to Yasmin.

'Talk to her,' I urged.

'You know what happens when I try to talk to her. She does exactly the opposite of what I want her to do!'

'We're not talking about your wants,' I said drily. 'We're talking about your daughter and what *she* wants.'

'I'm tired. All I get for my efforts is a kick in the butt. I don't know what to do with her. She's told me quite frankly to stay out of her life. When I was her age I was running my own business and was well on my way to making a success of it.' She paused, her eyes clouding with pain and bitterness. 'God,' she sighed. 'Being a mother is a thankless job. You're damned if you do and you're damned if you don't.'

I didn't raise the issue again but watched with concern as Soraya became increasingly detached from us, avoiding us – especially Yasmin. I tried to talk to her, tried to give her advice but, like Yasmin, she had a contrary streak in her nature.

I stole a glance at her and noticed how drawn she looked. Her hair hung in limp uneven strands. I was worried that she might be anorexic, but didn't dare mention this concern for fear of the consequences. She seemed to bait Yasmin deliberately. Knowing how it riled Yasmin, she still wore her nose ring like a badge of defiance. Her only passion seemed to be her music.

Yasmin had surreptitiously encouraged her in the early years, hoping she'd develop an interest in classical music. I suppose she envisaged Soraya as an acclaimed musician, playing in the London Philharmonic Orchestra.

Soraya, ignoring her mother's wishes, indulged her passion for jazz. With typical perversity, she had paid her own way through the Royal College of Music by playing gigs with local groups, or busking in the Underground.

Her music was haunting and soulful, reflecting the range of her own emotions. It was as though everything that was dammed up inside her found release in music.

Life was such a contradiction, I mused. Hindsight was all very well and yet, at critical points in our lives, we could never have imagined that things would have worked out the way they did. I might have been dead from an overdose of Valium. Yasmin might never have been raped, or she might never have returned to South Africa.

'Don't think about it,' Rosita often said when I brooded about the past. 'Don't ever think back to those times. Think only of the future. That's why God gave you eyes in the front of your head. If he'd wanted you to look back, he'd have given you eyes in the back of your head too.'

Rosita could always make me smile.

There was no man in my life. All I had were the wonderful memories of Sayeed, my one great love. Knowing nothing of this, Yasmin urged me to find a man and settle down before I passed my prime.

'If you wait much longer, no man will want you,' she said with her usual candour.

I couldn't have cared less. I had no time to waste on wanting a man. It was too debilitating. I decided that I would never tell her about Sayeed.

As for marriage and children – I had seen all the problems the young people of the nineties were having with drugs and AIDS and was glad I didn't have to experience the anxieties of the parents of my generation.

Yasmin and I had grown up in much gentler times, and so had Soraya. But Soraya's life had been disrupted when she was wrenched from a caring environment and taken to a strange city in a strange country, thousands of miles from the warmth of her family and the healing comfort of the African sun.

There were still so many unresolved issues between Yasmin and Soraya, issues which Yasmin refused to tackle even though her daughter was an adult and would probably have understood and accepted the truth.

Yasmin had never been able to deal with the entire truth. It was as if her mind had an automatic selective mechanism which chose only what she wanted to hear, or what others wanted to know.

She had made a grave mistake by not telling Soraya the truth about her father and the rape. The web of lies spun in those early days had become more tangled and I knew that some day, like weeds, they would sprout and choke the life out of their relationship.

46

'WHAT'S WRONG, Soraya?' I ventured tentatively, as the cabin attendant brought around the drinks trolley, aware that I was probing into territory Soraya had declared strictly out of bounds.

Startled, Soraya glanced at me, shook her head and turned away. I noticed again that she looked drawn, her profile much sharper, her cheeks hollow.

Nana, always intuitive about us, had worried constantly about Soraya. She said that she was like a lost soul, trapped between two worlds, searching for something she might never find.

'I just hope Yasmin's sins aren't visited on her,' she had once said with a prophetic air.

I tried to concentrate on my book. We were all going to miss Nana terribly. I had last seen her the year before when we had gone home to celebrate her ninetieth birthday. Soraya had come with me. Yasmin was in the States on business and couldn't make it.

My first trip home in 1992 had been two years before the first democratic elections. I had finally had my South African citizenship reinstated and my passport returned. It had taken almost a year of wrangling with the authorities, who were still part of the old guard and still driven by misguided loyalties. They seemed to drag their feet deliberately. But when my passport finally arrived, I was ecstatic. I didn't know whether to laugh at the absurdity of the whole issue, or to cry with joy. I wanted to leave for South Africa immediately, but of course I couldn't. I had another novel, *Strangers in Love*, to finish.

I returned again for the historic 1994 election. It was to be a quick trip, primarily to cast my vote. At the time I thought it was the single most significant act of my life. I was finally liberated. The old South African government had stolen my life, my history and my identity. They had stolen my breath. But I was returning. I was coming home. A mist had lifted and I could see the sun again.

I felt almost triumphant as I stepped off the plane. When the black immigration officer smiled at me and said 'Welcome', I felt vindicated.

It had been pure joy to see Nana and Ma again. Nana was in good health and as spirited as ever. We sat up till all hours of the night, talking and laughing. I left ten days later, promising that I would return soon with Yasmin and Soraya.

My next trip was the one with Soraya. We drove Ma and Nana to Johannesburg for a short holiday because Nana wanted to visit some of her family.

The trip had a dual purpose for me. Not only did I want to celebrate Nana's birthday, but I also wanted to attend Clive Faurie's trial. While I was still in London I'd heard that he and two other men had been returned to South Africa from Australia to stand trial for Sissie Skosana's murder.

While waiting outside the court I saw Clive and his lawyer enter the building. He had grown a beard and had put on weight, but there was no mistaking him.

'Clive?' I said as he passed me.

He turned and for a brief instant our glances locked. He hesitated for a moment and then hurried past. At that moment I knew, even before I heard his testimony, that he was responsible for the deaths of Sissie, Joe and Tiny. We should have known. We should have suspected. I berated myself for having been so trusting.

As the trial progressed, I was stunned to learn that he had been a Special Branch informant and that he had lured Sissie away from her flat to her death. Her decapitated body had been dumped in the ocean. He claimed that he had had nothing to do with the actual killing. The trial lasted for months. We were to hear more about the case during the Truth and Reconciliation Commission hearings, when the hideous truth was revealed in his testimony.

The hearings took place after I had left for London and Ma sent me newspaper clippings of the case. Clive's statement was mind-numbing. The violence was so ghastly that at first I thought the whole story was a fabrication. No one could be capable of such inhumanity.

An ugliness had crept into my safe little world, shaking its foundations.

'Were you ever really in love?' Soraya asked suddenly.

I nodded slowly, thoughtfully, finally understanding the cause of her strange mood swings.

'Is it always so painful?'

'Yes. It always comes with pain.'

'How did you deal with it?' she asked.

I took a deep breath, remembering all too clearly the pain, the feeling of being abandoned, the agony and aching sense of loss.

'That bad?' she said.

I smiled wryly.

She closed her eyes and leaned back in her seat. I watched her for a moment. Her question had brought Sayeed back into focus. He was always in my mind, sometimes just waiting in the wings ready to take centre stage.

Soraya, looking wistful, turned away.

As we began our descent into Johannesburg International Airport I wondered how my mother was coping. I had promised everyone that I would be gone for a few weeks only. Three weeks at the most. Long enough to assist my mother in packing up forty years of her life. Yasmin and I were hoping she'd join us in England. With Nana gone there was no longer any point to her staying on at McBain.

I thought about the desolation at McBain: the pale-yellow sun-scorched veld dotted with dry scrub. A desolation that, ironically, I had yearned for in those dark days in London.

When I was a child the loneliness had been unbearably painful. It imprisoned me, stunted my growth. How could I forget our futile expectations when we first arrived, or the dawning realisation that that was it – that was our home.

With nowhere else to go after our eviction from Soetstroom, we had ended up living like squatters in the veld while we tried to regroup. Perhaps McBain was the kind of place one had to leave in order to appreciate.

As I grew older it became easier to incorporate that lonely past into my present. Our lives had unfolded in ways I would never have believed possible. We had travelled a long road.

This was especially true of Yasmin. Who could have imagined that she had come from McBain, a God-forsaken dot in the veld?

Although my personal journey from McBain had been fraught with heartache and at times had seemed an endless battle, I had learned some valuable lessons. Nana always said that struggle was part of life. In the young, she said, it built backbone. But she didn't say what it did to decent, hard-working people like my father who, demoralised by the struggle, lost the spirit to fight back, or my mother, who gave up hope that our lives would ever improve.

Nana never gave up hope. She was the one who kept us afloat, buoying us with her wisdom and humour. Now she was gone.

Soraya turned to me with a sad smile. 'I'm going to miss Nana,' she said.

'Me too.'

Soraya had never seemed to share our worries about Ma and Nana being so far away from us and alone at McBain. God, how I'd begged them in my years of exile to join us in England. I was terrified that something might happen to them and that I would never see them again.

Nana, stubborn as ever, refused even to consider such an idea. She was too old to go traipsing around the world, she said, and she'd heard how miserable England was, especially London.

'I'm not leaving this place for some damp little hole in that circus,' she said.

'It's very peaceful where Yasmin lives,' I said, as though this would change her mind. 'You'll love it, Nana. Really.'

When I left all those years ago, I had suggested they follow. But even then Nana had shaken her head. 'I'm going to die right here with my boots on.'

I remembered those words. She had gone exactly as she had wished, peacefully, without a day's illness.

I was reminded of my father's death. He, too, had died peacefully. He and Nana had expected so little from their lives.

If only Papa had been alive today, I thought, there was so much we could have done for him. He had longed to return to India – if only for one last time. But in those days we didn't have the money for such a trip. Now that we – Yasmin and I – could at last afford to do it, it was too late.

Twenty-one years too late.

For my father all the good things, the things he anticipated with so much joy, arrived too late: money, Yasmin, the restoration of his sight.

All of it too late.

47

THE SERVICE for Nana was held in the Methodist Church. Although Nana had claimed to be Methodist, it was difficult to imagine her as a church-going Christian. She had always criticised organised religion, insisting that spirituality was more important than dogma.

The minister spoke about her devotion to her family and her willingness to help others. It was a moving tribute and few left the service dry-eyed. Yasmin's absence was conspicuous. Those who knew her went out of their way to enquire after her.

Yasmin had called the night before the funeral and had cried over the phone. Ma was obviously disappointed about her not being there, but in the end she accepted that Yasmin was in no condition to travel.

We buried Nana in the city, in the same cemetery as my father but in a different section since she was Christian. After the funeral my mother turned to me with a sigh and said: '*Ja*, now the two old friends can take care of each other.'

My mother would feel Nana's death more than any of us. Without Nana, McBain would never be the same. She had been an integral part of all our lives, but especially my mother's. Although she was gone, her presence at McBain was everywhere.

The night after the funeral my mother stood in the kitchen doorway. 'I'm going to miss her so,' she said. We wept again, Ma and I comforting each other while Soraya, looking totally lost, sobbed quietly in Nana's chair. I had not realised until that moment just how much Soraya had loved Nana.

A day or two later I tackled the question of whether my mother should remain at McBain.

'You can't stay here on your own, Ma. It's not safe. Yasmin and I think . . .'

'It's all very well for you to think and for her to send messages,' Ma snapped. 'She should've been here for Nana's funeral.'

'You know what happened,' I reminded her.

'I know,' she said, calming down. 'I just think it was so stupid of her to go riding, knowing she had a flight to catch a few days later.'

I understood my mother's disappointment and made no further comment. She expected me to agree with her.

'There's no use being angry with me,' I muttered.

'If only I could depend on her,' she said. 'Just once.'

'She'll get here as soon as she can,' I offered, hoping that Yasmin would arrive the following week as planned. I needed her there to help me convince Ma it would be better for her to make the move to England. Ma alone at McBain was too much of a problem. Our lives were complicated enough without further needless worry.

I knew that this was not going to be an easy task. My mother was a stubborn woman.

'I'm not going to be bullied into a decision,' she told me later. 'I'll make the decision when I'm good and ready. And I'm not ready.'

And that was where the matter rested for a few days.

I phoned Melissa and explained the situation. My agent was understanding. 'We'll wait for the next draft of *Forbidden Love*,' she said. 'It's a great story. Elise says she'll fax you some suggestions.'

'I don't have a fax machine, Melissa.'

'What about e-mail?'

'I don't have e-mail either. I'm in the backwoods . . .'

'Oh,' she said thinking this over. 'Never mind, we'll find a way. How's the family?'

'They're fine, thank you. We're expecting Yasmin soon.'

'Great!' Melissa said. 'I'll courier Elise's suggestions to her and she can bring them to you.'

'Well . . .'

'It's not a problem. I'll sort it out with her.'

'All right,' I sighed. There was no point trying to explain that I didn't have the time to do any writing. Besides, I preferred to write in my own space. Although my flat was small, I knew where everything was. The untidy litter on my desk was comforting. It was in that cramped space that I created the intoxicating world of romance. I would never live the kind of life I wrote about, but I could imagine it. It was so real that I could almost touch and smell it.

I would never have thought that I'd have the strength to drag myself out of the hole I had fallen into during the dark years. My life then had seemed so pointless. The prospect of enduring that misery for the rest of my life was too terrifying to contemplate.

Later, when I was recovering, trying to summon my strength and get on with my life – even if it was one step at a time – all I had to sustain me were my dreams.

I remembered how my mother used to tell us that one couldn't have everything one wanted in life.

It was a lesson she had taken from her own life. She had obviously had to make difficult choices and had made the sacrifices expected of her.

She had paid the price. But whatever the price, my mother had locked it all away. Her secrets remained safe.

48

MY MOTHER was still reluctant to leave McBain, even after Yasmin had telephoned and begged her to make a decision.

Yasmin also spoke to Soraya. 'Talk to Ma, Soraya. She'll listen to you.'

'I'm doing nothing of the kind. Don't drag me into this,' Soraya said and handed the phone back to me.

'That damn child,' Yasmin muttered. 'She's more than anyone can handle. Let Ma deal with her for a change. She thinks she's such an angel.'

'Why? What happened?' I asked.

'Never mind,' Yasmin snapped.

My mother remained noncommittal about moving and I became increasingly impatient. I wanted to get home, back to my own space and back to my writing.

'But things have changed in this country,' she said when I raised the issue again. 'I might be better off staying.'

'Alone . . . here in the bundu?' I was aghast that she would even consider such a thing.

'The people here know me . . . no harm will come to me.'

'Nonsense! The papers are full of stories about people being robbed and murdered. We won't have a moment's peace knowing you're here by yourself. It's a long way for us to fly back and forth from London. We'd like you closer.'

Ma looked so hurt and vulnerable that I put my arms around her and held her for a moment. Like my grandmother, she had always been fiercely independent. And despite my impatience, I understood how difficult it was for her to sever her ties with McBain. I remembered how unbearably lonely I had felt in London, especially when I found myself suddenly exiled.

'I have my own life,' Ma told me. 'I don't want to be under anyone's feet. What am I going to do there? I don't want to be a burden.'

'You won't be,' I assured her.

'I'm too old to start my life over in a strange country. All my friends are here.'

Soraya kept out of these discussions. But I persisted and Yasmin reinforced me by phone. It was going to be a difficult adjustment for my mother, but having her near would make our own lives so much easier.

Of course she would have to start a new life. Of course she would have to make new friends and establish herself in a strange community. There was no assurance that it was going to be easy.

Often, during the miserable London winters, I had imagined the villagers on the veranda in front of the store enjoying their long and loud discussions. There had been times when I ached to feel the warmth of the sun, to watch the night sky from our stoep – a scene which was uniquely ours.

Yet now I wondered if I would want to live anywhere else. London had finally become home. I was eligible for a British passport. The transition could be total, and yet I hesitated.

Perhaps I'm too old for change, I mused. I'd read somewhere that after forty change could be upsetting, but after seventy it was as traumatic as the death of a partner or a divorce. I didn't know why I expected my mother to make the move without any qualms.

'You're pushing her too hard,' Soraya said. 'She'll make a decision when she's ready. She's just buried Nana, remember?'

She was right. But what about all the clearing out and the packing? There wasn't much time. How were we going to manage it all?

'You and Meena can help me sort out some of the rubbish,'

Ma said casually. 'Between Nana and your Papa, nothing was ever thrown away.'

'What about you, Ma? Soraya teased. 'I don't remember you throwing anything away, either.'

As Soraya and I started the enormous task of sorting and disposing, I was constantly reminded of my life at McBain. My thoughts turned especially to those early days of upheaval when we had been powerless to control the course of our lives.

I should have been glad to put McBain behind me, to bury it with some of my more unhappy childhood memories, but when I gazed out over the desolate landscape and realised that this might be my last visit, I was seized by pangs of nostalgia.

Why would I feel so sad at shutting the door on this place? Why would I miss this pathetic little railway siding? We had never really considered it home. It was just a 'place', a barren spot in the veld.

'This place was my life,' Ma said. 'I know I shouldn't have regrets about leaving . . . but I do.'

Ma waved in the direction of a small brick building at the far end of the property. 'But,' she said with a sigh of resignation, 'I suppose I've done enough here. Someone else can take over the school. It's time the villagers got off their backsides and did something for themselves.'

She and Nana had built and run the one-roomed schoolhouse which the village children attended.

By the end of the week, Ma seemed reconciled to the idea of leaving, but every task stabbed her with memories and regrets.

She was clearing Nana's clothes from the wardrobe when she turned to me. 'Nana had a good life, didn't she?' she asked uncertainly. 'It wasn't much in terms of material comforts, but it was good. Wasn't it?' Sniffing, she patted her pockets for a tissue.

'She had a good life, Ma,' I reassured her. 'Despite all her grumbling, she was happy. She had a long and happy life.'

I had begun to realise that it would be impossible to wind up my mother's affairs within the time I had given myself. I had to accept that I was going to be away from home for longer than planned. Winding up the business and setting in motion the wheels for disposing of the property was not something that could be done quickly. I was pleased that Soraya was there to share the work. She tackled the clearing and sorting quietly and efficiently.

'I want to go through everything myself, Soraya,' Ma said. 'I don't want things just thrown out.'

'Ma . . .' we both groaned.

'I'm not throwing my stuff away,' she said firmly.

Soraya and I were sitting in the midst of mountains of old clothes and rubbish that should have been discarded years ago. Gladys brought in a tea-tray. As she limped towards us I got up to take the tray from her.

Gladys had been with us for as long as I could remember. Her hair had splotches of white and she complained about pains in her legs, just as Nana had. Despite her age, though, Gladys insisted on walking the two miles to McBain each day. Ma had suggested that she stay at McBain, but she refused to leave her home in the village.

Ma looked at Gladys with troubled eyes. She was worried about what would happen to her.

'You can't take care of the whole world, Ma,' I said.

'It's not the whole world worrying me, just Gladys,' Ma said quietly. 'She's part of this family. She was there for all of you.'

'I think we can all contribute towards a pension for her, something substantial for her to retire on. I'll make the arrangements before we leave.'

Ma nodded. 'That's a good idea,' she said. 'At least that'll give me some peace of mind.'

Soraya smiled encouragingly at Ma. I watched the two of them together. Soraya had always been such a comfort to my mother. I could not imagine what our lives would have been like without her, especially after Yasmin left.

The visit to McBain was proving more stressful than I had

imagined. But Soraya knew instinctively how to handle Ma when my patience was exhausted.

The house was starting to look empty.

'It feels like the soul has gone out of it,' Ma said, echoing my sentiments.

There was a sense that it had already been abandoned. Our footsteps echoed hollowly as we walked across the bare floorboards. Although Ma appeared to be resigned to the move, she still seemed resistant to the idea of giving up her home. The memories it held were important to her.

'What are you going to do with this, Ma?' Soraya asked, indicating a bronze plaque with a Koranic verse in Arabic that hung in the front room.

'I don't know. There are some words missing and it doesn't mean anything without them. I'll probably throw it out.'

'Don't,' I said. 'I'll take it.'

'Why?' Ma asked.

I shrugged. 'I just don't want to see it tossed out.' It had belonged to my father and I wanted it as a keepsake.

'Don't tell me you're going to take it back to London with you?' Soraya teased.

I didn't say anything.

The plaque was the only religious item in our home. When the morning sun caught it, the gold lettering still sparkled, highlighting the words. Papa told us that several of the letters had fallen off. Traces of glue where the letters had been had calcified against the metal backing.

Soraya absently dusted the plaque with the hem of her T-shirt.

I remembered how my parents had argued about the plaque when Papa wanted to hang it in the house.

'Not in this room!' Ma had exclaimed when she found Papa and me hammering a nail into the wall in the front room.

'In a Muslim household this room is the right and proper place for it,' Papa said firmly.

To me the plaque assumed spiritual qualities – like a religious icon that would protect my father and ultimately restore his failing health.

Papa's frailty at that time was cause for increasing concern. He was no longer able to make *Fijr*, the early morning prayer performed before sunrise. He only made *Maghrib*, the sunset prayer, and even this eventually became too much for him.

I studied the verse, thinking of my father and my grandmother and the way our lives had unravelled and then, by some miracle, had come together again. I thought about the years we had spent at McBain. There had been both good and bad times. Looking back then, even the bad times seemed to have been an integral part of growing up there.

49

THE COTTAGES across the railway tracks at the McBain siding lay in ruins, all of them abandoned long ago by their occupants. The white railway workers had moved back into town when their jobs became redundant, and the Bothas had disappeared without trace.

The view from our kitchen window was a disheartening one. There used to be life at the cottages across the tracks, especially when a train was expected. Now the buildings, once such solid structures, had been gutted. All that remained were smoke-blackened hulks. Ma thought it a miracle that squatters had not yet invaded the place. It was only a matter of time, though; and one more reason why she could not stay there on her own.

'This place not only holds our history, but also a lot of tragedy,' Ma said, joining me at the window. 'We never found out what happened to Elsa Botha. The women of McBain have had a lot of heartache.'

'What about you, Ma?'

'We didn't have many choices,' my mother said with a sigh. 'We travelled the road already chosen for us – husbands, babies and the kitchen. Today's women are lucky to have choices.'

She paused and then she said: 'I'm sorry you had to go through so much on your own, Meena. We didn't know what was going on. You were so far away . . . and not able to come back. It's hard to believe the terrible things the old government did. We're only beginning to hear about it now, at the Truth and Reconciliation hearings. Dear God, who could have imagined that all of this was going on right here amongst us. Right under our noses.' Ma shuddered. 'I suppose we were lucky. All they took from us was our home and they tore our family apart, but look what they did to others . . .'

There was a sadness, a heart-rending wistfulness about my mother as she gazed at the cottages.

'I don't know how I can leave this place. It's so close to my soul and yet there's been so much tragedy. Your father, Nana, Daniel, Birdie, Niels . . . Yasmin and Elsa both threw their lives away here. In a way I'm glad Yasmin got out when she did. I suppose it's to her credit that she's such a fighter. Look what happened to poor Elsa.'

'Nana used to say that the first born in each generation on her side was a girl, a strong girl,' I said.

'Each of them cursed,' Ma added. 'That's why I worry so about Soraya.'

'What do you mean, Ma?' I asked.

But my mother walked away, as though regretting her words. I knew that I would get nothing more out of her and strolled down to the siding to take a look at the cottages. The pathway along the embankment on the other side of the tracks had long since eroded. I noticed that the old apricot tree was still standing in the Bothas' backyard. I looked along the tracks, the rails glinting in the sun as they disappeared out of sight just beyond the crossing.

I found Soraya lounging in a canvas chair on the stoep. Oblivious to the world around her, she had her feet up on a small table, her walkman plugged into her ears. I admired her ability to switch off like this.

The phone call she had received that morning, and Ma's gentle enquiries about it, had obviously exasperated her. She had taken the phone into her room and had shut the door behind her. She emerged almost an hour later, eyes red and puffy from crying.

When Ma saw how distressed she was, she asked: 'What's wrong, Soraya? Who was on the phone?' But Soraya ignored her. She returned the phone to its place on the kitchen counter and then went outside without saying anything to either of us.

She was lying with her eyes closed. Sensing my presence, though, she opened her eyes. Reluctantly, she switched off the walkman and unplugged her ears.

'Want to talk?' I asked.

She didn't say anything.

I was uncomfortably conscious of the fact that I was prying.

'Ma and I both noticed you were upset and I thought you might want to talk,' I said quietly.

She rose abruptly, the walkman clattering to the ground. 'There's nothing to talk about,' she said. Baffled, I watched her as she stalked off.

It had been Ma's idea to approach her, obviously not one of her better ones. But Ma's concern for the welfare of her family outweighed considerations of tact or discretion. She was concerned about the phone call and perhaps she had reason to be. Still, if I had been in Soraya's shoes I would probably have been resentful about the intrusion too.

I remained on the stoep long after Soraya had gone, thinking about McBain's secrets and how they had affected our lives.

A few days later I found Ma gazing out the kitchen window. She seemed quite relaxed. Almost as if she were aware of my eyes on her, she turned and smiled at me. Then she moved away from the window and joined us at the table. The day after the phone call, Soraya herself had made a brief call, once again in the privacy of her room. Ma and I had exchanged glances, but said nothing to her.

It was just like the old days when Nana was still with us. We would all gather round the kitchen table while Nana made the tea. Ma and I recalled how fussy she had been about the tea-making ritual. It had to be done her way, or not at all.

Ma said absently: 'I ought to keep the garden watered.'

'What for?' I asked. 'We're done with McBain. Remember?'

'Yes, but it's a sin to neglect plants, especially when it's so difficult to grow them here. Besides, it's not as if I'm leaving tomorrow.'

Soraya pushed her chair back. 'I'll take care of it, Ma,' she said and went off to water the small patch of garden.

Ma had started the garden when we first moved to McBain. The ground was as hard as rock, but she had managed to coax some plants and vegetables into life. The chickens had taken a fancy to the garden and had destroyed the vegetable patch. Ma had decided to plant flowers instead. They were all hardy varieties: succulents and marigolds with an assortment of perennials. But the chickens had made a mess of this too, developing an appetite for marigolds. As a result their egg-yolks were a bright marigold colour. After this round of destruction, Ma fenced off the patch of garden with chicken wire.

From the kitchen window we watched Soraya watering the plants with an ancient patched hose – probably the same one we had brought with us from Soetstroom all those years ago.

'She's so lovely, isn't she?' Ma said. 'She's always had such a good heart. If only your Papa were alive to see her now. She says she wants to go to India to look up his ancestral home.' Ma paused thoughtfully. 'Look, I know there's something troubling her. I can see it. But she's an adult – she's got her own life. I don't suppose you know what's going on?'

'No,' I said.

'I wonder who that phone call was from? Could it be a boyfriend? She is seeing someone, isn't she?'

'James? I think that's his name. She never talks about him.'

'Why not?' Ma asked. 'Haven't you met him?'

I shook my head. 'None of them last long enough for an introduction to the family.'

'I entrusted her to you and Yasmin. Both of you are useless.' Ma looked at me with disgust.

'She's very secretive about her life,' I protested. 'You try and get information out of her.'

'I will.'

'Good luck,' I muttered.

We watched Soraya spraying water on the flowers.

'I can't believe that neither of you know what's going on. And you're on the spot. All Yasmin could tell me was that she was sharing a flat with a woman. A postgraduate student at the university. She never talks about her either. Do you know anything about her?'

'No, I don't.'

'She used to be such an open and forthright child. Now look at her. Never talks about herself. Makes you wonder, doesn't it?'

'Ma, that's the way young people are nowadays,' I said.

One night when we were relaxing in the kitchen after supper, Soraya brought out her London photographs. Ma got her glasses and made the tea and we sat around the kitchen table. There were several photographs taken in Yasmin and Neville's garden on the estate.

'Neville looks like he's put on weight,' Ma remarked.

'Since his retirement,' Soraya said.

'Do you see much of them these days?' Ma asked me.

'About twice a month.'

'Don't you live in the same city?'

'Yasmin lives in the country, Ma,' I said with a smile as I took the pictures from her.

'What about you, Soraya? Do you see much of Neville?'

'Not lately. I used to see a lot more of him . . .' She shrugged. 'He changed a lot after he and Yasmin separated. And I've been so busy with research for my thesis.'

'Also, Yasmin and Neville have this on and off relationship,' I added.

Soraya, toying with the pictures, nodded agreement.

'But that's all sorted out – their separation was a long time ago,' Ma said.

'They separated again for a few months about three years ago,' I said.

'I didn't know!' Ma said, astonished.

Soraya gathered the pictures. Ma seemed downcast. She was

clearly not impressed with the way her family was drifting from her sphere of influence.

'Tell me what's going on, Soraya,' she said.

'I don't know much either, Ma,' Soraya replied. 'As I said, I hardly see them these days.'

Ma frowned her disapproval.

'Well, tell me what you've been up to,' Ma said after a moment's hesitation.

Soraya got up and walked across the room.

'Whatever's upsetting you, I'd like to help.' Ma patted the chair next to her.

Soraya returned and sat down. Ma waited patiently as Soraya studied first her nails, then the two platinum rings she wore on her right hand.

She looked up. 'There really is nothing to tell, Ma. What I need is some space – please. I came here to get away from Yasmin, but now you people are constantly picking on me.'

'*You people!*' my mother said, her back straightening in indignation.

Soraya pushed her chair back.

'I don't like it when you talk to me so disrespectfully, Soraya. We didn't raise you like that.'

Soraya returned her gaze to her fingers. After a long moment of silence, she looked up and met Ma's eyes.

'I'm sorry, Ma,' she murmured.

'That settles it,' Ma said, a biting tone in her voice. The breach of respect by the youngest member of her family was too much to bear. 'I'm not going to England. I've always said I didn't want to be underfoot. Everyone wants to be free. Everyone wants *space*.' She started to get out of her chair.

Soraya, looking rueful, reached for Ma's hand and gently drew her back. 'Sit, Ma,' she said.

'It hurts, Soraya. I would do anything for you, you know that. But it hurts terribly when you speak to me like that.'

'Ma, I've just got a few personal problems,' she said. 'Nothing I can't handle. I'm sorry.'

'What sort of problems?'

'Nothing important,' Soraya said. 'Let it go now. Please?'

'I want to help,' Ma insisted.

Soraya rolled her eyes at me. I looked away, not wanting to be drawn into taking sides. But I studied Soraya covertly, searching for clues.

The silence in the kitchen became almost oppressive as Ma waited for Soraya to continue.

But Soraya got up. 'I'm tired,' she said. 'I'm going to bed.'

'Sit down,' Ma said sharply.

Soraya hesitated.

'Please sit down, Soraya,' Ma said in a gentler tone.

'I'm tired,' Soraya repeated. 'I'd like to turn in.'

'Can I get you something?' Ma asked.

'Nothing, thanks, Ma. I'll see you in the morning. Goodnight.' She turned on her heel and left the room.

We watched her go, Ma shaking her head despairingly.

'I wonder if Yasmin knows what the problem is,' Ma said picking up her glasses.

I shrugged.

'We're one family,' Ma remarked sarcastically. 'You live in the same city and yet it seems to me you might as well be living on another planet.'

I bit my tongue.

Ma put her glasses on again and returned her attention to the photos.

'Yasmin looks thin,' she said, studying one of the pictures before handing it to me. 'She's lost a lot of weight. Their garden is lovely. Do you think Neville's enjoying his retirement?'

In her own way, Ma was gently probing for clues to explain Soraya's secretive behaviour and why we were not the tightly knit family she expected us to be.

'I think Neville's bored,' I said. 'He expected to do some travelling with Yasmin, but she's always on the go. You know what she's like.'

Ma said nothing for a while. Then: 'We haven't had much

time to talk,' she said. 'It's been all work since you got here. I hope we can relax for a few days when all of this is done. I'm just sorry that Yasmin didn't come as well.'

'She'll be here, I'm sure,' I murmured.

Yoked by guilt, I was the least again. Lately, my mother and I would be laughing together one moment and the next I was in full retreat.

Ma stared pensively around her. It was clear that she was having doubts again. It was as if she expected to draw her strength from McBain. She sensed that there was a problem with Soraya and wanted to protect her. She thought she could, by sheer will, take over Soraya's problems.

She wanted to telephone Yasmin immediately to find out what was wrong with Soraya. I persuaded her not to. There was no sense getting everyone upset.

I sighed wearily, got up out of my chair and said goodnight to my mother.

50

THE NEXT few days were difficult. Ma was vacillating again.

'Ma, would you please stop worrying about Soraya,' I said as I peeled potatoes. 'She's more than capable of finding a solution to whatever the problem is. I think you and Yasmin should stop treating her like a child. She's a grown woman. Neither of you will allow her to grow up. You're each, in your own way, holding on to her.'

Cooking was a diversion for my mother. It had always been.

'A knife doesn't work properly, you're wasting half the potato,' she said irritably, taking the potatoes from me and finding the potato peeler in the drawer. I watched her brisk movements as she quickly finished the task. She was clearly reluctant to listen to what I was saying.

'I tried so hard with Yasmin. I wanted her to be happy. Both of you. I wanted you all to be happy. Yasmin more so because of what happened.'

Ma rinsed the potatoes under the tap and dried her hands on her apron.

'It's not easy being a mother. I promised your father I'd take care of Soraya.'

'I know, Ma. But you have to let go.'

'What do you know about letting go – about raising children? Dammit, Meena. I let her go to England – to you and Yasmin – hoping she'd have a better life. But look at her. She's miserable. Your father must be turning in his grave.' She pounded the chillies viciously.

Later that day, when we were sitting in the kitchen after lunch, my mother calmly declared: 'I won't be able to go back with you. I'll never sell this place in time.'

'Ma, please, we've been through this so many times,' I said.

Ma shook her head and sighed. 'Who in their right mind is going to buy this place? And I can't just abandon it and run off with you to England.'

'You can't stay here on your own,' Soraya said.

Ma tried to catch my eye, but I looked away.

'All right,' she snapped. 'Rush back if *you* want to, but I'll come when I'm good and ready.'

'No, Ma,' I said firmly. 'After Nana's funeral we agreed that you'd return with us. I'm not changing plans now.'

Ma frowned, examining my face for something more. She was looking for understanding but found none.

'I don't know what to do,' she said. I got up and went to my mother. I put my arm around her shoulders.

'It's clear. You agreed.'

Ma shook her head. 'You people are bulldozing me into a decision I don't want to make.'

'For goodness' sake, Ma,' Soraya cried in exasperation. Then in a gentler tone, she said: 'What do you really want to do, Ma? Do you want to stay here on your own? Do you think that would be wise? You're always telling us to do the right thing. Don't you think it's your turn now?'

Ma gazed at Soraya and tears gathered in her eyes. I went outside, leaving the two of them together.

I had suspected that something like this might happen. Had I not seen it coming? My mother had come up with a new excuse each day. I wanted to get home. My life had been put on hold because of her. I had problems of my own and here I was trying to sort out her problems – and she was resisting me every step of the way.

'I'm going out for a while,' I heard my mother say later to Gladys. 'Ask Florence to clean out the cupboards.'

'Where are you going, Ma?' I asked, but she ignored the

question and headed for the *bakkie*, the small pick-up she had bought years ago to transport goods for the shop.

Soraya joined me on the stoep and we watched as my mother drove away. It felt like the old days. I was beginning to feel the same anxiety to escape.

When Gladys left that afternoon, I walked her to the gate. Half-way there she paused and, turning to me, said in Afrikaans, 'You must see about Soraya. She's not right.'

'What do you mean?' I asked.

'I don't want to talk too much.'

'Gladys please . . . tell me what's going on.'

But Gladys felt she had said enough.

My mother seemed to have run out of excuses.

'We've already cleared out the shop. If I stay, it means starting all over again.'

Although we had already done a great deal of the sorting and packing, her comment added impetus to our efforts and the painstaking process of sifting through her history began in earnest. There were boxes of old letters, photographs, accounts, ledgers and baby clothes that had belonged first to Yasmin and then to me. Soraya's baby clothes were all there too, neatly folded and packed away in boxes. We found Ma going through one of these boxes, carefully examining its contents. I watched my mother warily, not fully trusting that she would stick to her decision. It was like being on a see-saw with her.

'Look, Soraya, this was yours,' Ma said, holding up a baby's knitted outfit with an intricate lacy pattern. 'Nana sat up night after night, knitting it for you. Isn't it lovely?' Ma stroked the garment, running her fingers over the pattern.

'What do you want to do with it, Ma?' Soraya asked quietly, hoping to distract my mother from another emotional scene.

'Take it as a keepsake, my child,' Ma said, digging deeper into the box and extracting an embroidered crib cover. She was about to hold this up too. I put up my hand to stop her.

'Wait, Ma. You can't do this. We have to get rid of these

things. Why don't we pack up all this stuff and give it to some charity?'

'Or why don't we have a sale – right here in the shop,' Soraya suggested.

'What a good idea!' Ma said delightedly. 'We'll have a big sale. Everything must go. Cheap!'

'We'll put some signs up in town advertising the sale,' Soraya said.

'I'm putting you in charge,' Ma said. 'You're good at these things.'

'OK.' Soraya looked relieved.

Yasmin phoned from London wanting to know about the progress we'd made. Ma was standing right beside me and so I wasn't able to say much. Yasmin seemed to understand and asked leading questions, which I could answer with a simple 'yes' or 'no'. Ma listened suspiciously. Yasmin seemed to realise that we were having problems.

'How's your leg?' I asked.

'Much better,' Yasmin replied. 'I have a walking cast now. Do you want me to come?'

'No . . . not necessary. We'll manage. Soraya will help.'

'I'd better come,' she said. 'It doesn't sound as though you're making much headway. Meena, let me talk to Ma.'

I handed the phone to my mother and went outside. Soraya had wandered off, making it clear she had no intention of speaking to Yasmin. But Ma insisted. She called Soraya and she came reluctantly. Ma handed the phone to her and joined me outside. Soraya was on the phone for at least five minutes. She didn't say much, but seemed to be listening carefully to what Yasmin had to say. Eventually she came outside to join us. She looked furious, but Ma had no qualms about questioning her.

'What did Yasmin say?'

'Nothing,' Soraya muttered.

'Didn't seem like nothing to me,' Ma said.

'Ma, I don't have to tell you that Yasmin makes a drama out

of every little thing. It's just about my studies. I had to send in some documentation. Nothing major.'

But it was clear to me that she was not telling us everything. She put on a bright smile for our benefit, but I knew better, and so did Ma.

'Will the two of you stop being such worrywarts,' she said. 'I'll be back there soon and I'll get my life sorted out. Yasmin lives with pressure and she tries to put pressure on everyone around her. I hate it. It's so stressful.'

'She's your mother,' Ma said.

'Don't remind me.'

'That's not a nice thing to say.'

'I'm sure the feeling between us is mutual.'

'I think you're making a mistake,' Ma said. 'I know Yasmin. I know she's crazy, but I also know that she loves you.'

Soraya shrugged.

'I know what I'm talking about. If Nana was still alive, she'd have told you so too. Do you think Yasmin will come?'

'Of course,' Soraya said. 'She'll be here to take the credit for organising us, broken leg and all.'

Although we laughed at this remark, both Ma and I were worried about Soraya. There was a brittleness about her. Her laughter was too sharp and too loud and had a dangerous edge to it. I remembered when Yasmin had come home to McBain to fetch her. Soraya had had the same edge to her laughter then.

51

THE RAIN earlier that day had brought with it swarms of flying ants and the stoep was littered with their wings. Ma and I sat in the dark, the lights turned off. The sky had cleared and the night was brilliant with the full moon. I had almost forgotten how magical evenings at McBain could be, especially the early evenings when the sunset turned the veld into flaming colours which softened to shades of indigo as the shadows fell.

That scene at McBain was so clearly imprinted on my mind that *Shades of Indigo* became a title for one of my books.

'You never talk about yourself or your life,' my mother remarked.

'There's nothing much to say, Ma.'

Ma thought about my response for a moment. 'I still pray that you'll find yourself a good man and have kids of your own. You'll know then what I had to go through with the two of you – and now with Soraya.'

This was a subject my mother often returned to. It was obviously of concern to her that I was not married; that I had not given her grandchildren; that I was going to be alone. Her precious daughter Yasmin was married and had everything – a business, a husband, a child. And then there was me . . .

The topic shifted as my mother's mind darted restlessly from one thought to another.

'I hope Soraya settles down soon too,' she said.

'She's her own person, Ma.'

'Her own person, huh,' Ma muttered churlishly.

'She's not a child, Ma. She's a woman.'

'She's going to end up being a spinster like you,' Ma said.

'Don't interfere,' I warned.

'I promised your father I'd always take care of Soraya,' she said, her voice breaking. 'I gave him my solemn promise.'

'Ma . . .'

'She's not strong like you and Yasmin.'

'I'm sure she's much stronger than you give her credit for. She has to be. She's Yasmin's child, after all.'

Strains of Soraya's flute drifted to us on the still air. The music was hauntingly sad. Both Ma and I fell silent, listening. Then Ma began to cry quietly.

With a pang of sadness, I realised that my mother was growing old. The lines had deepened around her eyes and her hair was streaked with grey. She had slowed down considerably over the past few days, probably from sheer exhaustion.

'I worry about you people all the time,' she said.

'There's no need, Ma. We're doing fine.'

'A mother never stops worrying.'

I smiled into the darkness.

'The other day when she made that long distance call,' Ma said, 'I thought she was talking to her room-mate, but it sounded more like she was talking to a lover. They were having an argument.'

'That's possible,' I replied, 'but I don't think she's serious about anyone.'

'I don't have much faith in what you or Yasmin think. Neither of you seems to know a damn thing about Soraya.'

'That's not fair, Ma.'

'I'll have a talk with Soraya myself,' she said somewhat caustically.

The following week we managed to dispose of the contents of most of the boxes. The same bargain hunters who had come to the earlier sale returned to snap up what remained in the store.

Although Ma seemed pleased with the results of the sale, she was still reluctant to sell Nana's clothes.

'It's too soon, Meena,' she said. 'It's too soon.'

We despaired that she would ever get rid of the stuff. But in the end Ma seemed to brace herself and almost blindly tossed Nana's belongings into a box, which Soraya and I sorted. Soraya put a value on the items and tagged them. Most of them were sold as well.

There were still boxes of papers to go through. I found Papa's shoe box full of Irish Sweepstake tickets which Ma had stored in the old trunk. I tossed these out immediately. We built a bonfire in an old petrol drum and burnt the papers. But there were still several boxes left.

I went through the ledgers from the early years at McBain. There were still accounts outstanding. I couldn't believe that my parents had been so negligent about collecting.

Papa would have said: 'You can't knock blood out of a stone. If people don't have money, they can't pay you.'

Tallying the amounts, I found there was four thousand rands in bad debts – a fortune in those days. There was no point mentioning any of this to my mother. She had enough on her mind.

In another box I found the rusty bicycle bell which had belonged to my old bike and a pair of Papa's old glasses, the ones with the black horn-rimmed frames and lenses as thick as glass blocks.

Everything belonged to the distant past.

We were in the kitchen again, clearing away the last of the supper dishes while Ma made the tea.

'Any more pictures to show us?' Ma asked Soraya.

She shook her head.

'So where's the boyfriend's photo?' Ma teased.

I knew there was a purpose behind the teasing. Soraya suspected this too and scowled.

'Come on,' Ma said. 'Get them.'

'I told you before. I'm not seeing anyone,' Soraya said sharply.

'Come on, you must have someone special in your life,' Ma

said, looking at me for support.

Soraya shook her head again.

'But you're a lovely young woman, how can that be?' Ma asked.

Soraya smiled grimly. 'There's no special man in my life, Ma.' She met Ma's gaze squarely then lowered her head and tiredly pinched her eyes. 'I think I'll get into bed and curl up with my book. No tea for me thanks, Ma,' she said.

Ma frowned and looked at me for an explanation.

'I told you not to pry,' I said.

'That's the trouble with you people. No one knows what's going on. You live amongst strangers, people different in their thinking from us. They're uncaring people.'

'Not all of them,' I said. After all those years I had learned to understand the English and had made good friends amongst them.

Ma's lip curled scornfully. 'Here people stick together. Families are close.'

'Ma, that was true of the sixties. But it's the nineties now. Things have changed since we grew up here.'

My mother's expression tightened, her eyes clouding.

That night neither my mother nor I could sleep. Around two o'clock, I heard her getting up. I wondered what was keeping her awake. There was no need for her to worry about the packing because Soraya and I had taken care of most of it already. Soraya had even taped a list of contents to each box to make things easy to find.

My mother went into the kitchen. I heard her running the tap to fill the kettle. In my mind's eye I saw her at the sink, glancing through the window as she plugged in the kettle. A few minutes later the toilet flushed. I thought of getting up and joining her for a cup of tea, but rolled over instead, praying for sleep. A cup clinked against a saucer and a few moments later my mother padded back to her room. I was too restless to remain in bed. My mother heard me stumbling around in the dark and switched on her light.

'What's wrong?' she asked.

'Can't sleep,' I muttered.

'Nor can I.'

I sat on the edge of her bed. She moved over and I slipped in under the covers. It was not a warm, spontaneous gesture. It was as though she felt obliged to invite me into the bed because I expected it.

'Remember how we used to get up at three o'clock during Ramadan?' I said as I snuggled under the covers.

'Do you still fast?'

'No.'

Ma wriggled into a comfortable position and pulled the blanket up under her chin.

'Shall I turn off the light?' I asked.

She nodded.

Ma and I lay in the dark. She turned her back to me and lay on her side. I gently massaged her shoulders.

'Hmm, that feels good,' she murmured sleepily.

For so many years my mother and I had struggled to reach some kind of understanding and still I had the sense that something was missing between us.

My mother had never been demonstrative and had kept herself aloof, even from her daughters. I had always been closer to Nana. Now, though, my feelings about my mother had matured somewhat. These days we tried to base our relationship on respect. It seemed to be working. At least I hoped so.

My mother snored lightly and I eased away from her. The sun would soon be up.

I remembered how we used to be up before dawn during Ramadan. I used to be quite diligent about fasting. I missed only the days when I was menstruating, a time when a woman was considered unclean and not permitted to fast. Papa had fasted too, even though it was hard on him. Ma used to discourage him, saying that he needed to keep up his strength.

At three o'clock each morning I got up to prepare something

to eat and if Papa wished it I would prepare a tray for him too. Sometimes Nana got up to join us, but not for the purposes of fasting. Nana was a Christian, as Ma had been before she married my father and converted to Islam.

By the time I got up, Soraya had already been up for ages. We went through the last of the boxes.

'I wonder what these are?' Soraya said, holding up a bundle of letters secured with a rubber band.

'Whose are they?' I asked.

'Ma's,' she said.

I struggled up off my knees, stiff from crouching over the boxes, and examined her find.

'All of them for Ma?' I asked.

She nodded.

I took them from her and glanced at the envelopes. The distinctive handwriting wasn't one that I recognised. Intrigued, I flipped through the envelopes which were neatly arranged in some kind of order.

I was about to remove them from the rubber band when I caught Soraya's reproachful look.

'They're Ma's letters,' she said. 'They're probably private.'

'Then put them back in the box,' I said, handing them to her. 'And tell Ma where they are.'

Much to my relief, we had finally found an estate agent Ma felt she could trust. She was bringing a prospective buyer to look at the property. It sounded quite encouraging. The government had announced plans to build a new road and bridge to eliminate the blind railway crossing, site of so many accidents. The new road, apparently, was to pass right by our property.

Poor Papa. That had been his dream. Years too late for him it was becoming a reality.

The agent told us that, since the announcement, a large oil company had made enquiries about our property. They were looking at it for one of their multi-facility filling stations.

'I'll fly out next week,' Yasmin said on the phone.

'Why?' I asked. 'We can deal with this.'

'I understand more about financing than either of you. I want to make sure that Ma gets the best deal.'

'What about your business?' I asked.

'Don't worry. There are enough people here to take care of it for a week or so.'

Ma chuckled. 'That girl will never change,' she said affectionately. 'Oh well, let her come. She has lots of money to waste. She can also say goodbye to the place. Not that it meant anything to her, of course.'

In that uncanny way she had of suddenly reading my thoughts, Ma said: 'I know you're anxious to get back. I wish you would go. I'm perfectly able to handle things here now. You and Soraya have been a big help to me, but if you want to go, I can finish what's left to do.'

'I'll go back with you,' I said firmly.

'I don't suppose you really have anything to rush back to,' Ma remarked. 'Not like Yasmin.'

I smiled wryly.

'You're a good person, Meena. I would have thought any man with a grain of sense would have snapped you up a long time ago.'

We were back to her favourite topic. I was getting irritated with my mother's obsessive concern about me being alone.

'Is there really no one in your life?' she asked.

I shook my head.

'I really prayed you'd find someone. What happened?'

'I haven't met anyone I want to share my life with.'

'It's terrible to be alone when you're old.'

'I'll cross that bridge when I get to it,' I said.

'We all need companionship.'

'Sometimes one pays too high a price. I've seen how unhappy some of my married friends are.'

'Why is it so difficult to find a good man?' Ma asked.

'Perhaps I'm looking for too much.'

'That's not what happens in your books, though. People fall in love all the time. They're miserable, they separate, they come together and in the end they live happily ever after. How can you write about things you've never experienced?'

'I didn't know you read my work,' I said with a touch of sarcasm.

'I even liked a few of them.'

I grimaced. 'You never approved of my writing. Never thought it was work. Yasmin too. She won't even talk to me about what I do. She thinks I write trash.'

Ma sighed. 'You and I . . . there's always been this thing between us. It's always been there like a wall and I haven't been able to break through it.'

'That's exactly the way I feel,' I said.

She turned away. She obviously did not want to pursue this line of discussion, but I did.

'I tried,' I said. 'I tried very hard when I was growing up, but you never seemed to have time for me. It was always Yasmin. Yasmin gobbled us all up. We didn't exist.'

'That's the biggest load of rubbish I've ever heard,' Ma said indignantly. 'I don't know what more I could have done for you.'

'All I wanted was recognition,' I whispered, my voice trembling. 'I didn't even expect love.'

'You were everything to us. You were there when we needed you, Meena. Nana and I would never have made it without your help.'

'Why didn't you tell me this at the time? I didn't think there was anything I could do to satisfy you.'

'I tried,' my mother said quietly.

'Obviously you didn't try hard enough.'

Hurt by my remark, Ma was silent.

'I was disappointed that you had spent all that time and energy on teacher training and then gave it up,' she said.

I didn't respond.

'Why don't you go back to teaching, Meena?'

I laughed at the sheer insanity of such a suggestion. She just couldn't stop herself from being critical. She never tried this with Yasmin because Yasmin knew how to deal with her.

Like Nana, my mother would criticise Yasmin behind her back but never to her face. With me it was different. Ma felt free to say what she wanted, when she wanted.

I loved my mother. I wanted her close, yet there was always tension when we were together. We would never be as close as she and Yasmin. There was a special bond between them. One sensed it in the way my mother talked about her, or looked at her photograph, eyes softening. She never looked at me in quite the same way.

Yasmin had suggested that Ma should alternate living between our two homes, but said that of course she knew how disruptive and unrealistic such an arrangement could be. In the end, she told me that she would be quite content for me to take on the day-to-day responsibility, while she would take Ma on occasional outings – the 'fun' daughter.

'Look,' Ma said, 'I don't want to come to your home and be made to feel unwelcome.'

There it was again. I could feel my blood pressure rising. I got up and went into the house.

I was furious that I allowed my mother to do this to me. The demons had been liberated again, probably because Yasmin was coming. Over the last twenty years, since Yasmin and I had gone our separate ways, my mother had learned how to play us off against each other.

Yasmin laughed it off. But with me it simmered, contained, until my mother and I were together for a while. Then the resentment between us erupted like a volcano. When the air cleared, it started all over again, building towards the next explosion. She never criticised Yasmin, no matter what the problems – and there were many – between her and Neville, most of them of Yasmin's creation.

The air was thickening.

Storm clouds were sailing in.

Yasmin was coming home.

52

MY MOTHER'S conversation had left me bristling and for a moment I had been tempted to tell her about Sayeed. Fortunately, I had restrained myself. It would only have given her more ammunition for criticism.

My affair had lasted three brief years and, like some of my other experiences, had ended abruptly and painfully. But unlike any of my other experiences it had shaken the very foundations of my drab little existence, changing for ever my perceptions of love and relationships and adding a new dimension to my writing.

It had happened at a time in my life when I needed change. I was in a dull, mind-numbing space, filled with restless yearning. It was a time of transition for me. My first novel had just been published and I was anxious to get started on the next one. It was in that period of waiting when, like a screw trapped in a groove, my life was going round and round and I wanted to do something outrageous, something totally different, something that would catapult me into a more exciting life.

Sayeed had turned my life upside down. He had swept me out of the ordinary and challenged me.

I missed him terribly. The thought had once crossed my mind that the tragedy of his death might, in some perverse way, have liberated something primal inside me which had given my writing the depth it had lacked before.

'I want to burn my letters,' my mother said. 'I'm going to get rid of all the things that have tied me to the past.'

I suspected it would be as difficult for her to burn her letters as it had been for her to dispose of the old clothes and treasures she'd gathered around her through her lifetime. I volunteered to help and collected the boxes of papers, carrying them into the backyard to the old petrol drum where the ashes from the previous bout of burning still remained. My mother's letters, still tied in a neat bundle, were lying on top of one of the boxes. I untied the letters and resisted the finality of the task by sorting them. Once again I came across the envelopes with the curiously upright and very precise writing.

I opened one of them and looked at the date – 1949. Then I looked at the name on the last page. Nathaniel. Nathaniel *Basson*. The man my mother had been in love with before she met my father. I scanned the letter, and then began to read more carefully. When I'd finished reading the first letter, I opened another envelope. And then another.

It was strange to read outpourings of love for my mother from a man other than my father. At first I felt angry. Betrayed. Here was a man declaring his undying love for my mother. He was willing to risk my grandmother's wrath by eloping with her. Although penniless, and having spent time in jail, he said he wanted to be a proper father to his child.

Stunned, I sat down on an empty crate. My mother's shadow loomed over me. I looked up. Without a word she took the letters from me, threw them into the drum and set them alight.

'Ma,' I whispered, ashamed of having peered into a life she had tried to keep from us.

She stared at me with angry eyes.

'I'm sorry,' I said quietly.

'So you know,' she said.

'Yes.'

'I don't see that it's going to make any difference to your life,' she said.

'Your secret is safe with me, Ma.'

Without a word, my mother tossed the rest of the letters into the flames, peering into the drum to make sure they were all burning. I waited for her to express her anger, but she didn't say a word. Her silence was more condemning than words could ever have been.

I waited, but she clearly thought that no further explanation was warranted, and for the rest of the day she all but ignored me.

My mother's silence was painful as I, too, was struggling to sift through my feelings, struggling to deal with the hurt and the feeling of betrayal. For most of my life, my mother had gazed down at me from a pedestal and I was devastated to discover that she had always had feet of clay.

Soraya and I drove into the city to meet Yasmin at the airport. We waited impatiently for her flight to arrive.

I was anxious to get back to McBain because the estate agent had phoned to say she was bringing an offer. Ma, afraid of missing her, had decided to wait at home. Soraya wasn't keen to accompany me but after much persuasion she eventually agreed.

On the drive to the airport I wondered absently how Yasmin would manage with her broken leg, but I needn't have worried. The flight arrived on time and Yasmin, in a walking cast, emerged, two of the cabin attendants assisting her down the steps. A wheelchair arrived on the tarmac and one of the ground staff wheeled Yasmin into the terminal.

Soraya was unusually quiet.

Yasmin spotted us, smiled, waved and dismissed her entourage. As usual, she looked effortlessly elegant. Just looking at her made me self-conscious about the weight I had gained. Unlike Yasmin, I was constantly changing from one diet to another. My sister never seemed to have any problems, mundane or otherwise.

Reading my mother's letters had changed my feelings towards Yasmin. My relationship with her had shifted. I no longer felt wounded. Perhaps now, knowing the truth, it was not necessary for me to feel threatened. I would probably never judge her as harshly as I had in the past. All my feelings about my past, my father and Yasmin, might finally be resolved. Perhaps I could put it all to rest now. She would always be the focus of my mother's life. Nothing would change for me. I would still be on the outside.

I embraced my sister. Yasmin flashed an angry look at Soraya and pecked her on the cheek. The air was thick with hostility.

On the way home we dropped in at Aishaben's for a short visit. She, too, was alone now. Cassimbhai had died about five years after Papa. She and Ma were still close.

I knew she was going to miss my mother. I issued an open invitation for her to visit us in England and to stay as long as she liked. I suspected, though, that she would not come, whatever the inducement. But the invitation seemed to console her.

Yasmin and Soraya were silent on the drive home. I tried to make light conversation, but the atmosphere between them was heavy. Yasmin sat in the back, responding in monosyllables, staring stonily out of the window.

I tried in vain to determine the cause of the tension. It was clear that something had happened between them, maybe even before Soraya had left London, which might have accounted for her peculiar moods.

We were hot and tired and I stopped at a café in town for refreshments. Because I knew my mother would be concerned if we were late, I called her from the café. The estate agent had not yet arrived. I asked her if she wanted to speak to Yasmin but she declined, saying we'd be home soon enough.

From where I stood at the phone, I had a clear view of Yasmin and Soraya, heads together, locked in argument. As I walked back towards them I heard Yasmin say: 'Why, Soraya? You've got the whole world at your feet. You're beautiful, you're intelligent, you could have any man you want. Why, in heaven's name, are you doing this?'

Soraya sat back in her chair and turned her sullen gaze to the street. 'Stay out of my life,' she said coldly.

'Not when it concerns me. How could you do this to us, to yourself?'

Yasmin was about to say something more. But she looked up and saw me and fell silent.

'What's up?' I asked as I sat down to finish my tea.

'Nothing,' Soraya said, abruptly. She pushed her chair back and got up.

'What did Ma have to say?' Yasmin asked.

Something was seriously wrong. I could tell from that blank, hurt look in Yasmin's eyes as she watched Soraya walk away.

'Ma's waiting for us,' I said. 'What's going on? Soraya looks like thunder.'

But Yasmin was obviously not going to tell me anything. She scowled at the wall behind me while she waited for me to finish my tea. I paid the waitress and helped Yasmin up.

Soraya was waiting at the car. 'I can't believe you had the gall to snoop into my personal life,' she said, picking up the argument where she had left off in the café. 'How dare you?'

'I didn't snoop. The letter was lying on your bed when you stayed over for the Easter weekend. I recognised the handwriting.'

'What were you doing in my room?'

'That's not the point!' Yasmin yelled, momentarily losing her balance and falling against the car door.

She recovered, her face livid.

I struggled to get the car door open so that I could help Yasmin into the back seat. Soraya wasn't lifting a finger.

'Come on, you two,' I said, having succeeded in stuffing Yasmin into the back seat. Soraya was at the driver's side. I glared at her over the roof of the car. 'What is all this about?'

Neither said anything as Soraya slipped in behind the wheel and I got into the back with Yasmin.

Soraya shoved the key into the ignition with such fury that I expected it to snap.

'Stop,' I said sharply, opening the door. 'I'm not sitting in this car with the two of you at each other's throats. Soraya, move over. I'll drive.'

We changed seats. Yasmin stared morosely out of the window.

'What on earth is going on between the two of you?' I asked Yasmin.

'Let her tell you,' she snapped.

I tried to catch Soraya's eye.

'Tell her,' Yasmin urged. 'Tell her about your affair with a married man!'

Startled, I glanced into the rear-view mirror, almost swerving into a ditch. I straightened the car and pulled off the road.

'Is this true, Soraya?' I asked as I turned off the ignition, almost too afraid to look at her.

Soraya had changed colour, the pallor of her skin almost the same shade of beige as her sweater. She turned away, but not before I saw the look of contempt she flashed at Yasmin. I opened my door and got out. Soraya got out of the car too, as though unable to bear being enclosed in the same space with Yasmin.

Yasmin remained in the car, sitting perfectly still, staring at the horizon.

'Are you sure, Yasmin?' I said.

'Ask her!' Yasmin shouted angrily.

'Is this true, Soraya?'

Soraya frowned, head up, chin jutting.

'Who is the man?'

Neither of them said anything.

'Do you know him?' I asked Yasmin.

'Of course. He's a friend.'

'Who?'

'Douglas Pilkington,' Yasmin said before Soraya could answer. 'Gwen and Douglas have been friends of ours for umpteen years. Can you imagine how I feel about this? Gwen trusted us. Trusted her!' Yasmin pointed an accusing finger at Soraya. She struggled out of the car and, leaning over the roof, said: 'You've wrecked Gwen's marriage! God, you're wicked!'

'Their marriage was over a long time ago,' Soraya said, her face angry. 'Neither of us planned this, Meena. It just happened. We fell in love, OK? It happens all the time.'

'It just happened . . .' Yasmin mocked. 'Love! What do you know about any of these things? You attach yourself to the first man who comes along, a man like Douglas – kind and considerate, and married. For goodness' sake, Soraya, he's old enough to be your father! How could you be so stupid?'

'Don't you dare judge me! Who do you think you are?'

'I don't want you making the same mistakes I did, Soraya,' Yasmin said. 'Nana said that taking a man from his family would never bring me happiness. And it hasn't.'

'I hate you!'

'That's fine,' Yasmin said. 'Hate me now. But down the line you'll thank me.'

'Never! All you've done is screw up my life!'

'Soraya!' I cried, appalled.

'Well, it's true. And I wish you'd both stay out of my business. It's my life. I'll do what I want. I'm not a child and I'm certainly not asking your permission to live my life the way I want. I don't have to answer to anyone.'

'Stop it! Stop it, both of you!' I cried, my brain trying to make sense of the situation. 'Soraya, I can't believe this is true.'

Then I thought of my own life and my three years with Sayeed. What was it about the McBain women? All of us, in one way or another, had had disastrous love lives with married men. It made me wonder if there was some fatal flaw in our genes.

'She's abandoned her music career to be a mistress,' Yasmin snapped.

'I'm not his mistress! He doesn't keep me! But if it makes either of you feel any better, I've already decided to end the relationship.'

'Isn't it a bit late?' Yasmin asked. 'You've already messed up Gwen's life. She's leaving Douglas. Did you know that? After thirty years of marriage, she's leaving him. So much for your decision.'

Soraya turned away.

Yasmin banged her fist on the roof of the car.

'Stupid girl! Why didn't you think of the consequences before?'

'We have to talk about this reasonably,' I said. 'All these accusations are not helping.' Exasperated, I ran a hand through my hair.

Nana always used to have the answers. She knew about things like this and why they happened. I prayed for her wisdom and guidance.

How could Douglas have got involved with Soraya?

Suddenly I felt aggrieved by all that men were capable of, not only Douglas, but Jonathan, Neville, and Sayeed too.

We got back into the car. Soraya sat in the front.

'How did this happen, Soraya?' I asked.

She shrugged, her pained gaze meeting mine, her eyes pleading. 'Please, Meena, don't tell Ma. I'll tell her myself.'

'Well, you'd better get on with it soon, because if you don't I will,' Yasmin threatened from the back seat.

We've had everything happen to us, and now this, I thought as I started the car and swung back on to the road. Yasmin and Soraya were silent and I was thankful that the sniping had ceased for the moment.

Soraya leaned back against the headrest, her face turned to the sun. Unlike Yasmin, who was still scowling, her expression was remarkably serene.

I thought I could see a pattern emerging that explained Soraya's behaviour. First there had been Papa, who adored her. Then there was Neville, who was kind and loving, but who had two other children. And now there was Douglas. Why were Yasmin and I so shocked that she should fall in love with an older man? Guilty ourselves of searching for happiness in the wrong place, we were now so blinded by self-righteous indignation that we couldn't see the obvious.

I said a little prayer hoping that Nana, wherever she was, would hear and reach out with solutions.

'Look, I said, trying to sound calm and rational. 'Don't say anything to Ma. She might not want to leave when she hears about this. You know what she's like. I'm sure we can get this straightened out between the three of us.' I glanced at Soraya and then tried to catch Yasmin's eye in the mirror but she was still staring out the window, obviously seething.

Amazing, I thought wryly. Something always happened when Yasmin was around.

She had hardly arrived and already there was drama.

53

MA WAS waiting on the stoep to meet us when we drove through the gate at McBain. She was so thrilled to see Yasmin that she failed to notice the tense atmosphere.

'How's the leg?' she asked.

'Healing nicely, thanks, Ma.'

Ma took Yasmin's arm and helped her up the steps to the house. Soraya, scowling, picked up one of the suitcases. I brought the other.

Later, when we had the chance to sit down and Ma had put the kettle on the stove, talk of Nana and the funeral started her crying again. Yasmin said she wanted to visit the cemetery, and Ma said that we could do that before we left.

'So, what's happening, Yasmin?' Ma asked.

Yasmin was silent. Her eyes found Soraya. Soraya looked away. For the first time Ma noticed that something was wrong.

'What is it?' she asked again, this time more insistently.

'Nothing,' Yasmin said, flashing Soraya a warning look.

Ma intercepted the look and frowned.

Soraya got up and walked towards the doorway. She paused briefly and then descended the steps into the yard.

'Leave her,' I said. 'Let her go.'

Yasmin and I talked well into the night. Topics ranged from Nana to Soraya and the state of our own lives. I began to realise that Yasmin had reached a crisis in her personal life.

'I want to sell the business, Meena. But don't say anything to the others yet. I want to wait for the right time to tell Ma.'

'What does Neville have to say about this?' I asked.

She didn't reply. I should have known that Yasmin only gave out what she wanted you to know.

'You've pursued your dreams,' I said then, 'and you're still unhappy. I've never been able to figure out what it is you really want from life. What is it you want, Yasmin?'

She thought about the question. 'I don't know. I just feel so damn restless. I've had everything I've ever wanted and now I'm tired of it all.'

It was quite mystifying to me that Yasmin had everything one could dream of, except happiness. Nana used to say that one had to create one's own happiness. It didn't come from other people.

'I want to do something useful,' Yasmin continued. 'I've been offered a very good price for the business. I've got to make a decision soon. A couple of months ago I knew what I wanted to do. And now this thing with Soraya has happened.'

'Your decision about your life has nothing to do with Soraya,' I said. 'You were the one who once told me that children have to leave the nest, that one can't hang on to them for ever, and that one has to live one's own life. Remember?'

She hugged me. I felt closer to her than we'd been in years. It was like the old closeness we had shared as girls.

We turned off the light long after midnight and, although Yasmin fell asleep immediately, I lay awake in the darkness thinking about our conversation.

Ma was in the kitchen with Yasmin when Soraya and I joined them the next morning. Ma was obviously upset. Yasmin reached for Soraya's hand.

'Soraya, come and sit down. Ma wants to talk to you.'

Ma obviously knew everything. Soraya sat down in the chair opposite Yasmin.

Taking a deep breath, Yasmin said quietly: 'I've told Ma the whole story, Soraya.'

Soraya glared at her mother, but said nothing.

'I knew something was wrong,' Ma said, reaching out for her. 'You couldn't keep this from me for ever, you know. It's all this secretiveness that got you into trouble in the first place. We're a family. We have to stick together.'

Avoiding Ma's eyes, Soraya slowly got out of her chair and walked out the door on to the back stoep. Yasmin struggled up and limped after her.

'My poor Soraya,' Ma said. 'How could something like this happen and you not know about it?'

'Me!' I cried indignantly. 'I hardly ever see Soraya.'

'And you!' Ma said, pointing an accusing finger at Yasmin as she returned to the kitchen. 'All you've done is run around the world, wrapped up in your own self-importance. Now look what's happened!' Ma was furious.

'Ma,' I offered timidly, 'it's not the end of the world. She says it was a mistake and it's over. I think we should move on.'

'And how do you expect Gwen to move on?' Yasmin asked.

Ma cast a troubled glance through the open door. Obviously distressed, Soraya was standing in the yard, hugging her pain to herself. She looked totally forsaken.

'Drama, always drama. Some day you girls will be the death of me.'

I went to the kitchen window and looked out at Soraya. Her shoulders were shaking.

'Go to her,' I said to Yasmin.

'She doesn't want me.'

'Don't give up on her, Yasmin. Go to her,' I insisted.

Yasmin went to her daughter. Ma and I watched from the window as she tried to put her arm around Soraya. Soraya drew back, her posture rigid. Yasmin tried again, looking helpless. I suddenly realised that Yasmin was afraid; she didn't know what to do. Ma walked away, as though the scene was too painful for her to watch. But I remained at the window.

'You're such a hypocrite,' I heard Soraya say. 'You're on to me about my life, but look at the way you've messed yours up!'

Yasmin's face lost its colour. 'What do you mean?'

'Neville told me that things aren't working out between you and that you may be separating again.'

'Rubbish! You know that's not true. It's just that Neville can't stand me being away from home so often.'

'Well, why are you?'

'You know that my business takes me away.'

'That's what you've always said,' Soraya said scornfully. 'Ever since I can remember that's been your stock response. You were never there for us.'

'Have you done this to hurt me?' Yasmin asked.

'Why do you think you're so important? Why does the whole world have to revolve around you?'

Soraya walked away towards the railway tracks. Yasmin stood, hands dangling at her sides, looking utterly bereft. I went out to her.

Soraya returned about half an hour later. She shunned Yasmin's efforts to make up with her and without a word to any of us she got into the car.

'God, kids!' Yasmin exclaimed, clutching her head as Soraya sped away. 'She's so difficult. So damn stubborn. I don't know why she has this grudge against me. What have I done to her? She goes out of her way to make my life hell!'

'Maybe she's right,' Ma said. 'Maybe you just weren't around for her when she needed you.'

'When I wasn't there, Neville was.'

'A girl needs her mother while she's growing up.'

'Ma, I was trying to make a success of my life, so I could give her everything she wanted.'

'Did you?' Ma asked.

'She went to the best schools . . .'

'That's not enough, Yasmin. She needed you, her mother. You took her away from a good home here, where she was loved and cared for, and you took her to a strange city, thousands of miles away from us and all you gave her to replace that love and caring was things. No wonder she's confused.'

Yasmin lowered her head. 'I thought I was doing what was best for her.'

'No, you were doing what was best for Yasmin,' Ma said, sharply. 'Nana and I worried about Soraya. We worried about her all the time.'

Yasmin furtively brushed away her tears.

Angry with her, Ma got up and left us.

Late that afternoon, in the midst of our family crisis, the estate agent called. It was her second visit since Yasmin's arrival. When she spread out the papers on the table, we set aside personal issues and concentrated on the offer.

'It's a big company and they're going to make a lot of money from the property,' Yasmin said. 'What they're offering is peanuts. We should ask for more.'

'I don't want to lose the sale,' Ma said doubtfully.

Yasmin shook her head. 'Nonsense. If they want it they'll be willing to pay more for it.'

'You may be making a mistake,' the agent said.

But Yasmin ignored her and blithely altered the amount offered for the property. 'Our first house was stolen from us. It's not going to happen again.' She handed the pen to my mother to initial the changes.

In principle, Ma agreed with Yasmin, but she was clearly nervous about making unreasonable demands.

Yasmin, however, was nonchalant. 'Don't worry, Ma, just wait and see.'

It was dusk when we walked the estate agent to the door and watched her drive away.

Yasmin put her arm around Ma's shoulders. 'Now if only I could handle my personal problems so easily,' she laughed, the laughter belying her troubled expression as her eyes anxiously searched the road, looking for Soraya's car. A few sets of headlights approached, but they all swept past McBain.

We returned indoors. Yasmin was restless and agitated.

I went to our room to lie down. Yasmin followed, shutting

the door behind her.

'Don't tell me you're going to bed,' she said.

'I have a headache.'

She tossed her small cabin bag on to the bed and unzipped it. Lying on top of the contents was a brown manila envelope. Even before she said anything, I knew it was from Elise.

'With all that's been going on, I almost forgot,' she said. 'Elise sent this.'

I took the envelope from her and tore it open. There were about thirty pages of my typed manuscript with some notations in Elise's handwriting. I was relieved to see that there weren't too many. It could wait until I got home.

There was another, smaller envelope inside the manila envelope. I shook it out. It was addressed to me, care of my publishers, but there was no return address on it. I slit the envelope open. It contained a single typed page. I looked to see who it was from and almost choked when I read the name. Jonathan.

'What is it?' Yasmin asked.

'It's a letter from Jonathan. What a damned cheek after all these years.' I handed her the page. 'He wants to meet me. Can you believe it?'

'Well, perhaps you should meet him,' she said.

'You must be out of your mind . . .'

Yasmin interrupted. 'I wonder how he knew where to contact you. I don't quite picture him as a reader of romances.'

'He probably saw one of my television interviews,' I said indignantly.

'Give the man a chance, Meena,' Yasmin said handing the letter back to me. 'He seems nice enough.'

'Oh sure,' I said scornfully.

I wasn't in the least bit interested, but it was curious that he had suddenly decided to look for me.

He said in the letter that there were reasons why he had not contacted me when I had first arrived in London all those years ago. He wanted to explain what had happened.

'He probably has some lame-brain excuse,' I muttered. 'Anyway, who cares? It was such a long time ago. Why would it matter now?'

Yasmin smiled surreptitiously, obviously thinking that she knew me better than I knew myself.

I slid Jonathan's letter back into the manila envelope and placed it on the dresser.

Then, as I lay back on the bed, I thought it might not be such a bad idea to consider his invitation. I was always looking for new material. Perhaps an encounter with him would provide me with a few interesting ideas for my next project.

I dismissed the thought as quickly as it had surfaced. I had too many things on my mind and Jonathan and his explanations were not priorities.

54

WHEN SORAYA was still not home by eight, Yasmin and I drove the *bakkie* into town.

We drove around the town's few restaurants and nightspots, but there was no sign of the rented car or Soraya.

'Where could she be?' Yasmin asked anxiously.

'She's had quite a day,' I reminded her. 'And it didn't help the way you blurted everything out to Ma.'

Yasmin pursed her lips. 'Ma seems to have taken the whole thing in her stride. As usual, she's laid the blame on me. Soraya messes up, and I get the blame.'

'Soraya is your daughter.'

'I don't want her to make the same mistakes. Remember how when I was raped some people said I'd probably asked for it.'

'Rubbish! You didn't deserve what happened to you.'

'Underneath all the success my life really is quite a mess, isn't it?' she said.

I didn't respond.

'I don't want Soraya to some day have the same regrets that I have.'

Yasmin was tormented by feelings that none of us really understood. Yet I still felt compelled to make her face up to what was happening between her and her daughter.

'Some problems will have to be resolved by your conscience, Yas, but right now you have to think of Soraya. You must help her get through this difficult time. And Ma's right. You did neglect her. You took her away from McBain, and then you neglected her.'

'She had everything she needed.'

'She had everything but her mother,' I said.

Yasmin sighed dejectedly. 'I don't know how to deal with her. She's made it clear that she has her own life and doesn't need me.'

'That's the pain talking,' I said. 'Perhaps this has to do with you and Neville?'

'In spite of everything, I tried to provide a stable home for her.'

'In spite of what?' I asked.

She shrugged.

I waited for her to speak. I was determined to get to the bottom of things. There were too many secrets in our family. Too many bones rattling in the closets.

'Oh for heaven's sake,' she snapped impatiently. 'It's the usual thing.'

'Like what?' I persisted.

'Neville and I are splitting up. We've grown apart. I've offered to sell my business, but he says the gesture is too little too late. I've worked hard for what I have, Meena. I can't just throw it away.' Then, with a shrug, she said: 'Anyway, we've reached a stalemate.'

'What's going to happen?'

'I don't know.'

'Yasmin . . .'

'He wants to rent a camper and go fishing. It's not my style. I'm not ready to retire. I'll sell the business, but I want to do something else with my life.'

'And he resents that?'

'I don't know. Maybe there's more to it than he's telling me. It's too late, Meena. Nothing is going to fix our marriage. That's why I want Soraya to get out of this mess with Douglas.'

'There must be something more, Yasmin. It's not like Neville to give up on you. He's known you for too long and he's lived through the worst of times with you. What really happened?'

She was silent for a long time. Then: 'He wanted a child,' she said simply. 'There was no room in my life for another child. I already had Soraya. And so I lied. I told him I had had my tubes tied after Soraya.'

She paused.

'Despite all my precautions, I fell pregnant two years after we were married. At that stage I hadn't even come to terms with Soraya yet.' She gazed out into the darkness. 'I had an abortion. I thought my secret was safe. Then five years ago he found some old hospital bills while he was cleaning out the attic. If I could place a marker at various points of my life, and go back to change things, that would be one of them.'

'How could you, Yasmin? How could you live a life of such deception?'

'I already had a child and I couldn't take care of her. How could I possibly have coped with another? Some of us are cut out to be mothers – clearly I'm not.'

'Poor Neville,' I said.

'Rubbish!'

'Yas . . .'

'Now he's suggesting that it might not even have been his child. Can you imagine that? I have never been unfaithful to him. What we had is broken. Nothing I say or do will fix it.'

'Does Ma know about any of this?' I asked.

'No. And don't you mention a word about it to anyone. You think you know someone, but you never do, no matter how long you live with them.'

I listened to the rationalisations. This was the alter-ego talking. Yasmin was hurting. She cared for Neville and I saw the tears before she brushed them away. She didn't want anyone to know how miserable she was.

'You should make things up with Soraya,' I said.

She nodded. 'Of course I will. I do love her, but I can't condone what she's done.'

'Soraya's searching for something. Ma and I both picked it up. She's been trying to find some missing element in her life – I think maybe she's looking for a father. I think you should tell her the truth about her father. What she needs is closure.'

'Never! It will only create more problems. The past is dead and buried.'

I shook my head. 'I think you're wrong about that. I think she needs to know the truth now. She's a woman, she can deal with whatever you have to say.'

'No,' Yasmin said. 'She'll never understand.'

'The only father-figures in her life were Papa and Neville. You must tell her the truth about her biological father,' I insisted.

We had by then driven past most of the likely places where Soraya might be, but there was no sign of her.

'You must keep the channels open between the two of you, Yas,' I urged.

'I've tried, but these days we can't even have a normal conversation.'

'If Nana were alive she would've told Soraya to go back immediately to face the music with Gwen.'

Yasmin made no comment.

'Do you want to stop at the police station?' I asked.

'Should we?' she asked, suddenly panic-stricken. 'Do you think something might have happened?'

'Probably not. But let's check anyway.' We drove to the police station. I helped her out of the car and into the building. We asked whether there had been any reports of accidents. The African constable glanced at us curiously.

'There have been some,' he said cautiously.

'We're from McBain . . .'

'Oh, *ja*! I know the place. How is Mrs Mohammed?'

'She's fine,' I said.

'Are you the daughter?'

I nodded.

'Your name is Meena?' he asked.

'Yes,' I said a little hesitantly, aware, of course, that many people in the area knew our family.

'Oh, ho!' he cried, seizing my hand. 'I am Sandile's brother Vulani. You remember Sandile?'

'Yes, of course,' I said. 'Where is he? How is he?'

'He is a doctor. He's in London.'

'I live in London, too!' I said excitedly. 'You must give me his phone number and his address.'

'Come again. I will bring it.' Vulani beamed while Yasmin drummed her manicured nails on the desk, waiting for me to ask about Soraya.

'We'll talk again,' I said. 'Right now we're a bit worried about my niece. We had an argument and she drove away. It's late and we haven't heard from her. This is her mother,' I said, gesturing towards Yasmin. 'We were wondering if you might have heard something?'

Vulani smiled at Yasmin, who nodded regally. He checked his records and obligingly made some phone calls. There was no report about a young woman being found. Now we had dealt with this worry, Yasmin was even more agitated.

She wanted to get home immediately in case Soraya had returned while we were away.

'I'll stop by soon,' I said to Vulani. 'I look forward to seeing Sandile again. It's been a long time.'

He walked us to the door. 'Go carefully,' he said in Xhosa.

Soraya was not home and we spent a frightful night waiting. We lay in bed, listening for the telephone, hoping it might ring, yet dreading that it might bring bad news.

She returned the following morning. Even I was cross with her for not having contacted us.

'I was at a hotel in town.'

'We went to town to look for you,' I said.

'Why?' she asked sharply.

'We were worried about you, Soraya,' Yasmin said.

'I expected a little more consideration from you,' Ma added.

'We were all worried sick,' Yasmin said, her voice rising angrily. 'Do you know what terrible thoughts I had? I was almost out of my mind.'

Soraya just looked at her. How the tables had turned, I

thought, remembering the times Yasmin had caused us the same kind of anxiety.

'You could have phoned,' Yasmin insisted. 'They have phones in hotels, don't they?'

'I didn't feel like talking to you,' she said. 'I still don't. I phoned Neville.'

'Neville?' Yasmin said.

Soraya met her mother's gaze. 'I spoke to him about Douglas.'

'And?'

'He said that if it hadn't been me, it would have been someone else.'

Furious, Yasmin struggled out of her chair. She grabbed hold of Soraya's arm to support herself, her grip vice-like, and led her to the bedroom. She shut the door behind them. They were in there for a long time.

Yasmin and Soraya were alike in so many respects. Perhaps that was why they weren't able to get on. I hoped that they would eventually resolve their problems and become friends. I didn't want Soraya to be alienated from her mother the way I had been from both my parents.

I thought of my father and Yasmin, and how expert she had been at playing up to him. She had been the focus of his life, just as Soraya had become later on.

Poor Nana – how she must have squirmed inwardly whenever she saw my father with Yasmin while I, like a stranger in their midst, stood to one side watching, my heart aching for a bit of the love that my parents lavished on my sister.

55

THE COUNTER-OFFER for McBain, hammered out by Yasmin, was accepted. The agent showed us the cheque for the deposit, which Yasmin had written in as a condition of the sale. With the sale suddenly becoming a reality, Ma began to waver again.

'Perhaps I should have rented the place out,' she said. 'Selling is so final.'

'Nonsense, Ma,' Yasmin scolded. 'Come on now, snap out of it. It's a done deal.'

'I certainly didn't expect them to accept the counter-offer,' said the agent, slightly awed by Yasmin.

'I told you,' Yasmin said, pleased with herself. 'If you want something badly enough, the price is never an issue.'

'You certainly know your stuff,' Ma said, giving her a hug. She was pleased with Yasmin's accomplishment and set aside her reservations for the moment.

'You're free now, Ma,' Soraya added.

'One is never free, child. Never.' Ma's expression was still anxious.

'I thought you'd be relieved,' Yasmin said.

'Of course I am, but this has been my home for a long time, you know.'

Soraya and I traded glances over the rims of our teacups.

'My mother is buried in this country and so is your father. Who will look after their graves when I'm gone? I just wonder if I'll ever come back here again.'

'Of course you will, Ma,' Yasmin said. 'You can come and

visit whenever you want to. You know you'll always be welcome at Aishaben's.'

Ma turned and gave her a long look, then she smiled – a smile tinged with sadness. 'I'm leaving a lot behind me – my whole history – a past, friends, loved ones . . . I don't know.'

That afternoon Ma quietly disappeared. Yasmin and I saw her driving away.

'Where on earth does she go?' I asked.

'Don't tell me you don't know?' Yasmin said.

I shook my head.

She laughed. 'You are so naïve, little sister,' she said, eyes twinkling with amusement.

'What do you mean?' I asked, piqued by her attitude.

'Ma goes to see Sergeant Klein.'

'Nonsense. That man must be ancient by now.'

'He's in a nursing home in town. She goes to visit him there.'

'But why?'

'They've been friends for a long time, ever since Papa died.'

I looked at her incredulously, but then remembered that Sergeant Klein seemed always to have been around; even on the day of our eviction from Soetstroom he had been there to watch out for us.

'I think he may even have been in love with her,' Yasmin said. 'Perhaps Ma knew, and that's why she turned to him for help. She knew she could trust him.'

'How do you know all this?'

'I asked her.'

'Where's Sergeant Klein's family?' I wanted to know.

'His wife died a long time ago. And his children don't have much time for him.'

'But if he's in a nursing home . . .?'

'Look, I don't know all the details,' she said irritably. 'If you want to know, ask Ma.'

I knew that I could never ask my mother, not after the incident with the letters.

That evening as Ma and Soraya were preparing supper, Ma's eyes moistened, she turned her head and quietly brushed away the tears.

'Why are you crying, Ma?' Soraya asked.

For a long while Ma didn't say anything, then she said: 'I was just thinking of all the terrible things that happened before you left South Africa, my child, all those years ago.'

I remembered too.

Despite Ma's protests about all the work she still had to do, she made no move to get out of her chair. We remained on the stoep, a luxurious laziness creeping over us in the glorious sunshine. Exhaustion had set in. For weeks now we had packed and unpacked, carried, ripped, thrown out, agonised and laughed.

Everything was under control.

Then the phone rang. The call was for Soraya. Ma, who had answered the phone, told us that it was a man.

'I'd have been quite happy to have stayed here with her,' Ma said quietly as Soraya went to the phone. 'In time she'd have forgotten about him.'

Yasmin, obviously pained by Ma's remark, turned away.

Ma glared at us. 'You've made a fine mess between the two of you.'

'Did you really think Soraya would bury herself here at McBain, Ma?' Yasmin asked.

Ma didn't reply.

Soraya returned.

'Who was that on the phone?' Ma asked.

Soraya ignored the question. We waited, but Soraya said no more.

I studied her, trying to determine what Gladys had meant when she said that Soraya was 'not right'. I wanted to believe that she was fine now that everything was out in the open. We had all done our share of digging, trying to find further ammunition to fire at her. Ma was wrong though. What Soraya probably needed was to get back to London to sort her life out. The sooner the better, I thought.

Soraya went inside and then returned a little while later. 'May I make a long distance call, Ma?' She saw the look on Yasmin's face. 'Don't worry,' she said, 'I'm just calling a friend.'

'What about her friends?' Ma asked us. 'Are they all white?'

Yasmin nodded.

'Don't you have friends from other backgrounds? What about other South Africans, people who share our way of thinking?' Ma frowned. 'You people have forgotten where you come from. Yasmin married a white man and has white friends – I think it's a very narrow outlook.'

It was difficult to make Ma understand that because we had lived abroad for such a long time, we had become assimilated into a different culture. We were no longer South African. It was only the childhood memories that kept us connected – and in my case it was a connection not to South Africa, but to McBain.

56

ALL THE packing was done. Ma, Yasmin and I were having coffee on the stoep, enjoying the morning air. Gladys was in the kitchen with Soraya, who was playing her flute. Although still cool and pleasant at that early hour, the weather forecast had predicted another scorching day.

I could hear the murmur of Gladys's voice as she talked to Soraya above the sound of the flute.

My attention returned to my mother and Yasmin who were revisiting the past.

'Remember the day Hermanus Steyn arrived, using the excuse of the rabies scare?' Yasmin asked.

'There *was* a rabies outbreak,' Ma said. 'I heard about it on the radio.'

'And he took advantage of that to come and snoop,' Yasmin said.

'Who would have thought that such an important man would die such a lonely death?' I said, lazily fanning my face with an old straw hat. 'I guess that's what Nana meant by Divine Retribution.'

We had heard long after the event that Hermanus Steyn had been thrown by his horse and had died alone in the veld. His body, half devoured by jackals, was found three days later.

'It was pretty grim, wasn't it?' Yasmin shuddered.

'In those days it was just one thing after another,' Ma said.

'I've always wondered how Hermanus Steyn heard about my plans to take Soraya out of the country,' Yasmin said.

'Remember the party line?' Ma replied. 'No doubt the De

Wets overheard us and told him.'

'What turmoil over a dog!'

'It was a dreadful time for all of us,' Ma said.

'It was an awful time,' Yasmin agreed.

'But it was a good thing he was there to help with Birdie,' I said.

'And the old man died without ever acknowledging his grandchild,' Yasmin added bitterly.

'At least he tried to make amends in his own way,' Ma said.

I'd been half-listening to the conversation and half-listening to Soraya playing the flute. I registered vaguely that the music had stopped.

'I confronted him, you know,' Yasmin went on, 'the day Birdie was killed. And he still wouldn't admit that Cobus had raped me. According to him it wasn't rape at all. That insistence on protecting his son. I could never have forgiven him for that. But if only he had said, just once, Soraya is my son's child . . .'

As Yasmin spoke, I looked up and choked back a cry. Soraya was standing in the doorway. It was clear she had heard every word.

She stepped forward, her eyes like daggers.

'So what happened, Yasmin? Couldn't you get yourself an abortion? What a shame. How disappointing for you.'

Yasmin paled.

'All these years,' Soraya said very quietly, 'you've been lying to me. Couldn't you have told me the truth? Just once, could you not have told the truth? Any of you?'

Yasmin struggled to find words.

'I was afraid,' Yasmin said. 'I was afraid.'

'And perhaps I would have understood,' Soraya said, her cold glance sweeping our faces, condemning us all. 'But you all turned my life into a lie. My whole existence is a fabrication.'

Gladys stood in the doorway watching the drama unfold. Speechless with anxiety, Yasmin reached for her daughter.

'Please, Soraya,' she pleaded. 'It's all in the past. Let's bury it.'

'Bury it? All you've done since you've got here is dig up the past. Why can't you dig up the truth for a change?'

Now came the anger. Her lips were white and tears streamed down her cheeks. I started to get out of my chair.

'No!' she cried sharply. 'Don't touch me. Any of you.' She walked slowly into the house. We heard the bedroom door close softly.

Yasmin's expression was gaunt as she looked at Ma for help. We had never seen Soraya like this.

'Go to her, Yasmin,' Ma said.

Yasmin limped into the house. Then we heard their raised voices.

'I'm going back to London tomorrow!' Soraya shouted. 'I can't stand being under the same roof as you.'

'Calm down, Soraya,' Yasmin said. 'Be reasonable.'

'Reasonable? Why reason with a liar? Why would you start telling the truth now?'

'There's nothing more to it,' Yasmin said.

'Go to hell! I don't want to talk to you. You make me sick!'

'We were only trying to protect you.'

'Protect me!' she cried scornfully. 'What you were trying to do was control me . . .'

'Please, just be rational about this . . .'

We heard first the bedroom door slam, then the back door. It sounded like two gunshots.

Yasmin returned. She limped to a chair and sank into it.

'Give her time to cool off,' Ma said.

Eventually Yasmin fell asleep on the sofa, exhausted. I studied her face in repose, long lustrous lashes spread against the upper ridge of her cheek. There was an innocence there. I felt a warm rush of affection for my sister. Asleep, she looked so childlike, so vulnerable. I was glad now that Ma had burnt all her letters.

Yasmin would never hear the secret of her paternity from me. Some things, in this case even the truth, were better buried for ever.

Yasmin was still asleep when I left the house and went in search of Soraya. I found her sitting on a rock in the shade of a tree that Ma had planted near the schoolhouse.

She watched me approach with listless eyes, her face wan, all the vitality drained out of her.

'May I join you?' I asked.

She moved over and made room for me on the rock. We sat in silence for a long time. She was trying to affect indifference. But I knew her well. I knew that beneath the detachment was turmoil and agony. I waited patiently for her to say something. I didn't want to intrude on her space. She had to be the one to speak first.

Eventually, in a low voice that trembled with emotion, she asked: 'Why, Meena? Why has Yasmin turned our lives into such hell with all her lies?'

'She was trying to protect you, Soraya. She loves you.'

'She's incapable of love. I can't understand why Ma allowed her to take me away.'

I couldn't bring myself to answer because I didn't want to cause her further pain. I knew that she was angry not only with Yasmin, but that she also blamed Ma and me for the deception. I feared that anything I said would only make matters worse. I prayed for guidance. Then I picked my words carefully.

'Ma was heart-broken when you left,' I said. 'And Papa doted on you. You were the centre of our lives.'

'But not Yasmin's life,' she said coldly.

'Yes, Yasmin left. She had her reasons. But you were there to connect us to her. You gave us hope and you filled a void in our lives. You turned a tragedy into a blessing. You might not have had Yasmin, Soraya, but you were loved, deeply loved . . .'

Still she said nothing. She was waiting for me to make my point and I was taking a long time getting there.

'What I'm trying to say,' I continued, 'is that regardless of what happened, what you believed or what you were told, you were always loved.'

'Yasmin could hardly wait to get away from me. She abandoned me.'

'We might not agree about her reasons for leaving,' I replied, 'but, believe me, she was devastated by everything that had happened. How could she not have been? She was brutally raped, completely traumatised. She was young and had no idea what to do. She didn't want to tell the family because Cobus had threatened to kill all of us if she did.'

Soraya looked at me in disbelief.

'It's true. I found her. We were terrified that Cobus would carry out his threat. There was no one who could help us.'

Soraya leaned back against the tree. She avoided my eyes, but I could tell that she was moved. But still she resisted my attempts to rationalise Yasmin's behaviour.

But I persevered because I wanted her to understand and to grasp the desperate nature of Yasmin's situation in its particular time frame.

'Yasmin was a restless teenager,' I said. 'I became restless and dissatisfied myself as I got older, so I understood what it was like for her. She was a beautiful young girl trapped in a small town where she wasn't allowed to be herself, to be free.'

What we had gone through during the apartheid years must have seemed absurd and improbable to Soraya. One had to have had first-hand experience to truly comprehend it.

'It was terrible growing up under apartheid, knowing there was more to life than you would ever be able to experience,' I said. 'It was like having your legs cut off just as you were learning to walk. You saw others – whites – living differently, having what you could never have simply because you were not the right colour. It made you bitter. Yasmin was beautiful and vivacious and thought she had the world at her feet, but she was stopped dead by the system which controlled our lives.'

Soraya was toying absently with the hem of her T-shirt. I could tell that she had taken in every word. Her eyes were bright with tears.

'Despite the fact that Yasmin had more in her little finger than all the white girls in Soetstroom put together, she was always on the outside looking in. They were envious of her because she was beautiful and confident, but at the same time they disdained her, knowing that she would never be their equal because she was a coolie *meid*. That's what they used to call us.'

Soraya's eyes met mine. She had stopped resisting me. She was listening and beginning to understand the forces that had shaped Yasmin's character.

'She loved to ride. At one point she wanted to be an equestrienne.' I smiled as I remembered that particular phase in Yasmin's life. 'She used to borrow Blitzen, the mare that belonged to the chief.'

'I remember the horse,' Soraya said. 'It died some time in the eighties – just before Neville and Yasmin and I came for a visit.'

'Cobus Steyn, the man who raped your mother, was the blight of our lives.' I spoke with the patience and clarity I would have used to a child. 'They were Afrikaners with a lot of influence – his father Hermanus was the local MP. From the time he was a young boy, Cobus did everything he could to make our lives unbearable.'

'And I suppose because he was white, nothing could be done about it.'

'Exactly. His father was a powerful man in the community – he was above the law. That was another reason we didn't go to the police when Yasmin was raped. In those days, the law was so convoluted that a white man who raped a non-white woman usually got off scot-free, while the woman went to jail. The woman was blamed for enticing the man. We were terrified that the same fate awaited Yasmin.'

I paused. Soraya was not ignorant about what life had been like under apartheid for it was something we had often talked about but, although she was listening politely, this was clearly not what she wanted to hear.

'The rape itself was so traumatic for all of us,' I continued, 'that we could not even contemplate the thought of Yasmin going to jail. So we kept quiet. We didn't lose our lives, but we paid the price in other ways. Yasmin can be regarded as a casualty of apartheid, Soraya.'

'So I was conceived when Yasmin was raped,' she said pointedly.

I nodded. Suddenly I wished that I hadn't started all this. I knew what her next question would be, and I knew that I couldn't answer it. How could I possibly tell her the truth?

'Did she try to get an abortion?' Soraya asked starkly.

I didn't answer immediately.

'Tell me the truth, Meena.'

I gazed at the horizon hoping that the hills that had always given me solace would now give me inspiration.

Soraya waited. I couldn't bring myself to say the words.

Still she waited, her eyes riveted on me, searching for the truth.

I took a deep breath. Then I nodded and met her gaze.

'Abortion was a consideration. Imagine what it was like for her, a young girl who had been raped, who had no recourse to the law, and had to be reminded of her violation for the rest of her life.'

Soraya got up and took a few steps into the sunlight. I watched her, waiting for her to speak.

Finally, she turned back to me.

'I understand, Meena. I'm not stupid.'

'But it didn't happen, Soraya. And you were raised by a loving family who adored you.'

'All my life Yasmin was there, imposing her will on me, making decisions for me,' Soraya said. 'I could never break free. I only wanted something precious for myself.'

I knew what she was talking about.

'Douglas had a wife, Soraya,' I said gently.

Soraya's eyes filled with tears. I got up and put my arms around her.

'Don't blame Yasmin,' I said.

Soraya cried against my shoulder. Her tears were bitter and anguished. Surprised by the intensity of her reaction, I had no words to comfort her. I could only hold her, trying to console her with my silent love, until there were no tears left – only the dry racking sobs of despair.

It was better that the tears flowed. Now, perhaps, the healing could begin.

57

SORAYA HAD gone for a walk. She told me she wanted to be alone for a while.

'I'll go and look for her,' Ma said when she hadn't returned by mid-afternoon.

'She's probably walking along the tracks,' I said.

'I don't know where this track business got started. First Meena and now Soraya.' Ma got up, wincing. She paused to press her hands into the small of her back and then slowly descended the steps.

'Oh, yes,' she said, turning back. 'I'd like to prepare one last big meal. A farewell dinner. Meena, see if you can find the boxes with the dishes.'

'For goodness' sake, Ma,' I groaned.

Ma ignored my protest. 'You won't have to repack the boxes. I'll leave my dishes for Gladys. Soraya labelled all the boxes, so it shouldn't be a problem finding them. Come on, you two, we've been lazing around long enough. There's work to be done.' Ma marched off.

'I wish this were all over,' I mumbled. 'I want to get home.'

'So do I,' said Yasmin. 'I've finally made up my mind to sell my business and my label to the American company. They've been interested for some time now. I really should leave soon.'

'I'm sure it can be arranged. But Ma won't leave until the sale has been completed,' I said.

'The transfer should be through soon. Would you mind staying on with Ma until then?'

I didn't say anything. Yasmin had clearly taken for granted that I would stay.

We went into the kitchen to begin the preparations for dinner. I looked out the window and saw Ma and Soraya walking away from the house. They were walking slowly, heads down, deep in conversation. Occasionally Ma stopped to gesture, pointing to the hills and to McBain.

Yasmin joined me at the window.

'Yas,' I said. 'Please don't be upset. Soraya and I had a long talk.'

'Why didn't she come and speak to me?'

'You'll have ample opportunity to fill in the gaps,' I said. 'Give her time.'

Ma and Soraya were gone for a long time. Eventually I sent Florence to find them. She returned a while later to say that they were on their way back.

We watched as Ma and Soraya carefully picked their way past the pot-holes in the driveway. Ma was holding on to Soraya's arm.

When they reached the stoep Soraya glanced up, saw her mother, brushed past her and went into the house. Ma joined us, her eyes full of sadness. She had been crying.

'Are you all right, Ma?' I asked.

She nodded, but I could tell that something quite upsetting had happened between her and Soraya.

'We were getting worried about you,' I said.

Ma drew a deep breath as if gathering her thoughts.

'We walked way past the crossing before turning back,' she said.

Soraya returned to the stoep, avoiding Yasmin's eyes.

'Tell them, Soraya,' Ma said.

Soraya paused, anxious eyes darting to Yasmin and then back to Ma.

'About your decision,' Ma urged, as if cueing her.

Soraya said: 'I'm staying on. I'll leave with Ma.' She directed this comment at no one in particular.

Yasmin was concerned. 'Don't you think you should get back?' she said. 'The longer you're away the worse it'll be for you.'

'Soraya and I've had a long talk,' Ma said. 'We've discussed all sorts of things.'

Yasmin's eyes narrowed, her mouth opened as if to respond, but Ma flashed her a warning glance.

'Please, no more fighting. Come. Let's go talk.'

Yasmin and I followed her into the kitchen, but Soraya remained outside.

'As soon as things are settled here and we have the cheque, Soraya and I'll follow. It shouldn't be much longer now,' Ma said as we sat down.

I knew intuitively that there was a lot more behind this decision, but I didn't want to think about all the possibilities. I wanted to go home.

My mother wanted to be positive. She said that all the negativity was attracting a Bad Karma.

I smiled. It was a typical Nana-comment. My mother didn't believe in things like karma. It seemed that much had changed in my mother's thinking. She also seemed a lot less inflexible and was definitely more relaxed.

'I wonder where all this is going to end,' I mused aloud.

'I don't know, Meena. It's up to Soraya and Yasmin now.' Ma looked pointedly at Yasmin. 'I've put it all in the hands of the Good Lord. He'll take care of us. Perhaps getting rid of McBain will give us a new beginning. I wish your Nana was here. She always knew what to do.'

She paused, then looked first at me and then at Yasmin.

'How soon do you want to leave?' she asked.

'Monday,' Yasmin said. 'I have to contact the American group and set up a meeting with my lawyers. I must get back as soon as possible. But I'm worried about Soraya.'

Soraya came into the kitchen at that point. She stood in the doorway, her eyes lowered, focusing on her rings, her fingers, the back of her hands – anywhere but on the faces around her.

'We shouldn't be longer than a week or two,' Ma said.

'Good, then I'll leave with you, Yasmin,' I said.

Yasmin nodded quickly, then looked at Ma for confirmation.

'It's fine,' Ma said. 'Everything here is practically done.'

'I'm sure everything will be all right,' Yasmin said. 'The agent seems to be reliable.'

'She'd better be,' Ma said sharply. 'I can't take any more problems. In these last few days I've had enough for a lifetime.'

Yasmin glanced at Ma, but Ma had that pursed, closed-mouth look which we knew so well.

'What's going on, Ma?' Yasmin demanded.

'I want the two of you to bury this thing between you,' Ma said. 'You're going to need each other, you know.'

Yasmin sighed, pushed her chair back and went to her daughter. She put her arms around her. The two of them clung to each other for a brief moment, then Soraya released her mother.

We sat down to the evening meal, none of us with much of an appetite, but since Ma had cooked we were obliged to eat. After the supper dishes had been cleared, Yasmin said: 'Ma, now remember, you're not to stay on at McBain after we're gone. You either stay in the city with Aishaben or at a hotel in town. It's not safe out here on your own.'

Ma rolled her eyes at me.

'Soraya, I don't want you people coming back here after we've gone. Is that clear?' Yasmin said.

'Oh, for crying out aloud! We're not children!' Soraya exclaimed irritably.

'Now, look here,' Yasmin started. She was about to fire another salvo at Soraya, but caught my eye. I gave an imperceptible shake of my head and Yasmin swallowed her words, smiling thinly. 'I'm sorry,' she muttered.

Soraya turned from Yasmin and started to move away.

'Give her a hug,' I whispered to Yasmin.

Yasmin followed Soraya out of the room. The door closed behind her.

'It's time, Ma,' I said. She knew what I meant.

'Soraya says the two of you spoke.'

'Yes.'

'I'm glad.'

'They need to talk,' I said, 'or this will be between them for the rest of their lives.'

We heard raised voices, and then the sound of crying.

Much later, Soraya and Yasmin joined us in the kitchen. Their eyes were red and swollen. I could see that the two of them had touched on a lot of pain.

With a wry smile, Yasmin said: 'You were right, Ma. I should have done this a long time ago.'

Ma put an arm around each of them, but there was something in her face, a look of anxiety, that made me wonder whether the storm was truly over.

'There now,' Ma said. 'The two of you can go home and Soraya and I will follow.'

'Are you sure that's what you want, Soraya?' Yasmin asked gently.

'Yes,' Soraya said. She was still a little distant.

'That's settled then,' Yasmin said with a smile of relief.

The phone rang and Yasmin went to answer it.

'It's for you, Ma,' she called.

'Who is it?'

'The nursing home.'

Ma took the phone from her and listened, her expression slowly crumpling. After she had hung up she stood motionless for a few moments, her hand resting on the phone.

'What's wrong, Ma?' I asked.

'Another friend gone,' she sighed, her voice catching. She turned away and went outside.

'Sergeant Klein.' Yasmin mouthed at me.

I waited for a few minutes and then went outside to comfort my mother.

A few days before Yasmin and I were due to leave, Gladys drew me aside. 'You people must look well after my Soraya,' she said in Afrikaans. 'I may never see her again after she leaves.'

'We will, Gladys, but she's a big girl now.'

'Sometimes you people are too hard on her.'

I was surprised that Gladys would think we were too hard on her or that we would expect too much of her.

I watched my mother and Soraya. There appeared to be something new in their relationship. I noticed the look in my mother's eyes, the protectiveness that had emerged in the last few days.

Everything movable had been disposed of. Whatever remained would be given to Gladys. We had already made one trip to the village, the *bakkie* filled with boxes.

Ma had worried about the place standing vacant, but Gladys said she'd send someone to stay in the house. The agent passed on Ma's concerns to the purchasing company and they moved up the possession date. The paperwork and transfers were completed in record time. It didn't matter to my mother that the house was eventually going to be demolished; she could not reconcile herself to leaving it empty and abandoned. If she had her way, she would have stayed on right to the bitter end.

'What are you going to do with the *bakkie*, Ma?' I asked.

'Father Menzies at the Seminary wants to buy it,' she said. 'He'll pick it up before we leave.'

The agent promised that the cheque would be delivered before Ma left. She assured us that the purchaser was a reputable company and there was no need for concern; our deal was a drop in the bucket for them.

Ma and Soraya were to drive us to the airport in the rented car. They would keep the car for a few days longer. Ma said that she and Soraya might spend a few days with Aishaben before driving out to McBain for the last time. Ma assured us that if they were late, they'd stay over at a hotel in town.

'Just a few more things I want to clear out,' Ma explained. 'It won't take long.'

I stole a glance at Soraya. She seemed composed and a lot

calmer than I had seen her in some time.

On the day of our departure Ma was waiting on the stoep, gazing into the distance. She had still not let go. She'd find many reasons to return.

While the others were occupied outside, I sneaked off to the kitchen window to take a last look at the tracks and the deserted railway cottages. To my surprise, I noticed smoke curling up from the chimney at the Bothas' cottage. I was about to turn away, thinking that squatters had probably moved in, when I noticed a woman, unmistakably Elsa, standing in the yard. As if sensing me at the window, she looked in my direction. I waved, but there was no answering wave and then she went indoors.

'For goodness' sake, Meena, will you hurry up!' Yasmin said impatiently. 'I still want to stop at the cemetery.'

I went with her. I wanted to tell her about Elsa, but I didn't think she would care.

We said our goodbyes to Gladys.

'Go well,' Gladys said in Xhosa, hugging first Yasmin and then me. She started to cry. I tried to control the tears, but by this time they were running freely. Yasmin clung to Gladys for a moment longer and then turned away quickly.

'Stay well, Gladys,' I responded.

We stopped off at Aishaben to say goodbye and then made a quick stop at the cemetery where Yasmin placed flowers on Nana's and Papa's graves.

At the airport Soraya clung a little longer to Yasmin than I would have expected. Yasmin, convinced that the conflict was over, hugged her daughter.

'I didn't want you to be hurt, Soraya,' she whispered. 'I'm so sorry.'

'I'm sorry too,' Soraya said.

In the bus which took us across the tarmac to our plane, I wondered what new secrets my mother had become privy to. In my mind's eyes I saw her face the day she and Soraya had returned from their long walk along the tracks.

Yasmin imperceptibly raised a tissue to her eyes. I assumed that our departure was a relief from all the tension. I doubted that she would ever miss McBain but then, with Yasmin, one never knew.

Once on board the plane I realised how exhausted I was. Yasmin was irritated when she realised that the parcel so carefully wrapped in brown paper, which I was lugging with me, was the plaque I had taken from McBain. It was something of Papa's that I wanted to keep. I was glad now, as the flight attendant took the parcel from me to stow elsewhere, that Yasmin had upgraded my economy class ticket to first class.

'Did you have to drag that old thing with you?' she complained as we took our seats.

She didn't understand. How could she? She had never had to compete for our father's – my father's – attention. She had had it, whether she was there or not.

Grateful for the comfort of the first class seat, I stretched out and breathed a sigh of relief. At last I could allow myself to relax. I was on my way home. I felt like Tiffany on her way to Zurich to meet her lover. *Tomorrow My Love* had been my fourth book.

Yasmin seemed preoccupied. I guessed that she had already switched off McBain and tuned in to her business in London.

It was nice to share this time with her – we rarely had the opportunity to be together like this when we were in London. Yasmin was always on the run. Nana had once remarked that it was as though she were trying to outrun herself.

We taxied on to the runway. The flight attendant strolled through the cabin checking that our seat belts were buckled.

I stole a glance at Yasmin and mused about the irony that Yasmin, who had been Papa's entire life, was not even his daughter and I, who was his daughter, had always been treated like an outsider.

Life works in mysterious ways, Nana used to say.

It could not have worked more mysteriously than it had in our family.

'Think we'll ever see this part of the world again?' Yasmin asked.

'Who knows? Remember, Nana used to say don't ever throw the key away. You never know when you might want to go through that door again.'

'Well, I will definitely not be coming this way again,' she said with finality.

58

WE WERE preparing for our descent into Johannesburg International Airport where we were to connect with our London flight.

We were both relaxed. In a few hours we'd be on our way home.

The flight attendant approached.

'Excuse me, Mrs Kingsley, Miss Mohammed,' she said.

Yasmin and I both glanced up.

'We've just had a message for you, Mrs Kingsley,' she said gravely.

'Yes?' Yasmin said.

'There's a family emergency. We were asked to notify you. The message is from your mother. She would like you to return immediately.'

I was concerned by the seriousness of her tone.

'Did she say what kind of emergency?' Yasmin asked.

'There's been an accident. Your mother wants you to meet her at the hospital,' the attendant said.

'Is our mother all right?' I was alarmed now.

'What about my daughter?' Yasmin wanted to know.

The attendant shrugged. 'I'm sorry. I have no idea. All I have is the message which was relayed to us. There's a flight back at two o'clock. You'll have enough time to make it. I've taken the liberty of reserving two seats for you.'

'Is there a phone we can use?' Yasmin asked.

'We'll be landing in a few minutes. It would be better to call once we're on the ground,' she said.

We phoned the hospital as soon as we landed. The duty sister confirmed that Ma and Soraya had been admitted to casualty. She told us that they'd been in an accident, but that there was nothing conclusive to report yet. The doctor hadn't seen Ma, but she was sitting up, talking. Soraya was still in radiology.

'It can't be that bad then, can it?' Yasmin said to me after the phone call. 'If they were badly injured, they'd have told us, I'm sure . . . Dammit, Soraya drives too fast. I've warned her . . .' Yasmin started, but I stopped her pointless speculations.

The flight back to the city was the longest hour and a quarter of my life. Yasmin and I explored every possible scenario. We hired a car at the airport and drove back to the city. On our way we passed two wrecked cars being towed away. I had a sick feeling in the pit of my stomach.

'That looks like our car,' Yasmin said, craning her neck as we passed. It was a total wreck and I didn't want to contemplate the condition of its passengers.

Ma was lying in a bed in the casualty ward looking very pale and shaken. Apart from some bruises and a cut above one eye, which had already been attended to, she appeared relatively unscathed. The nurse taking care of her assured us that her injuries were not serious. They were waiting to take her for X-rays and then the doctor would decide what to do with her. The nurse thought it likely she'd be admitted for a day or two, for observation.

Yasmin wanted to know about Soraya.

'How is she?' she pleaded.

'I don't know,' the nurse said. 'It's too soon to tell. She has a serious head injury. But the doctor will tell you more as soon as she's out of surgery.'

'I have to know, please,' Yasmin said.

'Of course. You'll know as soon as possible.'

'Yasmin, I signed the consent papers for surgery,' Ma said.

'Ma, how bad is she?'

Ma was distraught. 'No one has said anything to me. She was taken away in a separate ambulance. The waiting is driving me mad. Isn't there someone who can tell us something?' She struggled to sit up.

'Ma, you heard. She's in surgery,' I said.

'What exactly happened?' Yasmin asked.

'A minibus taxi was overtaking a truck. He came out of nowhere. He couldn't make it and we tried to swerve out of his way. We had just left the airport. Oh my God, Yasmin . . .' she cried.

Yasmin had gone pale.

'You've got to be strong for Soraya's sake, my child,' Ma said taking Yasmin's hand.

'Ma's right,' I said. 'We have to be calm. I'm sure we'll hear soon. There's no point jumping to conclusions.'

But Yasmin had not heard a word. She hurried away, determined to find someone, anyone, who could give us information about Soraya's condition.

'Meena, I didn't want to say anything in front of Yasmin,' Ma sobbed, 'but it doesn't look good. God alone knows why I was spared.'

My mother wept in my arms while we waited for Yasmin to return.

She came back after a while, but all she could tell us was that Soraya was still in surgery.

An attendant fetched Ma to take her for X-rays. I wanted to go with her, but she instructed me to stay with Yasmin. 'Come and tell me if there's any news,' she said as they wheeled her out of the room.

Ma had her X-rays and returned to casualty. Still there was no news of Soraya.

We had only a vague awareness of the passage of time. None of us had any inkling of how long we had waited.

Yasmin was like a caged animal, pacing and muttering under her breath.

Finally a doctor came to speak to us. When I saw him striding towards us, my legs buckled and I had to sit down.

'I'm Dr Rubinstein. You must be Mrs Kingsley,' he said. Yasmin, pale and anxious, leapt to her feet. I still wasn't able to stand.

'She's in recovery,' the doctor said.

'How is she?' Yasmin demanded. 'We've been waiting for ages. Why hasn't anyone told us anything?'

'Yasmin, please, let the doctor speak,' Ma admonished gently.

The doctor, looking grim and exhausted, continued. 'It's been a long day for all of us. We've stabilised her. She's had massive head injuries. We've reduced the bleeding in her cranium.'

Yasmin gasped and swayed unsteadily. One of the nurses lowered her into a chair.

'Go on, Doctor,' Ma said calmly. She knew then that she had to be strong for us.

'She's suffered no abdominal trauma. All her injuries seem to be confined to her face and head. So we'll be able to save the baby. The foetus is about sixteen weeks. It's a little girl.'

Yasmin turned her bewildered eyes on the doctor.

'What baby?' she whispered.

She looked at Ma.

'Did you know about this?' she asked.

Ma nodded.

'Why didn't you tell me?'

'Yasmin, this is not the time. Let's hear what the doctor has to say,' I said.

'The next twenty-four hours are critical,' he said.

'Will she be all right?' Yasmin asked.

Dr Rubinstein looked at her. 'I don't know, Mrs Kingsley. I don't know. We'll all just have to wait.'

We were allowed to see Soraya. Her face was so badly injured and so swollen that her features were barely recognisable.

'Oh God,' Yasmin cried when she saw her. 'My poor baby.'

Soraya was unconscious, her head swathed in bandages. Tubes led in and out of her body. She was hooked up to several monitoring machines, one of them a respirator. The pipping sound from the heart-monitor provided incongruous reassurance in the silence of the room.

'She must be in so much pain,' Yasmin said, her voice full of anguish.

'She can't feel any pain,' the nurse assured her.

'I hope the baby is going to be all right,' Ma said.

But Yasmin didn't want to hear about the baby. She showed no interest in what Ma had to say. Her sole concern was Soraya. Nothing else mattered.

We sat with Soraya for the rest of that day, all of the next day and the days which followed. Aishaben joined us in our vigil. We took turns phoning home to England to inform family and friends about the accident and to advise them of Soraya's condition.

Neville said he'd come immediately.

Yasmin needed him. It needed a moment like this, a moment of tragedy, to bring them together and to bind them as nothing else would.

We waited for some sign from Soraya, some sign that she was aware of us being there with her. But there was nothing. We held her hand, we spoke to her. Yasmin pleaded with her to open her eyes. Ma prayed. Friends stopped in to pray with her, but there was no sign of life from Soraya. Not the slightest hint that she was still with us.

Neville arrived a few days later. He was able to comfort Yasmin. Soraya's flat-mate Jess phoned, concerned about her. Neville spoke to her. Yasmin was in no condition to speak to anyone. She was on the point of collapse, but would not leave Soraya's side.

I stayed at the hospital for four days and then finally had to get away. I went to Aishaben's to rest and change my clothes. Ma, who had been discharged a few days earlier, came with me. When we returned to the hospital I urged Yasmin to take a rest, but she wouldn't hear of it.

After a week of constant vigil, Neville insisted that she have a break. He told her that she would be of no use to Soraya in the state she was in. Yasmin finally agreed. I drove her to Aishaben's. Although she was silent I sensed a change in her and hoped that she had finally confronted the fact that Soraya might never recover.

But she clung tenaciously to the hope that Soraya would regain consciousness, even when Dr Rubinstein took her aside and told her that the damage to Soraya's brain was irreversible. The only way they could keep her alive was on life-support.

'What about the baby?' Yasmin asked, for the first time showing an interest.

'We can keep your daughter alive until we're able to deliver the baby by Caesarean section,' the doctor said. 'It's been done before.'

'What about Soraya?'

'There's nothing we can do for her, Mrs Kingsley,' he said gently. 'We've done a number of tests, and there's no brain activity. But your granddaughter stands a good chance if we can keep your daughter's heart going. We're feeding her through tubes so the baby should develop normally.'

'Oh, God,' Yasmin whimpered, covering her face. 'Oh, God.'

Ma and I both knew that Soraya was not going to emerge from her coma. She was lost to us. But Yasmin thought that with her strength alone, she could will Soraya back to life.

Her will, though, was not enough.

Dr Rubinstein spoke to Yasmin again. He said there was a young girl waiting for Soraya's heart. Soraya's blood type was AB negative, a rare group, and so was the young girl's.

'You must consider this, Mrs Kingsley. Remember, we're keeping your daughter alive artificially – for the sake of the baby.'

Yasmin stared at him mutely, unable to comprehend what he was saying. She just couldn't deal with the reality.

Ma asked me to drive out to McBain to fetch Gladys and Florence from the village.

'Gladys will want to be here for Soraya,' Ma said.

I left before dawn, driving the familiar road to McBain. I thought of Soraya, lying so still in her hospital bed. She had already left everything behind. Her life had been cut short just as it was beginning to make some sense to her. Then there were those of us she had left behind, sitting and waiting.

The sun came up, hovering just above the koppies, bathing the sky in a soft light. It seemed as if the world had been created anew and I wondered what surprises this dawn would have in store for us.

Gladys was so distraught by what she saw of Soraya that Ma had to lead her outside to comfort her.

Yasmin became calm and stoic. It was as though she had turned a page – perhaps a whole chapter. If her daughter was going to be lost to her, which she wasn't convinced of, there was a granddaughter waiting to make her way into the world.

Gladys stayed in a spare room at Aishaben's. She was at the hospital each day, doing whatever she could for Soraya and for us. Yasmin hoped that Gladys's presence would somehow be acknowledged by Soraya, but it was a vain hope. There was no indication from Soraya that she was aware of anything at all. Despite all that the doctor had told her, Yasmin still cherished the hope that Soraya would come out of the coma.

'It's in God's hands,' Gladys said to Ma. It was what Nana would have said.

Ma wept quietly – for Soraya, for Yasmin and for Nana. At this time of crisis and tragedy, she missed not having her own mother to comfort her. I remembered how, during one of our dark spells, Nana had held her to her breast and comforted her as though she were a small child again, caressing her hair and humming to her.

A week later I drove Gladys back to her village. She hardly spoke a word during the drive back. It was as though something within her had withered too.

'Did you know that Soraya was pregnant?' I asked.

She nodded.

'How did you know, Gladys?'

'She told me,' she said simply.

59

A MONTH passed and still there was no change in Soraya. Yasmin spent hours talking to her, pleading with her, playing her favourite music to her. She could not and would not let go.

Christmas came and went.

A psychologist came to see Yasmin. Afterwards she was seen by a counsellor who spent hours talking to her, comforting her. But Yasmin still believed that any day now Soraya would sit up and talk to us.

Lying in a narrow cot, in a hospital she had never been in before, attached to two machines, one breathing for her, the other monitoring her heartbeats, seemed so far removed from Soraya's life. But she could never have known that all her living, her music and her loving had been in vain.

Her hair had grown back after the surgery. With her face relaxed, she looked like a young child again. Yasmin bestowed all the attention she could on Soraya, as if trying to compensate for the time she had missed with her. She washed Soraya, massaged her legs, turned her frequently. And all of it with the loving patience of a mother tending an infant.

Yasmin's layers had been peeled away. Soraya's accident had forced her to look inside herself to find spaces she had never before had an opportunity to explore.

Douglas Pilkington arrived. Neville picked him up at the airport. He had prudently kept the news of Douglas's arrival from Yasmin for fear of upsetting her.

At first Yasmin was angry. But eventually she conceded that

he had a right to be there.

'What harm can it do now?' she said.

Later she took Douglas aside and asked him about the baby.

'Did you know she was pregnant?'

He nodded. 'I planned to marry her, Yasmin. Gwen and I are getting a divorce. Our relationship was over a long time ago.' He paused and drew his hand through his hair in a gesture of weariness. 'Soraya told me over the phone that she was pregnant. She also told me that she wasn't going to marry me. She told me that it was all over between us.'

Yasmin gained some solace from his words, realising that Soraya had told her the truth.

Douglas looked devastated when he saw Soraya. It was clear then how much he loved her. We left him alone with her for a while. He sat by her bed, talking to her, telling her how much he missed her.

Soraya had told me, and Douglas confirmed it, that they had fallen in love. When I had first heard about the affair, I was angry with Douglas, ready to blame him. But when I saw him at her bedside, my heart went out to him. He stayed for a week and was with her each day.

'He's come to say goodbye,' I said to Ma.

My mother sat with her head in her hands. We had all shed so many tears for Soraya that there was nothing left. There was just another black hole in the collective soul of our family, one more strip ripped from the canvas.

Poor Douglas. Soraya had no idea that he was there, that he had rushed all the way from London to be with her. If only she could have heard the outpourings from his heart. It was not the tawdry little affair Yasmin had imagined it to be. Douglas's love for Soraya finally vindicated her.

Douglas and Neville spoke to Yasmin at length about letting Soraya go. Ma and I had already let go. There was no point hanging on. The person lying on that bed was not Soraya. Soraya's spirit was long gone. All that was left was the body that was being kept alive artificially to nurture the baby she carried.

Yasmin wandered the corridors of the hospital like a ghost. The staff watched her sympathetically. They understood what she was going through. They comforted her when they could and tried to lift her spirits. But Yasmin could not be reached; she had slipped beyond the point of feeling anything. She was being driven by sheer will. An iron will to keep Soraya alive.

'I can't let her go,' Yasmin wept quietly. 'I can't. She's all I've got.'

I could feel her shoulder blades protruding as I wrapped my arms around her. She had wasted away right before our eyes. I held her like a sister, as though we had twin souls.

'What should I do, Meena?' she cried. I was as close to her now as I could ever be. Tragedy had drawn us all together.

'You know what has to be done, Yasmin.' Frantic and terrified, she clung to me, her thin arms locked around my neck.

'If only I had a chance to do things over, Meena,' she sobbed against my shoulder.

I told myself that whatever happened would be determined by some other power, a power greater than ours. Yasmin had always believed that only we control our destinies and yet even she had been brought to her knees. For the first time since I could remember, she began praying.

It took another two weeks of painful deliberation before Yasmin made the first tentative admission that the doctors might be right about Soraya. That it was all over. It was the end of February. We'd been camped in and around the hospital for months. The doctors confirmed that the baby would have been due in mid-April. They kept a close eye on the development of the foetus, ready to operate at a moment's notice to ensure its survival.

A few days later Yasmin seemed to come to her senses. It was obvious in her eyes, even before she spoke. The old Yasmin was back, strong and decisive as ever.

Her first decision was to move Soraya into a private room. She arranged with the hospital to have another cot brought in and she moved into Soraya's room.

She laid down the law about us not crying in the room. She gave Neville a list of things she wanted, including a stereo and some CDs. She bought books and tapes and read to Soraya to stimulate the baby. She touched Soraya constantly, and played the music she loved.

Neville was there every day for Yasmin. He brushed her hair, massaged her shoulders, cared for her and loved her.

My mother was strong. She had reserves of strength I never imagined possible. It was as if she had spent her whole life preparing for this moment; the moment when the most important decision in our lives had to be made.

Ma told Yasmin what she and Soraya had talked about. Soraya was looking forward to having the baby. She was going to tell Yasmin when they got back to London. She was going to raise the baby on her own. She was certain that it would be a girl.

'But she didn't show,' Yasmin said. 'I would never have known.'

'She was very small, Yasmin. I would not have known either, if she hadn't told me.'

'But why didn't she come to me?' Yasmin demanded. 'I'm her mother!'

'She didn't want criticism. She wanted support.'

Yasmin dropped her head, her hands hanging between her knees, shoulders bowed as she stared at the floor. 'I've made so many mistakes,' she whispered.

Ma put her arm around her. 'There's always a reason for the way things happen in life. Nana would have told you that there's a greater design behind all of this.'

'I can't see it,' she muttered.

'Soraya even chose a name for her baby. She told me she liked the name Ashleigh. She wanted the baby named Ashleigh Fatima Mohammed. She wanted it spelt with the "l-e-i-g-h".'

For the first time in weeks, Yasmin broke down.

The doctors had again spoken to her about donating Soraya's organs, but Yasmin found the idea repulsive. She was not going to kill her daughter so that some stranger could benefit.

'Yasmin, please,' I said. 'You must think of Soraya too. It's what she would have wanted.'

'I've been praying for a miracle, Meena.'

'The miracle is there, growing inside her.'

'If I'm to bury her, I want to bury her whole, not with parts missing.'

'Soraya was an unselfish person,' I said. 'She would have wanted to help in this way. She always wanted to make the world a better place. Now's her chance. You can't take it away from her.'

Yasmin shook her head.

'I know it's what she would have wanted,' I urged.

The question of the donation of Soraya's organs was something that we could not resolve. Yasmin still stubbornly resisted. I knew it was going to be a long and difficult wait for all of us. I wanted to go home for a while. Ma thought it was a good idea.

Yasmin suggested that Neville accompany me back to London to attend to the sale of her business. She gave him power of attorney. Although she had briefed her lawyers by telephone, she wanted Neville there to make sure that everything went smoothly.

I promised to be back soon, within a few weeks. I thought that Yasmin might need me, even though she seemed to have regained her strength and determination.

Neville and I left for London a few days later.

We kept in constant contact with Ma and Yasmin.

Neville returned after three weeks when the business of the sale had been concluded. I wasn't quite ready to return. I spoke to Ma who told me that there was no need to rush back. Soraya's condition had not changed.

I flew back a month later, at the end of March.

The day after I arrived, the baby was in distress and the doctors prepared to perform an emergency Caesarean section.

They advised Yasmin that it was time to say goodbye to Soraya. They were going to remove her from the life-support system immediately after delivering the baby.

Now that the time had come and we had to say goodbye, we couldn't bring ourselves to do so. Ma couldn't let go. She clung to Soraya, pleading with her to open her eyes. The nurses led her from the ward as Yasmin went in for the last time.

When she came out of the room we knew that it was all over. We watched Soraya's body being wheeled to surgery. I put an arm around Yasmin's shoulders and walked her away. A new life was starting, and somewhere a young girl was waiting for Soraya's heart.

The baby was beautiful. We all crowded around the nursery, peering through the window where she was being kept in an incubator. Yasmin was the only one allowed into the nursery.

A few days later we held a service for Soraya. Then she was cremated. Yasmin wanted to take her ashes back to London, but Ma persuaded her to bury them in Nana's grave. It was the best place for her.

All her short life had been a search for her special place. A place where she could find peace and contentment. In death she was to find that place at last.

Yasmin waited for her granddaughter with more patience than I could ever have imagined possible. She and Neville were like two doting parents.

She spent each day at the hospital until Ashleigh was discharged. Then she took her to the hotel where they were staying. She would not let her out of her sight. She was absolutely devoted to her.

I returned to London, leaving Ma, Neville and Yasmin behind. They were going to remain in South Africa until the baby was strong enough to travel. Yasmin was not taking any chances.

The last thing I saw as the plane flew north and the clouds parted below us was the reddish-brown African landscape.

I wanted to close this chapter of my life. We all had to get on with our lives now. I thought about our blessings, our struggles, the times of despair in our lives, and how Yasmin and I had both managed to rise above it.

Yasmin would never be able to return to her old life. That was all in the past now. It had taken the death of the daughter she had not wanted in the beginning to alter the course of her life.

After all that had happened, I wondered how I would ever write again. But deep down I knew that I would, just as I had after Sayeed died.

For the first time in ages I felt terribly alone and wanted someone in my life, someone to console and comfort me, someone to hold me and ease the pain.

I thrust these thoughts from my mind. I needed to start working right away. Work was always a panacea. I remembered the manila envelope Yasmin had brought from my editor which was still in my briefcase. It had travelled unopened to and from London with me.

I settled back in my window seat, opened my briefcase and extracted the envelope. I had to start focusing, I thought as I slipped the pages out of the envelope. But my mind was in too much of a whirl to concentrate. I was about to return the pages to the envelope when I remembered Jonathan's letter. I read it again and then I lowered the table in front of my seat, found my reading-glasses and pencil and slowly worked through the first page of my manuscript.

Forbidden Love was waiting.

My publishers were waiting.

There could be no looking back.